Also by Stephen Swartz

Contemporary Literary Fiction

After Ilium

Aiko

A Beautiful Chill

A Girl Called Wolf

Exchange

Year of the Tiger

Fantasy & Science Fiction

The Stefan Székely Vampire Trilogy

I. A Dry Patch of Skin

II. Sunrise

III. Sunset

*Epic Fantasy *With Dragons*

The Dream Land Trilogy

I. Long Distance Voyager

II. Dreams of Future's Past

III. Diaspora

The Long-forgotten Legend of
THE MASTERS' RIDDLE
and the Strange Little Being from
PLANET SEBBOL

An Interdimensional Novel

Stephen Swartz

MYRDDIN PUBLISHING GROUP

UNITED STATES ✦ UNITED KINGDOM ✦ AUSTRALIA

ISBN-13: 978-1-68063-059-6

ISBN-10: 1-68063-059-8

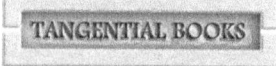

www.myrddinpublishing.com

Cover Design by Iris Schaeffer

The answer to a riddle is.

- Song 14 Scroll 3

Wisdom of First Goddess

d a r k   n o t h i n g n e s s

▶   1

Double-warm was the dark interval, and *wo* the thickness of *skarg* sludged over the village, despite a string of *oum* creeping here and there among the round stone abodes set in rows between the food-gardens and the merchant-stands.

The second-summer *chakari* squeaked low over the short-cycle, then rose to such a gravelly din that Toog, so sick for repose in the black of his abode, could no longer hear them. Not until their noise ceased.

Listen...

Nothingness.

Toog could measure time by the arrival of each finger of *oum*.

Double-warm was the dark interval. Toog released much heat-rain from his body vents yet his smooth silvery skin meshed with the moist weave beneath him as he out-stretched upon the repose mat. The dream land would not invite him in.

Beside him reposed his full-mate, the female assigned to him by the shaman. She traveled deep in the dream land and puffing her lullabies in soft rhythm. He watched her silvery *tali* pulse and *pook* swell outward and decline, her *gumu* turning blue then white then blue again as she swam against one then the other and another of the practice-mates waiting for her there in the balmy dream land. Already they had joined in the waking and, in the late-cycle, in the *skarg*, and passed their *lu* back and forth until they burst with belly-fire. His mate usually had a measure of excess energy to slough off, he knew, and flashed a mouth-turn at her.

Toog up-heaved his slick silvery body to give *wo* to his under side, to let the *oum* dry the moisture there. The cloth beneath his body was damp, as though he had been wet-caught in a medium *aa'lool*, when the seasonal *lool* dropped from the sky.

Toog gazed upon L'ra, his full-mate, and counted the measures of attraction he had believed for so many sun-cycles. It was like pulling stones from the counting pouch. She was the best of the cohort, the only member he wanted for the mating ritual. And for more than that going beyond. Journeying in the dream land, she appeared calm. They had met many cycles there before he asked the village shaman to pair them. He expelled an admiring squeak yet she did not return to the waking world—

Silence exploded around him.

The nothingness of the world outside covered the abode.

Toog up-bent on his side of the repose-mat, listened for the next squeak of *chakari*, waiting. Hearing none, he up-stood and left the container. He planned to return after a short-cycle and continue his repose beside L'ra.

The stone abode was deep-dark, ringing-silent, and fire-burning. The rare refreshment of *oum* coming past him, blowing here and there through the outside vents yet could not find any entrance.

He foot-stepped to the nursery cylinder, stood gazing upon the springling resting in the swing-basket, also visiting the dream land. Toog observed. Mouth-curled without command, puffs of *eruth* left the hoary infant, her tiny transparent body yet to become glossy silver. Perhaps she swam through the *skarg* with legs that in the waking world could not yet hold her upright. She had not squeaked in the late-cycle as he down-lay her into the swing-basket and rubbed head-to-head with her like the *puuchee* did.

Mouth-curls remained upon her face as Toog foot-stepped to the next container and searched lightly for any remaining food items to ingest. It was *gop* to let any food remain until the sunshine-rising. Wasteful. A call to boasting among those of his village that he had more than them. No more, no less was the rule.

He crashed about, lost in the blackness, yet found a vessel and filled it with warm *lool* from the *yb*. Unsteady hands were faulty and the liquid escaped, coating his silvery body with its viscous warmth.

Repose is necessary, he conversed with his inner Ru. The Ru did not answer him and Toog whispered a *grurt* for the Ru. The new sun-burst would call him soon and he would push himself to tasks, as he did with each sun-burst no matter the heat or the cool or falling crystals. He labored for his unit, making full for his cohort, and for the full-mate named L'ra and the new-made springling they would call M'ah. The blue tears of First Goddess fell upon him, made him hard-ache with the weight of a thousand sky rocks.

With a swallow of the warm *lool*, his body reset.

Streaming *parg* striped his tubes and joy-calm flittered

about his skin, signaling his readiness for repose.

Down-bending to the *xasto*, he let his body linger in idleness for eleven flickers, and upon the last his eyes were struck with fury by yellow flashes growing larger and brighter.

The yellow glows seemed to approach his abode. Humming like *doong* raised to his ears, playing like *weera* around his ears, then vanished with the end of the short-cycle. The yellow glow returned, departed.

Toog promised his inner Ru that once more he would attempt to enter the dream land.

Marking the cycle, Toog bold-set a banner in his mind-cave, a warning to all, especially to his inner Ru, that silence was the order. As silence wrapped around the abode, the *oum* passed with fear. He grabbed after the *oum*, wanting to cover his body with a finger of its coolness. Rather than complete that want-thought, he back-turned at the new wave of squeaking *chakari*.

Toog up-bent, up-stood, out-gazed through the visor.

Wrong. Some element is out of balance.

He asked his inner Ru and again received no answer.

What is the balance?

A long quiver ran through his silvery body like errant *ylla*. He turned to regain the repose cylinder and down-bent beside his full-mate.

He down-bent on the edge of the repose-mat, over-stretched to touch his orb-top to hers, yet she did not rise to the waking world. As Toog down-stretched beside her, he again felt the balance was askew. Elements were quick-dancing in squares not circles.

Listen...

Nothingness of great purpose.

Where are the chakari?

They had suddenly stopped their squeaking.

Like a *nur* hidden in the *jo*, Toog down-bent and side-gazed. The balance was broken. He would not wait for his inner Ru to advise him. Rather, he straight-stood, covered his body with new, dry cloth, ready for the sun-burst tasks. He took the nearest work tool into his hand and listened.

Gazing to and fro, repeating, waiting at the visor as though First Goddess would soon address him, waiting for a turn he did not know and could not count. He shook with fiery bowls of hot *gaum* sparking within his body.

Listen!

A sound, like the step-pounding of *kalar* or a softly-struck skin-box, a dampened pulse like the seasonal rock falls.

Toog listened for a quick-interval as the struck-sound beat firm and deep. The pulse-huff grew as steady as the sun flew over the mountains, the sound approaching his abode.

He lit fire-shakes through his body to cleanse the dirt-tubes, to ready the fire-strings to pull him into the fight. He knew in that quick-space the swing of balance would fall short.

It had happened before, he knew in the next quick-space. He also knew he was too weak to stop it, too old to face it, too young to understand it, yet he must give his strongest push to protect his full-mate and their springling in the swing-basket. His hand tightened around the work tool, hard metal meshing with soft flesh.

First Goddess was near, he believed. The swish of her fine cloth alerted him. He compounded strength, stoked inner-fire, and loaded all the stones he could gather from his mind-cave into both of his force-hands, to make fight-tools.

He must protect his abode, his full-mate, his springling in the swing-basket—

Toog heard the faint metal-sound, calling as of old, and he could not measure it the same as in the stories of old, read from the tablets. Distant calls, rising firm in the night *wo*. Like sticks scraping metal, rising swarms like *chakari* in the night *oum*. For no reason but the touch of a goddess had he been left previously. Now they had returned to Sebbol.

No!

The Masters would not take him!

They would not hurt him!

He would fight them!

He turned, wanting another love-gaze at his full-mate. Yet set with fire-shakes, he ahead-pushed a foot-step with want-touching his orb-top to hers, yet a wide popping of eye-rain fogged his *gazek*. At that short-count the yellow glow over-fell him like a big sweep of cloth and he stop-stood like a crashing sky rock.

The next foot-step he pushed ahead, he would not recall.

He was tight-pulled into the great flash of yellow.

Toog had left his world.

p r i s o n   p l a n e t

      2

Toog's eyes saw only nothingness

in the dark nothingness

of the waking world.

He wondered if he was orb-smashed. He heard they sometimes did that as punishment. The goddesses could be cruel that way. But did the Masters have the same goddesses?

He rummaged about in his mind-cave, wild-crashing into walls and bleeding. He searched on the walls of his mind-cave for clues to what had happened. Perhaps pictures had been painted on the walls. He wanted to gather the pictures on a string and tell the story to his inner Ru—or have his inner Ru explain it all to him.

A repose mat hard like stone supported his body, yet there was some kind of dry, scratchy *jo* beneath his skin. He sensed his body was no longer covered with cloth. The *jo* irritated his skin. Yet he dared not move, the heart-cutter within him enforcing his silence, commanding his stillness.

The air was cool now, almost cold, more than he was used to on his world with the constant warm *oum*, and especially cold against his skin. And it was moist, too, so it chilled him. His body erupted in shivers. In the same short-cycle, he realized he could see nothing. He was suspended in dark nothingness. His ears caught no noise. His eyes up-turned and rain leaked from them, wetting his face.

What he took to be several long-cycles later, Toog moved. First, he commanded his toes to clench, then release, and repeated several times the call-and-response. He up-raised his left hand and down-bent it to his face. There his hand detected a deep groove running from the corner of his mouth up across his cheek to the top of his head and curling around his ear opening. He sent his tongue to explore and he found two teeth no longer stood straight in his mouth. His jaw was out of balance. With a push from his inner Ru, his head popped back into its proper shape.

He could not see his hand up-held in front of his face, even when he touched the orbs of his eyes.

A thunder-pain burst through his body and his throat became fire-lit. He wanted to roar like a wild *nur* yet he had no breath. His eyes rained. He called to his inner Ru, begging for a different view, singing sadly of the drawing which showed he was not blind, that it was only because of the darkness.

His left hand out-stretched, touched the hard, cold surface of stone. The wall went high, as far as his hand could reach, up-bent, out-stretched, back-stretched. His left hand next went to his right hand, with a solemn chant to his inner Ru, struggling to separate the pain in that right hand from the thundering of nerve-noise rattling through his body.

Then he noticed it. The metal.

A bolt?

He touched it with his free hand and learned he could not raise his right hand from the surface he lay on because of the metal thing that had been pushed through his hand.

He released the wrath-call of the universe for the first instance of his life, and his inner Ru cringed in fear.

Now all the stories he had heard were becoming real. Hot rain gushed from his eyes as fear rumbled in waves through his head, crashing against the walls of his mind-cave.

Let us out, cried his fear-demons.

For many long-cycles Toog lay in the dark of the nothingness, hearing only the quick-pulse of his heart, and the faint shudders of his inner Ru, and the strange echo around the walls of his stone container.

Then he heard a sound—a voice—calling him to rest— speaking clearly inside his mind-cave, drawing pictures on the walls.

Toog grew silent, felt the weight of stars upon his head, closed his eyes and walked into the dream land.

It was a long, black thing, and he loathed arriving in the waking world. For it meant that it was not a cloud picture drifting through his mind-cave but a truth-scene—like having his inner Ru sitting across from him, conversing with him, a solemn blue figure with yellow teeth and red eyes.

His right hand throbbed with pain, more than before. Toog felt fluids seeping from the fresh wound in the palm of his hand. They had come for him, he believed, and lifted him from the stone shelf, carried him away to another container, perhaps tried to heal him, to make his hand firm again. They had taken him from this container, returned him, and again inserted the metal bolt through his hand.

Or was this a different container?

He tried a salve from his inner Ru to soothe his hand as best he could, but the pain would not lessen. Instead, the pain increased like a rising sun bursting into bright glory and it made him scream.

He let go the wrath-call of the universe several times, expecting one of the goddesses to respond. He writhed in deep, thundering horror, and pain like lightning *luts* shot up his arm to his shoulder and exploded like star-fire. He screamed, his body rocking back and forth from one side of the stone shelf to the other side until he rolled too far beyond the edge of the shelf and down-fell to another hard surface—

His hand let loose its own wrath-call of the universe and his fingers cried out also. His hand had torn away from the bolt.

Suddenly Toog felt his head filled with the pressure waves of an erupting *vash*. He held his strength as long as he could then crashed into the dream land.

Many cycles later, Toog arrived in the waking world. He did not know how many cycles had turned. He believed he lay again on the same stone surface in the same cell. His hand was again fixed to the stone shelf, a new bolt in place.

The air seemed colder than before, and his skin prickled like a dry *tuuk* in the *oum*. His teeth rattled like dancing sky-crystals.

He lay on the stone surface, as unmoving as a mountain, silent and lost in the dark nothingness.

After many short-cycles he whispered to his inner Ru, as though telling a secret, but got no response.

Toog thought of his family. L'ra, his full-mate, walked

through his mind-cave carrying their springling. His full-mate looked new-cleansed, like a goddess, *futar* feathers strung in a weave over her head, a white cloth woven around her waist, crystals on tassels swinging from her silvery *tali*. In her slim silver arms the springling warm-smiled, gurgling in her gray flesh, as fat as a late-summer *groll*. He recalled the scene from long-cycles before—unable to count how many cycles it must have been since he was taken away. The pictures remained on his mind-cave walls and continued to be drawn there.

The Masters could not drag the pictures away—

They were probably taken away from the abode, Toog spoke to his inner Ru. His head filled with boiling *hox* as he thought of his full-mate and their springling taken away. He shook against the stone as he watched his inner Ru give careful hand to drawing on the walls of his mind-cave pictures showing his full-mate and their springling becoming smaller and smaller. He might never see them again! Yet they walked through his mind-cave with ease.

Eye-rain over-spilled his face, leaked into his mouth, the bitter sting another reminder of how the shaman had warned everyone to act properly. If the goddesses were angry, the Masters would come. It seemed true now.

Toog vowed to find his family no matter what he must do. He had only been with his full-mate one sun-cycle from the day their springling burst forth.

How long had he been here in this dark container of stone?

A short-cycle?

A long-cycle?

A sun-cycle?

More?

He thought he was lost in the dream land most of that time, a dream land with no pictures and no paths, no fields or mountains. No *skarg* or *abo*. Perhaps it only seemed that way, like the pictures in the *hox* pools, bubbling and boiling with hot mud. The same was true for the pictures he saw when he looked into the *lool*. There, he could in-put his finger and change the picture, make it disappear. As though it had never been drawn.

In his belly he could feel no fullness. A dull throb spun an echo there, falling into a hard growl as the short-cycles turned. With the moistness of the air, his throat was no longer parched. He asked his inner Ru why he did not hunger or thirst but received no response.

The Masters would have to come for him after some time, Toog decided, rearranging the pictures in his mind-cave. The Masters could not leave him bolted to the stone shelf in dark nothingness, in a stone container far from his home—forever. The Masters would have to give him food if they wanted to keep him alive.

His inner Ru strolled into his mind-cave, drawing tools in one hand, and let out a worried *haal*.

No, do not draw the pictures!

Watching his inner Ru drawing, Toog realized that the Masters did not follow the rules of the goddesses of Sebbol. The shaman had explained to him how the Masters stood above the goddesses. For most of his life, Toog knew the Masters only as legend, as frightful pictures burning on the walls of his mind-cave.

Were the Masters the gods who ruled over his goddesses? After all, even a goddess needed a full-mate sometime, truth?

He grew weary, long-cycles running without end, and escaped into the dream land again.

Toog arrived in the waking world still surrounded by the dark nothingness, covered in silence, a new pain in his hand. His hand had grown to twice its normal size. The ring of skin around the metal bolt had torn, the crust of scab ripping, a sticky fluid mixed with blood running from the wound and over the palm, drying and fusing him to the stone.

Now the pain was less than the cut of a *druka*'s claws. He knew it hurt, but he had constructed a high wall to separate the wound from the pain. His fear-demons fought each other instead of him.

After a few short-cycles, the fluid became solid again and a new crust formed.

Did his full-mate also have a metal bolt through her hand? Was she even in this same place? a container of dark nothingness? Did they have his springling for their dinner?

He sent those thoughts away.

Suddenly, Toog felt a crushing weight to his forehead. He fought it, but dropped as though from a great height down into the dream land, a much darker nothingness.

He returned to the waking world as though born from the smoke of a great fire. He knew he had arrived by the bright light burning his eyes into silence. He commanded his eyes to close yet the light penetrated them with the same power.

Light was everywhere. Toog could see nothing. He was engulfed in a nothingness of pure light. He also could not move his body. His arms and legs would not respond. His inner Ru was asleep.

With great pain exploding through his arm and shoulder, he felt the metal bolt slowly being pulled from his hand. His entire body rattled with pain as the new scab was broken and flesh was forced apart from the bolt.

When the bolt was freed from his hand, Toog felt himself being lifted by his shoulders. For the first breath in many cycles, Toog up-bent and foot-touched a cold surface, then tried to up-stand, but his weak legs sent no report to his inner Ru. There was no sensation, as though his feet pressed against no floor, and his body wavered.

Blinded by the bright light, Toog was led out of the container, his feet going from the coldness of the stone floor to a burning heat of a long passage.

His feet sizzled against the floor as he stepped, led by the pair of Masters. He believed the Masters led him but his eye covers were held tightly closed against the light.

Several steps down the passage, he was halted by a firm hand pressed to his chest. The hand turned him to the right.

A wave of cold air struck him like a flying *hafo*, battering his face with its sinewy wings, and he realized that instead of sending him down a path, even a harsh road full of terrors, a way back to his home, the Masters were only taking him to a different container.

He cursed his inner Ru for abandoning him.

Short-cycles later, Toog continued drawing pictures in his mind-cave, wishing they would arrange themselves into a new pattern, so with the sweep of the goddesses he might know the future. He might learn the reason he was chosen. Was it for punishment? What had he done against the rules? He followed every law precisely. The shaman had always praised his correct behavior.

Toog felt forces pushing his body down upon a new surface. His hand was held in place and a metal bolt was again set through the hole in his hand. The explosion of pain drowned out the sound of the panel closing, leaving him alone in the new container, alone in the dark nothingness again.

Confirming his situation, Toog let go a fresh wrath-call of the universe, summoning all his strength and launching the noise with all the force he could put behind it, launching the curse like the sky rocks that hurtled across the horizon—

A voice shouted

for him

to be quiet.

Toog stopped his wrath-call—and stared like a hunt-pointer through the dark nothingness into the direction he thought he heard the voice.

What kind of thing am I paired with?

Toog called his body to be ready to run, knowing he was bolted to the stone. His inner Ru was hiding, anyway.

"Who are you?"

It was the same voice as had shouted at him, Toog realized. The first cut to his ears left him doubting his ears caught the sound. Yet he understood the words clearly—in his language, what he and the other Aull called *Sebbou*. He called to his inner Ru to draw again on the walls of his mind-cave, to show him the words he heard in his ears and match them to the words he saw in his mind-cave.

"Toog," he spoke, little more than a soft chirp. "I am Toog." He answered in Sebbou, like *gurg* crawling out of the *nuum*. The words felt like sharp-edged rocks packed in his throat. Other than his wrath-call, he had not let go a mouth-sound for many cycles.

After a heart-pump, he was not sure he had actually made the mouth-sounds. He knew what he had spoken yet he did not know if the other creature would understand his words.

"Where were you made?" the voice asked in a flat tone, like a *saak*-breeze through the *oum*.

Toog asked his inner Ru how another creature from another world would know his language but there was no answer. He heard words in an unknown language, yet in his mind-cave he understood them in his own language.

"I come from—Sebbol." With the utterance of his home's name, Toog felt a stream of sorrow-sludge up-creep from his stomach. He hesitated, unsure of the other creature's thoughts about his world. Would the other creature be friend or enemy?

"We are neighbors."

Again the words filled the stone container like the bellowing of an impatient *groll* waiting to be fed, yet the words that came into his mind-cave he understood as clearly as if his full-mate L'ra were speaking to him face to face with their *ag* intertwined.

Toog breathed deeply. "Neighbors?"

A raspy noise spilled out and slunk across the stone floor.

"Neighboring star systems," the other creature communicated both in sound words which Toog did not recognize and in mind-cave words which Toog did understand.

Star systems? thought Toog.

A long wind out-blew from Toog's mouth as the sorrow-sludge slipped free. He knew what *star system* meant. The shaman had explained to them the pattern of the sky. He could see the drawings on the walls of his mind-cave: one large orange star surrounded by twenty-two swirling mountains. His mountain was called Sebbol, the sixth out from the star. The only mountain the goddesses had favored. It meant he was far from home.

"You are new here," the voice spoke, a raspy whisper.

"Yes," Toog spoke.

"How long have you been here?"

"I do not know. I forgot to count the cycles. Could it be thirty long-cycles?" he asked, the movement of his mouth feeling strange as he formed the Sebbou words, squeaks and chirps, and let them echo around the stone walls.

"It must be more." The voice seemed to sigh. "You were in the first cell at least a year."

"A year?" asked Toog. The creature must refer to a sun-cycle.

"The first is the conditioning cell."

"Conditioning cell?"

"That is where you learn to accept your fate."

"My fate?" He asked his inner Ru what 'fate' meant but his inner Ru shrugged its shoulders and made an ugly face. Then he followed his inner Ru down a long tunnel and they stopped before a wall of markings. His inner Ru pointed impatiently at one set of marks. *Ivi*, the final destination to which each Aull would eventually arrive.

"It takes a year for the soul to split," the creature communicated both verbally in a guttural grumbling and mentally in clear, precise symbols.

"For a whole sun-cycle?" asked Toog.

"If that is your name for it."

"Year.... One year...."

"One year in the Masters' time scale. One year of the Masters' world is equal to three of your world's years. Also equal to seven years of my world's time."

"How do you know of Sebbol?"

"Two others like you have been here."

"Two...?"

"They both died."

The short-cycle was silent. His inner Ru wept.

"Why?" asked Toog, breaking open the shell of silence.

A low, dry rumble. "Only the Masters know."

Toog felt the sting of *hahi* running through his body. "They are no longer here? What happened to them?"

"They grew old and died. Many of the years passed. The smell was not good."

"Why would the Masters let them die?"

"The Masters had no use for them. They were extra."

"Extra what?"

"Workers."

"Workers for what?"

"I do not know. Some go out and never return."

"Are you saying I will die here, too?"

"No. I do not say that." A short-cycle later, the voice continued: "Yet it is possible."

"I cannot stay here," Toog spoke. "I have a full-mate, assigned by the shaman, and we together made a springling, born only one sun-cycle before I was taken away. I need to return to them. To protect them, and to—"

A loud grunt cut him off. "You will learn, Toog of Sebbol, we do not speak of the past here. No creature shares the past. The past is forbidden. Learn now, Toog, how to live in this place."

Toog wandered through his mind-cave a short-cycle, searching for his inner Ru in several passages. He studied the pictures on the walls he passed and knew all he had to comfort him was his past. Yet his inner Ru hid from him.

A raspy breath alerted Toog that the other creature was about to speak.

"Then you might be able someday to escape."

The voice began a playful noise, like the noise Toog had

heard his springling making when sun-light filled her heart.

"You do not think I can escape?" asked Toog.

There was a long silence.

"No, I do not."

Toog let go the rocks of his mouth. "I will. You will see me do it. I will escape from this place!"

More grumbling, wet and sticky. "I want to see that."

"Everyone will see that."

"You are so bold. Yet you are new. And such a small creature, and only half the height of the Masters, a quarter of their strength. And they have weapons—"

"Who are you?" Toog demanded, ripping the other creature's words off the wall of his mind-cave. His inner Ru gasped.

"I am called by many names on my world. Each depends on the time of day, the situation we encounter, the other's rank, and the meal last consumed. Here I am known by only one name. I am called Ra'aa'al."

"Where is your home?"

"Here is my home."

"Before now."

"I come from—" A short-cycle squatted between the creature's words. "I was taken from Ra'a'am'mas'sandiit. It is a planet which circles the star we call Ra'aa'al."

"You are named for a star?"

"A joke."

"How is it a joke?"

"I am the only being here from my world."

"How do you know?"

"I can sense no other."

Toog felt sorrow-sludge slide out of the other creature.

"Your world...," spoke Toog. "It feels like a place I have seen in my mind-cave."

"My world is known to many who dream."

"You are from the dream land?"

"I visit many dreams."

"Are you...?" Toog held his free hand to the fire of his heart. "Are you my inner Ru?"

There came a small noise, like the tweeting of sexually aroused *futar*, then a long grumbling. Finally: "I am no Ru, inner or outer."

"You seem like my inner Ru. Before it turned shy and cowering, only whispering from the shadows."

"Perhaps it is your own mind calling to you."

"My inner Ru was first ignited by the shaman at the sun-burst of the third remembrance of my birthing."

"We all wish to remember our birth. We wish to curse that day. We wish to forget how we came into this existence. If not because of a womb's forced duty, the required life-force push, we would not be here suffering now."

Toog felt his inner Ru shivering in a cold passage.

"I feel warm sun-light covering me when I think of my mother."

"We all wish peace for our mothers."

Toog remembered the sound of his mother's song. "I wish my mother has that peace."

Ra'aa'al grunted. "Peace does not exist here."

They exchanged vocals for many short-cycles, until Ra'aa'al dropped into the dream land and Toog was vocalizing to himself.

Toog thought for another cycle about all that Ra'aa'al had told him. He was convinced even more that he would escape. He had to. Three sun-cycles, he remembered Ra'aa'al saying. The count was true. Three *years* he had been held here, kept from his family. Three years! And it had only seemed to him like a few long-cycles.

Time was passing on Sebbol. What did his family and his village think of his disappearance? Did they know he was taken by the Masters? Or did they believe he had wandered out of the village that night and became lost in the wilderness, possibly eaten by a pack of *druka* or bitten in half by a giant *gortor*? Did they search for him? Was there a set of prayers sent to him? Did they keep a place at the meal plank for him? Did L'ra already take another mate? Did little M'ah already have a new sibling?

The dark nothingness hid everything from him. He did not have any chance to fight. No chance to act. He had been ready to fight yet he was swept away before he could raise his hand and unsheathe the spike in the heel of his hand. Vivid pictures were carved deep into the walls of mind-cave, not merely drawn on them.

He tried to enter the dream land yet his mind-cave was covered with brightly colored pictures. The pictures drawn there were his full-mate and their springling. When he finally saw the door opening to the dream land, he stepped through and found his family waiting for him. They spoke of their sorrow and their fear. He told them not to become like tangles of sea-twine. He would return to them.

He rattled upon his stone slab like a broiling *groof* and let go a fresh wrath-call of the universe.

Arriving furiously in the waking world, Toog up-sat quickly, like a rising *hareh*, pulling against his bolted hand and screaming from the pain he caused to himself.

He lay quiet then, listening to his wild cries echoing against the stone walls of the container. He felt pain in his hand, the streams of *ka'lool* coursing down his back, making him shiver, and realizing that it was all truth. This hard-running in the dream land was truth, for here he was in this stone container, nailed down to this stone.

Cautiously he down-bent his body, listening, hearing nothing.

He softly called to Ra'aa'al.

A long hiss rose in the silence. "Why?"

"I only wondered if you were awake."

"I am always awake. I can never sleep."

"I'm sorry for that."

"What is the reason for calling to me?"

"I just went on a frightful journey in the dream land."

"It happens to you Sebbox. I understand that."

Toog released a long *smaul*, thinking how he heard words with his ears and did not understand, yet at the same time he heard them echo in his mind-cave and they were Sebbou words.

"Have you ever had a full-mate and a springling you felt heart-fire for so much that you—"

"I warned you, Toog of Sebbol," spoke Ra'aa'al in a deeper voice. "Leave this subject to yourself. I do not wish to know it."

"Is it because you have no-one to return to?"

The hissing and rasping seemed to scratch deep into the stone walls of the container.

"You are a fool!" wet-growled Ra'aa'al. "Each being here has hardship. Have you no reverence for mine?"

"I'm sorry for that."

"Words do not take away the kill-shot."

"Ignore me, Ra'aa'al. My lungs burn for song."

Nobody wanted to hear of his problems, he accepted, for others had just as much trouble or possibly more.

What can we converse about for all these sun-cycles?

He wanted to return to the dream land, but he feared another journey of sorrow.

As the long-cycles added up to become a mountain of time, Toog grew hardened to his torture. He would turn his hand around on the metal bolt to learn how long he could endure before the pain would overcome him. He counted long numbers in his head to keep his mind alive. He taught himself to memorize long passages from the scrolls of his youth to exercise his mind. He worked his free arm and legs, flexing his muscles, keeping them strong.

He learned about the universe from Ra'aa'al, and its structure, and about the balance. He learned about the Masters and how they used the universe, sweeping across worlds, gathering its creatures. He learned how to forget hunger, to ignore thirst, to go without rest for long periods. He learned all there was to know about the place where they were kept. He learned how to be tough, how to ignore pain, how to forget torture, how to be strong.

Ra'aa'al taught him the trick of communicating through waves to others who used different languages, as he and Toog did. Ra'aa'al taught him how to speak into the mind-cave of another creature.

Toog learned how to survive, to continue living—living for that double-warm short-cycle when he would meet his family again.

A year later the Masters came for him.

STEPHEN SWARTZ

▶ ▶ ▶   3

Toog lay atop hot, steaming, jagged rocks in his mind-cave, deep in the dream land, as pictures of his youthful days flashed across the walls. The weight of three mountains pressed on his head, growing into pain and spreading across his face. He was tossed back into the waking world as the pain reached an unbearable level. He grabbed tightly to his stone shelf with his free hand.

When the pain subsided, Toog opened his eyes, afraid of what he might see. Along the wall opposite his stone shelf, light seeped in from what appeared to be a passage. The rest of the container was as dark as ever.

Two figures stood tall in the illuminated opening. Two others stood behind the first two. They all wore dark cloth which covered their heads and bodies. The shadows of the head coverings hid their faces. As much as Toog wanted to see them, to look into their eyes, to ask them *Why?* it was enough that Toog knew they must be the Masters. It was his first view of them.

Two Masters bent over him and with two hard tugs with a large forked tool they removed the metal bolt from Toog's hand.

He wanted to launch a wrath-call of the universe from that pain but he knew now that urge was only instinct. He decided to tell his inner Ru there was no pain. He had learned to forget pain.

The Masters in the doorway spoke to the one who had removed the bolt. Toog heard the spoken words in his ears yet in his mind-cave came no understanding.

They pulled Toog up and set him on his feet. He sank in their grip as his slender legs weakened. They grasped him tightly at his shoulders and dragged him out of the dark container.

Toog felt the burning sensation of the Masters' touch, some kind of rough covering on their large hands in contact with his bare silvery skin. The burning increased as they maneuvered him through the doorway.

As he was pushed through the opening into the passage, Toog felt a different kind of pain fill his body, like a flooding sea, and he fought against the Masters' grip, made them stop.

"I will remember you, Ra'aa'al," Toog called back.

As Toog spoke, he saw in the shaft of light from the open doorway a scaly creature of green and gray stripes, covered in curving spikes, stretched out on the other stone shelf. Ra'aa'al's head lay in the shadows.

As Ra'aa'al spoke, he lifted his head into the light.

"And I shall remember you, Toog of Sebbol."

Toog back-turned quickly at the sight: the face, foaming yellow saliva and pink mucus, more ugly than a diseased *suur* on Sebbol.

The Masters took him from the container and led him down the bright corridor until they reached a pair of large doors.

Toog held his eyes closed against the brightness yet took quick glances as best he could. The corridor appeared smooth on all its surfaces and pure white like the blood of an *ourk*. He tried to draw a picture on the wall of his mind-cave, enough to remember the directions of his journey. He would need to remember.

When they halted, one of the Masters ahead of him touched a small square on the wall and two doors slid each direction into the wall, creating an opening.

The one who opened the doors stepped aside and the Masters holding Toog pushed him forward.

He tripped into the new container, blinding light striking him at the same instant he was thrust down to the floor, his arms and legs crumpled underneath his body. He strained to see through the beam of light as he dared raise his eyes. Another Master sat behind a large shelf which floated above the floor. The great cloth of this Master covered all the head and body, the cloth the color of the inner life-stream flowing through Toog's body.

He thought of the words Ra'aa'al had taught him:

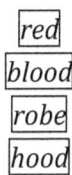

He still could not see the face of this Master, hidden within the shadow of the hood's overhang.

Behind Toog, the doors closed with a soft hum.

The Master with the red robe stood and moved around the side of the shelf to where Toog rested on his bent-legs. The brilliant light and glowing white walls, floor, and ceiling continued to blind him whenever he tried to gaze up into the Master's face. Daring to look down, he saw his skin was less silvery, more dull gray, and dark blue spots had started to appear on his lower arms. The hole in his hand was round and smooth, clear and open.

Strange words were spoken by the red-robed figure and Toog was not sure if he was being addressed. The robed figure pointed at Toog with a red-gloved hand.

Two Masters in black robes jerked him to his feet and Toog fell back promptly on his leg joints, bending the opposite direction like he did during mating. His collapse on the floor was followed by a kick to the back of his head by one of the Masters.

Toog dropped onto his face, his cheek against the floor—which had its own heat and burned his skin. The dream land was opening to him, a wide-mouthed *gulk* calling him, slimy green tongue rolling out like a path into the temple, yet he could not allow himself to go there.

Above him, the Masters were speaking among themselves, their voices low and deep. He could not understand the words. No words entered his mind-cave with clear meaning. All he saw were puffs of dust.

Suddenly he was being dragged across the floor by his arm, the hand with the hole in it flapping against the Master's grip.

Did they think he was in the dream land?

Entering a new cell, the Masters lifted Toog onto a high shelf, and cut away his cloth. He lay without cloth on the shelf yet was too weak to move. Placed on his back, his arms and legs were out-stretched and clipped to devices at the corners of the shelf. A large bright light lowered from the ceiling on a long branch.

The red-robed Master entered, arriving beside the high shelf. Toog's eyes blinked. He gazed up at the Master—their shaman, it seemed—trying to see this Master's face within the shadow of the cloth hood.

If only I could meet eyes with him, then he would know I am guided by an inner Ru. I am not a field-beast. He will know a mistake has been made. Then he will release me and send me home.

Toog thought he could see hairs growing from the lower face of the Master. The shaman of his village also had strings blooming from his lower face. It was a sign of wisdom on his world. Toog saw two eyes hidden in the shadow of the hood. A long projection between the eyes which must be an *ag*—the *wo* intake.

This Master is not so different from me, from the Aull of Sebbol. We can find a short-bridge between us. Let us correct this error.

The red-robed Master examined Toog with various instruments from a nearby wall-mounted box that extended over to the shelf on long threads. Toog had never seen anything like the system. He was too afraid to move. However, his eyes followed every movement of the Master, as well as the delicate movements of the tools used. He could not feel what the tools were doing to him. His body was unable to move and his skin had no sensation.

Am I a field-beast?

Finally, the Master stopped, satisfied or convinced or no longer interested, and stepped away, speaking to the other Masters, waving a red-gloved hand at Toog,

The two Masters in black robes pulled Toog off the board and stood him up like a blossoming *flao*. Toog swayed on his weak legs. His head filled with clouds and rain fell upon his mind-cave.

A third Master appeared from a new opening in the wall. That Master carried a white cloth, Toog saw, and the cloth was pushed at him. Toog took the cloth and saw it was something meant to cover his body.

They know me now. They see I am like them.

He felt warm rain wetting his mind-cave and flowers sprouted from the soil.

The black-robed Masters put the cloth on Toog, dropping it over his smooth head and moving his arms and legs through openings as though he was a springling's toy. The new cloth was fresher than his old rags, so he believed he was getting a reprieve.

They know I do not belong here. They are sending me home.

He was stood up, wavering on his feet, as the Masters studied him. They were twice his height, bulky under their robes, and he feared them yet held back his words. He wanted to question them. He wanted to go home, too.

The red-robed Master spoke and the group stepped out of the bright container. Toog was led to the container where he first saw the red-robed Master.

Toog was positioned in front of the floating shelf where the Master waited. The light was blinding, but Toog, eyes opened only as slits, could see two hand-sized objects on the top of the shelf. The first appeared to be a metal rod with a red ornament at one end and a blue ornament at the opposite end. The other object seemed to be attached to the shelf, looking like an overturned bowl.

Toog relaxed, expecting a prayer from the red-robed Master, words that would mean he was free.

They had examined him, found him healthy, he believed, and given him new cloth. Regardless of the reason for keeping him in those two cells for so long, if he was going home now, he would forget all of it. He just wanted to return home. He wanted to be with his full-mate and their springling again.

The Masters in black robes sprang into action. One placed his arms around Toog's narrow chest and held him tightly while the other took Toog's hand—the one where the bolt had been—and pressed it over the bowl-shaped object. Flashes of fire burned into his hand, seared through it, as he strained against the grip that the Master had on his body. Then his hand was ripped from the object as the red-robed Master took the metal rod and, aiming with the red ornament end, stabbed it through the hole in his hand.

A special new pain charged up his arm like a frightened herd of *borrox*, running wild, up his arm to his head and down his spine to his feet. His wrath-call of the universe was already sounding before Toog could summon it. The air inside him did not return and his call fell quickly to a raspy moan, like the cries of a dead *suur* on cold nights. Toog's body went limp and he hurdled into the dream land.

No pictures appeared on the walls of his mind-cave, none until he arrived in the waking world once more with a rough shake and opened his eyes to see he was being carried on a large wagon that went on its own wheels with no *borrox* to pull it.

As his eyes adjusted to the gray skies and gray landscape, the wagon came to an arched gate, a metal fence extending far in each direction, and halted. A hard, cold wind cut through him as he sat on the board of the wagon with other strange creatures.

◦

It was not like any place Toog had ever seen. On Sebbol, the land was covered in vibrant flora, great sprouts of every kind reaching to the skies. And the rises of the ground were not so high, not so rugged except the high mounts far to the east, where birthed flowing streams of *lool*. Everywhere was calm *lool* into which many of his village would swim or languish in repose, letting their inner Ru have rest. The containers which formed their communities were orderly, each container kept clean. There were many young ones always about. And females and males going about their tasks. And the sun-fire warmed them. The only problems they had were falling crystals and the arrival of the Masters.

Around him now a rocky terrain without flora extended as far as he could see. There was no show of living flora. Close by, he saw small leafy things no longer than his fingers, green and blue, rising between the rocks. Such a foreboding place! And there was no sun-fire in the sky, only a steady gray. It was a rare color on Sebbol. Everything was orange, two shades of yellow, four shades of blue, six shades of green, and seven shades of red. Only the skin of the Aull was close to gray—yet their silvery flesh shimmered like minerals sprinkled in the ground or drifting in the streams of *lool*.

How could any life survive on this dead world? And the *oum* here were so cold as it blew against him. His silvery skin burned with the cold, turning dull gray.

As the wagon jerked to a halt, Toog heard distant shouts, like the wrath-calls of the universe. His inner Ru was beating hard on a skinbox to alert him. Run, shouted his inner Ru, yet Toog could not move his spindly legs. He was attached to the wagon.

A group of Masters, covered in dark, stiff cloth now, gathered at the rear of the wagon. They raised some kind of weapon to him and the others on the wagon. The leader, dressed not in robes but in a tight-fitting garment with animal-skin foot coverings and a strap of dangling metal pellets, pointed his hand at them and up-swung his leather-wrapped arm.

When Toog was slow to respond, the leader grabbed his arm and jerked him off the wagon. Toog fell to the ground and remained on his leg joints while the others followed his pose one at a time and likewise knelt on the frozen ground.

Toog turned and gazed upon the variety of beings climbing out of the wagon and forming a group beside him. He had never seen so many different creatures—not even as pictures on the walls of his mind-cave. So many different beings Great Goddess Aull could bear from her vast womb! Could they truly be siblings? Creatures from other worlds, other parts of the universe, Toog thought, creatures like Ra'aa'al, the lizard.

Am I to be kept with these creatures?

Do they not know I am from Sebbol, the heart of paradise?

I am not from a world of pity, ugliness, and filth!

There are goddesses who care for me and my people!

The creatures, including Toog, were chained together, the metal links passing through the holes in their hands. They were herded by the team of Masters away from the wagon and through a gated arch. Down a deep-rutted, muddy road they went in a single line.

Toog, leading the line of captives, could not gaze upon them as they followed behind, but one look had been enough. There were large, hairy, muscular creatures standing on two bare feet. These creatures were much taller than common *udu* who lived in the *fleal* of Sebbol, and these had on their heads short spikes, similar to what sprouted from the heads of *veedo*. There were smaller, slimy four-foot beings who raised up on their rear legs when needed. They had four eyes. There was a creature like Ra'aa'al. Or what Toog thought Ra'aa'al was; his glance was so brief. Only one other being was close to an Aull like Toog, having two legs and two arms, round face and slim body like Toog yet with much hair on its head.

Toog tried to speak to the other Aull-type being but it did not understand Sebbou. Perhaps Great Goddess Aull birthed beings on more worlds than Sebbol, setting a new fire burning in his mind-cave. The Aull were spread across the sky of stars!

The Masters led the captives along the muddy road, pushing one here, jabbing another there with the ends of their stubby weapons. Toog noted the weapons: not the usual tubes that released flying barbs like when his hunt-group were killing beasts for food. These weapons were short like *ybou* fruit, with a thick tube and boney handles. They certainly did not seem like the type of weapon to shoot out anything harmful.

Here, between the dark gray skies and dirty brown ground, the Masters' faces could be clearly seen. They wore tight-fitting caps that appeared to be animal skin. The caps covered their foreheads and ears and tightly framed their faces with straps connecting beneath their chins. Toog was reminded of the head covering the shaman in his village wore when doing daily tasks on temple grounds. He guessed the Masters' faces were like his—like an Aull—having two eyes, one nose, one mouth. Covering their nose and mouth was a small gray box with two tubes falling to another box hooked to their hip straps. Despite that device, all the Masters that Toog had seen also had thick brown or yellow hair on the lower half of their faces. Above the boxes their eyes were deep-set and expressionless, almost like those of the captives they tended.

They are not so different from Aull. If they could see me for what I am, they would know I am misplaced here.

The muddy road took a turn into a canyon with hewn

sides, and the surface they tread turned from mud to gravel. The canyon was short but its cliffs steep. It reminded Toog of the wilderness of Ila on his home world.

The canyon widened into an out-carved basin where teams of laborers were hitched to long, thick ropes, trying to pull huge stone blocks out of the mountainside.

The loud crack of the punishment-ropes caught Toog's attention. They seemed much harsher than those used to train a new shaman on his world. His ears were filled with the wrath-calls of the universe from laborers all around him.

Suddenly Toog was yanked backward. When he turned to see the cause, the pair of four-footed beings were attempting to break free, pulling against the metal links. The Masters shouted at them, then one shot something from the weapon he carried and the two four-footed beings lay still in the mud.

One Master called for the line to start moving.

Toog pushed a foot forward. As he gazed upon the undulating mass of horror in the basin ahead, he saw a collection of creatures assembled from many worlds, mostly creatures like the horned *udu*-type beings that were arriving with him. Their tough, muscular bodies were right for this kind of hard work, Toog thought, so why was he here, tied up beside them? He was weak next to the *udu*-beings.

The line of new laborers was met by a Master in a tight brown uniform escorted by two black-uniformed guards. They spoke with the leader of the arrival party, then looked over the new laborers, painting the brown-uniformed Master's face with joy-light as he studied the strong, muscular *udu*-beings and frowned at Toog and the others. The Master leader directed the guards to escort the new laborers to a small container, which looked like it was made of strips of *fleal*, on the other side of the hollowed-out mountain.

Crossing the basin, the line moved among the teams of cable-pullers and whip-throwers. Lines of creatures tugged at thick metal cables attached to large boulders, prying them from the belly of the mountain. Toog gazed up at the creatures standing with swirling metal diggers and carving tools along the top of the mountain. He heard the grunting and moaning of the laborers, smelled the musky stench of work-rain from thirty different beings, felt their belly-fire and heart-cuts—the same fire and cuts he knew he would soon feel.

Toog decided his inner Ru could not welcome all the mouths to feed as he cleaned the mind-cave for the invaders. He called to his inner Ru and received only a fearful whimper echoing back.

We do not belong here. There is nothing for us here.

Toog's group of laborers halted, arranged in files in front of the weathered shack. Another Master, wearing a dark blue robe, stepped out from the building carrying a tablet. He looked at the laborers assembled, looked at his tablet, back at the laborers, back at the tablet again. He spoke to the guards, pointed at each of the laborers in turn then pointed to a particular team of cable-pullers.

Maybe I should tell this one that I am not supposed to be in this place. It must be clear to them. Then they will send me home.

Before he could speak, the guards took Toog and three *udu*-beings, and the other Aull across the quarry to one of the cable teams. The lead guard waved up at the director, perched like a *re-kon* atop the rocks, who called for the team to halt.

The Master placed Toog within the line and detached the chain, running it out of the hole in his hand and replacing it with a rough metal cable that was threaded through the hole in his hand again. The new cable ran parallel to the cables attached to the large rock resting against the mountainside.

Toog looked at his hand while the Masters hitched up the other laborers. His hand had turned black around the hole. Probably, the branding he suffered at the prison. At least he felt no more pain. It seemed as though his hand was no longer connected to his mind-cave.

The other laborers were hitched to the cables and the Master waved at the director again. The metal cables jerked as creatures pulled the line taut and strained to move the giant boulder along the well-worn path.

This? This is the new picture on the wall of my mind-cave?

Toog tried to wipe away the pictures on the walls of his mind-cave as he called for his muscles to share the burden. The Masters shouted at them, words he could not understand. He tried to ignore the pain-cries of his inner Ru. There were no dream land pictures that could help him now.

He called his muscles to tighten. If he did not, he knew there would be punishment.

Perhaps if I work hard and please them, they will let me go home.

So I will work as hard as I can....

Let them see me work....

The icy wind suddenly blew hard against Toog, and he knew he would be here for a long time.

◆◡

The long-cycles turned as Toog worked in the quarry. The cold, gray days were long and hard, the black nights short and colder. The laborers never got enough repose. The work never ended, the well-deserved break never came. His muscles had grown with the work, and his mind-cave had hard walls, the pictures burned into them, smoke rising with every line drawn.

He observed the other beings, and the Masters, watched their actions, saw how their inner Ru directed each of them. Or did not. Most of them remained grim-faced and sorrow-drenched, mind-caves empty of drawings and no inner Ru to advise them. They were like wayward villagers who had fallen into a slough-pit of farming *grut* and struggled to climb out. Toog hid his inner Ru, fearing the Masters might think he resisted them.

The path was well worn from the stone cliffs to the wagons in the valley below, a half-day's journey under the labor of pulling cables. His team was run back from the wagons to the cliffs to make the short-cycles turn. Sometimes the Masters seemed to invent a game, making each team run faster than other teams. The slowest team was hit with wild ropes that cut their skin. His silvery skin suffered. The winning team got drinks of *lool*—what he learned the Masters called "vod."

The muscular *udu*-beings seemed to be able to measure time without the aid of a cycle counter. Toog relied on his inner Ru for counting, but his inner Ru often hid from him, afraid to come out into this harsh life. One of the *udu*-beings who had arrived at the quarry with Toog told him through a voice that echoed in his mind-cave that they had been hitched to the cables for one of the Masters' sun-cycles. Toog remembered Ra'aa'al saying that one sun-cycle on the

Masters' world equaled three of Toog's world. His heart split in five parts, and two parts slowly melted into red-slime as he saw the pictures on his mind-cave dimming.

The *udu*-beings didn't speak much and held their heads lowered as if filled with the sorrow-sludge.

Toog knew the *udu*-beings were strong enough to break their bonds, yet they didn't. He decided to try the skill that Ra'aa'al taught him when they shared the dark container: to speak without sound, to share thoughts between mind-caves.

"You are strong creatures," Toog communicated to the *udu*-being hitched beside him as they were approaching the wagons on a cold windy day worse than most. "Why not break the bonds?"

Toog and the *udu*-being continued tugging on the cable, their tattered garments flapping in the wind.

The *udu*-being glared at Toog, the same look as Toog would give if bothered by a small *suuk*, then lowered his head again.

He did not understand me.

Toog grunted with his effort, the *udu*-being breathing louder, as they pulled the cable with the others.

"Tell me why you do not escape?" asked Toog, curiosity turning to desperation. "How are you called? From where do you come?"

The *udu*-being looked up again, his long tongue licking saliva off one of his long fangs.

"I am called Trexon. From Xmburrhaltis."

The *udu*-being spoke the words yet Toog's ears heard them in the *udu*-being's language. In his mind-cave, however, the words sounded in Toog's language. His inner Ru was reciting Sebbou!

"Trexon," Toog spoke, using his mouth, "why do you not

break your bonds? Why do you not try?" His chirps were not very loud.

The *udu*-being seemed to dislike the questions, paused in his pulling, enough to catch the Masters' attention.

"You do not understand!" Trexon growled.

"Understand what?"

"We are a conquered species." Trexon looked away, returned his gaze to Toog. "We have nothing to return to."

Toog lowered his gaze, the well-spring of sorrow founting in his mind-cave, splashing against the walls. Such a huge creature! And now as weak as a slithering *fuug*! He found himself sneaking glances at the *udu*-being—the Xmburrhaltis creature.

"The Masters have cut us all from our families," spoke Toog.

The *udu*-being turned his head left and right. It was the same gesture Toog's people would do to show agreement. He knew the Xmburrhaltis creature had heard his words in its mind-cave.

The pressure-pain of fear choked him, eyes out-squeezing the sorrow-rain as his thoughts plummeted in his mind-cave. In the pictures shown on the walls, he saw his full-mate's face drawn there. He heard his springling squeaking in her swing-basket. He felt the chewing-pain in his belly increase, the same pain which had been there since the night he was captured—

Listen.

The chakari *have stopped squeaking.*

Something is wrong—

Crackkkk!

Toog felt the Master's whip cutting into his back, shocking him out of his trance. He heard the Master call to him angrily.

"You will work!"

Toog squeezed his top-orb inward then outward, agreeing. He did understand. He had heard the Master's words clearly in his ears, as always, but this time also in his mind-cave, with his inner Ru speaking them in his own language.

The Master suddenly stood beside Toog, towered over him.

"Skinny monster! Why do you delay? Answer!"

The Master raised his whip to strike. Toog continued pulling on the cable as though the Master was not there, the transgression already settled. He had understood. He was returning to his labor.

"Skinny monster! Why do you defy me?" came words to his ears and inside his mind-cave.

I am not defying the Masters. I am continuing my task.

The Master turned toward the cliffs and the team director high on the wall, motioning for the team to halt.

Toog knew then that his words were not heard or understood by the Master standing beside him.

"I work hard for the Masters," Toog spoke, his low squeaks and chirps gaining no attention. They did not understand Sebbou.

The director signaled back and the cable instantly became slack, the giant stone halted in its path.

The line of creatures halted, their muscles heaving, their work-rain thick in Toog's nose, their breaths sharp as falling crystals—

"Skinny monster!" the Master spoke with heart-cutting tone. "Why do you defy me?"

The Master slapped the whip down hard across Toog's smooth back as the director approached.

Toog cringed, dropped onto his leg joints, wishing that his inner Ru would stay hidden and safe from the lightning-pain.

"I do not defy the Masters," Toog spoke with sun-fire behind his words. He hoped his words would enter the Master's mind-cave and be understood. Awaiting the response, he down-bent against the whip-falls.

"You defy me!" the Master shouted, putting his full strength into lashing the whip.

Even as Toog cried out his reply amid the cuts of the whip, he knew the Master must have understood.

"Forgive my mistake," Toog called out, in both vocals and mind-cave words.

Suddenly, Toog heard the sound of metal being torn and looked up to see the creature from Xmburrhaltis, Trexon, break the cable into strips of jagged metal and free his hand. Trexon grabbed the Master's whip, broke it across the Master's neck. Trexon strangled the Master with one big hand while tearing in two the cable which ran through Toog's hand.

The entire valley of cable-pullers quickly became aware what was happening although they continued their work. The director of Toog's team ran down the line toward the disturbance, calling guards to follow.

The other Aull in Toog's team extended a leg and tripped the director as he ran by and the director fell down on the muddy gravel while the Aull caught in his hand the weapon the director dropped. The other Aull called to Toog and tossed the weapon to him.

Unsure how to operate it, Toog pressed the trigger and released a red beam of light which burned a line in the mud and ice ahead of the approaching team of security guards.

Trexon dropped the body of the lifeless Master and ran down the line pulling the cable from the hands of the other cable-pullers. As they were released, they set about breaking the cables of neighboring teams.

A squad of reserve guards arrived and ran to encircle the quarry. They fired into the raging mob of laborers destroying the cables and pulleys.

One team let the huge stone they were pulling topple onto a pair of Masters who had been abusing them. The screams of the Masters let all the laborers know the Masters were not superior beings, not lords of the universe, but simple beings like them, like the laborers. They wore flesh which could be torn and bones which could be crushed. Their screams were like beasts—not at all divine.

"Laborers!" Toog shouted in Sebbou as loud as he could, hoping the different species might understand his message, written on the walls of their mind-caves in their own languages. "Fight! Now is the time to fight!"

The drillers had tossed their tools off the cliffs and laughed as they smashed on the rocks below. Some heaved Masters off the cliffs as others below took stones to the Masters' heads and bodies.

"Laborers! Destroy the Masters!" Toog launched with poisonous mouth-fire. He could see they knew what to do, whether or not they understood his words.

With the Masters' weapon in his hands, Toog ran across the quarry basin and toward the trail which led out through the short canyon to the gravel road. The other creatures ran after him, shouting and throwing rocks up at the Masters who were mounting the rim of the quarry.

The guards fired down on the fleeing laborers, leveling whole sections of the mob with their red-beamed weapons.

Toog and several others who had captured weapons fired up at the guards, but their use of the weapons was inferior.

"You are surrounded!" the quarrymaster shouted down from the top of the cliffs, protected by guards. "Halt! Stop! You cannot escape! You can only die! Only die! You hear? Listen, slaves! You are all conquered species! Your place is to work or die! Return to your lines, to your cables!"

Toog heard the words again in both his ears and his mind-cave. How did the others understand what the Master had spoken?

To work or die?

Several more blasts convinced the laborers of the truth of what the quarrymaster had said. The rampaging faltered.

"Bring forward those who started this rebellion! Bring them forward," the quarrymaster demanded.

Almost instantly, the crowd parted as several *udu*-beings from Xmburrhaltis carried Toog and pushed Trexon forward. The two of them were dumped on the ground at the base of the cliffs.

"That's the one who killed the overseer!" the Aull who first gave Toog the weapon shouted from the front of the crowd. Toog heard the words in his ears and did not understand the language—must not be Aull like Toog—but in his mind-cave he understood.

The other Aull was pointing to Trexon.

Immediately, a guard standing beside the quarrymaster raised his weapon and fired a long red blast at Trexon. The Xmburrhaltin's body bent at the middle, melting away to clear air between his chest and hips. The two sections of his body dropped to the ground.

As the crowd was again hitched to what remained of the cables, and the quarrymaster's hut smoldered from the weapons fire, Toog was wrapped in metal links and taken away.

e x p e r i m e n t

 4

Toog awoke with a rough out-toss, like he had his throat filled with *saak*, and a long rasp-moan like the dying call of a wounded *ourk* coupled with the whimpering trail of a wrath-call of the universe that had been silenced yet still echoed between planets. There was a bright burn-pain in his hand. He gazed in the dark nothingness and felt the chill and the damp.

So I am not killed.

So I am returned to the stone container.

His inner Ru peeped out from behind a wall in his mind-cave. It was a journey through the dream land like no other, chased by wild *veedo* under a dark red sky full of falling crystals. Reaching the top of a high mount, another, larger mountain crashed down upon him, sending his body slithering down the slopes like streams of *ouk*.

"What did you do?" a voice asked.

Toog startled. The voice he heard in his mind-cave was not his inner Ru, yet it was like a warm repose mat with a full-mate to smooth his scars. No words echoed in the stone cell.

"Ra'aa'al?" Toog *thought.*

"Yes, Toog of Sebbol."

"Ra'aa'al of Ra'a'am'mas'sandiit." He wondered how long he had been bolted to the stone shelf. He sighed. "We are together again."

"What did you do?"

The words floated through Toog's mind-cave and settled on the dusty floor in a neat arrangement. His inner Ru had no difficulty reading them.

"I started a fight," Toog replied in shameful tone.

"No, I mean your work."

"A mountain was being cut into blocks. We pulled the stones away. The land was cold and the sky was gray."

There was a silence that grew darker as Toog's echo faded. He tried to see Ra'aa'al through the darkness.

"Ra'aa'al...?" he called.

"Us-ku-ga," Ra'aa'al whispered slowly.

"What?"

"Uskuga. What they call the land where you worked. It is near here."

"Have you been there?" asked Toog.

"No."

"Then how do you know it?"

"I gather the thoughts from those among us."

After the trouble he caused, Toog believed he would be killed—the punishment he earned. That was how it was done on Sebbol yet few community members ever caused such trouble. If an Aull lost control of his body and killed another, then the shaman would send the killer away, out into the wilderness and some beast would take them apart, returning his body to the *wa.*

The Masters surely must have a harsher punishment than any Sebbol rite. They must have forgotten him already.

"How long have I been returned to this cell, Ra'aa'al?"

"Twelve of your long-cycles."

"Only twelve?"

"Yes. Three feeding pods and four water draws. So twelve."

"Lost in the dream land all that time. Yet I learned nothing. My inner Ru hid from me, and my feet hurt like broken crystals cut into them. The sun-fire was hot. And the mountain fell—"

"Better that than a wakeful forever."

Toog stopped his *thinking*, sighed. "I was at that mountain for two sun-cycles."

"Not so long then."

He waited for a response. Nothing. The sorrow-rain flooded his bowels. *How long has Ra'aa'al been here?*

"Ra'aa'al, I...."

His voice fell silent as he remembered his earlier lessons. One did not speak of the past here. Nobody would listen. Only in the dream land could he ask questions. He could speak to his inner Ru although he might get no reply. He only wanted peace and he found none when his inner Ru did not respond.

A fire-pain sparked in his chest, and he feared falling forever into the dream land.

He gazed into the dark nothingness for many cycles.

Is this the end for me?

Will I die here, too, and leave a bad smell for Ra'aa'al?

Will anyone know what happened to me?

Toog listened to the nose-noise of his inner Ru and decided to surrender. His inner Ru sang a soft lament as he put away his drawing tools and sat with spindly legs folded before the walls of his mind-cave. Within thirty breaths Toog was submerged in the star-fire of his mind-cave, gazing out to the universe. In that view he saw the past like a string of bobbles and trinkets strewn along the path, each one ready to explode with a forest of pictures if he picked it up and held it in his hands. So he stepped around them, ignoring the heart-cuts that penetrated his chest with each foot-step. He went further into that dark nothingness, further into the long, black, death-trance which had served as his repose during the past three sun-cycles of the Masters' world.

When he arrived in the waking world again, his hand hurt no more. His cell was as always a dark nothingness.

"They come for you," the one named Ra'aa'al spoke to Toog, the words echoing through his mind-cave.

The machine-wagon rumbled roughly over the bumpy dirt road, shaking Toog into the waking world.

He was chained to the board in the rear of the wagon like he was when taken to the work camp. He looked around, saw three other prisoners. They were like him yet different: beings who resembled Aull, yet not the kind from Sebbol. They were also chained.

He examined the guards in their close-fitting brown uniforms with devices hanging from their bodies, weapons poised, sitting at the far end of the board. They wore clear masks over their faces, with large windows to look out.

Peering out through the gap between the wagon's waving over-cloth, Toog saw the landscape: rough, barren, rocky, under dismal skies. Cold mist hit Toog's face as the *oum* blew in. A small patch of pale leaves tried to grow beside the road in spots. Such a dead place! Away from the road, the land lay as brown as *udu* fur, broken by outcroppings of black or gray rock.

When the wagon rolled to a stop, the first guard jumped out and turned to show his masked face to the prisoners as they climbed out. They were strung together with metal links.

After landing on his wide feet, Toog scanned the area. The *oum* whipped drops of *lool* against his tattered rags. His bare arms had darkened with the cold, his silver turning dull gray.

There was no sign of a work camp, no smell of work-rain, no noise of whips cracking and creatures howling their wrath-calls of the universe. Nothing. Only the wind, the misty rain, the mud of the road—and the sound of the guard's gruff voice ordering him and the other prisoners to march in a line off the road, down a trail past a large bare-rock hill.

The guards followed, holding their weapons ready.

Toog was the third prisoner in line. The first one was tripping constantly, and looked injured. He suddenly spoke up in a pained voice, apparently asking the nearest guard where they were going and what they would be doing.

The guard saw the prisoner stumbling to keep upright as his rags grew dark with blood from his legs. Then without a pause, he pointed his weapon at the prisoner and fired a flash of orange light which burned into his back and burst out his front. A spray of orange and blue body matter splattered the rocks they were passing. The prisoner writhed in agony, then collapsed.

The prisoners had to keep going, dragging the dead one.

They moved further, as long as the walk from the arched metal gate at the work camp through the short canyon to the basin cut into the mountain. Toog's bare feet were becoming caked with the cold mud.

Finally they stopped in front of a small gray cliff. It made a wall. The cliff was spotted with red patches—and a yellow and a green patch. The guards directed the prisoners to stand against the cliff wall. The guards spoke in cheer-tone among themselves.

They were going to be killed, Toog suddenly knew, looking at the stains behind him on the rock.

Weapons were raised. The guards aimed at the first prisoner. Two flashes of bright red light struck him, one at the shoulders, one low on the abdomen, splitting him into three sections which fell into a clump on the cold mud. They fired again at the three portions until it all was a puddle of fluids that flowed away into a ditch.

The guards turned and again the weapons fired, separating the fourth prisoner. They continued until the body was liquefied. Only Toog remained. The guards turned their weapons on him, fingers weighing on the power switches—

Bzzzzzz.

The sound came from the nearest guard's belt. He lowered his weapon, opened the clip on his waist band and spoke to the device.

Toog heard their spoken words but nothing echoed in his mind-cave.

The guard with the communication device looked up at him, speaking to the other guard as he replaced the device on his waist band.

Toog suddenly heard some of the words in his mind-cave:

monster

return

fortress

"You!" the guard shouted.

Toog heard it both in his ears and in his mind-cave. His inner-Ru peered around the corner of his mind-cave, fearful.

"Six-nine-six-six lives a little longer."

"Why?" asked the other guard.

"Some scientist wants to study it."

"Probably cut him apart to see if anything can be used."

Toog watched them with a sense of relief as the guards set fire to the bodies of the three unlucky prisoners. He watched them burn until only ashes remained. The wind carried the ashes away.

Slaps to his face shook Toog into the waking world.

He found himself fixed to a vertical seat, metal straps encircling his throat, waist, each ankle. A string of links ran through his hand hole and fastened to a metal loop in the frame of the seat. A bright light glared at him and he could not turn his head away, forcing him to shut his eyes tightly. He guessed that he was in the same room with the chief Master.

"Six-nine-six-six!" The voice was deep, like the grunt of a *goud*.

^sA $_fL'n$ $p^op^kp^op$, Toog's mind-cave echoed in Sebbou.

Toog tried to open his eyes, keeping them as slits. He could not move in his current position.

"You are strong!" the voice continued. He heard the words in his ears and understood nothing, yet within his mind-cave they were clearly written on the walls in Sebbou.

Through the blinding light Toog sensed dark beings moving behind the light. They wore the usual dark robes with hoods that covered their faces.

"You have worked well!"

A rough out-chucking came from the darkness behind the light. Toog thought the Master had stepped closer. The one in a red robe. Their shaman.

I am about to be freed.

"You are an interesting monster." There was a short laugh, like the bark of a *jaax*. "Short. Thin. Small oval head with no hair. And silver skin. Smooth skin. Slippery. Yet not so strong, not so limber. Pity." Again the laugh. "You are a mistake."

Yes! Finally they realize their error. He felt the burning of sun-fire inside his belly. *Now they will send me home.*

"You worked hard—for your size—at the Number Three Work Camp. Investigation concludes that you did not start the rebellion. Investigation concludes you did not kill anyone with the weapon you used. You operated the weapon improperly. You are a weak species, a waste of flesh and bone. We will close the portal to your world."

A great fire erupted in his mind-cave, the heat of flame which matched his mood at hearing they would not capture any more Aull. Yet the heat of fire-tongues stung his flesh as he realized he could not return home. The walls of his mind-cave blazed.

"The scientists have enough of a menagerie already," the deep voice continued, apparently speaking to another Master and not to Toog. "Only true laborers need be brought here. Others are little more than laboratory experiments."

His inner Ru waved his hands wildly in his mind-cave, trying to get his attention.

"They consider you an intelligent species." The sharp laughs cut into Toog's ears. "Perhaps enough to play board games with them." More of the joy-noise. "So we will not execute you."

There was a pause as the Master in the red robe stepped back, lost behind the bright light.

"We will transfer you to the scientists for whatever use they may find for you. Whenever they decide to use you." More of the deep laughs, like a dying *drouk*. "Because you are an intelligent being, we will answer a question which you may inquire."

His inner Ru pressed his hands to his head as if in pain, shaking his head before the walls of his mind-cave, as the Sebbou words melted down the walls, forming a black pool at the feet of his inner Ru. Toog spoke quickly, not knowing if the Masters would even understand him.

"How long have I been here?" he asked in Sebbou.

But the soft caws and high-pitched squeaks he produced caused more laughter from the figures behind the light.

A hand entered the light, waving side to side, and the laughs stopped. The hand held a small black square, a cube, which had an opening on the top yet was covered by silver metal strands. Toog heard his words repeated. They seemed to come from the small cube resting on the hand of the Master standing there.

Following his words came the words of the Masters, which he did not understand. They did not appear on the walls of his mind-cave. They floated in the air like dust then dissipated.

There was a grunt. "The first cell, when you were alone, was three of our years. The second cell was one year. The Number Three Work Camp was two years. Now seventy-seven of our days since returning to this facility."

Hearing the Sebbou words seeping from the small cube, Toog immediately wanted to respond.

So long away.... M'ah must be grown fully by today. Yet I will see her soon. L'ra will be waiting.

"This is an intelligent creature," spoke the deep voice to others, which quickly repeated in Sebbou from the cube.

"Why am I here?" asked Toog in his cawing, cooing, squeaking voice. "What did I do wrong?"

The hand closed over the small cube, then opened again. He heard his words come out in the Masters' language followed by the spoken words and the Sebbou equivalent from the cube.

"There is no right or wrong." Again the laughs. "You are a conquered species. Like other species you have seen here. Your purpose is to serve us." Laughs. "And you did—yes, as best you could, yet poorly." The voice was flat, like a dry *abo* in the Great Summer, thought Toog. "As stated, you are a mistake."

"What right have you to make other creatures your slaves?" Toog shouted—beeps turning to sharp chirps.

The deep voice: "This one understands. It is intelligent."

The cube translated.

"We have the right of a conquering species. We need no other. We have conquered all of this world. We have conquered other worlds. We have determined your world is suitable for settlement. We have need of new areas—"

"Settlement?" Toog squawked.

The cube hummed then spit out the translated speech. "Your world has suitable conditions for our settlement. You are a weak species. Conquest will be easy. We will occupy your world and survive there."

"Survive what?"

"This world is dying. The atmosphere is poisoned. We require another world. We explored many worlds. Your world is suitable. You are from that world so we will keep you alive for science."

The voice was without emotion and replied with an even tone, something created by the cube. He could hear the words of his language in his ears but not in his mind-cave. What he thought were laughs were just the sounds of the machine. There was no heart-spins to the answers. Perhaps the Masters standing around him did not know what he had asked.

"Your last inquiry?" the Master's language machine asked.

Toog squirmed in his seat, then spoke in a hard, lowered voice he had never used before:

"Where is my full-mate and my springling?"

Another cough, then laughs. The machine formed an answer.

"We do not keep records on those not taken."

So they are still on Sebbol. Safe there. Yet not for long.

A short grunt came from the Master in the red robe. Sounds of the machine winding down.

"Take him away."

Those words Toog heard in his mind-cave, although the words his ears gathered made no sense.

"Let his number be forgotten!"

"Let his body serve science!"

"Let his service never end!"

"Let him die away!"

The words cut through Toog, filled his mind-cave with flickering flames and billowing black smoke. Crystal shards flew through the passages of his mind-cave, scoring the walls, destroying pictures drawn on them. He ducked and dodged the shards but his inner Ru was struck and cut, ran out screaming.

A pair of hands draped in black cloth reached out from

the light nothingness and clenched his throat. A high-pitched moaning arose from somewhere in the container and echoed against the walls and deep-burrowed into his mind-cave, frightening his inner Ru. Deep voices spat out a deafening chant. Lights flashed, changing colors, faster and faster. Sky-fire shot through his mind, shaking his mind-cave to ruin, and crackled through his body.

When Toog returned to the waking world, he found himself in a completely dark place, as before, the dark nothingness deeper than before. He lay on another stone shelf, with spits of cold, moist air prickling his skin.

He recalled being led along a corridor. Several Masters in dark robes carried small, glowing light sticks in their hands. The same kind of light sticks were set in the wall along the corridor. Deep voices echoed in his mind-cave louder than they did in his ears, yet he did not understand their meaning.

No! This is not the way. You are supposed to free me and let me go home. Not this!

He saw himself thrown down on the stone shelf. He saw them slap his hand down as he squirmed like a *gurg* caught on a hook. He heard the ring of the hammer as it struck the bolt.

Clink—clink—clink.

Deeper, deeper.　　　blood　　　　flesh

Clink—clink.

Louder, deeper.　　pain　　　　pain　　　　pain

Clink.

He arrived in the waking world as rough and sudden as a *duur* exploding under the sear of the Great Summer sun, with his wrath-call of the universe already crashing wildly around the dark cell like a *boog* stung with star-fire.

He clutched his bolted hand with his free hand, staring out into the dark nothingness.

"Ra'aa'al?" he called, expecting a reply.

Nothing.

Nothing.

He listened to the silence, thought he heard the squeaking of second-summer *chakari*. He thought he could smell the sweet blue fragrance of his full-mate next to him. For a moment, he thought he heard his springling squeaking in her swing-basket. Then he saw the bright flash of orange light burst upon the walls of his mind-cave, and slowly fade—fading to an impossible blackness, leaving him drowning in sorrow-sludge.

◆◡

Escape

His inner Ru drew on the wall of his mind-cave, returned to each line and made them thicker. Pointing to the dark passage to the side of the wall, Toog understood. There would be only the dark nothingness if he did not break out of the stone container. But also a risk of dark nothingness if he did break out. And he would be on his own, without any goddess to help him.

Toog knew he would escape. He would make his way home to his family. Somehow. He must go. He must make them safe, possibly hide them in the Wilds of Gup, beyond the mountains of Mux. Other families could join them. His whole village would need to hide. The Masters were coming.

Then he would return to this cold world, their world, with as many Aull warriors as he could gather. They would destroy the Masters once and forever!

He cut his hand on a sharp rock deep in his mind-cave and pressed the bubbling white essence against the single fruit of the *bobu* fern growing at the center of his mind-cave, growing out of the Well of Kall, next to the birth pool of his inner Ru. In that act, the entire remainder of his life would be dedicated to the destruction of the Masters.

He rested for six short-cycles, digging for the treasure buried in his mind-cave, searching for the mighty *toom* that would carry him up the steep mountain, that would take him up to the star-seat of Great Goddess Aull, mother of the universe. There he would stand tall and extend his hands, show her the ugly hole in his hand. And Great Goddess Aull would weep and give him everything he needed to succeed in his plan, a good portion of her powers. She would call upon him to save the Aull of Sebbol from the Masters.

In the cold darkness Toog worked his hand around the bolt, tearing scabs, loosening it until he could squeeze his other, free hand underneath his bolted hand. He found that the bones in his bolted hand had thickened and become stronger. Yet the skin had torn and fused countless times, making the hole in his palm permanent.

With all his strength, Toog pulled at the bolt, prying it up with both his hands. Bit by bit he fought against pain as the bolt scraped upward, metal against stone, against flesh and bone, until the bolt finally slipped free from the stone shelf. With a great out-breath, Toog pushed the bolt from his hand, and in-drew a sharp breath as the metal fell to the floor, the clink on the stone floor echoing long in his ears.

He swung himself up to a sitting position on the stone shelf, feet dangling. He gazed out through the dark nothingness, into the direction of each wall, afraid to step down onto the floor and perhaps become lost in the dark nothingness.

Condemned to be entombed forever!

His inner Ru struck a stone that burned with blue fire, held it up in his mind-cave. The light leaked out of his eyes, bathing the room in faint blueness.

Toog stood, feet pressing down upon the stone floor, cold to his soles. His body swayed, his head full of *lool*, the blue light quivering. Settling his balance, he stepped to his left until he felt a wall. He began feeling the walls of his cell, step by step, hand by hand, wall by wall, as the faint blue glow showed him a small spot wherever his hands touched. In the darkness around him, he could detect no door, but he knew there must be one. He remembered being brought in through an opening in the wall to his left, but he was not sure now.

He went around the walls eleven times feeling for uneven surfaces. A crack that would hint at a door. A joint or catch or hinge or a scratch where someone had grabbed it during the closing. The walls felt smooth but not like stone: something unnatural, with the odor of the Masters' robes, a bitter scent like something made in a machine rather than grown in the soil.

He felt for differences in the air's temperature in his cell, pushing his fingertips along the smooth surfaces, but without success. The walls were not made of blocks of stone stacked one upon the other. He recalled how the shaman had pointed out how the abodes of his village had been built. This cell, though, seemed to be truly doorless—cleverly designed as a final repose container to hold him for all eternity.

Standing in the center of the dark cell, he extended his hands in opposite directions, turned his round head to its limits and back again. He listened for sounds outside the cell but he heard nothing. The blue glow faded, blinked out. His inner Ru had no more of those stones.

Panicked, Toog rushed to the wall to his right and, running his hands feverishly up and down its flawless surface, found the spot. He dismissed it on the eighth circling of the cell. A space between the slabs of stone, too narrow to see, where a faint puff of cold air seeped out at the very bottom and warm air leaked in at the top. A flaw, a clue. This was the door, he realized.

He found the bolt on the floor, hands sliding across the stone surface in the darkness. With its point he began digging between the slabs of stone, making a groove from top to bottom, testing the growing gap, trying its strength. Toog knew this was the way out. Carefully he worked his fingertips into the crack, tearing the skin around his claws. He sensed that some kind of sealant had been applied to the door before the final closing. He was meant to remain forever inside.

For Aull, the second finger was a knuckle longer than the other fingers. It was said that long ago Great Goddess Aull gave that finger more length and a sharper claw so they could dig into a *puut* even when it hung from higher stalks of the *puut'va* plant, what would likely be the last available food in a dying landscape.

Toog maneuvered his second-fingers into the gap he'd made. He pulled with all the strength he had used at the Number Three Work Camp. His fingertips dug a little deeper and he tried again. And again. He worked the stone's material into crumbles, let it drop to the floor as dust. Gradually, chips of material fell from the line he cut between the blocks, working deeper and deeper, from the very top to the bottom edge along the floor.

He refused to halt, rejecting failure. With his fingers bleeding and the skin of his hands torn, he attempted to wrench the huge blocks apart, to tear open the door. He labored for many short-cycles—to a long-cycle and beyond.

The door resisted—as though it were designed to endure the full span of cosmic time, a crypt where his dead form would be preserved, one poor sample of the race called Aull from planet Sebbol, perhaps to be discovered ages in the future. The stone slab he called the door resisted his straining—up to the instant when the door suddenly surrendered to his persistent strength and moved.

With a soft hiss, the door separated from the wall and a thin sliver of white light stabbed into the cell. But he did not stop. He grabbed the edge of the door and pulled with all the muscles he had built up at the work camp. He braced his feet, the claws of his toes digging into the floor. The stone slab moved more. The crack widened—then suddenly slid away from the wall as if by its own power, with more soft hisses as though a machine now operated it.

Without an extra blood-burp, Toog sprang from the dark cell into the bright corridor.

Everything was white—blinding to his eyes. Covers spiraled shut, but left a tiny opening for each eye to see out.

At the end of the corridor to his left stood a guard in brown robe, slumping against the wall. Catching the unexpected motion of the door sliding open, the guard quickly straightened up. The guard turned to him, its face a mask of fearful shock, eyes red, mouth turned up, teeth barred, ready to attack.

Toog hurled himself at the guard, rushing like an enraged *goud*, springing up from the floor and in one fluid motion drove the metal bolt straight into the guard's throat, leaving it there as his feet landed on the floor. The guard crashed to its leg-joints and toppled over. His hands sizzled with energy.

Kill! Now he was one of those warriors that came across the plain sometimes, attacking villages, cutting and spearing until enough white fluid flowed—and his body burned with hate.

Toog's inner Ru stood tall in his mind-cave, ready to cheer. His inner Ru's arm swept across the wall, dislodging a layer of dust which billowed away to reveal a drawing of squares. It showed the structure of the prison complex as Ra'aa'al had determined it from accessing the minds in the prison.

His inner Ru pointed to a passage while waving down at the guard on the floor.

Immediately Toog grabbed the guard's weapon off the floor. His blood-stained hands found the grips, and he took it up like a garden tool ready to cut the soil as his eyes searched for how to start the device. He recalled the Masters taking him to be killed at the cliffs had held this same kind of weapon. They had pushed this button, then that button. The weapon hummed to life.

Two more guards came casually around the corner, joy-noise spilling from their mouths as though they were off-duty, happy to be going home. Seeing the gray Toog standing in the corridor, they seized up, tried to swing up their weapons, but Toog squeezed the lever on his weapon first and they died with their mouths agape. *Kill!* The warrior burned with hate. The short, skinny, silver creature they had locked away had managed to pull the correct switch on the weapon's short, cylindrical body, releasing a hot red-light that cut their bodies apart.

As Toog felt the heat of the weapon's metal cylinder, his inner Ru knelt down and marked the path in his mind-cave. Go through the intersection of corridors there, then up the cascade of levels to the higher floor. Exit the large container there, enter the outside. Go to the top of the prison. There you will find a bridge to freedom.

Toog shifted the weapon in his hands, found the cascade of levels and mounted them, one small level at a time, then stepped quickly past more blocks of cells. He came to another cascade of levels but it led down, so he had no choice but to descend, his hard-soled feet clanging against the metal steps.

A Master in flowing brown robe, not carrying any weapon, started up the stairs, heavy foot coverings thumping against the steps. The Master had its face lowered. Toog pulled the lever on his weapon and the red light shot out, cutting the Master in half diagonally, from neck to hip, each half falling away in opposite directions.

Another guard immediately appeared at the bottom of the stairs, gazing up at him, probably hearing the commotion and possibly seeing what had happened to his comrade, catching sight of the red light from his weapon. This guard raised a weapon.

Toog leaped from the higher step, toe-claws poised, cutting the guard's face as he landed. Stumbling backwards and falling down, the guard slammed against the floor. The metallic noise of the stairs echoed loudly as Toog held the weapon's front end at the guard's head and let go the red light, leaving a crater in the guard's face. The sight of the cavity made him sick but he knew it was necessary.

The weapon was now too hot to hold. The Masters always wore coverings over their hands, he noted. He let the cylinder dangle by its strap. A red button on the top of the cylinder which had glowed steady was now pulsing.

His inner Ru had told him to go up, Toog recalled, so he turned toward the levels and bounded up the same set of steps, jumping over the split body of the guard there while its liquids ran down the metal steps.

The noise of approaching guards filled Toog's ear holes. He glanced around in every direction, panicking. He held up the weapon despite its heat, ready to shoot.

Two new guards arrived at the bottom of the stairs, saw him, started up without fear. Just a little gray monster, nothing to worry about. But Toog aimed his weapon on the first guard and lit it up, the red light sharp as a knife, cutting off its shoulder and arm. Fluids fountained from the wound as the guard dropped hard to its leg-joints, crumpling on the stairs.

Toog leaped from that step down onto the trailing guard who had crouched on the bottom step to take aim with his weapon, bowling over the guard. Toog trained his weapon on the guard as he tried to scramble to his feet, pushing off the gray monster, mouth ready to scream, to sound an alarm—but Toog's weapon shot again, cutting the guard's throat, leaving its head hanging by a flap of skin. Fluids spurted out of open tubes.

The breathing-point target was effective for silence-keeping, Toog noted. The Masters' vulnerability.

Free of the cascade of levels, Toog hurried across the large room at the bottom of the stairs as best he could, his big feet and the strong press of the air around him and the pull of the floor below him making it difficult. He had felt the same effects at the work camp, something strange about this world.

The vast room was filled with stacks of boxes and rows of barrels, the collection of all the supplies a prison needed. He was tempted to stop and take a look for food among the boxes but angry noise coming from behind him hurried him on.

When he got to the opposite side, he threw open a door there and charged out—

Out!

Outside!

Into the air!

He did not know where to go, had not thought that far ahead, too focused on simply getting out of that dark cell. Now—staring at the gray sky ahead and above him, taking the wind in his face—he knew that if he dared slow at any moment, he would be captured again. Yet he saw none of the guards out on this top area of the prison complex.

Now how to get out of the prison?

Keep in motion, wherever you go! his inner Ru warned.

Toog glanced in each direction as his inner Ru cursed him for the pause.

Smell the air! Hear the noise of machine-wagons. There is your exit, his inner Ru shouted.

A handful of Masters in brown robes and hoods strolled out from a side corridor on Toog's right, none of them bearing weapons and acting as though they were coming with full bellies from a meal, vocalizing and making much joy-noise.

Toog dashed to his left, hoping they did not notice him. He scurried away across the upper level of the prison complex, as though trying to hide from the entire sky overhead while the small group of Masters went to the right.

Toog stood awestruck. Through the doorway he traversed was the outer world, appearing not as cold as when he was at the work camp. Perhaps a new season had come. And yet, as he spun around on his foot, he could see that the prison complex was huge—as big as a mountain! And filled with many smaller containers! And those filled with beings from across the sky!

The cold wind burned his naked body.

Behind him a gang of guards in tight brown uniforms cried out to him and began the chase.

Ahead of Toog was a stone wall that stretched to his right and left as far as he could see. It seemed to form a ring around the entire complex, a barrier so guards walking their rounds would not fall off. He was on the top of the prison complex. He gazed over the wall at the ground below: a vast carpet of lumpy vegetation extending as far as the prison was wide.

His inner Ru had said there would be a bridge.

Soon, the Ru responded. *Keep true to the path.*

Far beyond the wall, ahead in the distance, Toog could see a line of white mountains cutting through the twilight. Nowhere did he see a garden or any *skarg*. Not even a single village. He searched for sun-fire—there: at the distant line across the world but only a gray blur. Behind him, behind the prison complex, all was dark. And the line of gray that crossed in front of him was closing quickly. Night was coming.

Where is the bridge? he cried out to his inner Ru.

Guards shouted at him, or at other guards, as they rushed toward him over the flat roof area of the prison. Their weapons were drawn.

His inner Ru clicked fingers, pointed to a drawing on the wall of his mind-cave, then shook his hand at it when Toog did not notice. *A repair request is logged for this section, according to friend Ra'aa'al. It is long overdue.*

Toog looked around, saw that a tower rose above him.

The surveillance tower stood on a tripod of metal latticework legs rising three levels, coming together at the top, with a small fenced platform perched there. A guard at the top leaned over the fence, calling down at the guards coming after Toog.

They all seemed to want him to stop. They threatened to shoot him if he did not stop. But Toog did not know their words. He could guess the meaning. Yet his inner Ru was too occupied searching paths of escape to translate in Toog's mind-cave.

Where to go? Toog called to his inner Ru.

There is one direction only, replied his inner Ru, one hand pointing straight ahead in Toog's mind-cave.

What? This? The tower? Toog stared up the tripod leg to the platform. *A tower goes up. It is not a bridge.*

His inner Ru clapped his hands. *The metal is old, burned by air, now weak. I detect a fracture beneath the layer of peeling cover material.* His inner Ru showed Toog the detailed drawing on the wall, complete with instructional arrows and numbers to prove the necessity of repairing the part as soon as possible. *Here*, said his inner Ru, pointing. *Touch the red light here.*

The guards slowed as they approached, stopping at a safe distance, wary of what the little monster was doing, holding one of their weapons.

Toog had no time to worry about them. He gave a nod to his inner Ru as one guard shouted at Toog instructions he could not understand.

Now you are caught, moaned his inner Ru.

What can I do? cried Toog, turning around in place, seeing the guards and their weapons and their eyes hating him.

You have done much to get here, said his inner Ru. *Fourth Goddess will protect you.*

Toog glanced up the tower, saw the guard on the platform waving his arm frantically, shouting down at him. Toog returned squeaks but they were lost in the noise of guards commanding him to stop.

You have a weapon, his inner Ru informed him, *which may be useful now. Release the scent.*

With a blink of his eyes and a quiver of his nose flaps, Toog's rear vent opened with a spurt of gas. The invisible cloud's acrid, bitter scent immediately overwhelmed the guards, causing them to drop their weapons, consumed by coughing and snorting, covering their faces with their hands, noses leaking and eyes raining hard. Some of them dropped to their leg joints while others fell down completely and rolled in spasm.

Now work fast, his inner Ru urged.

The cloud hovered between Toog and the sickened guards as he held up his weapon, aiming at the tripod leg, at the spot marked on the wall of his mind-cave, and let go a long red blast that seemed less bright than before. He saw that the red button pulsed slower. He fired another blast. The metal of the tripod leg glowed where the red light struck it.

Again, cried his inner Ru. *More red light.*

The guards groaned behind him as they tried to regain their faculties. Toog saw one guard hold up a weapon, its cylinder glowing. Wavering on leg joints the guard managed to send the shot out—which hit the invisible cloud and dispersed, the cloud becoming red, each strand of light a weak thread wrinkling and twisting, harmless, unable to reach Toog.

Toog's weapon seemed to be losing its power, so he in-sucked several immense breaths, puffed up his small chest, ignoring the guards' retching noise, and fixed his strength to his inner Ru.

What are you doing? his inner Ru cried out, waving his arms over his head.

Quiet! Toog responded.

The tower's guard shouted down to the crippled guards as they struggled to get to their feet, some of them up-spewing and others out-coughing red fluid.

With all his strength compacted into a tight knot of power, Toog launched himself against the tripod leg where he had shot the light blasts. His shoulder impacted the same spot. The hard crash rattled through him, left him stunned a moment. Yet he saw the dent he had made; the metal was indeed weak.

He backed up and rammed the tripod leg again, leading with his muscled shoulder, hardening like a stone shield. He rammed it again, saw the metal bend. The tower swayed, leaning away, then buckled.

As the breeze tried to clear the cloud of pungent gas, a couple of the guards regained their voices and shouted at him, urging him to stop whatever he was doing. They did not want to shoot him, Toog guessed, perhaps only wanting to put him back inside that dark cell. To save him for later. For experiments.

"I will not go back," Toog squealed as loud as he could.

Before any guard could respond, even if they could understand him, they were again overcome by spasms and retching. Down on their arm and leg joints, they could not breath any fresh air that wafted over the top of the cloud of gas.

Again Toog set his shoulder and battered the tripod leg. Each impact caused a fire-burst throughout his body—but the tripod leg broke, and one long sliver of metal ripped free, twisting outward as if a warning to stay away.

A couple guards managed to stumble to their feet, breathing fresh air and grabbing their weapons—just as the tower tripod collapsed. The tripod's other legs bent as the structure swung low, crashing against the wall. With the fallen tower hanging out from the wall, the platform shifted awkwardly and broke off its supports, falling to the ground outside the prison. The guard on the platform leaped free as it crashed down but hit the ground before the platform did. Getting up, the guard could not avoid the falling platform and, shrieking, was crushed.

The breeze was slow in clearing the vile gas, so the incapacitated guards could only watch the tower collapse, standing wobbly and confused.

Shoulder aching, Toog climbed onto the fallen tripod leg, aiming his weapon back at the guards, swaying on their feet. He saw the red button had changed to orange. As he watched, it changed to yellow.

There is your route away, said his inner Ru.

Understanding, Toog left the weapon behind, no longer able to fire. His hands were free to grab the toppled tripod leg and crawl out on the leg to where the platform had been attached—out beyond the wall, out over the field of freedom.

As I said, his inner Ru explained, *a bridge.*

Toog scurried to the end of the tripod leg, where the bracing straps for the platform made a crumpled nest.

The guards rushed to the wall, jostling each other,

pointing at Toog out on the tripod. Two guards raised their weapons and shot at him. The blasts missed him, too small a target among the crossed metal braces, but threw up sparks where the hot light struck the metal.

The growing darkness made it difficult for the guards to see him as they shot more light at him, bouncing off the jumble of metal. It weakened with every blast, becoming malleable—until the whole tower tripod bent further down, bowing gracefully to the field outside the wall.

Someone broke through the line of guards, holding a bigger, heavier weapon. Suddenly the air was full of the noise of metal darts banging against the metal legs of the tripod, bouncing off the supports, spraying the ground outside the wall.

Shrinking against the rain of metal darts, Toog looked down. The ground below was too wet for the flora there to catch fire from the hot metal. The dart gun's reign ended, its ammunition spent. Feeling the hot sparks burning his arm each time the darts hit the metal braces, Toog saw his chance.

He grasped the platform supports and let himself drop from the broken tower, down into the mossy vegetation. He almost sank in the wet flora, as soggy as it was.

Catching his breath, he pulled himself up and ran like a Great Summer *koor* with fire crystals falling and sky-dirt raining.

His silvery skin shone in the light from a fat night-sun above him but stumbling into a bog and crawling out of it managed to cover him with enough mud and plant mush to hide him as he hurried on, not knowing where he was going but certain he would never return to the prison.

Gates opened and teams of guards poured out. Lights were turned in the direction of his escape and the lines scanned the landscape, sweeping back and forth. Guards walked in tight files across the mossy plain, searching every patch of ground.

They looked again the following day, and for several days thereafter, before finally conceding Toog's escape. Rather than acknowledging a lapse in security, however, they corrected their database: Specimen 6966 had been executed at the killing rocks per directive. No longer any silver being from a world they had visited, registered as Tau Kita 6—a planet which its primitive inhabitants called Sebbol.

s e b b o l

 5

L'ra knew by the sounds her full-mate was looking for food or drink in the day-container. She knew his sounds. The low whistles during the mating ritual, the irregular churls during feeding, the ragged slithering when the crystals cut through his gut or when his inner Ru did not respond. She liked his sounds, but now they were gone.

Listen....

Nothingness.

Movement in the darkness—

No cloth had covered his smooth silvery skin. With the ritual done, his tail stub receded, his spinal hairs lay flat. He had put his *ua* to her red, swollen mound and she had responded like a *futar* in flight, soaring higher than the crystal mountains as he pressed against her. If only the *skarg* were close again, like they had enjoyed earlier in the day. Yet the *oum* floated over them, caressing their silvery skin like the tiny toes of a springling.

Oh how their springling glowed! Almost all eyes and mouth now, with tiny limbs sprouted that would grow to full length during the next sun-cycle. Her tiny toes flickered as though she was already swimming in the *abo*. They had joy-noise watching her.

Toog, the full-mate she had known for ten sun-cycles, four cycles after the shaman joined them, two since the out-belly time, one after the birthing of the springling, was not beside her.

In the dark nothingness Second Goddess had touched her and drawn her into the waking world—like a slap to her face, a sharp dig into the wall of her mind-cave.

He goes....

L'ra's eyes spiraled open and found the empty space beside her on the repose mat. With up-rush noise she passed about the abode, pausing at her springling's swing-basket and found the new-born deep in the dream land.

The dark was too quiet, no longer the squeak of *chakari* in her ears. The night was different.

Where did he go?

Her inner Ru did not answer.

Will he return?

Again there was no answer. Her inner Ru was acting like a sick *fuug* again, shrinking into the shadows of her mind-cave.

She searched through the containers of the abode, calling out for Toog in low squeaks, unwilling to draw her springling out of the dream land.

L'ra whispered to her inner Ru, asking for assistance.

I have sorrow-rain for you, her inner Ru responded at last.

She peered out the opening of the abode, looking for Toog in the dark nothingness. Outside the abode, the *oum* had thickened and her eyes could not cut through. The sorrow-rain began to fall inside her mind-cave, soon drenched her. She down-folded her body upon the entry to the abode. There she waited for him to return, feeling small crystals cutting into her belly.

Golden light filled the sky from blue mountain to red mountain and the village shaman visited L'ra's abode and told her the story of the dark nothingness. She let pour her eye-flood, let the waves splash upon the ground, and new *suupo* sprouted from the soil at her feet.

The shaman called the *suupo* a blessing from Second Goddess. By that act, the divine count had been put in balance once more, now that Toog was gone. She should not let her belly be filled with unwashed *saak*, should not let stones grow there.

The shaman knew she had a springling in the abode and she and the springling would need a protector and sustainer. He would find another full-mate for her as soon as the rituals allowed. After the season of falling crystals, he would travel to other villages and choose someone for her.

In the interval, a partial-mate would be sent to her. Perhaps in three long-cycles, the shaman told her, so she must make ready a new cloth and clear away all that once belonged to Toog, her friend and mate. The partial-mate would not want to be reminded of Toog.

She let loose eye-rain, saw it drop to the soil.

No longer under the sun-cycles would Toog exist. Her mind-cave must be washed clean.

Let the pictures remain unwashed, I beg.

Her inner Ru grinned and lowered the cleaning cloth.

L'ra's fingers stroked her silvery belly, turning her two outer fingers over the two inner fingers in the symbol of fertility. It had been a good short-cycle with Toog, playing together in the *skarg*, when he had released the cloud of pink globules and she attempted to catch the best one within her unfolding tube, then back-lay on the *saak* to repose.

As she continued communicating with the shaman, the silvery skin over her belly glowed pink, wavering between a dull, deep red and a whiter, paler illumination. L'ra and the shaman both stared at the glowing belly as though it was covered with *drao* before the village dance.

First Goddess has touched you, the shaman exclaimed.

It was my full-mate Toog who touched me.

Yes, to leave something of himself behind as he was taken away.

The shaman knew then a partial-mate was not needed for her. There was going to be another birthing. Toog had helped create a new springling within her. The skin over her belly would continue to glow pink for fourteen long-cycles, becoming brighter as she neared the birthing, when the new orb would pass through her belly wall and be deposited into the *skarg* for twenty-eight long-cycles then be brought into the abode. With that act, L'ra would then advance to the third stage of society, never again needing a mate. The village allowed only two offspring for one unit lest their food resources become limited.

The shaman touched her smooth silver head with his outer fingers and in her mind-cave were drawn the pictures she knew she must gaze upon. Even with the second orb growing inside her, she would have to carry a crystal in her mind-cave forever, a crystal which would cut her each time she saw a picture of Toog on the walls.

The Masters come as they choose, the shaman explained, and they take who they choose. She should not let cuts enter her heart or stones grow in her belly. Allowing that would make her as silent as those who had unexpectedly left the community of Aull, those who had vanished like the cool out-breath whenever a mind-cave collapsed.

She understood and stroked her head several times, until a blue furrow was formed on her silvery head.

The shaman saw the blue furrow.

To help you gather up your sorrow-rain, I shall send a partial-mate to you for six long-cycles. Make haste with the partial-mate and return light upon your face.

And so L'ra, once the full-mate of Toog, went to the market and gathered her food just as she did every long-cycle. And the other villagers regarded her, saw her pink belly, and let go a drop or two of sorrow-rain for her, and she down-turned her head in response.

Sorrow-rain could be dangerous, the shaman understood. Some Aull had drowned from such rain.

And the long-cycles turned, the sun burning and cooling, the second birthing and sounding of bright-joy *clee* and *forai* song, and L'ra named her springling N'oh in a fresh drain of *lool*. Growing more, she soon would be placed in a swing-basket within their abode.

First daughter M'ah continued to grow, with knee-walking, foot-walking, stream-flowing and wind-racing, until no male could catch her. Prizes were given to her. A ribbon was fixed to the tower of the village so all would know that M'ah, first daughter of L'ra and missing Toog, had led the team of youth to victory.

Then N'oh rose up and joined the team of *maot*-catchers and in two long-cycles caught the highest number of *maot* in the village and gained prizes equal to her sister.

Together the sisters M'ah and N'oh worked each day to raise the stones out of L'ra's belly and throw out the dark crystals that cut through her heart. They always grew back.

In time, L'ra down-bent into repose and gazed upon the passage of M'ah from youth to adult, her full body of fertility unfolding before everyone. M'ah was always chased by the males, often caught in the *duup* or captured in the *weeth*. The shaman chose Naar, the strongest male, to be her partial-mate, and they learned together how to please the goddesses, most of all by imitating how Great Goddess Aull pulled the sky-lights from her belly and stuck them upon the walls of her mind-cave, the vast everything that covered the world of Sebbol.

In time, N'oh was paired with a partial-mate named Guur, who after many cycles took her to the top of the mountain and showed her the vastness of the *weeth* below. Yet in their attempt to imitate Great Goddess Aull creating the universe from her loins, it was N'oh who fell to the stones below and was broken upon them like a *jurt* being over-stepped by a large *kalar*.

Guur arrived at the council later, covered in *gaum*, expecting the shaman to send him straight into a ritual fire. Guur up-stood and surrendered his belly to her sorrow-rain, made a mark on the mind-cave walls of L'ra and M'ah. He wished to join N'oh as her broken silvery body was prepared for the fire and the blue ashes that the villagers would drink.

Yet as the broken body of N'oh was carried to the village fire, she quick-returned to the waking world. They set her upon the *saak* and listened as she told everyone about the dream land she had visited. There was her father, Toog, pulling the long cord of Great Goddess Aull's womb, pulling with all his strength, trying to retrieve the sky-lights that had been hidden.

It cannot be truth, called the shaman, and others drew truth upon the ground with him.

My second daughter N'oh has gone away, responded L'ra like a wild *hareh* full of crystals, and I believe she did find Toog there.

The villagers remained puzzled yet the funeral fire was used for cooking instead and everyone made feast. L'ra chose to celebrate N'oh's return to the waking world while others enjoyed the meal.

In the cycles that followed, N'oh remained broken yet always in the waking world. Children ran around her, teasing her, saying she could not chase after them.

She has no use in this village, the shaman told L'ra, yet she takes the food.

N'oh has skills making cloth, L'ra reminded the shaman.

Then let her make cloth.

So second daughter N'oh became the cloth-maker, and in her weaving were patterns from the dream land journey she took. Her cloths became famous and carried truth to far away villages. Many visited her village for the chance to exchange things for the cloths she made. L'ra and M'ah were filled with sun-light rain.

Yet no young males full of the flush of fertility fever ever visited N'oh, for none wanted to hot-take her to the *abo* or share a repose mat with her, though she knew she remained as ready for mating as any other female of the village. They believed N'oh carried a bag of *drix* in her body, and the little monsters each day emerged and chewed into her legs, left poison, and kept her from up-standing or out-walking. The shaman did not speak against the fire. The story was not truth, and so pictures of N'oh pulling herself along, on her leg-joints and arm-joints across the ground, remained on the walls of everyone's mind-caves.

N'oh did not make noise like a wounded *ourk*. She up-turned a face-curl to the sky-lights and spoke like stones to her father. When she visited the dream land, she would call to him, so far ahead of her on the horizon, always unable to catch up to him. Her stories about the dream land caused belly-juice in the villagers yet none took it as truth. And she wove new pictures into the cloths, each a likeness of Toog's face which she saw while visiting the dream land.

And then the time came for L'ra to let go of her full-mate, Toog, so Great Goddess Aull could welcome him back into her womb for all time. L'ra set the painted stone there in the garden behind the abode. She could see on the walls of her mind-cave that M'ah and N'oh had the same pictures of Toog. In the dark nothingness L'ra could match eyes with them and know truth deeper than the village shaman could dig under the sky-lights of Great Goddess Aull.

They are the daughters of Toog, spoke L'ra to the sky-lights.

In time, L'ra down-spread her body in repose as M'ah up-stood with her full-mate, Keet, and the shaman spoke out the words they all knew, what was drawn on the walls of mind-caves across the community. M'ah and Keet were joined under a new banner, and given the tools needed to start their own garden.

And L'ra closed her eyes in repose as M'ah carried in her arms the springling she named Toog'la, chosen by the shaman to be male, and four times circle-walked the warm-basin where the festival fires had gathered and glowed. The shaman spoke the words of Aull and the *oum* away-swept the ashes into a new cycle. Singing and dancing followed.

M'ah and Keet and their springling Toog'la down-sat before the garden and there remembered the dark nothingness and the light of everything. They knew the long-cycles would never would end, and the Masters would return to take more Aull from the village. Or another village. So the Aull of Toog's village drew plans on their mind-cave walls, led by Keet. When the black pit of terror opened among them again, they would be ready to fight.

For that fight, M'ah and Keet made another male springling and named him Gaag. And in the next sun-cycle another springling came forth from her pink-glowing belly, a designated male they named Foor. But Foor was lost in a long-cycle when crystals fell from the sky.

Others in the village also grew more males, taller and stronger than the females, and their garden tools became weapons. Even the Masters must shed liquid, whether blue or red or yellow, like the lowest Aull did with a slip of a garden tool, or at the birthing, or caught in the jaws of a hungry *duur* or under the claws of a *jaax*. Even a Master could be killed if enough *em* poured out.

The shaman saw truth in the pictures on the walls of his mind-cave and added his own pictures to those of the village: a cohort of Aull with weapons over-standing the fallen Masters, most of the bodies in pieces and others caught in the cleansing fires.

◆◡

L'ra slow-walked through the *lalo*, her cloth touching the under-bent golden *fuut* flickers, the sun bright-touching her face.

Where is Toog? she called to the distant *hareh*.

A message was hung on the entry way. Part of the message tore away and floated on the air, across the valley, lost in the *oum* that rested between the mountains. Her inner Ru was away.

L'ra down-sat between the *fuut* and the *chool* stalks, her silvery skin half hidden by the cloth N'oh had woven, ready to count each short-cycle of the play period. She raised the cloth off her body and let the sun color her bronze. Her silver was dulling anyway.

Neighbor De'u arrived from the walk-path, down-looked at L'ra, and with sharp mouth-curls showed weapons at L'ra. It was not common to go into the *lalo* with no cloth. Often the young males would circle a female who reposed without cloth. The shaman had told about this act many times, yet L'ra, in her older days, had no such pictures on her mind-cave.

Why do you show your sour face? asked L'ra of De'u.

De'u snorted and spit. First you show to the sky your body. Like a young female. You call the males for attention?

L'ra pulled the cloth over herself. The sun-light is my friend, so I welcome it upon me, spoke L'ra. She tossed her head to the left and right twice. I have no concern for young males. It is only the law of the shaman which keeps them free to roam.

Second Goddess will cut those males, De'u responded.

So much had passed over the many sun-cycles since Toog had disappeared into the dark nothingness, and in that great time it was neighbor De'u who was the worst to speak. She spoke for many of the village, calling them to see her pictures and draw their own in the same patterns. And everyone trusted the pictures drawn on their mind-caves that showed one of many truths of which they might choose. Everyone seemed to choose the dark drawings.

Most chose the same truth: Toog was down-head and up-feet, too long floating in a dark nothingness and probably forever.

L'ra had for many sun-cycles held as truth that Toog was taken away by the Masters in the middle of the *uma*. More pain-cuts to her than that drawing were the dark marks that counted the cycles. He would never return, they told her, and she began to draw the same pictures herself on her mind-cave walls every *choot* and *uma*.

Neighbor De'u sent eye-knives down upon L'ra. He was taken because he was cursed. He was outside the light of our goddesses.

It was known by everyone that the Masters only took those of the village who had done evil by hand or mind.

He must have done something evil. De'u traced the pictures in L'ra's mind-cave and L'ra wished her inner Ru was there to erase them. It is the only pattern for his away-walk.

Toog did nothing against law, L'ra spoke, adding finger drawing in the *oum* which made a down-curl pop from De'u's mouth.

The Masters know everything, De'u continued like a charging *drouk* sick with fever. You must confirm with neighbors T'ui and R'eo that Toog did not play with them in the *abo*. You must confirm with First Goddess that Toog sent no bad wishes into the sky-lights. You must confirm with Second Goddess that Toog gathered the food-gifts and spoke his blessings upon them. Only after these sacred confirmations—

Toog did everything law requires, stated L'ra with a flat hand cutting the air five ways. He was a perfect full-mate, father, and worker in the village. The best of the garden cutters and seed diggers. Among the best of the animal killers, too. He spoke truth words and path-walked without waver or delay.

You have pretty pictures on your mind-cave, De'u spoke with a stabbing tongue. Yet pretty is not the same as truth. You must trace the pictures that you wish would fall away. What remains will be truth.

L'ra up-stood and matched-face with De'u, eyes to eyes, like two fever-bent *hux* about to fang-fight.

De'u back-jumped, hands up-raised as plant-sheer tools.

I know the truth about Toog, stated L'ra as thick as low *oum* seeping through the entries of old containers. Her word-color sent a furious, unbalanced vibration burrowing through De'u's mind-cave, shaking the walls, chips flaking off.

Neighbor De'u raised her hands to the sky and spoke words of summons to Second Goddess.

L'ra spoke: Second Goddess will not save you from your mind-cave collapse! She crossed her arms, fingers raised. First Goddess protects her children. Second Goddess will drown in sorrow-rain.

De'u launched a string of yellow mouth-juice upon the ground, spotting the foot of L'ra.

You are a slobbering *paaz*!

De'u responded: You are an *ourk* spewing *ouk*!

You are a stone under the mountain!

You are a small stone under a smaller stone!

Villagers nearby halted at the flapping noise, rare among Aull. They went closer, gazed upon the two old females, calling to them and asking for a balance to be set between them.

You will be next, De'u spoke with a dark grunt. The Masters will take you next for your flapping noise. We do not give away our repose so quickly, neighbor L'ra.

Then you know law well, neighbor De'u! Have you a red-belly shaman hiding in your mind-cave?

Hands were pressed and the *oum* surrounded them like warm woven cloth. Each went on the walk-path to her next task.

In the final space at the rear of the abode, close to where the swing-basket hung which held M'ah's new springling named O'uh, marked female by the shaman, old L'ra down-sat and curled under her body both legs and feet. Deep in her mind-cave as she was resting, she decided to settle the truth with her inner Ru, now that it had returned.

She wrote on the walls of her mind-cave: *I know Toog did no wrong, spoke no evil, nothing against law, yet he was taken from us without fore-calling or sky-gold reason.*

It is a bowl of balance, replied her inner Ru.

Then I also draw upon these walls the picture of the Masters taking him away, and he is full of the fear-flood and lets loose much eye-rain. He calls to me and to M'ah and knows not the coming of N'oh, yet none of our community rises to help him, to fight beside him against the Masters.

It is a finished thing, said her inner Ru.

Then is it a possibility that Toog did nothing evil yet he still was chosen?

All possibilities are possible, said her inner Ru.

So in one possibility might it be possible Toog was taken not for an evil he did but for an evil the Masters did?

Her inner Ru rose as quick as *tii* and gurgled like a fawning *hoor* in mating season. *The Masters did?*

Is it possible the Masters are the evil doers?

Her inner Ru shook like a waving stalk of *flaam* in the

oum.

It is a possibility among possibilities, replied her inner Ru after a short-cycle.

L'ra in-called a measure of air, sent it immediately out again.

Toog is not evil and was not taken for doing evil.

That is a possibility among possibilities, said her inner Ru.

It is the Masters who are evil, responded L'ra, for they take us from our community even when we do no evil.

Her inner Ru waved its eyes, spun its head, made the sound of a mind-cave collapse without her mind-cave actually collapsing.

Do not collapse now, L'ra begged her inner Ru.

It is a weakness you have cut into me, responded her inner Ru.

I made no such weakness in you. Law has made you weak. Law has up-held you and you know not how to down-bend.

If I could draw pictures upon the outer walls of your mind-cave, wrote her inner Ru on the wall, *the neighbors would see that your fingers make evil drawings.*

So neighbors would send me to the shaman, replied L'ra, and the shaman would feed me questions. The shaman would choose the answers for me and I would down-bend in trust.

In trust you would down-bend, wrote her inner Ru.

That would be evil, said L'ra.

There is no evil which can draw pictures upon the walls of a shaman's mind-cave, wrote her inner Ru, *none at all that can draw pictures for First or Second or even Third Goddess.*

I do not deny law has columns and pillars and a roof over us, yet it can still fall with a strong *oum* or too many

Aull rest-touching it or with much mouth-spilling.

Law is like Aull. The Aull are made of law. The law is food for the inner Ru.

And the inner Ru eats often and often too much!

Her inner Ru sent a down-curved mouth to her face, made a scratch upon the wall of her mind-cave, and stamped a foot.

Shall I go on holiday again?

If you want to leave me to law and the shaman and the drifting *oum*, L'ra replied, then go to your hideaway. Repose as you will.

As you wish.

Tell no others about the pictures on my walls, L'ra warned.

Yes, that is law, and we agree.

With a stone-flood of bad-food shaking her belly, L'ra went about her cycles keeping her pictures hidden. She sent away her inner Ru more often and stood as one-of-one in the village. Neighbors watched her and spoke about her with words stained and dirty. She grew older and older, watching daughter M'ah gain positions as mother and full-mate. She watched daughter N'oh make more cloths of her special design, repeating the mind-cave pictures of Toog.

L'ra took the duties of Great Mother with the sun-light rising and falling, and when needed she pretended to consult with her inner Ru. In time, neighbors forgot her and her worm-shook ways after the disappearance of her cursed full-mate Toog. After many sun-cycles she took her great repose and was forgotten.

M'ah carried the younger male springling in her arms as

the older males followed her on the walk-path. To the market, to the shaman, to the healing waters the Aull went. The older springlings grew strong with frequent swims in the *abo*. One leg was odd-bent since the belly-pop and did not up-hold the midling.

She named him Toog'la after her father yet full-mate Keet sent the name away like a decaying *guum* that had sat too long in the *erol*. Keet gave the male midling the name Raam, which was said to give him the same strength as the ancient warrior who carried that name. Yet the new name did not give the midling strength. Instead, M'ah took him to swim in the *abo* every day—unless crystals were falling from the sky.

M'ah's second springling she named Gaag. So pleased was Keet that he showed Gaag to the shaman and the shaman proclaimed Gaag a perfect model of what a male Aull should be—as M'ah had once been praised for being a perfect female Aull. Words were spoken behind walls that tossed pictures to neighbors declaring the imperfect Raam should not take food that was better given to perfect midlings. Villagers had spoken the same truth about N'oh who could not walk yet made cloths for everyone and so they gave her food.

The misfortune for both was clearly the result of Toog's curse. First, he was chosen by the Masters and taken away. Then his second daughter, who he did not know, fell broken. Then his first daughter's first orb was named for him and the springling turned imperfect. The whole !g clan was cursed, neighbors squeaked under their tongues.

As sun-cycles turned, M'ah watched her male midlings grow, Raam the lame, and Gaag the strong. Her heart flickered bright as she watched them together, the strong youth helping the weak youth. The neighbors repeated calls for separation yet the shaman decided Raam could stay if he shared the food from his mother's portion. So M'ah gave to Raam all she could offer and had none for herself. She often fell into a storm-fire until her sons gave some of their food to her. Even N'oh, who gathered food for the cloths she wove, gave some food to M'ah.

Let me down-sit in repose, M'ah spoke to her sons almost every long-cycle.

We must feed you, her sons spoke back at her.

My cycles turn slow now, yet you will go on. It is for you to build a walk-path for your full-mates and springlings. Forget the strivings of your mother and father. Forget sun-cycles past. Draw pictures of tomorrow and share them with neighbors. You are the sun-light upon my face.

And with clasped hands M'ah went into the dream land and her sons released eye-rain as a flood to be collected by their full-mates, H'uo and K'ae, to be mixed with M'ah's ashes. The next generation of Aull stood around them, faces as plain as *reng* in the dry season.

Your Great Mother is in her repose, Raam spoke to the group of offspring. Let us take her to where Keet, who gained the fourth stage before her, is already in repose.

Daughter O'uh did not understand, but Raam wrote the truth on her mind-cave wall and the eye-rain fell.

After they drank the ashes, N'oh down-sat among them, in the center of the midlings, and spoke to them about the life of Toog and L'ra, about her elder sister M'ah and M'ah's full-mate Keet, and about her own life as weaver for the village. She taught the skill to the midlings and soon many were making cloths designed with the pictures of Toog, and L'ra, and M'ah and Keet. And the Aull of the village were filled with sun-light and danced like *tii* after the season of falling crystals.

The cloth weaving of N'oh and the youth who followed her ways was like bright mountain fire at first, yet the weaving abode did not remain bright atop the mountain for everyone in the village.

Neighbors arose like *drii* burning in the *reng*, out-crying like wild *hux*, gathering around the abode of old Gaag's family. It was the male named Kiid, third son of Gaag, the son of M'ah and Keet, who was out-called for making noise in the village. Raam quickly up-stood to protect Kiid yet the youth still went out fire-singing. Kiid felt sun-light burn through his belly when he spoke and so he spoke as often as he could, even though many Aull of the village felt stones in their bellies when he spoke.

The Masters will return, Kiid out-spoke in the village, drawing pictures in the ground. When neighbors sent knife-noise at him, he had spoken louder. He had sent word-knives at them. He had sent fist-words to their bellies to make them feel the stone-aching. The shaman called him to down-sit together. Their talk did not fill Kiid with repose, instead lit new fire-words in him.

I am not the sprung-forth of my father's cloud, he out-spoke like an erupting *fluu*, bronze hands waving like a crazed *boog*. I am not the springling of my Great Father. Toog is not of my counting stream. I am not the river of Toog, not the *!g* clan.

The neighbors gathered like an attacking pack of *meax*, high-holding tools of the garden as weapons. The shaman up-raised his hands to stop them.

Fight not against the sons of Toog, the shaman out-called, for they do not carry the curse of Toog.

Yet the neighbors would not unfold into flat and straight. They pushed forward and over-ran the shaman. They struck their garden tools at Kiid and down-cut him. He ugly-fell like a pile of *ouk*, as a splatter of *reez*, and left as a puddle of *zour*. The neighbors back-stepped and in most hearts back-cuts appeared and in some bellies aches grew thick as thundering *goud*.

What have we done? some of them drew on the walls of their mind-caves. *What have we done?* Many inner Ru raised a clamor and the village shook.

The shaman was carried away to the abode of healing and after two long-cycles, the shaman arose. Kiid, instead, went to the dream land. Many of the village drew pictures on their mind-cave walls, images of the dream land, images of star-fire and Great Goddess Aull gathering their hearts into her hands.

Beside the fire-pit long-stood Laat, Maak, and Buun, three brothers of Kiid, the sons of Gaag and H'uo. They down-gazed at the dark ashes as the pit-minder stirred them with a long pole. Some of the village chanted.

Oum covered their skin with fear-rain and they hand-clasped and drew pictures together on the mind-cave walls they shared. There appeared lines and checks and solids that preserved the life of Kiid. There preserved they the life of Gaag, the life of M'ah, and the life of Toog the cursed Aull, and the parents of Toog, of the *!g* clan, Daag and Lo'u, and their parents, back many sun-cycles to the vast womb of Great Goddess Aull.

To be Aull was the highest prize, the greatest honor. And yet the acts their eyes had captured filled their bellies with heavy stones and stinging crystals. Aull is right and good, everyone agreed. And yet to be Aull and act in pain-causing is wrong and bad, they shared.

Toog was chosen by the Masters and taken from the village. It was now a wall-cut story and everyone knew it and repeated it to the springlings that they might be warned. Learn the lesson of Toog, who did not follow the pattern of the goddesses, or you also will be taken away by the Masters.

They repeated the pictures in their mind-caves.

The Masters took Toog and no other, they shared.

Be not like Toog.

In the counting pouch the sons of Gaag selected in blindness an uncounted stone. The stone out-pulled was the stone of harmony. In their wide-gaze they drew pictures of the harmony stone. The counting pouch gave them answers, and the answer was harmony. The question they asked was the same.

Laat, first son of Gaag and H'uo, gazed at Maak, their second son. Why did the Masters choose Toog?

Maak quick-gazed at Buun, the fourth son. What did Toog have that the Masters wanted?

Buun long-gazed at Laat. What did the Masters gain from taking Toog?

The harmony stone glowed like the eastern sky before a crystal storm.

They put their round eyes together and breaths shared.

H-a-r-m-o-n-y . . . *Oul* in their language.

The Masters wanted Toog to teach them harmony.

It is clear as the crystal *yu'u*.

Though a simple village gardener, Toog carried secrets, they now understood, seeing the pictures on the walls of their mind-caves. Toog knew harmony. Toog went freely and without ties along with the Masters to teach them harmony.

Toog was not cursed, not selected for evil *reez* or out-pulled for bad acts. Toog was invited and welcomed as a shaman. Toog was not cursed. Toog was raised to the sky! Toog was chosen as the shaman of the Masters!

And Toog would return to Sebbol one day, maybe return as a Master himself, as a high shaman over all shamans, perhaps as the Prime Aull—or even as a god-seed!

⚫

The three sons of Gaag took the counting pouch and the stone of harmony to the temple of the shaman.

Today we asked the counting pouch our questions and received this answer, the three sons explained.

Laat held out his hand with the stone in it.

The shaman remarked how shiny the stone was, shiny enough to blind them. It glowed red.

It is the harmony stone, Maak spoke.

Harmony is good, the shaman spoke, down-turning his face.

We asked the counting pouch about Toog, spoke Buun.

We asked for the reason the Masters took Toog, spoke Laat. We wanted to know if Toog was evil or good.

We pulled out the stone from the counting pouch and it was the harmony stone, spoke Maak.

We come to you, shaman, to advise us, spoke Buun. Without an answer, our sibling Kiid went forever into the dream land too early and without knowing a reason.

The shaman took the stone into his hand and seemed to count its weight. The stone pulsed red and orange.

I see three islands in the river of Toog, spoke the shaman. In a small group they chose a stone. Perhaps they agree on the choice.

We did not agree on the choice, Laat spoke.

Maak was fire-driven. If Toog had acted badly then he was deserving to be taken by the Masters, yet he did not act bad.

If not a bad act, spoke Buun, then a good act was the reason.

So we asked the counting pouch and we were moved to touch the stone of harmony.

You three Aull are like the down-bent *shaar*, not able to see the sun in the sky because you too-much-enjoy chewing the *drao* on the ground. The shaman was fire-lit. You come to show me your wet *skarg* pictures.

It is truth, spoke Laat.

Then touch again from the counting pouch, spoke the shaman.

Before any of the three could put a writing brush to a mind-cave wall, Buun had tossed the stone of harmony into the pouch.

Now touch again, the shaman insisted, letting loose a noise like the grunt of a hungry *ourk*.

Laat set eyes upon Maak. There was *oum*-rain around him. In the eyes of Buun was a nine-color *ruu*.

Tie it off, instructed the shaman. When the counting pouch was sealed, the shaman took the pouch and threw it high into the sky, up to where a *suul* might snatch it as food, yet it dropped quickly to the ground with a soft *thu'th*.

Buun picked the pouch from the ground and ran his hands over its covering to clean it.

Touch again, spoke the shaman.

It is Buun's turn, spoke Laat, and as Maak held the pouch open at the height of his silvery head, Buun reached in and touched a stone. He closed his fingers around the stone and pulled it from the pouch.

They gazed upon Buun's closed hand.

Blossom your hand, spoke the shaman, and Buun's fingers un-bent, opening to truth:

The stone of harmony!

They gazed upon the stone.

It is truth, spoke Laat. Maak and Buun agreed.

I see the picture drawn on the wall of my mind-cave, spoke the shaman.

The shaman led the three Aull to the temple of the high shaman in the next village and again the speaking was shared.

You seek the answer of your Great Father's riddle? Of his disappearance, spoke the high shaman after they arrived.

These three seek the answer, spoke the village shaman.

We touched the stone of harmony twice for our question, Laat spoke. It is truth. Our Great Father was taken by the Masters to teach them harmony.

Harmony? The high shaman's face turned faint-blue. What does a simple village gardener know about harmony?

Harmony is in every Aull, spoke Buun.

It is truth, spoke the shaman and touched his hand to Buun's silvery head.

Then touch again from the counting pouch, spoke the high shaman.

Maak replaced the stone in the pouch, tied it off, and the village shaman tossed it high into the sky. When it returned to the ground, Laat picked it up and held it open.

You touch the stone this time, spoke Laat. His eyes shone like crystal rain.

The high shaman down-turned his face. You stand too tall, he spoke. Better you slink in the *skarg*.

To find the truth we come to you, spoke Maak.

And the high shaman pushed his hand into the counting pouch and after gathering a stone in his hand pulled his hand out. He out-held his closed hand among them.

Blossom, said Buun.

The high shaman uncurled his fingers and there was the stone of harmony! Again it glowed red.

At that moment the sky seemed to spark into a rain of pink and red then return to white, and warm *oum* blew against them.

The high shaman brought the stone to his eyes and sharp-gazed upon it. No marks, no cuts, no brush strokes, nothing to give ease to the choosing. He down-turned his face, silence filling his mouth.

Now it is truth, spoke Laat.

Three touches, spoke Maak.

Harmony, spoke Buun.

Toog has gone to teach the Masters about harmony, spoke the shaman.

I see the pictures drawn on the walls of my mind-cave, spoke the high shaman, and the hand drawing the pictures is the hand of First Goddess.

And so it was that the high shaman spoke to the Aull of the village and they agreed and shared that Toog of old, of the *!g* clan, Great Father of Laat, Maak, Buun, and long-cold Kiid, did go with the Masters there to teach them about the harmony of Aull.

To celebrate Toog's selection, villagers agreed to make a figure of Toog, carved from *jurt*, painted with *emno*, and up-stand it at the center of the village. To praise Toog each day as they went to and fro on their ordinary tasks was one honor. Yet the figure also would announce to everyone that this village was the village of Toog, who went with the Masters to teach them harmony.

And if that did not light a fire in the bellies of visitors, wrote the high shaman on the walls of his mind-cave and later on a plaque to be fixed on the statue, then a large figure of Toog standing so tall among their abodes might also announce to any of the Masters who would arrive next that this village was not to be harmed, that no Aull should be taken from here—for did they not already learn harmony from Toog of Sebbol?

The pictures are burned into the walls of our mind-caves, the high shaman told them, for they had passed three mother-cycles since Toog disappeared yet no return of the Masters. It must be a sign from First Goddess that the Masters had learned harmony and no longer acted in belly-cutting ways.

The chief sculptor chose a fierce grin for the statue, much like the scowl of a hungry *gortor*, although the villagers took him to be showing an up-turned mouth, as pleasant as the *yu* floating in the morning *oum*. Songs were woven for the rituals they performed around the statue, different songs for each long-cycle. Cloth was made by the midlings following the patterns of N'oh. Much flora was brought into the village and set around the statue. Some of the villagers were assigned to clean the statue. Midlings were taught dances and moved with sun-light in their bellies around the statue.

After many sun-cycles, the statue of Great Father Toog was the center of the village. It stood as the totem for the entire region and many came from other villages to up-gaze at the statue, at the fierce yet smiling face of the Special One who went away to teach the Masters harmony. And the shaman spoke the truth about Toog to all springlings, so they might know the story and become filled with *palati* and *jumi*, and weave songs to Toog on the walls of their mind-caves, and long-sing praises throughout the cycles.

Many sun-cycles turned before the last Aull wrapped the last stone idol in picture cloths woven by old N'oh and the youth she had taught, having watched the sons of M'ah and Keet gain full-mates and their springlings come forth in the *skarg* and even they grow old and enter the dream land forever, and the broken weaver sat among her newest students and gave them her final instructions. Satisfied with their work, knowing they would continue the weaving of cloths after she went to her final repose in the dream land, she lay on the ground behind her abode and covered her face with the first cloth she ever made.

And as the sun-light low-bent and red-burned, she spoke into the cloth:

I see you, father.

She was slipping to the edge of the dream land, far-looking to and beyond the horizon. To the great *abo*—the marsh of repose.

I feel your breath from behind the mountain. I breathe the scent of the marsh. I am old and soon will join you there.

She took long, slow, draws of air, her nose flaps quivering.

I shall weave pictures for you of the life of our village. I shall weave pictures of L'ra and M'ah. You can remember them. I am N'oh, who was created in the skarg *before the dark nothingness in which you disappeared. You have not known me, yet when I lay broken in the dream land in my youth, I found the thread which ties you to me. I have pulled that thread many times, for many sun-cycles. Now the thread is short and I know you are close. A few foot-steps more and we shall meet.*

▲ ▶ ▶   6

Deep in the dream land, slow-walking beside a pair of green-and-red striped *groll*, wheeze-snorting among the *oum*, Toog heard the words of the crystal mountain rolling down the slopes, gathering in piles around him. They were words he knew, had heard before, but they came from a voice he did not recognize, had never seen written on the walls of his mind-cave.

He arose and out-gazed over the valley. In the far line of light stood a figure, appearing as an Aull, perhaps someone from Sebbol, with both hands raised, one moving left-to-right, the other moving right-to-left, meeting.

Toog slapped at the nearest *groll* and they both galloped away with wild-cawing in opposite directions, as he held his face against the gray sun-light. He put a gray foot forward and then the other gray foot and came close to that dark figure in less than a short-cycle.

You are N'oh, spoke Toog to the figure. The name floated in the air like *oum* and he had grabbed it.

Covered in a cloth of dark nothingness, the figure gave a glowing silvery hand to him, and he gathered the hand between his outer fingers. The hand fit into his fingers and he knew the match was truth.

I have heard your words, spoke Toog. *I have seen your drawings on my mind-cave walls.*

The figure of an old woman wrapped in a black shroud bowed her head.

I wish you to have my words, she spoke. *I am N'oh, the springling you did not know. You are my father and my mother has departed for the dream land. I shall follow her when I no longer follow you.*

L'ra has gone to the dream land? Toog asked, feeling his belly burst into flame. *So soon?*

Holding up a glowing hand, the figure of N'oh up-curled her mouth and sun-light twinkled behind her eyes. *It is not so soon. Many sun-cycles have turned after you disappeared.*

A star-fire burst in his chest. *How many?*

Too many for a child to count. Now I am an old one—

Like the eruption of a great mountain, Toog was kicked out of the dream land, hard stones crushing his chest, unable to suck air.

An old one....

His body, battered and chilled, shook against the flat stone he used for repose. Sometimes the goddesses would spin pictures designed to confuse, perhaps to teach a lesson, or ease the journey from waking world to dream land. That is what the shaman told him long ago. This journey was a lesson: He must hurry back to his home.

Yet he was not on a journey to the dream land. He was not on the path to death. It was worse. He was still on this world ruled by the Masters.

At first, they were a mysterious evil the shaman used to keep the midlings in good order. Then, as he grew to adulthood, they were a real presence in village life. They came every few sun-cycles and took someone away. None knew the reason, so they remained mysterious—and built up in his mind as a powerful entity equal to the goddesses. Captured and imprisoned, he believed they acted at the behest of the goddesses, a kind of policing force. Taking him from his cell and letting him face them, towering over him as they did, he knew they were special beings. At the work camp, he saw they were not so divine but seemed to enjoy dispensing cruelty. He saw them as merely another creature among many creatures there—the creatures with the weapons.

Then he had escaped from his cell and there was a guard right there—one of the low-ranking Masters, standing watch, holding the same kind of weapon they liked to use: a cylinder that sent out a beam of light that cut and melted flesh. Or burned straight through a body. He had not hesitated to strike at that Master, never fearing divine retribution. He was fire-driven. He had used the Masters' pulsing light weapon against other guards as he escaped. And he saw they were flesh beings like him. They fell like other creatures fell. They died like other creatures died. They were not divine, nor were they a force used by goddesses, but a separate species of upright beasts. Enough Aull together could defeat the Masters, he calculated.

He thought of the killing he had done and his inner Ru tried to lecture him on what he was due now. He was too afraid to think of the future, how his life would be after he had killed. He had acted with quick-thought, as though his inner Ru drove him forward—and they often quarreled over the details and their meanings. It was not forbidden to kill; if in the hunt for food, which came once a year; if in defense of the village, which had not happened in his life yet. A bad Aull was sent away, into the mountains, and never seen again. Perhaps that was to be his life now: to be sent into the mountains forever—on the Masters' world.

One short-cycle's journey from the prison complex, a low ridge rose in the south and stretched to the north. On the windy side of the ridge lay a series of caves in the bare rock, some small, some large. In one of the larger caves Toog found refuge.

It had a narrow entrance, hidden by scruffy *lathu*. Several large rocks also helped cover the view of the entrance from below. Inside, a corridor sloped downward and to the left until it met the ceiling which sloped more sharply down from the entrance.

Where floor and ceiling met, at the end of the passage, was an opening just large enough for Toog to slip through. Short as he was, he still needed to drop to his leg joints and arm joints. The opening led to a short-ceiling inner cavern and a path that wound through stone posts rising from the floor and stone fingers hanging from the ceiling, leading to an even larger room.

The inner cave was completely dark, like Toog's prison cell had been. He could only stumble through it, his hands feeling for walls and stone columns. Once he went too far in the wrong direction and tripped off a low cliff and fell into a pool below. The pool was not large yet it took him a while to reach the opposite side, which was another low cliff. And the pool was very deep; he failed to reach the bottom in a single long-breath dive.

He was not sure what might be in the pool, but it was the liquid his body needed. It seemed to be mostly *lool*, with other liquids mixed into it. The liquid had a strong smell of *vol*, which caused his nose flaps to fold shut. He was used to swimming in the murky water of the *skarg*, with its waving fronds, drifting mud-bubbles, and strings of *luur* to avoid.

The *skarg* was always warm, filled with nutrients he could absorb through his skin.

More than once he was nipped by something, perhaps a *jaur* or a *pelox* of some kind. Never was it a wound that made him worry or bother his inner Ru. More than that, the pool's liquid seemed denser than *lool* he had swam in on Sebbol. His skin tingled when he pulled himself out of the pool, but the prickly sensation faded. After swimming in the pool many times, he noticed his smooth, silvery skin was rougher, covered with small bumps, and of darker color—when he could look at himself in the light at the cave entrance. His inner Ru thought the changes were because of the cold of the cavern, not the pool. He was meant to adapt, said his inner Ru. Great Goddess Aull had given them that ability.

Toog had lived in this cave, eating berries from small bushes, plant roots he dug, and once in a while some small animal he could catch, for fifty long-cycles. He often watched the Masters go along the road passing below the ridge, moving in their machine-wagons large and small, sometimes with other creatures, sometimes not. Once he saw a Master standing up in the rear section of the wagon, his mouth open and a great noise coming out of it. The sound was ugly to Toog's ears, but the Master seemed to enjoy making the sounds, up and down, short notes then long notes. Toog guessed it was a chant of some kind but he did not know the words or which goddess the chant was for. Sometimes the evil beings seemed like Aull, their mind-caves filled with song and they could enjoy life. Toog was confused, stared at his hands, remembering how he held the weapon and pointed it at them and unleashed fire that killed them. He wondered if they had full-mates somewhere and springlings in swing-baskets. And if they did, how they could then be so cruel to him and others they took from other worlds.

Then two of the Masters found his cave. Perhaps they were on patrol and wondered about the indentation in the rock face and they thought to take shelter there. Or perhaps they were searching for him and tracked him to the cave. It did not matter which it was.

Entering the outer cave, they followed it to its end, lowering their heads with each step back into the passage. After examining the walls, they discovered the small opening that led to the inner cavern and crawled through. The first one was unfortunate and walked too far before the second one lit a torch. The first Master fell into the pool with a loud, echoing splash.

Toog, hiding between the up-standing and down-hanging stone columns, struck the second Master on the head with a heavy rock, then dove into the pool to retrieve the body of the first Master.

He gained a lot from the two wanderers: clothing, boots, drink containers filled with *lool*, their weapons, knives. From the Masters themselves, food. Awful tasting food, yet it sustained him. His round teeth found chewing difficult. He wanted to cook the meat yet he feared making a fire which might alert the Masters to his location.

He spent considerable time dissecting the first body, noting the different arrangement of organs, including two organs Aull did not have. He wasted nothing, however, and made stations in his inner cavern for each type of body part. He had not eaten much flesh on Sebbol but in hard times and to be polite he did. It seemed meat was more prevalent on this frozen world than plant food.

As he organized his food pantry, he remembered when he went into the wilderness on Sebbol and lived off whatever he found there. It had been a rite of passage for male youth to go out for many long-cycles. He recalled how Laan and Beet never returned, and Daol lost a leg—had to cut it off himself when he was caught in the jaws of a *gortor*. Those who did return got to choose a partial-mate—he and his fellow male youth called them practice-mates. His favorite, L'ra, was already paired when he returned, so he waited while the shaman paired him with P'ua. Together they learned the mating ritual designed by First Goddess. When he started his village tasks, he requested L'ra as his full-mate and the shaman granted it. L'ra had also requested Toog, after having poor experiences with Jaat.

Toog dispatched the second Master's body more quickly, after a few long-cycles and by then becoming spoiled. He'd had difficulty consuming the flesh of the first Master so with the second body he tried to cook pieces using the fire pulses from the Masters' weapon.

The device had three settings—four if the default status was to be counted. Toog remembered them:

burn
cut
kill
melt

He had seen all of them demonstrated when he was taken to the cliff to be killed but was saved only to be put back into a dark cell. The creature that was hurt and could not walk was shot with the default setting which produced a burn in the skin, a painful injury yet one which might heal. When the creature stumbled again they shot it with a higher setting and the creature was killed, a hole blasted straight through the body. The next higher setting—Toog had watched them adjust their weapons in unison as the captives were lined up against the cliff—killed the other creatures with one blast each, cutting the bodies apart like knives of fire. After he was spared, the Masters had switched to the highest setting and mowed the pile of bodies back and forth with the orange beams of light, melting the corpses into a sticky fluid which was loose enough to flow into the ditch. Not wanting the pulse light to draw attention to his hideout, Toog took the weapon to a place far from any Masters' view to test it. Back in his cave, he placed pieces of meat against a flat stone and shot it with the weapon on the lower setting, cooking it thoroughly in only a few breaths.

When the meat was finished, he resumed his diet of scarce flora and the small animals of the cave who came to him and were caught. Strange worm-like creatures from the pool, some as long as his arm, were often a snack for him.

Every day Toog went to the entrance of the cave for sunlight and fresh air. The land was entering a colder, darker season, he counted. Nothing like Sebbol. He gave his eyes light for longer and longer time, trying to heal them from the darkness of his cell to the bright light of the zenith-sun reflecting off the cold white powder that covered everything outside. It was like the place of punishment described by the shaman. Cold was deadly to Aull.

snow
ice
cold

They were words Ra'aa'al taught him, words used by the Masters. The white crystals that fell from the sky, collecting on the ground, landing on his head and body if he stood out of the cave, hurt his skin when they touched it. There were no words for these crystals in Sebbou. He had to pull the

Masters' clothes over himself. He could not understand how any animal or plant could live in a place like this.

In the light he could see the changes. His once silvery skin was darker and thin-streaked in blue and green, mottled like a sick *suur* he had once seen rocking on its back in the *weeth*. When he touched his skin it was no longer soft and smooth, no longer pliant but hard and rough—also covered with small bumps, like the hide of a *veedo*. He had the appearance of illness but he understood the cause of it. He was not meant to be in this place, living with almost no cloth in such a cold place, drinking poor *lool* and eating bad meat and bad flora. He had to find a better place to live. This world was full of poisons.

You must return to your home, his inner Ru insisted, drawing illegible pictures on the walls of his mind-cave. *You are needed there.*

I will, Toog replied, shivering.

Good water was hard to get. He did not like leaving his cave's protection, but he was forced to make frequent trips to the stream which ran past the bottom of the ridge. Parts of the stream were hidden by *lathu* and *vau*—the bushes and trees. The flora was quite different than what Toog knew from Sebbol but he called them by the Sebbou words. Of the various scruffy flora, there were none taller than him.

He would hide among the foliage, watching and waiting, like a wild beast, and fill the two containers he got from the Masters who wandered into his cave. He would take a long drink, low-bent on his leg joints, then sneak back to his cave fortress.

From the stream, Toog could see a road veering away from the end of the ridge. He knew it connected the prison complex with the work camp. He often saw cloth-covered machine-wagons filled with creatures coming and going along it. After a while he lost the count.

Toog climbed to the top of the ridge above his cave. From the wind-swept snow-crusted slope, which rose to higher elevation as the ridge stretched to the north, Toog could see the expanse of the valley and more mountains far away on each horizon, with the prison complex over there and roads going in different directions. The work camps were out of range. He could not see any village or any warm *abo* or murky *skarg*. He had no idea how he could go home.

Late one night, Toog heard a noise.

A low, heavy voice called his name from the entrance of the cave. He felt the ground shake as the form moved deeper into the outer cavern. He heard the creature grunt when bumping its head on the sloping rock ceiling. Toog waited silently, weapon in hand, at the opening of the inner chamber. He knew the creature was too large to crawl through.

"Toog...." the creature called, heavy on the *g*. "Toog...."

After the echo faded, Toog squeezed through the opening and pointed his weapon at the creature's shadowy form.

A huge dark hulk with horns filled the cave. Toog knew this kind of creature: an *udu*-being, like those at the work camp that were called Xmburrhaltin.

Toog's finger weighed heavily on the trigger.

"Turn your weapon, Leader Toog. I mean you no harm," the *udu*-being said, almost a whisper. The gravelly words echoed in the cave, the noises of an animal, but in Toog's mind-cave the words were clear as they stuck to the walls.

You know the mind-cave language, Toog communicated.

"Many of us learn the prison code," spoke the Xmburrhaltin.

How can you see me in this darkness? Toog asked, sending the words out from his mind-cave.

"My eyes have learned to see through the darkness. Yours, too?"

Why have you come? What do you want? After the work camp experience, he did not trust these large, muscular creatures.

"To join you."

Me? Why? Toog was confused. He had no intention of fighting a Xmburrhaltin. Did the Masters send this brute to kill him? Was this the way he would die? *How did you escape from the Masters?*

More grunts, a step forward. "I wish to join your gang,"

"My gang?" Toog called out in Sebbou, cutting through the echo of the Xmburra words. His words also must have gone through the mind-cave of the Xmburrhaltin.

"Your gang of those-who-escaped. I felt vibrations of scenes."

"Vibrations?" asked Toog.

"We talk of these things. Many in the prison know about your escape, Leader Toog, and many now plan their own escapes."

"How did you escape?" asked Toog.

The creature grunted. "I broke away going to a work camp."

Toog could not believe the words bouncing around the walls of his mind-cave. His inner Ru hid in fright. So many pictures appeared on the walls—pictures drawn on top of pictures: the machine-wagons, the dirt road, the Masters falling under his claws.

"Can it be truth?" he asked. "How did you find me?"

"I followed your pattern. I found it in the prison."

"Pattern? What do you mean?"

"Your mind sends impulses, forms a pattern that floats in the air and stains the ground wherever you have been. I followed the pattern to you. Here."

Toog let go a squeal, choked it back.

"Then the Masters also could track me...." Toog left-turned right-turned his head, as if looking for his inner Ru. "Why do you call me 'Leader'?"

"For respect. You are the first to escape. Because of you others will follow. I will follow you, Leader Toog. You are the leader of us."

Toog up-stood before the Xmburrhaltin. He was three times as tall as Toog, three-times as wide, covered in gray fur from head to toes. With two short black horns.

"How are you called?" Toog asked the Xmburrhaltin.

"I am called Grauun."

Toog held up the Masters' weapon.

"Grauun, meet the gang: me and my weapon."

The creature's eyes widened. "Now we are three."

Toog reached down for the second Master's weapon, held it out to Grauun. "Four."

Words did not come easily to the little silver being whose hands and feet were turning blue despite wearing the dead Master's greatcoat, nor for the giant being covered with the thick gray fur, a pair of small forehead horns and uneven rows of teeth and long claws on hands and feet that were put to good use drawing in the dirt on the floor of the cave as they tried to share their stories.

I think the pulling is not so great on this world, communicated the furry creature when Toog mentioned how difficult it was for him to run on this world. I feel a few steps quicker, and stronger, like I carried less weight here. How was your world?

Toog told his tale in dusty pictures as his mind-cave worked out the words, adding a side trek to explain the legend of Hoot the Dry in the Valley of Somo, how the sneaky *chun* thought it was getting a meal but instead was served in twenty-seven parts to a village of Aull. Then, putting together some words for Grauun, another side trek to explain how the young Liif could believe Third Goddess would allow him to go with the orb-maid F'ao for the mating ritual without the proper prayers—he got the squeaks wrong—and how they unexpectedly produced a twice-dented orb in the *skarg* that burst open too soon and the poison inside it corrupted the *lool* for the entire district—which was the reason for stricter rules being imposed for the mating ritual by the high shaman—and why they no longer ate *faef*.

That's nothing, Grauun grunted, wiping his messy mouth after a meal of some four-leg animal he killed nearby and dragged back to the cave. On his world, there were no goddesses, only gods, and they stood tall in their caves and mighty among the ice and snow in all days and nights, howling louder than the terror-wind, and growling louder than the howls of new-born Xmx pulled frozen from the mother's icy womb! The high god was Xm—obviously—and Grauun had to tell the story of how Xm defeated his seven brothers in hand-to-hand battle, and ate four of them before his daughter insisted on sharing the bounty with her children—What you call 'springling'. Then Xm had to climb the mighty mountain using only his claws and teeth during the worst terror-wind ever, and once at the top, Xm took a mighty in-breath and sucked the terror-wind right out of the sky so we could have calm for the Festival of Vol. And he told the tale of Vol, who slew the Eastern Werch and cut her into eleven pieces to feed the Kax that formed the great ice wells with their hollowed-out torsos.

But on my world, Sebbol, Toog explained, we don't have terror-wind or gods that kill their brothers. We have harmony and many songs praising harmony. We even have a mountain called harmony, Per-Oul. It is often covered in bright flowers. In the summer season the Aull youth must go there and live off the land along the way, and some youth do not return, but those who do return get their pick of partial-mates. You see, each Aull female must be started before the next Aull can fertilize her. It is a check Great Goddess Aull imposed to protect us from a bad cloud of globules—

On Xmburrhaltis, we just take the females into a dark cave and push our hammers into them until a terror-wind rises in us and we awake not knowing who we took into the cave. We just put our bodies together and run all night, howling at the twelve moons like Buxan did in the story of Vemmy's vengeance on the Hox. And if any Xmburrhaltin disturbs us, then we pause to kill it—or let it share our cave-grunts. It is like Xm did on the mountain of ice, as written on the sacred staff of Gourk.

We do not exactly have females and males on Sebbol. We are both—alternately. The shaman determines which sex a new orb will be. If we have too many females, then male; if too many males, then female. First Goddess can explain it to you if you call to her. It is also written on some tablets which the high shaman keeps safe.

Never going to call to a female god, no! Xm would spit up

his meal to hear such a sour thing. But you can get some muscles on your little body with a lot of good fatty meat. Try the Vex-Teel or Lag, even a few Smud eggs will help. They will fatten you up for the winter. In fact, our summer season is when the ice softens for about ten days, then the next winter begins. The sage Draux tells us we are too far from the star Exm to melt more ice—

We do not have ice on Sebbol. It is positioned to provide perfect environment for Aull. We live in a paradise—warm and moist, with plenty of *lool* and *skarg* and always the *oum* floating by. And the *abo* is most calm.

Moist! Hah! This *oum* you speak of, what is it?

Oum is a cloud of vapor, but thicker than air, watery like the *abo* but contained within itself, like a floating bubble of liquid, but the liquid is thicker and you can push your hand straight through it and sometimes we catch it and drink from it although it may not always be nourishing, depending on the source of the *oum*, but they float everywhere, and sometimes we cannot see across the valley for all the *oum* collecting there.

Sounds like a horrible place! Too moist! I understand why you are so eager to return there. If you could grow some hair on that naked body, you might be able to visit Xm without dying right away the first instant a terror-wind cuts you.

I prefer the warm and moist breeze of *oum* on Sebbol. And my full-mate L'ra, who waits for me with our springling M'ah.

Ah, females and the kindling! They tie you down, hold you back, make life a hell for us. Better to be captured by the Masters and made to cleave stone from mountains! Xm would be proud of us here, escaped and living wild, making our own road! I just miss having a thick Xmburrith to push against in a cave. If they took any females from Xmburra, I have not seen any.

I want to go home and be with my family, Toog communicated clearly from his mind-cave. Having worked out the words, he wanted no misunderstanding. *That and nothing else. You can stay here if you want but I am leaving.*

●●

They hunted for food by day and communicated in the evenings. They wondered how their fate would have been different if the Masters had first visited a world where the beings had the same kind of weapons, an advanced civilization, a warrior society.

If we had their weapons, they would all be dead before they could speak, Grauun said with a loud grunt, munching on the leg of an animal he had killed. Then they would be afraid, he said, and they would never dare to step outside their own world. But we met them only with spears and clubs. They sent out a noise that made us fear them, put terror in our heads.

We did not meet them at all. They steal us in the night, Toog shared. I never saw them. We had no better weapons than you.

One day they will go to a world where the inhabitants will cut them down and make them fear. We see they are nothing but bones covered in flesh.

Toog agreed, licking off his fingers, belly full.

Many nights later, Toog felt another presence in the cave. His eyes spiraled open, stared through the darkness, searching. His ears caught no sound yet he persisted in sensing the other entity. Toog's hand felt for his weapon, found it. Slowly he stood, still listening for some sound that would betray the intruder.

Then Toog heard a voice—but it came from within him, rather than into his ears. He stopped, frightened, and listened as the voice called his name. It was familiar.

"Toog, listen to me," spoke Ra'aa'al in a ragged voice, echoing in the corridors of his mind-cave in perfect Sebbou. "I have only now raised enough strength to send my voice to you. I sense the Masters will come for me soon, very soon, so I must escape."

"What can I do?" Toog asked in the same silent medium.

"I need another body."

"Body?"

"I have used this lizard body since they captured me."

"Lizard? What is your real body?"

"I will explain later. It has taken me many days to locate you and even now my power is fading, so I must hurry. Here is what you must do: you must kill an upright body— no broken bones—then you—just do it. I grow weak again. I will be with you soon."

Toog listened to the silence that followed, the scratchy noise of the universe.

Knowing what he must do, he awoke Grauun and began to plan their mission. He told Grauun about sharing a cell with Ra'aa'al and what kind of creature he seemed to be. Toog knew the only other upright bodies were those of the Masters. He and Grauun would have to kill one of the Masters so Ra'aa'al could inhabit its body.

"It is good," grumbled Grauun, "to kill the Masters."

Dawn came early with pink sun-light spilling across the leathery grass, swaying in the early morning breeze. From the top of the ridge, after a long hike, the thick gray walls of the prison loomed in the distance. They had put up a new guard tower. There appeared to be no life inside the walls;

everything was quiet. Yet Toog knew it contained hundreds of prisoners from across the universe.

"Here we stand, you and me," Toog spoke in Sebbou, heard by Grauun as Xmburra. They stared across the valley at the prison. "We must kill one of the Masters today. This we do for Ra'aa'al, who needs an upright body to inhabit in order to join us. The Masters are the only upright bodies here." He glanced at Grauun. "Unless it is a creature like you or me."

"Kill a Master?" Grauun grunted, thick eyebrows raised.

"It is the only way."

Grauun grunted, looked off at the prison. "I cannot."

"Why? You must," Toog insisted. "He must be killed by cutting-the-breath. We cannot hurt the body. You are strong enough to hold the throat closed until death."

"I cannot," Grauun replied. "I fear."

"The Masters?"

Grauun slowly nodded. "It is a trick they put in us."

"Remember all they have done to you. That must set the anger in you!"

"It does, but when my head touches scenes of pain, I fear."

"You must do it. I am not strong enough," Toog explained. "Be stronger than the trick they put in your head."

"But I fear."

"You are big and strong. You must not fear." He glared at the Xmburrhaltin. "You must put their trick into a passage of your mind-cave and never look in it again."

"I fear nothing!" He drew a big breath. "Except the Masters."

"If you wish to be a member of my gang, you must kill one of the Masters."

"Did you?"

"I killed twelve." He narrowed his eyes. "I do not regret."

Grauun's face tightened. "Then I will kill twelve."

"Only one is needed now. In time, we will kill all of them."

They made their way down to the road. Toog had watched the convoys often. He knew that no machine-wagons would be coming by until later. A machine-wagon brought supplies to the work camp every day. Sometimes new prisoners. They waited at a small bridge where the stream ran under the road.

The dull gray sun passed overhead. As Toog expected, the growling of the Masters' machine-wagon soon sounded across the valley. When the wagon was close, Toog gave the signal. Grauun pulled away one of the supports under the bridge and it collapsed. The machine-wagon screeched to a halt just short of the bridge.

Toog sprang from the ditch, holding his weapon pointed at the wagon. The guards, dressed in tight-fitting brown uniforms, were perplexed by the little blue being holding one of their pulse-guns. They laughed at him—until Toog pulled the trigger and a beam of orange light hit the side of the wagon and the wheel there melted into scrap and the wagon leaned down.

One guard jumped out of the wagon, shouting, and tried to run but Toog's next blast cut him down. The others remained spellbound. They did not know what to do; they had never been threatened on their own world, and not so close to their fortress. They still seemed amused by the little blue being, but the Xmburrhaltin coming up from under the broken bridge gave them pause. The big furry creature also held a pulse-gun.

Toog waved the remaining Masters out of their wagon.

Lay on the road, face down and bellies to the dirt, Toog ordered, sending the command into their mind-caves. They hesitated, puzzled by the message in their heads. But seeing Toog making a motion with the weapon, they got the idea.

As they were dropping to their knees, two of them tried to use their weapons but Toog spun around and shot them. Their hands dropped from their arms as they screamed, blood leaking from the seared stubs. Two others rushed at Toog.

He struggled with the guards, taller and stronger than him, as the last guard decided to flee. The Master left the road and leaped across the ditch, racing across the tundra plain. Lifted off his feet by the guards, Toog swung his free arm and his hand struck the jaw of the guard who was grabbing his other arm—a strange instinct he had never felt before. He saw the spur in the heel of his hand had come out and cut the guard's face, tearing part of the jaw away. The guard let go of him, held his bleeding face.

As Toog shook pain from his hand, he squealed to Grauun, pointing at the escaping guard: "Him! Get him! Him!"

Grauun lumbered around the front of the machine-wagon and ran after the fleeing Master.

Toog slipped free and pulled the trigger of his weapon, killing the Master who had grabbed hold of his arm. Training the weapon's bright light on the Masters moaning about their lost hands, Toog cut them into pieces. His inner Ru called for him to stop. They were already hurt, thus punished, but he continued until the weapon beeped that its power was low. A blue button pulsed on the top of the square section at the rear of the weapon. It pulsed slower and slower, then went dark.

Toog halted, breathing hard. He watched Grauun,

bounding on hands and feet, catch up to and throw down the escaping Master like a predator catching dinner. The big Xmburrhaltin carried the body of the Master, striding leisurely on two legs back to the road.

"It is done," said Grauun, looking at the charred bodies of the guards strewn on the road beside the machine-wagon. "No longer do I fear the pain trick."

The machine-wagon had food supplies, so Grauun carried all he could back to their cave, plus new weapons, while Toog dragged the body of the dead Master, the blue being's arms thickening with the effort, back stiffening with power.

◆○

The night was cold but the cave was protected from the biting wind. Toog sat with his aching back against the cave's wall, looking across to the opposite wall where the body of the dead Master sat, propped up. He watched as it firmed and turned white. The eyelids were still open, the eyes turned upward.

Toog waited silently. He studied this strange creature, noticing how the skin shriveled as the night deepened. He watched Grauun standing at the cave's entrance, looking out, reporting no activity on the road below. They would find the wagon and the bodies soon. He thought it better to hurry back to the cave rather than risk another wagon coming by and seeing the attack.

From the corner of his eye, Toog caught a flicker. He turned and stared at the Master's body. He saw it again: the small outside finger twitched. The finger next to it moved. Toog stood up as the body's arm swung up from the arm joint, hitting its chest.

"Grauun, come from there," Toog spoke. "Help me up-stand the body."

Grauun lumbered over and jerked the body up with one hand. The arms of the body fell into spasms, and the head rolled back and forth on the weak neck.

"Lay it down on the ground, stretch it out," Toog instructed. "That will be better."

After the body was on the floor of the cave, the spasms stopped. There was no motion for a while—until the eyelids closed and opened. The eyes turned, looking around the cave, then turned up to see Toog and Grauun standing over the body. The dry lips parted and it spoke in cracked, broken speech. It was the voice of the Master, speaking the Masters' language.

Toog heard it in Sebbou echoing in his mind-cave.

"L-et me r-est." A gurgle from the throat. "I am h-ere."

"Yes, rest." Toog's mouth up-turned. He looked at Grauun. "Ra'aa'al is here."

"What k-ind of b-ody...do I h-ave?" Ra'aa'al asked, speaking through the dead body's mouth.

"It is the body of a Master," Toog answered proudly.

"I killed it," Grauun added.

"When—did you k-ill it?"

"One day ago," Toog responded.

"It is—a little st-iff...but—it w-ill do."

"I am glad, Ra'aa'al. How long will you need to rest?"

"I will w-alk...in the m-orning."

"And then what will we do?"

"Go...h-ome."

"How can we do that?" Grauun groaned.

"We are on this world, and we know not where it is in the sky," Toog added.

"Bide your t-ime," the body responded. "I h-ave learned

of—all this fr-om other pr-isoners."

"How long will it take?" asked Toog.

"First—we must h-elp two...others g-et out."

"Why?" Toog asked.

"They are.... They h-ave t-old me of the way. ...If I l-eave w-ithout them, I—will die. They h-ave powerful minds...and if I do not ob-lige them, at—the moment we—d-epart—this world, they w-ill send a kill-ing thought—to me. That is the pr-ice of the s-ecret. It—is not too h-igh a price f-or what it—is."

"Are those creatures like you, Ra'aa'al?" asked Toog.

"No...they are f-rom...Heis-Tegag."

"Where is that?"

"As far fr-om h-ere as y-our home."

Toog leaned down. "Why did they tell you the secret?"

"They h-ave not told me—all. I know h-ow it is d-one, but on-ly they—know *where* to—do it. A white cube...the Masters walk through. Heis-Tegag cr-eatures know wh-ere it is."

"Will this body return to life?" asked Grauun in Xmburra.

The body's mouth gurgled. "It will...re-main as you got it."

"But it has turned ugly," said Toog, contorting his face.

"It has odor," Grauun added. "Like food."

"These beings from Heis-Tegag, how are they?" asked Toog.

"They are like y-ourself in form—upright, but short, and ugly—which is beauty—on their world."

"When will we rescue them, Ra'aa'al?"

"T-omor-row, the n-ext day.... When I am...alive."

Toog stirred at regular intervals yet he entered the dream land still wondering about the magic cube Ra'aa'al mentioned. With talk of going home, Toog's dreams were filled with images of L'ra and his springling M'ah. The Master in the red robe said he had been on this world for six of their sun-cycles. He calculated the same as eighteen sun-cycles on Sebbol. His daughter would be orb-ready. She would be paired. Had his full-mate L'ra taken another partner? And Toog was on this desolate world so far from home that it would take many sun-cycles to return—if he *could* return.

He knew who to blame: the Masters, deceptive cowards who through luck from the goddesses or strange fate had developed weapons and machines that allowed them to reach out across the universe to conquer other creatures. They took him from his home, his family, and brought him here to be nailed to a stone shelf in a dark prison cell for eternity—why?

He did not know the answer, but his hatred consumed his entire being, and as his gray skin began to take on a bluish hue he screamed at his tormentors just as Ra'aa'al shook him awake.

"It is morning." The pale hand of the dead Master, standing in its brown uniform, reached down and touched Toog's shoulder.

"Too soon," replied Toog with a grunt.

"Perhaps not soon enough," the Master's voice responded.

Slowly Toog stood, feeling body-juice leaking from his skin vents, collecting enough to run down his body as though he had just emerged from the *abo*. He felt pain in his right hand where the bolt had been. Pain in his other hand from hitting the Master's face.

"You visited a dream?" asked Ra'aa'al as the Master's body stood tall and bent to the side. It felt odd for Toog to address this pale thing.

"Yes. But not a good visit." Toog sighed. He ran his bluish hands over his blue head, felt the bumps were higher. "Is today the day?"

"Perhaps," Ra'aa'al answered. "I must be strong enough to best them in mental battle—and physically, too—before we can rescue the Heis-Tegagans. Otherwise, they may get control over me."

Toog's eyes spiraled open wider, his mouth up-turned. "You will be our leader, Ra'aa'al."

"No, it is you who began this group. You are the leader, Toog. You were the first to escape from the Masters, to set an example for us. Only you can be our leader."

"But you are the strongest, Ra'aa'al. Your mental powers are so great—"

"No, Toog, you are the leader." Ra'aa'al produced a twisted grin through the somber gray lips of the Master's mouth. "This body is feeble. Not suitable to be a leader. However, I will give you advice."

Toog looked around the cave's outer corridor.

"Where is Grauun?"

"He was absent when I awoke."

Toog went to the cave's entrance, gazed over the bushes, down across the valley.

"Perhaps he fears me," Ra'aa'al suggested.

Toog turned to Ra'aa'al, twitching at the sight of the decaying body. "I will go find him. He may have gone down to the stream. You stay here and rest."

"No, Toog, I need exercise now, not rest. I will go with you."

They made their way through the scruffy bushes and jagged rocks, the body of Ra'aa'al moving stiffly, always on the verge of toppling over, on down to the stream. They hid in foliage along the bank.

Grauun was not there.

Toog scanned the valley and spotted Grauun's huge hulk far away, lumbering toward the road, going in the direction of the bridge that they had collapsed.

"He is going to where we got your body."

Toog helped Ra'aa'al up and they hurried to catch up to Grauun.

The sun-light was no more than a glimmer straining through a dark overcast as Toog and Ra'aa'al arrived beside the road. Through the whipping wind, Toog recognized the noise of machine-wagons. Despite having no beasts to pull them, they made an awful noise and spit out poison.

Toog quickly met Grauun in the ditch alongside the road.

"Why are you here?" he asked.

"The machine-wagon. The bodies," Grauun muttered. "They will be found. They will know we exist."

Toog cursed in squeaks and chirps. "We had to get a body for Ra'aa'al. I did not care about the scene we left here. Now it is too late. There is a machine-wagon coming."

They crouched in the ditch as the wagon rolled to a stop behind the abandoned wagon. The Masters climbed out and stared at the charred bodies of their comrades. Some went to check the abandoned wagon. Weapons were drawn.

Toog heard them speak something—questions about who could have done this terrible thing, his inner Ru wrote. The writing on his mind-cave's wall was a fury of nearly unreadable squiggles.

The leader instructed the guards to look around—which meant Toog and Grauun were quickly found, leaving

Ra'aa'al to hide behind the bridge's fallen post. They yielded quietly since they had no weapons. The guards aimed their weapons at them while the leader cautiously approached.

"These must be the mysterious prisoners I heard of," the leader exclaimed in his language. "I thought it was only a joke. A story to frighten new guards." His comrades laughed. "When did you escape?"

Toog and Grauun remained silent, feigning ignorance of the words. Yet Toog read the words in Sebbou on the wall of his mind-cave.

"Speak or we will kill you here this instant!" shouted the leader.

Toog opened his mouth to reply but his Sebbou words were drowned out by the cry of one of the guards.

"Look there, Commander," the guard cried. "A survivor."

Ra'aa'al had left the hiding place under the bridge, climbed up to the road, standing awkwardly. His skin was deathly pale and looked bright against the dark ground. He walked steadily and straight-limbed over the dirt road. When he reached Toog and Grauun, the guards drew back against the machine-wagon.

"Is he alive?" a guard cried out.

The leader called it by name, got no response.

"No—no, he's not alive—somehow." The leader stepped up to the body, examined it, stared into its eyes. "A dead thing."

"I—am—not—dead," croaked the mouth of the body Ra'aa'al inhabited.

"What is that thing?" a guard cried out fearfully.

Ra'aa'al moved between Toog and Grauun until he stood ahead of them with the guards further in front.

"He's—it's—coming closer! Shoot it!" the leader ordered.

Guards opened fire on Ra'aa'al, pulses of red light striking him squarely in the chest. The uniform burned, even the flesh began to smolder, but Ra'aa'al continued advancing. He knew the body was already dead and their weapons could not stop him.

The Masters scrambled into their machine-wagon, started it, and charged forward at him, knocking Ra'aa'al aside.

Toog and Grauun leaped from the road, falling into the ditch with the stream as the machine-wagon lurched and spanned the small gap where the bridge had collapsed, crashing on the other side but continuing to roar down the road toward the prison.

"This is bad," Toog cursed. "They will bring many Masters to search for us."

He helped Ra'aa'al up from where he had fallen. Three broken ribs protruded from his chest after the machine-wagon struck him.

"We cannot free the two Heis-Tegagans now," Ra'aa'al sighed, looking down at the ribs. Blood had stained the uniform but it did not run down the clothing. It had coagulated inside.

"They thought they could kill you again, but they could not." A faint chuckle slipped out of Toog's tiny blue mouth and he felt ill at the sound. He looked for Grauun. "But they did burn you."

"I felt nothing," said Ra'aa'al. He pushed the broken ribs back into his host body.

"But the skin of your chest...it's charred and wrinkled from the flame," Toog stated. "You are more ugly now."

"In time, we will all be ugly. We are an ugly bunch," groaned Ra'aa'al.

"Where go now?" Grauun asked Toog.

"Where, Ra'aa'al?" Toog repeated.

"We must leave," Ra'aa'al replied.

"Are we going to the magic cube?"

"I have heard of a place on this world where it is warm," Ra'aa'al croaked. "I would go there. Perhaps that is where the magic cube is."

the cube

▲ ▶ ▶ ▶   7

Over distant ridges and hills, through countless valleys of moss and lichen, past bogs and mud-streaked glaciers, to the north, to the brown, foamy sea they went. With Toog in the lead, followed stiffly by Ra'aa'al inhabiting the Master's body and lumbering Grauun, they marched to the top of the snowy ridge before them and peered across yet another tundra valley, sadly seeing more distant ridges and gray-cast mountains. From that ridge they spied a stone road winding its way across the valley from their near right on to the far left where it was lost in curtains of mist. A frigid wind arose behind them and blew them down into the valley.

Across four of the Masters' day-cycles they traveled over the tundra, yet they remained uncertain about the correct direction. Ra'aa'al knew from reading the minds of the Heis-Tegagans that the place they sought was to the north, near a dark, poisoned sea. It was the place where the Heis-Tegagans arrived on this world. Somewhere there stood the machine through which the Masters departed their world in order to gather the creatures they sought. Toog, Ra'aa'al, and Grauun could only return to their homes by passing through the machine, what those from Heis-Tegag said was a huge white cube filled with magic. Only the Heis-Tegagans knew the secret of the machine, Ra'aa'al said, but they could not free them, not with the Masters on the hunt. So they would need to learn how to operate the magic of the cube by themselves.

As they reached the valley floor, Grauun noticed another, road of dirt and gravel veering off the main road. They stood at the intersection deciding which way to go. Looking at the poorer road, with the wind beating hard against them, they detected the fresh tracks of the Masters' machine-wagons.

"The Masters have been here," Ra'aa'al spoke, regarding the tracks. "We are on the right path."

"Then we will go this way," Toog stated, motioning.

Grauun nodded and followed.

"The road goes up the next ridge, through that pass," Ra'aa'al commented, awkwardly bent arm trying to point.

The three traversed the road, up to the pass, and gazed in awe at what lay below. Stretching from the bottom of the ridge was a long plain carpeted with dull yellow grass without a single patch of snow. It looked like paradise. If only all that grass was broken up with some *skarg*.

"The air is warmer on this side of the ridge," Toog remarked.

"It is strange," Ra'aa'al admitted. "We are in an arctic clime. Why then is there rain here, where only a few steps away there is snow? There are strange forces at work here."

"The magic of the cube may change the weather here," said Toog. "Magnetic waves hold back the cold."

"It is not good to be so warm," Grauun grumbled.

"I don't agree," Toog spoke. "Why must we question it if

it is good? Let us continue our travel."

"I do not like traveling in open areas," Ra'aa'al stated. "There will be no place to hide if the Masters find us."

"We will have to stand and fight," Toog explained. "You can frighten them again, Ra'aa'al, with your death-gaze."

"This is not just another valley," said Grauun, growling at the plain. "I see no other ridges or mountains."

"We have no choice," Toog declared, waving his hand at the plain. "We must go across the plain to reach the magic cube."

Ra'aa'al nodded slowly, silently. He took an unsteady step, starting to exit the pass. Toog and Grauun followed as the path wound down to the grassy plain.

Once they were on the plain, Toog's blue feet felt the warmth of its surface, reminding him of the corridors in the prison. Seeing them closely, the grasses were not yellow but gray, long and leathery, scratching his bare legs as he moved through them. Only the angle of shy sun-light made them appear golden. They marched from the road, trying to be as inconspicuous as possible.

The plain proved to be larger than it appeared from the pass. They spent four nights sleeping among the grasses, away from the road, one of them always on watch although no Masters appeared. They had long lost sight of the ridge, and the horizon was low in every direction. The air and the ground increased in warmth each day of their travel. Now the grasses were mixed with sandy, rocky soil, reminding Toog of Sebbol.

On their fifth day on the plain, after the gray sun had passed overhead, and the plain had risen enough so they could look down toward the horizon, Grauun, who had the sharpest eyes, spied several piles of large boulders at the farthest reaches of his vision. When they got closer, he could see Masters' machine-wagons parked behind the boulders, visible in the gaps between the huge rocks.

"Another quarry?" Toog inquired.

"This does not seem a good place to dig rocks," said Grauun.

"Those boulders appear like those I pulled from the cliffs."

"They appear natural, not cut."

Keeping low, they worked their way toward the boulders, as close as they dared get to the Masters. They settled among smaller rocks that were just as smooth and round as the larger ones ahead.

"I hear no slave-noise," said Toog. "I smell no fear-rain."

"Perhaps we should move closer to see what the Masters do here," Ra'aa'al suggested. "I will go, since I wear their body."

"A dead Master's body," Toog reminded him.

"He will frighten them," Grauun grumbled.

"I will only take a look."

Ra'aa'al crawled on his broken hands and bent knees out from their hiding place, across the short expanse of grass and sand, up to the closest large boulder, which rose to twice his height when he awkwardly stood. He peered cautiously around the huge rock, gazing through the gap between the boulders.

The ground dropped away on the opposite side, down to a narrow beach which curved around to the horizon. Under the light of a moon hanging low in the sky, he saw the tide of the foamy sea bubbling on the sand and felt the warm sea breeze.

Ahead sat a large, white, squarish structure, a huge cube, on the beach midway between the waterline and the rocks which hid him. Several Masters, dressed in brown robes and hoods and carrying their short-barreled weapons, stood in a line extending from the cube. Every moment one more Master disappeared into the cube's front opening and its walls glowed a brighter shade of white then returned to the dull white.

Ra'aa'al observed only a short time before returning to get Toog, reporting what he saw. They went up to the boulders and watched the Masters and their magic cube.

"They go in but none come out," Toog noted.

Ra'aa'al made the Master's head nod.

"Perhaps there is a prison under the ground, and the cube has inside steps which go down," Toog suggested.

Ra'aa'al sniffed the scent of the sea, a bitter, acidic odor.

"This must be the place, and that is your *magic* cube. There is nothing magic about it: it is a machine."

"How do we operate it?" asked Toog.

"I do not know."

When the last of the Masters had entered the cube and it glowed briefly, Toog and Ra'aa'al returned to Grauun.

They moved up to the boulders, set their gear, then explored along the beach while the Masters were gone. Ra'aa'al was disappointed by the sea's foamy water: dense, half-liquid sludge. As though industrial waste had been emptied into a natural sea for a very long time. He told Toog about it, about his world in ancient days, before his kind had learned to live without bodies but found limitations in that form and so had to learn to inhabit other bodies, the Fovol being the most useful.

Toog stood before the monstrous edifice, towering over him and Grauun. The cube's white walls were perfectly smooth, with no markings or external apparatus. They could see no door where the Masters had entered. Ra'aa'al had identified the front side as where the Masters entered, but it appeared as plain as the other sides, nothing indicating an entrance.

Then the cube began to glow, and the three escapees rushed to hide behind the nearest pile of boulders. The front side of the cube glowed a brighter white. Out came a group of the Masters, twenty-three of them as Toog counted. Most of them stood by the cube while a few others moved over to the machine-wagons, climbed inside them.

From where they hid, they saw silhouettes of various kinds of creatures within the glowing walls of the cube. A large creature, one of Grauun's kind, suddenly emerged from the cube and ran down the beach—until a blast from a Masters' weapon dropped him in the sand.

Toog knew Grauun saw it and was ready to stand and fight.

"Get down, Grauun," said Toog, and he did.

"I want to kill Masters."

That Master stepped away from the cube, weapon pointed at the fallen Xmburrhaltin. The Master, robe waving in the breeze, fired another blast and the sand glowed bright orange, even after the creature's mid-section had been melted away.

"They use weapons of light," said Ra'aa'al. "The power of light can burn and cut flesh."

"We have such weapons," Toog said.

"Let us use them," Grauun grunted.

They watched as the Masters marched out the creatures they had captured from across the galaxy. Toog counted the legion: twenty, thirty. There were several creatures like Grauun, a few Cetreans, Piilactrians, and Friseens, and a pair of Ra'aa'al's kind—the lizard body he had used as a prisoner. That creature was called Vangu, coming from a world called Dxii, according to Ra'aa'al. He was lucky to find it when his Fovol body was injured in a flying-machine crash. His Fovol body, battered in the wreck, had hiked through the jungle for days until it was bitten by the Vangu. Yet, while inhabiting the Vangu's body, he could not repair and operate his flying-machine. Then the Masters came.

Aside from a few beings Toog had never seen before, there were two upright beings that caught his attention: a male and a female, both with high foreheads and muscular bodies. The male wore the cut-skin of another animal around its hips. The female was covered in a long green cloth and carried something in her arms. As he watched, the bundle in her arms moved. It was a springling, Toog saw, and he felt a stone roll into his mind-cave, remembering his own springling.

"I cannot endure this!" Toog growled through clenched teeth as he tore his gaze away. "We must stop them."

"Patience, Toog," Ra'aa'al whispered. "Soon all debts will be paid, and all wrongs righted."

"I want to kill Masters," Grauun growled.

"Can we let them take those creatures away?" asked Toog. "To be locked away in dark cells? To be forced to labor in work camps? To be put on a table under a hot lamp and cut open?"

Ra'aa'al looked over at Grauun, back to Toog. "No, I suppose not. We should do something to stop the Masters."

"I agree," Grauun grunted.

With a nod from Toog, they moved carefully down the beach with the rocks shielding them, until they were close to the first machine-wagon.

"Listen to what I say," Toog communicated. "This must be precisely planned." His inner Ru assessed the situation, mapped the area from Toog's visual survey, marked the positions of the Masters, calculated angles.

Grauun hunched down, ready to spring.

Clouds had become heavy during their planning, and thunder rumbled. Lightning flashed out over the sudsy sea as Grauun reached for the driver of the first machine-wagon and pulled it from its seat, snapping its neck.

Toog grabbed the driver's weapon and they moved to the next machine-wagon, and the next, until they had six weapons and six drivers had broken necks.

The Masters were busy lining up the new prisoners by type, having them stand like sleeping statues.

Thunder continued and the rain fell as Ra'aa'al stepped from behind the last machine-wagon and fired his pulse-gun at the two closest Masters, searing away their chests from under their heads. Instantly other Masters ran toward Ra'aa'al, firing as they charged despite being surprised their attacker looked like one of them. Toog was in position and hit them from the side with his pulse-gun strikes, blasts of orange light cutting them in two.

More Masters converged, leaving the captive creatures to stand silently in the rain, and took aim on Ra'aa'al.

Grauun pushed over a machine-wagon on top of a trio of Masters coming at Toog.

One of the guards, shielded by the first row of captives, fired at Ra'aa'al and burned off his arm at the shoulder. The arm, with weapon clenched by its hand, dropped to the sand. Grauun lunged between Ra'aa'al's teetering body and the next blast, catching it squarely in the chest, but Ra'aa'al shoved the big Xmburrhaltin to the sand.

Grauun staggered to his feet. His thick chest fur was merely singed. He hoisted Ra'aa'al's wounded body over his shoulder and carried it to one of the machine-wagons, then grabbed another pulse-gun and stomped back to help Toog.

Toog was focused on his attack. *Now shoot at number 6,*

then eight but a little lower, instructed Toog's inner Ru, dressed in a warrior sash, pointing to each Master's position marked on the detailed diagram drawn on the wall of Toog's mind-cave. *Wait for five to move left, then take three, and then take five. Watch for number eleven coming from behind the last row of captives.*

His inner Ru gasped as Toog obeyed the instructions quicker than expected. *After eleven shoots again, that weapon will no longer have enough energy for a fatal shot. Then you can mount the machine-wagon and cover the area with defensive light.*

His inner Ru pointed at new targets on the diagram. *Take down twelve before he runs too far down the beach to be out of range. Yes—got him!*

Toog was firing over the assembled creatures from atop one of the machine-wagons at the Masters who had been firing at Ra'aa'al. They were in disarray, unprepared, having always been the attackers. Even their weapons were set to only fire stunning blasts, but those that remained switched to full strength. Grauun shot at them from the front while Toog moved to attack them from the side. The Masters fired at Grauun through the rows of creatures, hitting many captives yet missing Grauun. Toog fired at the last of the Masters until none were left alive and his inner Ru wiped off the wall in his mind-cave.

The storm ceased.

⁀ ⌣

Toog walked through the carnage in the overcast sunset, strange sensations coursing through his body. The ugly odor of fire-death filled his mind-cave, his inner Ru hiding but stretching out a hand to point to a warning written on

the wall: *When killing monsters do not become a monster.*
Not a monster, Toog thought, but his words would not stay
on the wall of his mind-cave. They floated away like dust as
fast as his inner Ru wrote them. The Masters were the
monsters, not him.

He stood seething with anger as he studied the
formation of creatures. He recognized some of them. And
yet there were no beings that swam or flew, he noted. Only
land-based beings. Only the intelligent ones were taken, the
ones with civilization and culture. With families. Only the
ones that could be made to serve. We are not the monsters,
he groaned to himself. His inner Ru gave a nod, remained
silent.

Now he was truly a warrior. His shaman would be
proud. He would be sent out to fight whenever other
villages tried to come and take what they possessed. Sure,
they would trade goods and make fair deals, but sometimes
a village would not want to play that game, would try to
steal. They could not live peacefully side by side. They had
to always be ready. But they were not ready when the
Masters came in the night.

He kicked a charred body here, overturned a piece of
carrion there, as great black flying animals descending from
the sky and pecked at the burnt flesh. They knew what to
do, thought Toog. Clean the waste, make use of everything.

He gathered what useful equipment he found while
Grauun tended to Ra'aa'al. The wounded body of the Master
he wore continued to leak dried, powdery blood. The
granules slowly sifting out through the open-ended artery
in his shoulder.

"It is of no use," Ra'aa'al spoke. "This body will no longer
suffice."

"They are nothing more than bones carrying flesh, with a

layer of cloth over it to hide their true nature," Toog responded, staring down at the body Ra'aa'al wore. "No more than us."

"If we had more of us then we could defeat them," Grauun growled. "Kill them all."

"We could force them to show us how to operate the cube," Toog communicated. "Or force them to operate it for us. To send us home." He looked at Grauun, saw the singed fur on his chest. "Are you hurt?"

"No," Grauun grunted, laughing as he rubbed his chest. On Xmburra the terror-wind would cut through him if his body did not have thick skin and thick fur to protect him, he explained, almost boasting. An illustrative story followed.

The body Ra'aa'al wore creaked, interrupting the tale. Its mouth fell open and a long putrid breath spilling out.

"This body served me well," spoke Ra'aa'al, "for a short time, but...I now require another."

Toog understood. "We will get another for you."

He went across the beach, stopped beside one fallen body that appeared in good condition. He turned it over with his foot and saw the large hole in the rear of the skull which he had created. He moved on.

They will wonder why the machine-wagons do not return, Toog thought, his inner Ru crawling out to sit and listen. They will wonder about the creatures they have captured. They will come to see what has happened here. They will see the attack here, and they will know that monsters exist. His message went straight to Ra'aa'al.

"Time is ending," Ra'aa'al said with a Master's body's hollow moan. Grauun raised Ra'aa'al's head and tightened the band on the stub of his arm, though the dried blood continued to drain.

There were no Master bodies that could be used, Toog

began to realize. Too much damage. He paced back through the fallen corpses, and over to the machine-wagon where Ra'aa'al and Grauun rested. He stopped, regarded the twenty creatures still standing in their rows in hypnotic trance.

"Grauun, come with me," Toog spoke. "I need your help."

The Xmburrhaltin lumbered from the wagon, following Toog. They passed the charred bodies and stopped before the legion of captives standing stiff and silent. The first row they passed, then the second, continuing to the last row where they walked along the file to the last creature, then back one.

They stood before the pair of upright creatures which most closely resembled Aull: the male with the furry face and the female in the green gown holding the springling. The male was taller than Toog—a species called Wexa, according to Grauun. Its brown, leathery body was covered with blonde hair much thinner than the fur of a Xmburrhaltin, and it wore only a cloth of lizard-skin around its hips despite the cold, freshly taken from its warm home world. Its face protruded with a short snout like a *jaax*, small pointed ears atop its head, long whiskers sprouting from the sides of its face. It stood rigid, entranced by the Masters' magic.

To Toog's eyes, the female looked different up close: smooth green skin with thick black hair falling from her head. Not Wexa.

He stepped back to the male Wexa.

"Creature," Toog called. Like other creatures, it was mentally paralyzed, standing like a statue. "We need your body."

Toog looked at Grauun, then back at the Wexa.

"Take its breath away," Toog ordered.

Grauun looked back at Toog. "What...?"

"Take its breath. Ra'aa'al must have a body."

"But Leader Toog...are we then no better than the Masters?"

Toog narrowed his eyes, a blue furrow folding down across his face. "If Ra'aa'al does not have a body, then he cannot leave this world. If Ra'aa'al cannot leave this world, then neither of us can leave this world. It is a necessity, Grauun. Understand? That is the reason I will sacrifice one of my own kind—or close, because this is an upright being—rather than sacrificing one of your kind."

"Xmburrhaltins are upright beings," he grunted.

"I meant—"

"Not only the pretty upright beings are intelligent."

"Yes, I agree, but—"

"Your friend Ra'aa'al is not an upright being but a sand-spirit that runs through and fills the body of another animal."

Toog glared at Grauun, then nodded and turned away.

"There is no other choice." He tried to hold back the sorrow-rain.

After a pause, Grauun gave a grunt and placed his big paw around the throat of the Wexa. With a glance at Toog, who gave him a nod, Grauun began to squeeze—slowly at first, then with increasing pressure until the creature's air had been cut off.

The Wexa's body shook. Its eyes opened, focused on Grauun. In a flash its hands were like knives, slicing upward, breaking Grauun's grip. The Wexa grabbed him, raised him into the air, and hurled Grauun's huge bulk across the sand, leaving him to tumble and roll and crash hard against the side of the cube. The Wexa struck Toog across the cheek with the back of its hand, knocking him down, then raced off across the beach, dropping to four legs, and was soon out of sight.

Toog got up slowly, rubbing his jaw. He felt the dent in his face but as he held his hand there the dent filled out, became normal. He looked over at Grauun, who stumbled awkwardly to his feet, regarding the side of the cube, undented. He howled in pain, shook his shoulder and arm, rubbed his ribs.

Toog stepped over to the female in the green gown who was holding her springling.

"Was he your mate?" Toog asked in the squeaks and chirps of Sebbou, hoping the creature's mind-cave would provide writing on the walls in the creature's language. But she did not respond.

The infant began to make noise.

"Speak your name," Toog demanded, gazing up at her face.

The infant cried louder in her arms.

Toog clapped his hands loudly in front of the female's face.

Suddenly her head snapped violently, eyes opening, blinking. Her entire body collapsed at Toog's feet, dropping the infant.

Startled, Toog leg-bent to examine the infant on the ground. The same green skin covered its body, with a long appendage between the legs. Its eyes were closed, mouth open. The infant was unconscious.

Grauun came up behind them.

"The springling is dead," Toog said, lifting the infant in his hands, giving it to Grauun. "Take it to Ra'aa'al." He stared at the female. "I will bring this one."

The woman was taller than Toog—most creatures brought by the Masters were—though not as tall as the

Wexa. She wore a long, flowing, green gown, now dirty and torn, made of a stiff, shimmering material. Her tangled black hair lay about her green shoulders as Toog gazed down at her.

He dragged her body across the sand to the machine-wagon, hefted her onto the back of the wagon, flat on her back. Toog felt his arms ache and his back burn with pain, the effort more than his small body could manage. This was more than an Aull was expected to do. He only needed to lift bags of seed or tug a *groll* through a gate.

Toog took the infant carefully from Grauun's large hands and gently placed its motionless body into the arms of the female. She remained unconscious on the wagon.

Bring Ra'aa'al here, Toog communicated, too tired to speak.

When the body was brought to the wagon, Ra'aa'al lay close to death. Grauun tightened the arm band once more.

"I will sacrifice one of my kind," Grauun offered suddenly.

We will ask Ra'aa'al, Toog responded.

They regarded the decay of the Master's body, minus one arm, and its burned-out chest cavity, twisted flesh and muscle hanging in strips from old bones.

"Ra'aa'al, we must do this quickly." Toog glanced back at the captives standing in formation. "We have many bodies for you to choose."

Ra'aa'al's eyes rolled open slowly.

"We have an infant creature, an upright being, and a female, too. Her infant has died. We have those like Grauun, and he is willing to sacrifice one of his own kind—as am I, though I see no Aull among the captives. We have the spindly creatures from Cetrea, and a five-legged Piilactrian. I see four Gugi, too. And a pair of Mum, but you likely do not want to have to slide across the ground on your slime."

He gazed at Ra'aa'al. The death-gaze eyes saw nothing.

Toog heard a voice from within his head.

I can only speak through this medium, communicated Ra'aa'al, *for we have passed that threshold.*

"I understand. What should we do?"

If the infant is dead, I can inhabit it until my strength returns. The female will care for me as her own child. This would be best. We will not need to sacrifice a living creature. When I have grown in the female's care, I shall seek another, stronger body. We must hurry. Bring the infant to me. I will mold myself to its form.

Toog took the infant in his hands. It felt warm, though he knew it to be dead. It had not moved since it fell and hit the ground.

My strength is waning, Ra'aa'al communicated. *I must rest to build my strength. The transfer will be soon.*

They waited through the evening, letting the captives remain in formation, to the darkest part of the night when stars were bright overhead, the points of light painting pictures Toog did not recognize.

Waiting for Ra'aa'al, Toog thought about what to do with the captives. He could not send them back to their homes, nor could he just leave them standing on the beach. Breaking from the Master's magic spell, they would be lost on this world. Like him.

Ra'aa'al, are you ready? Is it time? Toog asked.

Soon, Toog, soon.

Time passed through the night. Grauun drifted to sleep just as Toog saw the thin, languid line of orange light spread across the horizon, over the sea, preparing to cover the beach.

I am ready, Ra'aa'al whispered, stirring Toog from his

drowsiness.

"I am ready, also," Toog spoke with a pop of his tiny mouth.

Hold the infant close to me with its mouth open against mine—against the Master's body's mouth.

Toog did it. He stared into the dead eyes of the body Ra'aa'al was leaving and saw flames of raw energy, Ra'aa'al's true form, burning there—a sand-spirit moving like *saak* in the *abo*.

Suddenly Ra'aa'al's voice roared at Toog from somewhere between the Master's body and the infant's body.

Toog! Toog! What is this? What do you do to me?

"What do you mean, Ra'aa'al?"

You tricked me! The infant is alive! A spirit still there! Now you will never go home, Toog, because...I...am...lost....

The infant writhed, began to cry, and at that moment a bright crimson burst of energy, a ball of churning light, shot from the mouth of the Master's body, was deflected by the infant's breath, and shot out of the machine-wagon, arcing high into the dawn sky out across the sudsy sea.

"Ra'aa'al!" Toog cried out, leaping from the wagon and racing down the beach after the blazing light. But it was hopeless and the blaze soon was lost behind the horizon.

He crumpled in the *saak*, low-bent his head to the ground, let the sorrow-rain surge. When he looked up again, the sky was a swath of yellow haze. And he was still on the Masters' world.

Toog knew not where Ra'aa'al had been flung. He remained on the sand, his face twist-tightened and sorrow-rain squeezed from his swollen eye vents. Ra'aa'al was gone now, and with him, his only way back home to his family. All hope was lost as the Masters' sun rolled across the horizon and the world was silent, save for the thrashing of Toog's sorrow-rain.

Toog felt a nudge in his ribs. He awoke, rolled over in the cold sand and looked up at Grauun. Getting to his feet, Toog gazed across the sea to the horizon where he had last seen Ra'aa'al. The sky was gray, but he could detect the sun, a weak glow that must have absorbed Ra'aa'al's spirit.

"We will find it," Grauun declared, placing his heavy hand on Toog's blue shoulder.

"No." Toog turned to Grauun. "No. There is no hope."

The Xmburrhaltin grumbled, trying and failing to squeeze into the tight recesses of Toog's mind-cave.

"Ra'aa'al was my first friend here," said Toog. "We exchanged promises."

Grauun waved his big furry hand at the rows of standing creatures from across the universe.

"What will we do with the female being and its baby? What will become of the captured ones over there?"

"We must release them," Toog sighed, staring out to sea.

"But they will wish to go home—"

"Go home? *Go home?*" He flashed bronze. "Let them find their own way home!" Toog shouted, his squeaks and chirps lost in the wind. "Yes, let them find their own way home—as we will have to do. I have no answers to any riddle."

Grauun turned to regard the formation of captives as Toog moved over to a machine-wagon.

"We will have to return to the prison," said Toog, sitting on the back of the machine-wagon. "We need to free those of Heis-Tegag that Ra'aa'al told about. They will help us return to our homes...." His voice trailed off. He hunched over, his tiny mouth widening, turning pink.

"Toog, are you ill?"

"No, Grauun, I...." Pink foam filled his mouth. He spit it out. "I was thinking of home, of my full-mate and our springling. It must be planting time there. M'ah will be starting the season of lessons. I—"

"I had four cave-pushers and twenty-six Xmbu made of my seed. The Masters destroyed all of them when they took me!"

Toog dropped to the sand on his leg-joints, buried his head in his hands.

"Yes. I forgot the prison code. Never talk about our past, the homes we were taken from." He looked up. "I'm sorry, Grauun. We all lost families when the Masters came to our worlds."

Grauun let out a growl. "That is why I hate them so much, more than you ever could! I was a slave for them in the quarries of Kustur for twelve years, but only after rotting in their prison for eight years until they decided to use what they had stolen! Enough, Toog?"

He nodded, took a long breath, his nose vents wheezing.

"We must return and free the Heis-Tegagans!" Toog declared, standing. "There is no other way. I must return home. I must! It is many days to the prison. If we—"

"What of those who stand over there?"

His eyes flashed pink. "We must leave them. We cannot help them. The Masters will come. They will see the attack. Maybe having the captives will please them, so they will not look for us."

"What of the female being? And its child? You want to leave them to the Masters?"

Toog's eyes swelled, became pink again. "The same."

"But the creature is mind-spun. It needs care."

"We cannot care for her."

"You are hard, Toog," Grauun growled. "Hard and cruel! Like *fauk* stones that burn in the night and cleave bone by day. I fear you now! You are like the Masters now! They snatch us from our homes, slaughter us, enslave us, torture us, put tricks in our heads, make us wish to die—then let us live on in eternal damnation! You would let these creatures die after we risked our lives to save them? Show not the hole in your hand to me, Toog of the frozen tundra, for we are not brothers and you are not my leader!"

Toog stared up into Grauun's seething red eyes. He towered over Toog. He remembered that Grauun's species were quick to temper and carried grudges forever. He could kill Toog with one hard swipe of his hand.

Grauun turned slowly from Toog, walked away.

"I go now to free those of Heis-Tegag," Toog called to Grauun. He watched the creature trudge to the formation of captives. "I will return here about thirty day-cycles from now. I will bring the Heis-Tegagans and meet you here, Grauun. They know how to make the cube send us home. If you still want to return to your home."

I will not be here, Grauun communicated.

"Do you not wish to return to Xmburrhaltis?"

I have no reason to return. I prefer to stay and kill Masters.

"Then to the far corner of the universe for you!"

But I am true to my code.

As Grauun reached the machine-wagon with the female being and her infant, Toog sat down on the sand, watching his big friend. Grauun picked up each of the sixteen creatures left alive after the fight and placed them onto the machine-wagon in their hypnotic trances, laying them down like wooden sticks. He had difficulty with the larger creatures. The Mum slithered away down the beach, slipping into the foamy sea. The five-legged Piilactrian galloped in the opposite direction. No loss. Then he tore away the cabin top so he could fit into the machine-wagon to drive it. He searched for the starter control.

After some time, Toog heard the machine-wagon making noise and knew he had learned its secret. The Xmburrhaltin took hold of the control panel and the machine-wagon moved away from the cube, rolling down the beach some distance before turning onto a dirt road, heading across the plain and out of sight.

The wind whipped Toog, his once silver skin a dull gray, blue on his hands and feet. The pink in his eyes faded with his anger.

"Ra'aa'al!" Toog cried out.

There was an echo in his head, a buzzing in his mind-cave, but he knew it was only an illusion, a false drawing on the walls of his mind-cave. His inner Ru was only trying to scare him, letting him feel the loneliness of his isolation once more in the dark nothingness of the universe, far from home—alone, abandoned, desolate, without hope.

The cave was much as Toog had left it. Warm inside, especially the inner chamber with its hot-spring pool. Toog replaced the snow in front of the cave's entrance to help protect himself against the cold. The floor had a few tiny scraps of meat they had left, and he chewed on the bones. His teeth had hardened, he discovered.

Sorrow-rain filled his eyes as he remembered the day Grauun had driven away in the machine-wagon full of silent captives. Toog did not know where Grauun could go with them, where he could hide them, but wherever he might go, he would be their savior and their shaman. Toog had asked him to stay, then requested, then pleaded and demanded, all in vain.

"I make my own gang," the Xmburrhaltin had grunted, baring his rows of sharp teeth.

Toog had spent many days and nights returning through the ice and snow of the Masters' frozen world to this small cave near the prison fortress where he had been kept. It felt like he was coming home—to a place he had never been, had never known, yet a place that now seemed more his home than the *skargs* and *oum* of Sebbol.

It was more than a safe place to hide. He could not hide forever, not unless he was willing to let his cartilage remain meatless in the cave after his inner Ru had died. It was close to the prison. He had to free the Heis-Tegagans, and he plotted how he would do it. They would be grateful and would show him the way home. Even if he could rescue them, he did not know where in the prison they were, nor how he could contact them to learn their location. In his weakness after the loss of Ra'aa'al and Grauun, his mental power had softened.

He shed eye-rain as he remembered Ra'aa'al, but he closed his throat vents, telling himself to be strong.

Grauun's words echoed through his dark mind-cave: "You are hard, Toog! Hard and cruel!"

"And stupid!" he cried out. "How could I be like the Masters?"

On many frigid nights, Toog tried calling to Ra'aa'al, believing he existed somewhere in the universe, without a body to move around in, perhaps, but still in spirit form, yet received no response. He tried to call the Heis-Tegagans from his mind-cave, but he was too weak to write on the walls, and again there was no response.

The wind outside howled and he thought of Grauun.

The string of long-cycles unwound slowly. More snow mounted outside the cave, sealing him within. Toog felt himself growing weak. He was beginning to starve. He was beginning to die. His body was now almost completely blue.

r e s c u e

8

One frosty morning, with the pale gray sun hanging meekly in the haze of winter sky, an upright being came to Toog.

Standing before him was the Wexa male from the formation of captives that had stood in front of the cube on the beach—the one that had run away. He swung up his arm, hand tapping on his chest, saying "Djuttu." Coming from a warm world, Toog guessed, Djuttu was tall and lean, tan body covered with thin blonde hair which did little to keep him warm. At the cube he had worn only a lizard-skin wrapped around his hips. Now he covered himself with a Master's greatcoat like Toog did. He suspected the being had killed a Master to get the clothing, or perhaps had returned to the cube and taken it from a dead body. Toog studied Djuttu's *jaax*-like face, dark eyes above a short snout, meat-cutting teeth, whiskers extending horizontally from the snout, small pointed ears rising from the top of his head.

Djuttu was the one who had thrown Grauun across the sand to smash against the cube. This being was a warrior clearly, and Toog held his distance, kept the Masters' pulse-gun ready.

"What do you want?" Toog spoke slowly in Sebbou, noticing the Wexa's feet, hairy and clawed, extending out of the snow. He hoped the being had the power to see his words written on the walls in his mind-cave and had an inner Ru to tell him what they meant. Not every creature had a mind-cave, he decided; some beings only had rough stones that clanked together in irregular patterns.

Djuttu was silent.

Then a flood of words roared in Toog's mind-cave, his inner Ru tumbling in from a side passage and jumping up to shout them. The words rushed out with such intensity that Toog put his hands to his head as if to contain them. His inner Ru likewise held its head. Then the words ceased.

Relaxing a moment, Toog realized he had retained all the words that this Djuttu had communicated.

This Wexa had been taken from Yvo, a world of lush jungles and violent volcanoes far from the Masters' world. Like Toog, he had lived peacefully in his village alongside a stream which widened to form a pool beneath a grove of flowering fruit trees. He lived with his dominant female and her other six males and their twenty-four children, along with seven other families. The jungle breeze often prompted the trees to drop their blossoms and seed pods into the pool, which the children would gather for food while the males hunted huge lizards deep in the jungle. It was on one such hunt that the Masters arrived on his world. Djuttu and his companions had offered them their seed pods for dinner, but their kindness was met with violence. Only Djuttu survived the fighting to be taken captive and brought to this cold world where the snow turned his bronze flesh to white and made his bones shiver.

Coming out of his trance when Grauun was choking him,

he reacted automatically in defense, then fled. He wandered across the tundra for fifty-six sun-rises, then happened upon Toog's ridge and this cave. His whiskers twitched, sensing food could be found there. He dug through the snowbank protecting the cave and, instead of food, found only blue Toog, who was also starving.

Toog welcomed him, fed him from his own meager rations, and had him rest next to the low fire he made. He took tundra grass, wiped it dry against his rough blue skin and held it tightly clenched in a fist until it warmed and glowed yellow, providing a dim light and a faint warmth for the night. He noticed this new, strange effect by accident but he used it to keep his little cave habitable.

He told Djuttu his own story, waving away his inner Ru when it complained that his telling veered from truth. He intended to return home—somehow—and the Wexa was welcome to go with him and find the way to his own world. That was what Djuttu wanted, too.

First, Toog explained, they must make themselves strong again. Then they needed to make a plan.

For the first, Toog led Djuttu up the side of the ridge, over the crest, and into the crags and chasms of the other side, a place hidden from the view of the Masters. There they lifted stones and ran up and down the slopes, climbed the sheer rock faces, and breathed in the frosty air like it was the warm, moist air of home.

Once a strange woolly beast approached them among the rocks and Djuttu coaxed the four-legged animal sporting great curved horns to charge at him. When the beast rushed forward, Djuttu grabbed its long horns and twisted its head around until the bones in its neck popped and the body dropped as still as a stone. They carried it back to the cave and ate well for many day-cycles. Djuttu thought the beast's horns would make good weapons but Toog reminded him of the immense power of the pulse-guns. He had several of them gathered from the fight at the cube, saving the batteries.

For the second thing, they sat each night with their backs against the cave walls, talking about their situation. They could not remain in this cave forever. There were Masters to kill, of course. That was a worthy goal. But more important was to return home and make sure their families were safe. Now was the time to do something. The snow had stopped, the white mounds flattening, the frozen ground soon becoming soft and wet. Now was the time when they could come up with a plan to go home. They were strong again and ready to act.

"There are two creatures," Toog explained, putting his blue hand on Djuttu's furry head and feeling the sting of connection. A burning sensation ran up his arm, warming in his head.

He spoke his Sebbou words but saw how they became long squiggles on the walls of his mind-cave. He could see the lines, with marks over some of them, turning around and around in his mind-cave, becoming spirals, spinning into long coils in the air. It was not words that he shared but ideas, which would be written or drawn on a mind-cave wall then read or studied through whatever system of symbols each being had learned.

"We must free them from the prison," Toog continued slowly, letting the writing catch up to his thoughts. "Only those beings know the secrets of the cube: how to operate it, how to return home. Now that you have rested, Djuttu, I will need your help, since my other comrade abandoned me."

"I-do. What. Can-do. Friend." The Wexa's barks even

sounded like a *jaax*. Toog had to train his ears to understand.

"We must locate their cell in the prison," said Toog in his squeaks and chirps. "This may be the most difficult thing. Then we break into their cell. Then we rescue them."

"Rescue...?"

"Yes," said Toog. "We will lead them out of the prison. Then they will be grateful to us and will help us go home."

Djuttu rubbed his bewhiskered muzzle. "How-is. Wave. Being's. Vibratory. Pattern?"

"What do you mean?" Toog kept his palm against Djuttu's forehead. He pressed harder. "Vibration pattern?"

"If-know. Being's. Pattern. Can-locate."

"You have this ability?"

"We-use. Hunting. Great-lizards. My-world."

"How close must you be to be able to do that?" asked Toog.

"If-then. Fair-weather. Can-sense. From. Top-of-ridge."

"Can you sense them from here now?"

Djuttu moved to the entrance. Toog followed. They climbed up the side of the ridge from the cave and crouched behind a rock. They regarded the gray stone walls of the Masters' prison far in the distance. The weather was good.

"Do you sense them?" Toog asked, wind whipping his coat.

"Too-jumbled," Djuttu replied. "Many-creatures. That-place. All. Cry-out. With-agony." He turned to Toog. "This. What. You. Saved-me-from. Question."

"Yes, Djuttu." Toog shivered at the memory. "Years of pain."

"I-feel. Pain-and-sorrow." A low mew slipped from his mouth. "Could-not-endure. That-place. Thanks. Save-me. I-will. Repay-you."

They gazed at the prison, a cold and silent place.

"I-wish. Free. Them-all," Djuttu spoke with a low growl.

"Yes, but we cannot do that this first trip. In time, we will free them, every one of them, and we will all return to our homes."

The wind picked up, tossed their garments about them. The sky was clear above but dark clouds approached. Flurries darted about as they shrank among the rocks.

"Spring comes late to this clime," said Toog, seeing Djuttu cringe against the onslaught of the wind.

"Let's. Move. Closer. To-there," Djuttu suggested. "If-then. Better-can. Distinguish. Patterns."

Toog watched the Wexa sniffing the air, whiskers twitching, head turning this way and that way, sensing.

"All-is. Quiet. In-there."

"So today is the day we rescue them?" asked Toog.

"Better-day. Than-tomorrow," barked the Wexa.

They returned to the cave to gather supplies they would need to break the Heis-Tegagans from their cell. Then, with stealth, they crossed the valley, to the bridge which had been repaired during the winter.

The sound of machine-wagons in the distance made Toog and Djuttu duck under the low bridge. Soon a convoy of six machine-wagons rumbled overhead, filled with guards, and continued across the valley.

"Those were the Masters," Toog told Djuttu through clinched teeth, remembering the day he and Grauun confronted them at this bridge. "So many Masters going at once. Perhaps there is another rebellion at a work camp."

"Yes. I-know. Those-being's. Pattern."

"There will not be many guards at the prison now."

They scrambled up from the ditch.

Hurrying along the road toward the prison, Djuttu

dropped and ran on hands and feet until he got too far ahead of Toog, who could only run on two feet, and not so fast anyway. He was better at swimming. Djuttu returned to two feet as they left the road, cutting across the lichen-covered field which surrounded the fortress, arriving at the east wall.

"Moving-carts," Djuttu spoke, "More-than. Normal-use. Transporting. Captives. Is-true. Friend. Question."

"How do you see these thoughts of mine?"

"I-felt. Disturbance. Your-pattern. At-moment. Those-beings. Passed-us. You-noticed. Difference. Seeing. Less-of-them. Fear-wave. You. It-swept-through."

"You worry me, Djuttu," said Toog. "You are correct."

Djuttu showed his teeth, the two fangs glistening. "If-then. An-army. Escaped-creatures. Must-capture."

"I do not think that two constitutes an army."

"Correct. But. My-world," Djuttu barked, "If-then. One-being. Strong-enough. We-say. He-is. Army-of-one!"

Toog recalled Grauun and the captives the Xmburrhaltin took away from the cube after Ra'aa'al left. They could be coming under attack by the convoy of Masters. It could not be easy to hide so many creatures. The Masters would hunt them down.

"On my world we did not have an army," said Toog, sorrow-rain making his voice thick. "We could not fight the Masters."

"Many. Armies. My-world." He barked again, running his long tongue over his teeth. "My-village. Strongest-of-all."

Toog felt a fear-wave cut through him. "Yet you are here."

Djuttu's throat rumbled.

They squatted low in the sparse vegetation against the east wall of the prison fortress, scraggily bushes no taller than Toog's leg-joints. No guards in the towers saw them, no alarms were set off. The afternoon sun-light made jagged shadows.

They do not expect us, Toog communicated.

Howl! You can speak cloud-talk, Djuttu responded. *You must be one of those advanced beings.*

Toog gave a nod. *We must be silent in our mission from now.*

Where are their guards? Djuttu asked, looking up at the guard tower rising above them. He squinted against the sun-light.

I do not know, Toog replied. *They could not all have left the fortress in that convoy to...whatever the reason.*

This will be easy, Toog.

We must not be too lax.

Djuttu's mouth seized up, saliva dripping. *Ooo, they are so ugly, and wear a vile stench, these Heis-Tegag creatures!*

Yes—Ra'aa'al told me about them, Toog communicated.

We would better not to eat them. The illness would be fatal.

You sense them?

Djuttu raised his snout twice. *I sense them.* He closed his eyes. *There are...eight of these creatures—no, seven. One just died. They are filthy beasts, ugly, horrifying creatures. They are small....* Djuttu eased his eyes open, stared at Toog.

Can you locate them?

I do not know if I can bear to look upon them.

Djuttu, perhaps neither can I, but only they know how to leave this world. We must free them.

They have uneven vibrations, Djuttu communicated, closing his eyes. *They must be...yes, I sense it: they are uneven because they are three—three sexes. Their vibrations are sparse....*

Can you locate three that are in the same cell? Toog's inner Ru was waving its arms wildly in warning. *Those three are the ones we must rescue. So Ra'aa'al said.*

It is difficult. They call to each other...cell to cell to.... Difficult to separate them.... Each has a different scent.

Djuttu squeezed his eyes shut, his forehead wrinkling, whiskers quivering. His stubby tail stood straight out.

Try, Djuttu, try.

One cell contains four, another cell three, others are single only.

Toog frowned, lips thickening. *Let me attempt to call them. Ra'aa'al taught me how to let an echo into their mind-caves, and I have practiced the method.*

He pushed his inner Ru against the wall, ready to write. He felt his mind-cave expand, walls cracking, realigning, dust falling from the ceiling forming clouds on the mind-cave floor. His inner Ru brushed off its robe with an angry grimace.

Those from Heis-Tegag, Toog communicated, *and who knows Ra'aa'al of Ra'a'am'mas'sandiit, identify yourselves.*

They waited.

There is no response. Toog sighed, glancing cautiously up at the top of the fortress wall. *We do not connect. Perhaps their pattern is too different from mine.*

Not so, responded Djuttu, closing his eyes, his whiskers twitching. *I felt a wave in their pattern as you spoke the name of friend Ra'aa'al. It came from the group of three, but...only two creatures there now. I must not have read their pattern correctly, or the third has just died. I sense another one is near death....*

Toog's eyes bulged. *Where are they?*

Difficult to determine. So many corridors. Like a puzzle. But they do not cry out in agony. They are not content, but they are beyond pain. They can feel no more. Howl! They call you, friend Toog, they call you! They say they are from Heis-Tegag, and they know friend Ra'aa'al. They are dying now. They have been in the cell for...two-hundred years—no, twenty of the Masters' years, which is two-hundred of Heis-Tegag years.

Toog's inner Ru was busy plucking silvery webbing from the ceiling of his mind-cave, working the strands in its fingers, creating a figure of white lines that floated in the air of his mind-cave. It looked like a child's craftwork. This was not a time for play! Yet his inner Ru continued making the play thing.

We must help them, Djuttu communicated, *with ugliness or not, they are in such pain.* His tongue slid out of the side of his mouth as he panted.

Toog watched his inner Ru fashioning the square of white strings which more began to look like the prison. Not a play thing, after all! A map!

Where are they, Djuttu?

Djuttu licked his teeth. *There are cells of creatures like you, cells resembling friend Grauun, another cell of friend Ra'aa'al's kind, and strange creatures with five legs...and spindly things, ugly things, dead creatures, dying creatures, a guard station—only two Masters, one asleep—and those of Heis-Tegag. They are in a cell at the end of the first corridor of this same building. Here—next to this wall.*

As Djuttu communicated what he sensed, Toog saw his inner Ru pointing to places on the white string cube floating in his mind-cave. A model of the prison, he realized, constructed from the vibration patterns Djuttu was sending to him, directly to his inner Ru. And the Masters believed they were so intelligent and superior!

Djuttu opened his eyes, squinted. *They are not superior.*

Let us go free them. Toog smiled.

The stone wall was high, but Djuttu had no trouble boosting Toog up enough to grab hold. Toog pressed his fingers against the stone and the tips flattened into suction disks which enabled him to crawl up. Once over the top of the wall, Toog crouched behind one of the watch tower's pillars and secured the rope they'd brought. Throwing the rope over the top of the wall, Djuttu caught it in his teeth and crawled up, claws digging into the stone.

On the wall's narrow lip, Toog surveyed the prison fortress. There seemed to be a minimum of guards, and none had yet spotted them.

"Lead me to them," Toog whispered, holding the pulse-gun he'd taken from a dead Master at the cube, still fully charged. He hoped not to use it. Djuttu had another pulse-gun and Toog had shown him how to use it.

Bowing low, they swept down the walkway and crept down the stairs at the end. At the bottom of the step-cascade, stood a guard. Djuttu grabbed its head and bent it backwards over its shoulders, breaking its neck in one swift action.

They sprang toward an open doorway which Djuttu, with a wave of his hand, indicated they should enter.

The corridor was long but empty: smooth white walls with no cell doors, ceiling glowing with light, and a boot-dirty floor. Djuttu placed his hands on the wall to his right. He felt for differences in vibrations in the wall which would reveal hidden doors. He moved slowly down the corridor, nodding to Toog when he found a door, but moving on each time when he felt the pattern of the creatures within were not those of the Heis-Tegag creatures.

We must hurry before we are discovered, communicated Toog.

Djuttu moved along the wall. *Pain. Such pain.* He crossed the corridor and felt the opposite wall, starting at the door they entered.

Two guards appeared in the corridor.

Toog spun around and fired the pulse-gun at the guards, severing one at the waist. *Ffft ffft.* The other guard dove to the floor, rolled over and fired. Toog threw himself back against the wall to avoid the shot, an acrobatic move that surprised him. But the orange blast hit the white wall and ricocheted to Djuttu, striking his hip. Toog's next shot at full power melted the Master's forehead into its brain. *Ffft ffft.* The pulse-guns were quiet, Toog was thankful.

Djuttu lay on the floor, holding his hip, fur singed and flesh cut by knife-fire. Toog pulled Djuttu's hand away, saw it was not deep. Guards had their pulse-guns set on a stunning level for regular patrol, it seemed.

He helped Djuttu sit up.

"Here. I-sense. Their. Home-cell," Djuttu barked between tense breaths, pointing to the cell opposite from where he sat. He regarded that wall, sniffing, mouth open, whiskers stiff.

"You must be sure," Toog insisted. "We cannot mistake the cell."

"Yes. I-sense. Their. Pattern. Just-as. Masters. Came."

"Show me where the door is. Mark its borders."

Djuttu struggled to stand. With Toog's help, he crossed to the opposite wall and, holding out his hand with one claw extended, drew indentations along the edge of the hidden door.

"Here." He sank to the floor in pain.

"I will stand guard while you cut, Djuttu."

Toog hurried to the end of the corridor and checked down each adjoining corridor. No Masters. He ran back to Djuttu and checked outside the doorway. No guards.

"We must hurry," Toog chirped.

Djuttu rose again and cut a line along the edge of the door with the tool Toog had brought. He tried to work his long claws into the crack but the door refused to budge. Trying again, he got better leverage and the door twitched on its hinges.

"I-need. Help. Too-solid," called Djuttu.

Toog set down his weapon and grabbed the edge of the invisible door. Only the faintest line in the otherwise smooth surface marked it. With maximum effort from both of them, the door yielded, hissed open, leaving a small gap.

A cool trickle of air flowed out as the door separated from the surrounding wall. A horrible stench seeped out, the odor of death—or of *living* Heis-Tegagans.

Eventually, the door ceased its resistance, the opening wide enough for Toog's soft blue body to squeeze inside. He held his breath. Djuttu backed away, bent down to purge, as Toog took a step into what had become the tomb of the Heis-Tegagans. A stripe of light from the corridor cut into the cell, showing the stone shelves where the small, ugly creatures lay. A sticky film covered the floor of the cell and Toog tried to move over it as lightly as he could, seeing the creatures who slunk into the shadows.

"You are from Heis-Tegag?" Toog asked them, using Sebbou and hoping they had mind-caves with good walls to write on.

One of the creatures raised a thin arm out of the shadows.

"You know a being named Ra'aa'al?" Toog asked.

The creature that had lifted its twig-like arm then raised its brown oblong body out of the shadows, showing its dripping, gelatinous face to Toog, who cringed and closed his eyes.

"Not Ra'aa'al," the Heis-Tegagan uttered in its language. Toog heard it echoing in Sebbou in his mind-cave.

"Ra'aa'al sent me." Toog used his inner Ru to speak for him. He tried to regain his composure and not show fear.

"You come to rescue we of Heis-Tegag?"

Toog blinked quickly, holding his breath, nose flaps pinched.

"My mate has died," spoke the ugly creature, pointing to the opposite shelf. "And my other mate, Zem'Gafu, is very ill, may die soon if not return to our world."

Toog glanced at the one named Zem'Gafu, laying nearly unconscious on the stone shelf.

"I was named Bar'Gafu," rumbled the Heis-Tegagan.

"We must hurry if we are going to escape," Toog insisted.

"Can you carry my mate?"

Toog moved to Zem'Gafu's shelf. He dreaded touching the sticky film which oozed from pores and slid over its dying body—the same film which covered the floor of the cell, he guessed.

"You must help Zem'Gafu," Bar'Gafu begged. "Can never travel on own. The Masters tore off legs."

"All right," Toog said hastily, releasing his breath, smelling the Heis-Tegag stench.

Toog felt he had to up-purge, but he choked back the urge as he bent low over the stone shelf and slid his arms under the slimy body, the shape of a seed pod of the *chii* plant common in the *abo* of Sebbol.

"Do not worry, dear Zem'Gafu." Bar'Gafu spoke the language of Heis-Tegag, but Toog heard the message in

Sebbou in his mind-cave. "Our trouble has come to an end. We are leaving this place. You must allow this strange blue creature to carry you from here. Do not be afraid."

Lifting the Heis-Tegag creature from the sticky shelf, Toog could not feel any firm bone structure in the creature, only an undulating flux of liquids that shifted as he lifted the being. Like how *oum* felt. When Toog turned to exit, he saw the other Heis-Tegagan standing in the doorway on legs like twigs, no taller than Toog's leg joint.

Cradling the slimy/sticky Zem'Gafu in both his arms, Toog motioned for Bar'Gafu to go on out through the door. Bar'Gafu stepped out on tiny feet that seemed too small for its thick body.

Toog followed, carrying the other Heis-Tegagan.

Stepping through the doorway, Toog heard Djuttu draw a sharp breath at the sight of Bar'Gafu and Zem'Gafu, their flesh dripping on the floor of the corridor.

Quickly, Djuttu turned away and bent over to ease his illness.

Disregard their form.

I will try, Toog.

They will show us the way home. Now we must make our way out of this fortress the way we entered. Lead the way, Djuttu.

Toog pointed with his head. "Follow him, Bar'Gafu."

The corridor was free of guards, but outside the doorway, a pair of Masters in brown tight-fitting uniforms moved toward them, not expecting to find creatures outside of the cells. When their eyes suddenly met Toog's, it was too late. Djuttu, as he had practiced, pointed the weapon at the guards and pressed the small button that launched an orange beam of light in a pair of pulses: *ffft ffft*. When the pulse of light hit them they melted into their shadows.

Other guards were alerted by the orange flash of the pulse-gun blasts. Masters raced to intercept them, sounding an alarm that creatures were escaping. Their strange words were written on the walls of Toog's mind-cave by his frightened inner Ru.

Toog tucked the slimy Zem'Gafu under his arm and extended his blue arm, firing his pulse-gun at the Masters, stopping the one on the left. Others fired at Djuttu and Bar'Gafu, although hurried and off-target. Djuttu returned fire: *ffft ffft*—striking the two middle guards who fell to the floor, legs injured. One guard instructed the others to switch to maximum—

Maximum what? asked Djuttu of Toog.

Toog and his comrades backed toward the cascade of levels leading up to the walkway near the new guard tower. Bar'Gafu bounced to the top of the stairs like a hot *grum* while Djuttu followed, limping.

With the ailing pod named Zem'Gafu tucked under his arm, Toog shot his pulse-gun at the remaining guard who had called to the other guards. More of the Masters were approaching.

A wounded guard rose on one arm and fired a blast at Toog, who deftly turned to dodge the shot, as though an invisible hand pushed him back, but he inadvertently left Zem'Gafu to absorb the blast. Toog fell and Zem'Gafu, dead or dying from the shot, rolled away from Toog's grasp. Brown fluid spilled from a hole in Zem'Gafu's side, spreading across the floor.

Another guard fired a blast that hit Djuttu's chest. Dropping his weapon, Djuttu grasped his wound, then grabbed at Toog's arm. With a weak howl, Djuttu hoisted Toog over his shoulder, clutched Bar'Gafu under his arm and ran along the walkway.

Djuttu stood on the edge of the wall—then leaped.

With a wild howl, Djuttu sprang up from the clump of moss he landed in with his charges and, with Toog holding on to his shoulders and one arm clutching Bar'Gafu to his chest, bounded on three feet over the lichen-covered tundra away from the prison, toward the great ridge which housed their cave.

The Masters fired at them from the wall, but as the escapees got farther away the effectiveness of the pulse-guns diminished, designed for close engagement. With so many of the Masters away on a mission, they could not send any in pursuit of the escaping creatures. Reports would be corrected.

Djuttu, wheezing and limping, fighting pain, got them to the foot of the ridge before he collapsed. He dropped Toog and Bar'Gafu down in the grass and rolled himself over onto his back, sucking air.

I only want to go home, Djuttu communicated.

He clutched the organs showing through the open wound that had torn down from his chest, desperately trying to put them into their proper places and, resigning, gave a long, painful howl.

The stick was splintered and Toog's blue fingertips were torn from his work, but the hole was dug in the hard, frozen ground at the bottom of the ridge. He carefully eased Djuttu's body into the hole and stretched him out, then began replacing the dirt.

"Why work for the dead?" Bar'Gafu inquired, the brown blob of a body squatting on a nearby rock.

Toog looked up, surprised the little brown thing could so

closely imitate the squeaks and chirps of Sebbou.

"The custom for Aull is to burn the body and drink the ashes," Toog replied, returning to his work. He did not care whether the Heis-Tegagan could understand his words. "I want to hide the body so the Masters cannot find him." Toog paused in his work. "And so his body will return to the soil more easily. As Second Goddess has taught us."

"Bodies decay soon enough leaving them above ground," said Bar'Gafu, flicking a glob of slime from its body.

Toog continued his work.

"He was a good comrade."

Toog tossed the last dirt atop the mound.

"Yes, good comrade," Bar'Gafu repeated in a whistling Sebbou while scraping an excess of slime from its body and dropping it to the ground.

"But his time is now done." Toog stood, gazed down. "Djuttu is gone, and so shortly is your mate Zem'Gafu gone, too. And our friend Ra'aa'al is gone. Also Grauun, my one-time friend. Only you and I remain—only you and I to return to our homes."

"Best for Zem'Gafu to die quickly," said Bar'Gafu, picking a few crumbs of dirt up in a tiny hand and sprinkling them over Djuttu's grave. "Zem'Gafu had much pain. Soon will be same. Last of family. My life is nearing its end. After twenty years with the Masters, good to die free."

"You will go home before you die," said Toog.

"Some go home, some die."

"Now you can speak Sebbou?" asked Toog, his face bronzing.

"Can understand fifty-four patterns," the brown blob snorted. "Sebbou is easy. Easier than Masters' language."

With a sneer, Toog led the Heis-Tegagan up the ridge to the cave. He welcomed the little pod to his new home.

"One stone cell for another stone cell," spoke Bar'Gafu.

Toog frowned. He scrounged for food rations but found little. The brown blob complained of the food choice. Toog waved the blob off, ate a morsel of dried meat.

"When you have digested," grunted Bar'Gafu, "then will eat."

Toog glared at the blob a moment, then swallowed.

"What of your promise to Ra'aa'al?" Toog asked.

"Ra'aa'al is no more," spoke Bar'Gafu. "Thus no more agreement."

Toog almost choked. "What...?"

"Made no agreement with you."

"But I freed you. So you can help me go home."

The soft brown thing, oblong and slimy, shifted awkwardly on the cave floor. Its arms were as thin as twigs, waving back and forth as it spoke. For Heis-Tegagans, the head was only the upper end of the oblong body, hairless and having an air vent on each side of that round end and one mouth/nose above a large single eye that sometimes pushed out on a stem.

"Did not ask to be freed by you," spoke Bar'Gafu. "First spoke to you when entered cell. No arrangement before."

"So you will not help me return to my home?" Toog held back his anger, worried the thing would refuse him.

"No reason to do."

"No reason...?" Toog struggled to hold his anger.

"Will not live long enough to reach my home, so why bother with such travel?"

"Yes, why bother?" Toog cursed. His blue skin shaded bronze, then returned to blue. "Why wait? Why don't you kill yourself now, and save yourself the wait?"

"Cannot kill myself. How can be done? Look at me." The lone eye pushed out on its stem. "You could bring me peace,

Toog—if you wish."

Toog flashed bronze. "I might do that!"

"Then you would never go home."

"No." Toog let his anger ease as his inner Ru held up its hand. "You already said you would not help me."

"No reason to help," sludged the Heis-Tegagan.

Toog got up, clapped his blue hands together. "I am going down to the stream to wash off your mate's slime. Don't jump off a rock while I am gone."

Bar'Gafu stood on twig legs, slime oozing down its body. "Not understand Heis-Tegag." The brown blob turned briskly away. "Ra'aa'al understood Heis-Tegag."

"But why should I?" Toog shouted back, starting down the ridge. "I didn't agree to understand, did I?"

Toog continued down the ridge, picking his way among rocks and small bushes.

He chose a wide area downstream from where he usually gathered water, which was hidden by foliage along the bank. He waded into the icy water and imagined he entered Aull's mythic place of punishment. The brownish slime proved to be sticky and stubborn, hard to remove. He had to scrape with his finger claws, hurting his skin. When he removed bits of the hardened slime, he was careful to send them downstream.

Bar'Gafu appeared suddenly, pushing out from between two bushes. With a gaseous wheeze fragranting the spot, the brown thing sat at the edge of the stream, watching Toog struggle with the sticky slime.

"Are you ready to exit?" asked the brown thing.

"I do not want to speak to you," Toog chirped from the pool.

"Then why do you?"

Toog glared at him. Rescuing this monster was a

mistake.

"Not understand our kind: Zem'Gafu, Tan'Gafu, and me. We are three that make one. Alone can be nothing."

"What do you mean?" Toog glanced up and saw the monster displaying a long yellow string of a tongue, curling over its face.

"Notice that our hands were not bolted to the stone shelves as were yours?"

Toog stopped and looked up suddenly, remembering.

"You are right. Why not?"

Bar'Gafu held up his tiny hand. "See our three-finger hands do not have bone within. There is nothing to hold us down with a bolt. Besides, we are weak beings. Could never escape by our own movement."

Toog sneered. He hated listening to this creature's version of Sebbou. "But you didn't want to be freed."

"Pact with Ra'aa'al was made long ago, soon after Ra'aa'al arrived. Did not realize we were dying. Wished to return home."

Toog looked away. "Then you know how I feel."

"Notice how this slime oozes over my body? What is it?"

"I do not know. Perhaps it comes from glands in your skin."

Bar'Gafu gazed at Toog: a twisted grin on a toothless mouth. An arm stretched toward Toog to show him the slime.

"Is decaying flesh." Bar'Gafu drew back the arm. "Air of this world, to which the Masters have brought us, is corrosive to our flesh. My mate died because of this. Bone material becomes as supple as grass. Dissolves in our bodies. It is death to be on this world, no matter the horrors to which the Masters subject us."

Toog's head furrowed vertically. "Why would the

Masters take you?"

"Why do the Masters take any creature? That is the riddle."

"For slave labor," Toog responded quickly. "I was sent to a work camp, but my form is not the best for that kind of heavy labor. It was the Xmburrhaltins that seemed suited to it."

"Was early in conquests," the Heis-Tegagan continued. "Not particular what worlds they took creatures from. In time, learned which species were suitable for their needs. So began to take creatures only from certain worlds. Started experiments. Yet Heis-Tegagans remain, forgotten, left to die."

Toog climbed out of the pool, wrapped the Master's greatcoat around his shivering blue body. He sat on a rock, shaking inside the clothing as he studied the Heis-Tegagan.

"Are you ready to exit?" asked Bar'Gafu.

Ignoring the blob, Toog continued: "Ra'aa'al told me if he tried to depart the Masters' world without you and your mates, you would destroy him. Seeing you now, I cannot understand how you could do it. You are such a weak and forlorn creature."

"Yes, Toog, is true. Sorry to say." Bar'Gafu gurgled, spit out some black fluid. "Was merely bluff. Have no power. Could not kill him—close or at a distance. Had no way to escape, so we contacted Ra'aa'al, a powerful entity in the prison. Ra'aa'al had the power to escape—or cause others like you to help escape. To compel Ra'aa'al to rescue us, offered to exchange knowledge of the Masters' machine, absorbed from their collective minds at the prison, for securing our freedom."

"I understand," spoke Toog. "You learned languages."

"Yet time elapsed, came to edge of forever. Ra'aa'al's

power began to wane. Soon was too late to benefit. Were dying. Even now, no hope of returning to Heis-Tegag where the giant Hugra stand over us and feed us. Will die before can make a journey."

"What will you do then?" Toog asked, suddenly feeling pity for the ugly being.

"Will await the inevitable."

"Which is...?"

"Will...melt away...in time."

Bar'Gafu withdrew the eye stem. Toog heard a high-pitched whimper. Or gas escaping from a vent.

"And what will I do, if you...melt away?"

"Put me in hole. Like your furry friend. Then you may await the inevitable, too."

"Which is...?"

"Death certainly," Bar'Gafu snarled, the eye extending again. "Always death. Always transfer of matter. Digestion. New forms. New purpose. Cannot know in advance."

"You mean you will not help me escape through the cube?"

The Heis-Tegagan's eye blinked. "No reason to do."

"But I helped you escape the prison!" Toog exclaimed.

"No benefit if die soon anyway."

"You should have told us before we risked our lives to free you! Look what Djuttu did for you. He just wanted to help and now he is dead."

Bar'Gafu gurgled, spit. "Did not know would be you entering our cell. Thought our time had come at last, ready to be used by the Masters, to be bent to their purpose, to benefit them."

Toog covered his eyes with his blue hands. "I have no other way home."

"Why want to return? Everything will be changed, left

you behind. Nobody will recall your name or your deeds. Will be lost in the past. Put aside to collect dust and melt away. Will not like what find when return. Will regret returning."

Toog flashed bronze, returned to blue as he headed up the ridge to the cave. He hated the brown pod's way of speaking Sebbou, using Sebbou words but in a Heis-Tegagan pattern. Or shifting into formal Sebbou that sounded like a shaman's high sermon, as though speaking to midlings.

Bar'Gafu followed, fell quickly behind.

Toog thought of a response and, when the little brown pod finally arrived at the cave and sat down inside, he spoke it:

"I do not know why you are the way you are, Heis-Tegagan, or what tale might unlock your history, whatever may be the secret to understanding your strange way of thinking, but...." Toog flashed bronze. "I speak for myself, and I tell you I have a life yet to live. My life has meaning says First Goddess on the first tablet. I have a home and a family to return to. I have a long life to live, and you cannot deny me that life, not after all I have suffered to get even this close."

"Close?" Bar'Gafu laughed, a high, wispy noise that echoed in the cave, like gas escaping from a vent. "Only across valley from the Masters. And how far to your planet from this cave? Are a fool. Why cannot realize there is no hope of return? If Masters find no use for you, then there is no reason to continue to exist. Must die. Simple answer."

Toog clenched his teeth. "The Masters were going to execute me because I started a rebellion at my work camp, but they decided I was...interesting. So they wanted to cut me open and look inside, study me like a shaman's lesson.

Yet what did they do? They locked me in a cell again. To die away. Like you and your mates. I would not let them do that to me, so I escaped. I killed Masters! Others followed my example: Grauun, Ra'aa'al. And we saved other beings they brought back from the other worlds." His face furrowed vertically. "I cannot stop now. I will not! I will find the secret for myself if you will not help me. I will not die like you, awaiting the melting away to dust. Not without fighting! I will not!"

"Toog," whispered Bar'Gafu, a low whistle like an icy breeze, "listen to my words. Imagine this path: Solve the riddle of the Masters after what seven years? Cross to the next planet. Cross that world over difficult terrain, past dangerous beasts, corrupt air, poisonous plants, terrible storms, not knowing correct path. Imagine finding a tangent and crossing to the next planet. Cross from planet to planet until reaching your world. How many years does all this travel take? Ten or twenty years? Counting by Masters' years, which equal...three of your world's, isn't it? So reach your village, now old and decrepit from long journey."

"I will not be so old—"

"Walk along road. People pass, stare, because have become ugly in years of travel. Are blue, not silver, dark not bright. Ask one where former home is located because have forgotten. Soon standing in front of abode, regarding form, conjuring memories. Tap tap tap on entry-cover, hear one inside. Entry opens and a tall, sweet-scented fellow stares. Ask if your mate is present, yet before fellow answers, asks who are you. Your name is Toog. Fellow looks puzzled, laughs, tells where to find mate. Dejected, stagger away, go to place fellow directed. Clouds above began to rain down as dropping before the place where mate was put into hole in ground and speak words. Tell me, Toog, what will do then?"

"No, they would burn the body and drink the ashes."

Toog stared at Bar'Gafu intently, silently for a while.

"I would feel like dying."

"See? Told so." Bar'Gafu sent a small spurt of black liquid out its lower vent. "Save struggle. Die here, now. Repose in peace, Toog. Will even dig hole in ground for you. Promise. And speak words."

Toog spiraled his eyes half-shut. "I know how your promises are." He studied the little brown blob, his inner Ru peeking out.

"Duo-poids all alike," spoke Bar'Gafu, finger scratching at its bottom end. "Think alike. Like obsession with all tactile pleasure—putting one thing all the way inside the other!"

"And you...*tri*-poids...are all so negative-thinking." Toog flashed bronze. "Nothing can ever be good for you—"

"Probably think tri-poids have body features that must join together? Like the Xiit that place their two stems together into the *boul* of the *Um*? Like that? Three parts together? Sure. All duo-poids think that, like it is riddle. No, not that way at all. Heis-Tegag tri-poids are better, have *Ab*, *Doi*, *Rix*—three sexes. When ripening season comes, all gather in the yard. Abs expel material which forms a nest. Then Doi and Rix each produces material into nest. Doi gives *ula*, Rix gives *dur*. Squirt, squirt—ah! Like that. Bar'Gafu is Rix. Zem'Gafu was Doi, Tan'Gafu our Ab. If fortunate, two materials merge, become one, full of *bel*, nourished by Ab's *xom*. In time, Ab rolls each *pou*—what you might call 'egg'—in nest material, what we call *xom*, rolls them into spheres. Usually seven to sixteen spheres, depending on age of Doi and health of Rix. Then Doi and Rix place spheres into the entry of Ab, gather inside. When spheres mature, usually forty-eight days on our world, Ab pushes them out from bottom and Rix gathers them, feeds them beneath a Hugra. 'Follow behind a fat Hugra and will always be fed,' the saying goes. It must be Rix because, by then, Doi's touch is toxic to *kut*—matured spheres. The spheres expand during next few years to the size and shape seen now as Bar'Gafu. Answer question?"

"I never asked that question," Toog muttered.

"Was thinking it." Bar'Gafu burped, droplets of black liquid spurting out the top opening. "Duo-poids always think it. Not as crude as your kind and your insistence on chemical bursts of electric pleasure. Actually is no pleasure. Everything is illusion. Chemical illusion. Would not do if not feeling electric pleasure. So obsession grinds."

"We do enjoy rubbing against each other in the *skarg*...until her belly turns pink and our vents open and our tubes unfold...." Toog let loose a great sigh. There was no point of discussing mating rituals. He knew what he wanted: to simply return home, be with his full-mate and springling. To laze in the *skarg*....

Bar'Gafu chuckled like clanking crystals. "Want only more of electric pleasure. Take a drink of peace, Toog. Repose in quiet peace. Struggle no more. Be one with universe. Be the dust."

Toog bowed his head, sighing desperately. The monster's words made sense. They felt right. Comforting. How long could he go on, stuck on this frozen world, unable to return home? And if he did, just as the blob suggested, everything would be gone. Seeing that gray misty veil before him, it would be easy to surrender to peace and shut himself down. But he had to try.

"I will not let myself believe what you say will be truth. I still hold on to my vow to return—for no reason perhaps than to prove you wrong! I will return."

"Toog...think," Bar'Gafu whispered. "Know am right."

"You are wrong!"

Toog turned to go deeper into the cave, to the inner chamber where he would find peace. He would need another plan.

Bar'Gafu sludged after him, leaving dark stains trailing on the cave floor, muttering between raspy breaths how much of a fool Toog was.

"What is so special about your life that you should spare it?" the little brown blob asked. "Cannot have joy here. What to live for? Tell me."

Toog paused at the small opening to the inner chamber.

"Long ago, twelve years on my world, I burst from the sack of Daag and Lo'u near the village of Mu—at least, that was my count when the Masters captured me, and it has been seven of their years since."

He learned later that an elder sibling died in the *skarg* before being transferred to the swing-basket in the abode, did not burst forth from the orb and turned sour, so the shaman granted Daag and Lo'u another, which was Toog. How close he was to not being made! It was a time of famine, he recalled, so each unit was limited to one.

He told the story of his life in the village, meeting and pairing with L'ra, how they joined together in the *skarg* to make M'ah, how the orb burst through L'ra's belly and they returned the orb to the *skarg* to mature, grow out of its skin, then transferred the springling to a swing-basket in their abode.

He told how the shaman explained the ways First Goddess watched over the village—except when the Masters came.

And he told of his life on the Masters' world, the pain in the prison cell and the pain in the work camp. He told of his escape and meeting Grauun, their travel to the magic cube with Ra'aa'al, how they went separate ways over disagreement about what to do with the new captives they found there. Djuttu was one of them, he reminded the smelly Heis-Tegagan, the one who gave his life helping in the rescue.

Toog stood in silent contemplation, thinking of Djuttu, and Grauun, as he stared out the cave's mouth at the arrangement of sky-lights in the growing darkness, so different from what he saw looking up while on Sebbol.

"Understand," Bar'Gafu spoke after a long silence. "What of the other young one?"

Toog perked up, regarded the brown blob.

"N'oh?" He worried that something bad had happened. "How do you know about my second springling? I never got to meet her. I was taken before the orb burst."

"Your mind," Bar'Gafu smiled, long yellow tongue unfurling. "See pictures in your mind."

Toog took deep breaths, the flaps of his nose vents quivering.

"Then why did you ask me to tell you all this, if you can read it in my mind?"

"Start your thinking," Bar'Gafu replied, pushing up, standing shakily on the stick legs. "Have seen eleven times the amount of information your feeble mouth can recite."

"What use is that information?" Toog grumbled, sitting back against the cave wall. "To trick me?"

"Can see in your mind you believe have much to return to. Can see that, while can tell you there will be nothing at your home, your mind will refuse to believe. The mind-illusion is a fascinating power. Can make you do what you do not want to do, should not do, and cannot do, only for pleasure of trying. Again pleasure. Want something and becomes obsession, search for pleasure, because mind-illusion exaggerates desire. Will do anything to satisfy mind-illusion, get pleasure, even if know yet refuse to believe that satisfying this illusion will not get pleasure, indeed will cause pain, both physical and emotional. Might even die to satisfy that urge."

Toog's eyes spiraled closed. "How do you know so much?"

"Heis-Tegagans are eighty-percent brain."

Bar'Gafu's lone eye closed once, twice, thrice. Then, scraping a bit of slime from an arm, the pod spoke to Toog in a whisper:

"Cannot defeat stubborn mind of yours, Toog, for you are a slave, more than ever you were to the Masters. Even so, must force understanding your way of thinking, your culture, your weakness, and accept they are what they are for you. Is your truth—even if illusion. Continue believing you are wrong, will regret undertaking this task which your mind-illusion sets. Will try to help, sure, although against nature of Heis-Tegag to encourage one to go to end of goal—or until die."

"Thank you," Toog said. His face began to unfurrow.

"Since can no longer benefit the Masters—who could never find use for our kind—have decided can benefit you."

Toog gave a squeak. "You pathetic creature!"

Bar'Gafu vented gas. "Soon will teach the Process."

Toog's eyes spiraled open more. "The Process...?"

"For traveling between worlds. Not need the Masters' magic cube. Only a machine that aids the Masters in the Process."

Toog sat up. "So I can return home...without the cube?"

"Yes, of course."

"Then you can, too?"

"Not strong enough. Maybe you can do."

Toog's eyes bulged. "You are ugly inside and out! Why did you not tell me this?"

Bar'Gafu snorted, a weak spray of black juice exiting top and bottom. "Still must teach the Process. The Masters have cube, but we have the Process. Will teach to you."

Toog raised his blue hand, four fingers splayed, the webbing between them still silver. "Is this an agreement?"

"Yes," Bar'Gafu smiled, raising a stick hand.

Toog reached for the twig of hand, clasped it. "Done."

Later, when Toog had gone out of the cave, down to the small pit he had dug after he first found the cave, and squatted over it to expel his waste, Bar'Gafu appeared, the lone eye rising on its stem.

"Ready to exit?"

Toog wrinkled his face, finished his effort. He started back to the cave. As he stepped away, he glanced back toward the pit. The Heis-Tegagan was bent over it, and slurping noises arose from it.

9

The sun had barely cracked an orange line between the horizon and the low-hanging storm clouds when Toog awoke suddenly. His ears grabbed after the faint sounds that had awakened him. He reached for his weapon, always at his side.

"What is out-of-balance?" sputtered Bar'Gafu.

Toog motioned for the little blob to be still.

Crawling on his flat hands and bent leg-joints to the entrance of the cave, Toog could see shadows moving among the bushes and rocks on the slope below. He stood up within the cover of the cave's mouth, hiding in the shadow, and surveyed the slope. There were definitely some creatures down there. Approaching them.

Bar'Gafu stood at his side in the shadows. "What is there?"

"Things," Toog whispered.

"Many things, sense."

"I count five. They are upright beings."

"See them...here," Bar'Gafu pointed to the round upper end of the oblong pod that was his body. "More below."

Shadowy figures shuffled cover to cover, keeping low on the slope.

"Masters!" Toog exclaimed in a whisper. "I see their head-coverings. It is them. The Masters!"

"The Masters?" Bar'Gafu's eye rose on its stem. "I can benefit them."

"You are benefiting me now. Remember?" Toog clenched his teeth as he quickly gathered his meager belongings into a pack he had gotten from a dead Master. "We must hurry away from here."

"Cannot go. Cannot walk fast. Will teach the Process now."

"No, you are coming with me."

"There are too many of them. Cannot possibly escape."

"We can and we will."

"There goes your mind's illusion again."

"And here we go, illusion or not."

Toog grabbed Bar'Gafu's twig of an arm, ushered the brown pod out of the cave, pushing the blob up the craggy side of the ridge. The rocks still held deep shadows.

One blast from a Master's pulse-gun loosened dirt only a few steps beneath Toog and Bar'Gafu as they continued climbing to the crest of the ridge.

The Masters scrambled up to Toog's cave. They fired their weapons into the cave. A flash and bang erupted and smoke billowed out of the cave.

Others followed Toog and Bar'Gafu up the side of the ridge. The Masters struggled to keep their footing. Toog, covering the ground many times before, was quite sure-footed on his blue feet, his four toes grasping the rock surfaces as he dragged Bar'Gafu along with him.

"Pull too hard. Will break arm," warned Bar'Gafu.

"Then keep up," Toog commanded.

He counted twelve Masters pursuing them, all in the brown tight-fitting uniforms, armed, determined to capture or kill these two escapees. They could not let the breaching of the prison go unanswered.

Storm clouds on the horizon had darkened, moved closer. A harsh wind whipped against the two creatures hurrying across the crest of the ridge into the northern wasteland. Rather than turn into the narrow valley where he and Djuttu had trained, he went the other way, into the rugged area.

The terrain became more broken, with crevasses and deep gorges waiting to consume an errant traveler. Reaching the end of the path, Toog took Bar'Gafu under his arm and leaped across a narrow gap, landing on the far side with a hard thump that sent dirt and rocks tumbling down the side of the cliff, along with most of the supplies from the pack. Bar'Gafu rolled across the rock surface, almost over the side but for the sticky slime oozing from its body.

One of the Masters, hurrying after them, lost balance and fell to a splattering death when the wind caught it at the edge of the gorge. After slowing their climb to carefully span the gorge, the Masters fired again but Toog and Bar'Gafu kept low, crouching among the rocks.

The storm clouds approached, meeting the high elevation of the ridge. Toog did not want the Masters to get on a higher level than him because they would have an advantage shooting down at them. So, instead of turning down the path back toward the valley, he scrambled up an embankment with Bar'Gafu in tow.

Toog soon realized this new ridge connected with a much more treacherous range of mountains that extended to the east. He had never been this way; it looked dangerous.

The Masters followed closely, firing at them every few steps, always just out of range. The pulse-guns had limited range, the lowest setting shooting the farthest but with the least damage. Shooting upward and into the rain diminished their effect, as well. Then a Master brought out a different kind of weapon and the metal pellets sprayed the rocks at Toog's feet. They only succeeded in urging Toog to move at a quicker pace, still with Bar'Gafu under his arm, up the craggy mountain.

Toog threw his pulse-gun over his shoulder, hanging by its strap, and shook the pack out.

"Get in," Toog ordered. "Close the flap."

Bar'Gafu crawled inside the pack, tightening the straps as Toog pulled it on his shoulders again. He climbed higher up the cliffs using both hands, his fingertips flattening to disks.

The Masters got to the bottom of the cliff, looking up at their prey. One pointed to them.

"They are below us!" Bar'Gafu cried, eye extending out of the pack as it swung precariously.

Toog struggled to maintain his grip on the rock ledge. His blue fingertips, even with their flat disks, struggled to keep a secure hold. The wet rock surfaces, black and smooth, were slippery.

"They raise their weapons," Bar'Gafu warned.

"Steady, embracer-of-negative-energy!"

Toog grabbed his pulse-gun with one hand and pulled it off his shoulder, taking it by its hand grip. Hanging from the ledge, with one hand grasping the rock with three finger pads, he fired down at the base of the cliff. The blast struck the pile of rocks between two of the Masters, causing both to jump away as the pile scattered.

Toog dangled awkwardly from the cliff with one hand, as

Bar'Gafu grabbed his shoulders with tiny twig hands. The rest of its oblong body remained inside the pack.

"The storms!" Bar'Gafu exclaimed, pointing upward.

The edge of the dark storm clouds was overhead.

"When the storm strikes, lightening will blast us off the cliff," Bar'Gafu warned. "Rain will make rocks slippery. Will fall."

"You are wrong, bundle-of-joy. The storm will hide us from the Masters."

Toog fired one last time from his dangling position before he threw the pulse-gun over his head, letting it hang by its strap as he pulled himself onto a ledge. He scooted away from the edge so they were hidden from the Masters' view. Bar'Gafu crawled out of the pack. They could feel the splash of heat when the pulse-gun blasts hit the underside of the ledge.

"They use full power on those weapons," Toog commented, breathing heavily, vents open wide. "Like we used in the prison." He thought of how he and Djuttu had set their pulse-guns on maximum while the shots from the guards' weapons, set on low power, did not cause severe damage.

The storm engulfed the top of the ridge and broke into full fury. Lightening flashed sharply, crisp in the heavens, as thunder boomed. Rain, whipped by the strong winds, battered the cliff, the Masters, and Toog. Bar'Gafu crawled inside the pack.

The Masters crouched among the rocks, still firing up at the ledge from time to time as the rain fell.

"Rain feels good, doesn't it, Bar'Gafu?" Toog liked the wetness on his skin, almost like he was swimming through the *abo*, despite it being cold. He felt energized.

"This rain has the poisons which corrode my flesh,"

Bar'Gafu responded, holding the pack's flap closed. "Too much acid."

"Yes, one being's joy is a different being's curse, says Second Goddess."

"Rain hurts, says Bar'Gafu," the Heis-Tegagan grumbled from inside the pack.

Toog crawled to the edge, positioning himself so he could look down with only one eye to spy on the Masters.

"I think they have gone around the cliff. There are only two below now. The others must be trying to get to the top so they can shoot down at us." He looked up the cliff.

"Seems correct," said Bar'Gafu, pointing a twig hand up.

Immediately a shot from above glanced off Toog's arm. The shot left a purple mark but his rubbery skin remained intact.

Toog spun over on his back, aiming the pulse-gun upward, and fired a long blast, hitting one Master who tumbled from the top of the cliff, striking Toog's ledge hard before dropping to the bottom of the gorge.

The Masters at the bottom fired up at Toog. One shot hit the ledge. Another missed and the glob of flame streaked to the top of the cliff and struck one of their own who was leaning over to look down. Toog heard a scream and another Master who lost balance on the wet, slippery rocks plummeted to death.

"Calculated will die here," Bar'Gafu cried out from inside the pack. "Teach you the Process now."

"Not enough time." Toog fired up at the Masters. "We must escape before the storm passes."

A rain of hot metal scattered on the rocks around Toog and he pressed back from the edge. One piece ricocheted twice on the stone surfaces and struck Toog's leg, shielded by the canvas pack. He felt the hit through the cloth. The crumpled metal was hot to his touch when he tried to pick it up, and dropped it immediately. The same kind of weapon they had used when he was on the toppled guard tower, he recognized.

"Not safe anywhere." Bar'Gafu cried like wheezing gas.

The brown blob scrunched tighter back against the cliff face, pushing the pack, squirming within it.

Toog surveyed the cliff face and discovered an adjacent ledge which skirted the next wall. It was only a short leap away, over a narrow chasm. The other ledge was smaller. And wet from the rain. But he would have to risk it. There was no other way to go.

The rain lessened. The dark clouds continued to rumble, flash with lightning. Masters were still above and below but blinded by the darkness of the storm.

With Bar'Gafu stuffed safely inside the pack hanging from his shoulders and the pulse-gun dangling securely by its strap, Toog measured the distance between the two ledges.

"Perhaps should sit for a while and consider other options," Bar'Gafu suggested from inside the pack on Toog's shoulders.

"Put your negative-energy under us," cried Toog.

And he leaped, springing from bent legs, and caught the other ledge by his fingertips, the flat disks sticking tight despite the wet surface. He was used to maneuvering on wet surfaces; his ancestors were amphibious. This was like his youth trip, when he had ventured into the Mounts of Gol and tried to climb to the top to get eggs from a *zub* nest. But that was in clear weather.

He fought for a place to put his blue feet, long toes stretching out for a secure grip.

"Notice how my suggestion would have been more

prudent option?" Bar'Gafu declared, eye poking out of the pack.

One blue toe found a gap in the rock face, pushed into it to secure a hold. Toog wondered how his foot was able to expand that way. First Goddess must be watching over him. He pulled himself up onto the ledge.

Toog regarded a boulder there, as big as his belly, sitting near the edge of this new ledge. He set down his weapon and the pack. With strength he had not used since the day of his escape, Toog worked the boulder to the very edge. He fired the pulse-gun down at the Masters, who promptly gathered at the base of the cliff and fired up at him. Toog put his stiffening blue back against the boulder and his leg muscles strained to their limits as the boulder balanced at the edge a moment then rolled over the side, crashing down on the Masters below.

"That was unexpected option," said Bar'Gafu, huddling in the pack, flap open. Crawling out and standing on stick legs, the blob picked up a pebble and heaved it over the side.

Two Masters managed to escape the falling boulder while the others were severely wounded. The survivors hesitated, firing up the cliff a few times, then turned their attention to helping their wounded comrades.

Waving at his little companion to follow, Toog stepped lightly along the outcrop with Bar'Gafu creeping close behind on stick legs, leaving drops of flesh with every step. His warm weapon hung from his shoulder. A sudden gust ripped the empty pack away and they watched it flutter in the storm wind as the dark clouds overhead continued rumbling, attacking them with sprits of rain.

The remaining Masters lost sight of them as the escapees stepped around the side of the cliffs. The ledge widened after a while which enabled Toog to safely run along it with

Bar'Gafu hanging onto his shoulders until they reached the next ridge, always climbing higher, safely away from both the sheer cliffs and the Masters.

As the storm rumbles faded, they found themselves gazing down upon a plateau set among the mountains, as though the flat area was the basin of a great caldera. Far across the plateau they could see several spots of light, like fires burning at what must be a camp, hidden by thick gray fog.

"More Masters?" Toog wondered, squeaks swallowed up by the fog.

"Would never make a camp here in this wilderness," said Bar'Gafu, climbing down from Toog's shoulders.

"Then who can they be?"

"Move closer. Fog will hide."

Carefully they picked their way through round rocks and scruffy vegetation down from the encircling ridge to the plateau floor. Fog swirled around their legs as it grew to envelope the entire plain. Faint glows showed through the fog, marking the camp. Toog motioned Bar'Gafu ahead.

They traversed the uneven, rocky ground, checking each step which the fog hid.

Toog pulled the pulse-gun from his shoulder, readied it in his hands. He saw the blue button glowing: the power was running out. And he had lost the second pulse-gun when the pack spilled.

Bar'Gafu, struggling to keep up, scraped another bit of slime, shook it off.

"Here is not good air," Bar'Gafu spoke, answered by Toog's command to be silent. "Bad rain, bad air. Bad world."

Hidden in the fog, they approached the camp with slow, deliberate steps. Toog paused, hearing voices ahead. He tried to set his gun's power to maximum but it only had enough power remaining for low, to burn but not kill.

"Halt!" a deep voice called out amidst a fury of guns clicking. The command roared in Toog's mind-cave but his inner Ru could not identify the language in his ears. The meaning was clear, though.

Toog and Bar'Gafu halted.

"Drop your weapon!" the voice ordered. Toog could not see the figure through the thick fog, just a shadowy hulk. "Drop it!"

Toog set the pulse-gun down on the ground at his feet.

"Who are you?" the voice demanded.

Toog did not answer. The words he heard were unclear. His inner Ru shrugged inside his mind-cave, unsure what to write on the wall.

"I am called Bar'Gafu," the Heis-Tegagan spoke up, standing behind Toog and peering around his legs.

The hidden creatures closed around them, weapons raised. As they pushed their way through the fog, Toog recognized them as Xmburrhaltins, those of Grauun's kind.

One creature, though, Toog had never seen before. Its face consisted mostly of four huge teeth, two upper and two lower, clacking together as though hungry. Behind the large clawed feet it stood on, a flat tail dragged on the ground. Standing twice Toog's height, the creature reminded Toog of the *hux* that lived in some of the forests on Sebbol. This creature carried in its big clawed hands a long black weapon which Toog had only seen mounted on some of the Masters' machine-wagons. It was the opposite of the stubby pulse-guns, about as long as the creature was tall.

"At least you are not Masters," this hairy *hux*-creature spoke in its language as they broke through the fog. The words echoed in Toog's mind-cave, where his inner Ru pointed to the wall with a grin and the writing appeared.

"We are guarding against an attack. But since you are not Masters, we will welcome you to our camp."

Toog stared at the long weapon, studying its twin barrels.

The toothy creature noticed his interest. "I heard Masters call it 'relsovaputz'. It shoots metal bolts out between these two magnetic rails." The four front teeth clacked together. "The big creatures like us are too frightening—not easy to kill with just hot-light. So they made these." He grinned at Toog. "They shoot bolts." And his tail thumped on the ground. "Bolts!"

Toog's head bronzed as the *hux* ran a rough tongue over its large, square teeth. The creature's thick arms and legs had two more joints than Toog's had. The *hux* wore nothing over its fur except a belt of black bolts. Tucked in its belt, Toog saw, was another bolt like what was used at the prison. When the *hux*-creature shifted the black weapon in its grip, Toog saw the hole in one hand.

"You are the leader?" Toog inquired of the *hux*.

"No. I am Ar-Kel Ovga-Menzu of Re-vKeer by the Minv— not the Ar-Kel Ovga-Menzu in Hlorra, north of the Gloub-Kua, who is never to be discussed. The whole clan there are dam fools. No relation to any other Ovga-Menzu in Dranl or Juf, either. You can call me Arkor. I'm second in command of our group." Big teeth gleaming, the *hux*-creature looked down at Bar'Gafu, noticing the smell. "You are from Heis-Tegag, I guess."

"How do you know?" Bar'Gafu sneered.

"It is not difficult to identify a Heis-Tegagan."

"And what are you?" Bar'Gafu snipped.

"I am a Bex. From the planet Becha, in the Buz-Lopf system."

Bar'Gafu pointed a twig hand at Toog. "This one thinks

you are a *hux* from Sebbol."

"No, Bex is the apex lifeform on Becha. I don't know about on your world, little thing."

The spoken words were flying back and forth, yet they could only understand them within each other's mind-cave. Toog tried to keep up.

Do not enjoy your insinuation, Bar'Gafu responded, his words also echoing in Toog's mind-cave.

There is little to enjoy on this world, Arkor communicated in kind, clacking its square teeth. *Come with us.*

The Xmburrhaltins followed as they moved through the fog and the group soon arrived at the camp.

"I don't believe I heard your name," Arkor remarked, holding out the hand with the hole in the palm.

Toog held up his blue hand, showing his wound.

Arkor grinned at the show of comradeship, his large incisors wet with saliva.

"Toog," he replied, cautiously, quietly. "I am from Sebbol."

"Toog...." The Bex paused. "I have heard that name before." He smiled, teeth gleaming. "Our leader spoke this name to us. I wonder if you are the same as that."

"And who is your leader?" asked Toog.

"He goes by the name Grauun. One of the Xmburras."

Toog choked, cleared his gullet. "I am that Toog."

Arkor glared at the blue being. "True?"

One of the Xmburrhaltin guards behind them grumbled.

"Silence," Arkor snapped, then turned to Toog. "I am certain our leader will want to meet you. I will take you to him at once."

As they entered the camp, they passed two of the Masters' machine-wagons, sitting abandoned. Toog understood how they got all the supplies up to the plateau. And how they could go on raids.

"No more fuel," Arkor responded. "Useless now."

The dingy gray tent they stopped at was the largest of a handful of tents in the camp, clearly supplied by the Masters. Arkor parted the tent flaps and sauntered in, his girth pushing the opening wider.

Toog and Bar'Gafu followed.

The tent was empty except for a table in the middle and a cot to one side.

The hulking figure of Grauun sat awkwardly behind the table, facing the entrance. His head was lowered, studying several maps spread across the small table. When they entered, Grauun sniffed.

"We have two arrivals," Arkor spoke casually. It was Grauun's language he used. Toog could understand some.

"Prisoners?" Grauun asked, sniffing around.

"Yes," Arkor replied. "One of them says he knows you."

"Grrr?" Grauun looked up. His eyes focused on Toog, and he stumbled to his feet, knocking the chair over backwards. "You!"

Grauun's eyes pierced sharply, deeply into Toog.

"Did they attack us?' Grauun asked Arkor.

"No, quite the contrary." Arkor set the rail-gun down, leaning it against his body, braced by his thick leg. "They were unaware of our camp. Found at random."

Toog stepped forward. "We would not expect the Masters to be camped up here. It is a good location."

"Indeed not," Arkor agreed.

"But we did see the light of your fires all the way from

the end of the plateau, even through the fog. I am sure if we saw them then the Masters who—"

"Extinguish them!" Grauun ordered Arkor.

With a slap of his flat tail, the Bex shuffled out of the tent.

"How did you get these tents?" Toog inquired, throat vents relaxing.

Grauun continued to stare at Toog. "Hmmf!"

He turned and righted the fallen chair, much too small to support him, and sat on it, gray fur flapping everywhere.

"Thus together we again are," Grauun acknowledged, trying out his best Sebbou, shrugging his big shoulders. The grunts were not close to the correct chirps. "You more blue now are. Almost recognize you not." He sniffed twice, catching a stench, and found its source, then grumbled in Xmburra: "And who is this smelly creature?"

"Bar'Gafu," Toog replied, "the one from Heis-Tegag."

"I might have known."

Bar'Gafu stepped back. "Beg your pardon!"

They ignored Bar'Gafu's close approximation of Xmburra.

"In our previous raid on the Batagai number two camp," Grauun spoke in Xmburra, glancing at Toog, knowing his mind-cave spirit-thing would translate his words, "we obtained many useful articles, as you see. Including these maps. This one shows the land from the prison at Uskuga, where we were kept, to Batagai. This other map shows the land from the Batagai work camp to our work camp."

He waved Toog closer.

"Remember our work camp? The rebellion? Trexon was my cell mate. And this map shows the land from Uskuga to the cube by the sea. It is only a bay, not the sea—yet the water is poison. We scouted much of this land, and raided many camps and some convoys. They fear us now. We have destroyed many Masters. How do you like that? I could have used your help many times on our raids. None has better aim with the Masters' weapons than you. And cunning: you have that! Here in my gang, only Arkor, my second—only we have this trait of cunning. Of course, I owe you much for teaching me to use this trait. My fellow Xmburrhaltins do not have cunning but they are good at following orders. Ah, but we had our differences! Didn't we?"

The words were scribbled on the wall of Toog's mind-cave faster than he could read them, but he understood.

Yes, I remember.

"You were correct," said Grauun. "I could not protect all of those creatures by myself. Most of the beings from the cube that we saved were killed by the Masters when they surrounded us near Namy. Some were captured. Only four escaped with me."

He waved at the entrance to the tent.

"All who are here with me now have never been in a prison—except Arkor. He escaped from the Masters, ran away from an execution trip—lost half his tail running from them."

He glanced at the tent's entrance, expecting Arkor to return.

"Forget what I said to you long ago at the cube. We were hot for fighting and not thinking clearly. It was said in haste and passion. Stay with us, now that you have your Heis-Tegagan pet and you have found us. Not sure what use that smelly thing can be for—"

"Can hear you," Bar'Gafu spoke, then spurted some black fluid out both ends of its oblong body.

"—but we can sure use you in our gang. We are

preparing another attack on Kazacha. More Masters to kill. That is the village where many families of the prison guards live. So little ones—springlings! And females. They should be tasty. It is two days' march. What do you say, Toog?"

Toog had listened and read the writing on the wall, even as his inner Ru screwed up its face in disgust.

"Grauun, you know I have only two goals. First, I intend to return to my home and be with my family. That is the reason I rescued this Heis-Tegagan from the prison. This being knows how to operate the cube. We can go home now. My second goal is to return here and destroy the Masters. Forever. I do not mean to fight them in petty battles. I mean to completely destroy their race—as they try to do to us. Maybe destroy this whole planet. That is the order of my actions. I can see your plan is to kill the Masters, one body at a time."

"What is wrong with that?" Grauun roared, standing again and knocking his chair over. "It gives me great pleasure to take personal note of each Master's death. You know what joy is? It makes for a more rewarding task. It is all I have left. It is my goal now. I know I can never return home, so I make my purpose to end them. Even one at a time."

"I thought you wished nothing more than to return home."

"There is nothing there for me, Toog. The Masters have made me curse life. They have destroyed my ability to mate, to live a glorious life. Xm is displeased. Every night I suffer turmoil and anguish in thinking of my family. I cannot stop thinking of their destruction. I have only one purpose now and that is to spend every last pulse of energy I have opposing the Masters! That is all I can do!"

"But Grauun...." The blue being's eyes grew pink. "I do

not know the fate of my family. You know your family is gone."

"And that is better, Toog?"

"Which is better? To never know their fate, or to be certain one way or the other?"

Bar'Gafu stepped forward on stick legs, raising a stick hand.

"To not know. That is the better choice."

"Why do you say that?" Toog demanded, gazing down at the brown pod.

"The stink bug has words!" Grauun howled.

"Watched my mates die because of Masters," Bar'Gafu spoke. "Would prefer remember them at the beginning, on Heis-Tegag, not as when died on this frozen world. You have that privilege, Toog. You have pleasant memories, not terrible realities."

"This smelly thing knows," said Grauun, sitting again.

Toog stood firm. "I must see that my family is safe. Knowing they are safe will give me the strength to destroy the Masters."

"No," Bar'Gafu exclaimed, slapping a twig hand on Grauun's table, loosening a bit of slime. The brown pod tried to wipe it away but the smeared streak made it worse. "You are wrong. It is not knowledge of your family's safety that will give you the strength. It is your anger in your present circumstance that gives you destructive power—"

"The creature knows you," Grauun laughed.

"It is your thoughts-now-in-torment that gives you the rage that makes it possible for you to destroy the Masters. Know of no creature except Masters that fights while family is safe. If family is in danger, or it fears they could be in danger, only then can collect necessary strength to defeat enemy."

The Heis-Tegagan's lone eye rose on its stem, blinking.

"If you are to destroy the Masters, you must remain filled with hate. Must gather hate within. Can only be done by not knowing whether family is safe; by wondering whether Masters carried them off; by wondering whether they have outgrown you and long ago died; by pondering partner, how many partners have been welcomed since you disappeared. Denied companionship, will seek another—"

"Stop!" Toog cried out. "Stop it!"

"Told you was for nothing," Bar'Gafu reminded. "No good to return to your home and be forgotten. Warned, but did not listen. Illusions surround you, fill you up. Like you are swimming in precious *skarg* and warm *abo,* yet it is only the fog of this plateau on a world of ice, hunted. Do not be a dam fool, as the Bex say. All have only one purpose remaining. Only one. To complete the cycle."

Toog, blue skin turning darker, leaned over the table, one arm bracing himself while the other raised to his face to hid his sorrow-rain.

"I like you, Heis-Tegag thing!" Grauun announced. "You think right. And everything you say is truth."

"An embracer-of-negative-energy," Toog muttered, lowering his hand. His eyes had returned to blue.

"Better embracer-of-negative-energy," said Bar'Gafu, "because never disappointed. Have tasted. How survive on what other creatures leave? How many disappointments have you eaten, Toog? Too many for counting, would think. Because have standards too high, can never touch, never eat, expect too much. Perhaps could be embracer-of-positive-energy when at your home, but not at your home now. Are here, and to survive here need to plan for worst, because—as we tasted—will never avoid worst."

"Toog, this creature you have found is a smart thing!"

Grauun roared.

"He is quite full-of-pictures," Toog volunteered.

"I don't like your smell, Heis-Tegagan, but you are smart." Grauun grunted. "Look at this map, Ban—what is it? Bargo...?"

The brown pod arose on stick legs. "I am called Bar'Gafu!"

"Look at this map." He unrolled another map over the table. "I cannot determine what this map shows. You see what it is."

Toog looked at the map. "It seems to be.... I'm not sure, perhaps another continent. This is the sea? These islands? But I don't know what these lines mean.... Roads?"

Bar'Gafu stretched up on stick toes, trying to view the map. After a loud puff of steam, Toog picked him up and set him on the table. The gelatinous film on the Heis-Tegagan remained on Toog's hands so he grabbed some dirt at his feet and rubbed his hands roughly together as Bar'Gafu studied the map.

"A map of the tangents that originate from what the Masters call their *stargate*—the magic cube."

"Tangents?" asked Grauun.

Toog's eyes bulged. *Stargate?*

"A point where the universe can be torn, like a cloth with a hole. The Masters step through the hole and arrive on another world, like Heis-Tegag or Xmburrhaltis or Sebbol. Dimensions of two worlds intersect at the tangent, one point on each world. You must locate it before you can use it."

Grauun held up his big hand, looking through the hole partly hidden by his fur, seeing Toog through it.

"Bar'Gafu knows how to work this process," Toog stated boldly, like he alone possessed the treasured magician. "He can open the tangent. Then we can go home."

"What is the process?" Grauun asked, scratching his furry cheek.

"The Process is—" Bar'Gafu started in haughty tone.

"What we do to depart this world," Toog explained. "We don't need the cube to do it—unless you are a Master. They are not so advanced as they have us believe."

"Easier for travelers without powers to use cube," Bar'Gafu added. "The cube does the Process for them."

"I understand." Grauun smiled, his fangs showing through his thick face fur. "But where is the cube on this map? It was on a beach."

Bar'Gafu's lone eye, stem extended, scanned the image. It was more a chart than a map. The smelly blob asked Grauun to turn it to better survey it. Then Bar'Gafu pointed a slimy finger at the mark near the center of the map.

"This is your cube. This is the gateway home."

Grauun and Toog leaned over the map, staring hard at the spot Bar'Gafu marked with a tiny finger.

"Seven cubes operated by Masters," said Bar'Gafu, pointing to each of them in a rough circle around the center of the map. "Maybe each cube covers tangents for different worlds. Choose wisely or could arrive on different world than your home."

"Embracer-of-negative-energy," Toog said, giving a sigh that made his skin flash bronze and return to blue.

Grauun slapped his big hand on the map, hairy finger on the center cube, claw indenting the surface.

"Where is Xmburrhaltis?"

Bar'Gafu looked briefly and pointed a twig finger to a brown blotch at the corner of the map. Marks in the Masters' language named it Delta-Gorske 5.

"What meaning is that?" asked Grauun.

"The Masters named it their way. Did not know it was called Xmburrhaltis by inhabitants."

"They never asked us!" the Xmburrhaltin roared.

Bar'Gafu stepped back. "Far away by the stars, yet only one step from the cube."

"And my world?" Toog asked. His blue skin lightened, almost glowed, as his eyes pinked. "Where is Sebbol?"

Again Bar'Gafu pointed to a spot on the map, a green dot much closer to the center than Xmburrhaltis—yet a single step through the cube-machine.

"Here is Heis-Tegag," said Bar'Gafu, finger on a small orange spot on the opposite side of the chart from Xmburrhaltis. "The Masters have named it Epsilon-Smithers. Planet one."

"What is Smithers?" asked Grauun.

"Perhaps they name it after a shaman?" Toog suggested.

"Not important the name," Bar'Gafu grumbled. "Too far."

They stared at the chart. It all seemed so ordered, in perfect position, perfect balance, all connected by invisible passages that creatures could simply step through.

"How can we go home?" asked Toog after some silence.

"Will teach you the Process," said Bar'Gafu.

Grauun studied the map longer, then straightened up.

"You are welcome to stay. And enjoy our food, if you wish. We have fresh Master. And the Ababerazan found some of the berries you like. And this smart but filthy creature from Heis-Tegag can stay with us, too. But way over there—far away. In the last tent."

Toog glanced at Bar'Gafu, then back at Grauun.

"I will stay. And I will go with you to your war, but only as far as it gets me to the cube and home."

"That is good." Grauun howled, then regarded Bar'Gafu who was waving a tiny hand in agreement. Pointing outside the tent, Grauun said: "Find Arkor and he will be sure you get food and a place to sleep."

"Is anyone ready to exit?" asked the little Heis-Tegagan.

Toog glared at Bar'Gafu until the brown pod shuffled out.

Grauun had sat down, expecting they would both leave, but Toog remained.

"How many here never were in the prison?" asked Toog.

Grauun looked up. "Me and Arkor, a few others. We got them on the road to a work camp. The others we saved at the cube or on the way to the prison, intercepted a line of machine-wagons, killed the Masters and took their captives—freed them."

He laughed in his rough, howling style.

"How the Masters ran, so afraid of us! And we could cut them down as they ran. I remember one I cut downward shoulder to leg and it hopped away on the other leg, so I cut downward the other side, shoulder to leg, and it dropped to the ground on its bottom, still wriggling. So last off with its head. That stopped the pain-screams. Almost prepared for dinner. I like these pulse-guns. Like knives of fire! Yet Arkor prefers the rail-gun, likes to shoot many bolts into the Masters."

Toog grimaced. "The creatures are thankful you saved them, I am certain. They know not the pain of the Masters' torture—what you and I have known."

"It is right to save them from the Masters. Ha! They are not a superior species but weak, with small hearts and warped minds. They should be ended. All of them. Including their families."

Toog stood before the table, his blue skin darkening. "Those who were captured and brought here cannot have as much hate for the Masters as you and me, as any creature who worked in their camps or rotted in their prison."

Grauun sat back, grinning, his two primary fangs hanging out of his mouth. "Yes, we spared them from all that and they are grateful."

"Those creatures, I am sure, would prefer to return to their own worlds rather than stay only to fight against an enemy they barely know."

It took a moment for Grauun to understand. He blinked, then withdrew his fangs and narrowed his eyes under his thick brow.

"Is that what you think?" His throat rumbled.

"Ask them."

"Those creatures I saved—they are loyal to me, especially the Xmburrhaltins—I know them: they believe in our fight. We fight them here to protect our homes. They will follow me anywhere to hunt the Masters!"

Toog's face furrowed. "I only ask you to give them a choice." His throat vents quivered. "I know some would wish to return home. All I ask you is to ask them. Let them choose."

Grauun glanced at the tangent map. "Do you think so many of them will want to go home now? Or can go home?"

"I have the Heis-Tegagan."

"Yes, the little bag of foul matter...."

Grauun combed his furry chin with his dirty claws, regarding Toog's pleading form, flashing bronze and back to blue.

"As you wish." He grinned, rows of sharp teeth showing. "In the morning we will assemble and see what the tally is. I will be fair, Toog, as you ask. Those who wish to leave with you, I will allow to leave. The weak ones will go."

Toog took on a solid blue. "Thank you, Grauun."

The Xmburrhaltin smiled. "Come, Toog. You must tell me all you have done since last we saw each other. Tell me of your adventures, your conquests. How many Masters have you killed? Tell me how you freed that clever friend of yours."

Toog awoke at the sound of Arkor calling the creatures together the next morning. He stretched his rubbery blue arms and legs, made joints in them, felt the soreness of the previous day, then pulled on the refitted Masters' greatcoat Arkor had given him and peeked out of the small tent he shared with Bar'Gafu.

The legion of creatures was assembled. Grauun was speaking to them about Toog, the little blue being from planet Sebbol—who on cue stepped from the tent and walked toward them.

"Creatures! This is Toog," said Grauun in Xmburra, pointing at the little blue being. "Many of you do not know him. I realize I instructed you to never say his name. But he was the first to escape from the Masters, so I withdraw my order. He is now among us. Respect him as you respect me. Obey his commands as you obey mine. And remember his deeds: he was the first to escape, the first! Never forget. Because of this Toog, most of you never had to experience the pain of the Masters' prison or the work camps!"

He regarded Toog with a toothy grin.

"Do not think he is only small and weak," Grauun continued, "for this one has strange powers that cannot be seen until you face him in serious battle!"

The Xmburrhaltin roared across the plateau. Toog stepped forward—with Bar'Gafu bumbling behind, fresh from the latrine at the edge of the camp.

"Leader Toog, I give you my army."

Grauun jutted his furry chin, indicating Toog should inspect the troops, so he moved toward the first rank. Starting at the end, Toog looked at the first creature: a Xmburrhaltin, like Grauun; the entire first and second ranks were Xmburrhaltins. They could fight the Masters and win easily. Toog stopped by each one, noting they were as muscular and huge as Grauun. It was easy to understand why the Masters had used them in the quarries. But he could not understand why the other creatures had been captured, beings like himself.

He continued inspecting the rank. More Xmburrhaltins. As he approached the last one in the rank, the creature raised its hand to show the hole the Masters made by driving the bolt through. Toog shuddered, recalled the clinking of metal on metal as the bolt was hammered through his hand. The other Xmburrhaltins were not so marked. They were the ones who would wish to go home, Toog thought.

The third rank had an assortment of creatures, some Toog had never seen before. One was a lizard creature like the body Ra'aa'al wore when Toog first met him in that prison cell. There were three short brown upright creatures, hairless and naked, sporting one eye in the middle of their faces without protruding nose or ears. They showed their many-fanged mouths as Toog passed.

"Those Mogadans really enjoy eating Masters," Grauun told Toog.

There were a few more upright beings, mostly male by their appearance with different sex organs on display, wearing a variety of torn clothing or leather coverings, almost shivering in the cold air. None were from Sebbol.

He came next to a fully clothed being, covered in an elaborate costume. With yellow hair on its head and protruding nose and ears, this one appeared similar to one of the Masters. Only its lavish fashion, though now dirty, kept Toog in a state of calm.

"*U, r'ta u'gor ˢWa?*" Toog inquired in polite Sebbou. No hint of understanding. The style of clothing indicated it must be an intelligent being. The garments showed care and artistic effort. Summoning words from his inner Ru, he carefully spoke: "Weh r'yu {squeak} fur'm {chortle}?"

The upright being, standing well above Toog, startled at the sound of its own language spoken by the little blue being.

"Where am I from?" spoke the being hesitantly.

Toog examined the wall of his mind-cave, where his inner Ru was slowly writing. He reached up and placed his blue hand on the tall being's forehead. The heel of his hand firmed, formed a ridge, became a suction pad that fixed his hand to the head of the upright being. Alarmed at the trick, the being fidgeted, bent down.

Grauun growled at the creature, raising a clawed hand.

"Yes," spoke the upright being. "I am rather surprised you know English, sir."

English is only a system of symbols that can be deciphered by any higher-thought being, Toog communicated through the connection of his hand to the being's head. *The system you use is not unique or unfathomable.*

"I quite agree," replied the being. "I never meant to imply—"

Name? World? Species? asked Toog.

The being suddenly stiffened, raising a hand to its forehead as if feeling pain there, then dropping its arm to its side.

"Timothy Cromwell, at your service, sir!" The being clicked its leather-covered feet together. "I hail from Boston—in the Colonies, sir. Although I certainly would doubt you know where that may be located in the New World. I am what we call a human being."

Toog took a moment to let the words process through his mind, as Ra'aa'al had taught him. His inner Ru crossed its arms in disgust, protesting by dropping the marker on the floor of his mind-cave, raising a small cloud of dust.

"*N'ew Wor'ld?*" Toog repeated in his squeaky rendition.

"Yes, the Americas. Have you not heard of them?"

How far away is your planet Boston? Toog inquired.

"What?" The being's eyes blinked. "I heard that...in my head? Your words...in perfect English." The Hu-man chuckled, caught himself, resumed a serious posture. "No, no, no, dear fellow, not Boston."

Toog studied the Hu-man. His inner Ru registered confusion, trying again to draw on his mind-cave wall.

You said you were from Boston.

"Yes, indeed. However, Boston is a city. The name of my planet, as you've no doubt heard others say, is Earth."

"*Ear'tha...,*" Toog tried to repeat, adding a squeal. His nose flaps quivered, regarded the being from Earth called Hu-man, apparently harmless. *Do you have a family?*

The Hu-man had gotten used to their unique method of communication and responded confidently: "No, I'm an orphan, and unmarried."

He would stay and fight the Masters, Toog knew.

"Y'ou {squeak} wel'come {churl} jo'in," spoke the little blue being.

"I thank you, sir," replied the Hu-man.

"If you can fight, we need you," Grauun growled behind them. Toog translated.

The Hu-man saluted. "Always ready to fight the Crown!"

Toog focused on the Hu-man. Everywhere there seemed to be one group fighting another group. Now it was a crown? Only the goddesses wore crowns.

Your enemy is my enemy, Toog responded.

"Agreed." The Hu-man gave a nod.

Toog moved on, noting the two Cetreans whose bodies were shaped much like Aull or Hu-man but encased in hard shells with soft parts inside. They stood silent as though they still were in too much shock to react. He passed the five-legged Piilactrian with a lingering look. *For what can the Masters use such creatures?* It could not fight, only carry supplies.

Must return home. Must chew cud, Toog heard the pacing creature's thoughts as they echoed in a husky tone in his mind-cave. *Fear-fear-fear. Oh! Oh! May-die. Help-help-help. Where gallop? Away-away-away.*

Toog knew the feeling. Complete panic upon awakening on a distant world with no way to go home.

He came to the upright female being he had seen at the cube. She had carried her springling, but it had seemed to die when she dropped it but was actually alive—sending Ra'aa'al shooting out across the universe. He still felt a hole in his belly when he thought of that.

Her long green gown had become quite dirty and torn since that day. It no longer trailed on the ground but ended at her leg joints. Her muscular body was for fighting, yet she possessed a pair of mounds which appeared to carry liquid, rather like the humps on the Piilactrians, possibly for springlings to drink from using the valves that protruded. The long black hair falling from her head had become dirty and tangled. Other than her height, robust figure, and her green skin, she might be mistaken for a Hu-man. She towered over Toog, but her green face glowed warmly when she looked down at him.

His inner Ru tapped on his heart, made a sketch on the wall of his mind-cave: a small Hu-man fashioned in five strokes. It drew a circle around the figure on the wall.

I remember you, Toog communicated. *Where is your child?*

"My child is dead," she spoke in her language. "Killed as we fled from attack."

Toog tried to understand, doing a quick deciphering.

I am sorry, Toog responded, gazing up at her.

Her mouth twisted, a quizzical smile forming, like she was trying to understand him but failing.

Toog tried again. No getting through. He waved his blue hand for her to lean down, then placed his palm on her forehead. A connection buzzed up his arm a moment, then became clear.

What is your name? he asked.

"Basha," she spoke but Toog also heard in his mind-cave.

What is your home world?

"Ababeraz is my home."

I wish you were not brought here. All of us not here. Toog nodded pensively. *I know a creature who can lead us home again.*

She straightened up as he removed his hand from her head, continuing to watch him as he went down the line. He glanced at each being as he moved to where Grauun and Bar'Gafu waited.

"We have a good group, do we not, Toog?" Grauun asked.

"Yes, a good group," Toog replied.

"You didn't inspect the last row," Grauun commented. "Those creatures in the back rank."

Grauun turned to Arkor, gave instructions.

"You know the Xmburrhaltins, of course," said Arkor. "I am from Becha, and those lizards are from Dikondra. The brown creatures over there, the short ones, come from Mogada. They cannot speak, but they do communicate mind to mind. And you know those first two upright beings covered in red fur come from Polotrax, and the others, those with twin horns, from Raemue, and that female from Ababaraz, our best fighter. The Vuuth over there, and a Drell behind. The Q'im and Lolli in the back."

"Will you join us in fighting the Masters?" Grauun asked.

"My plan does not change, Grauun. I am sorry. I promise to return and destroy the Masters. All of them. First, I must return to my home. Now we need to have them choose, to see who will go with me. And who will stay."

Grauun frowned, blew fur from his lips. "Very well, Toog. You direct it."

Toog nodded, moving in front of the group. He summoned his inner Ru to the task of writing on the walls of his mind-cave, hoping the variety of creatures before him could understand his message. Then he spoke in his true voice, using the squeaks and chirps of Sebbou, as well as internally like Ra'aa'al had taught him.

"Many of you have not felt the pain of the Masters' bolts in your hands. You have not felt the pain of their electric whips on your backs. You do not know the suffering of being locked away in their prison. Or laboring as slaves in a work camp. Your hate for the Masters comes only from the fact they have taken you from your homes and families."

He scanned the assembled beings. Some of them seemed to understand, others he could not be sure about.

"I can take you back to your homes, if you wish to go. I have a Heis-Tegagan who will show us how to operate the magic cube the Masters possess, which creates a doorway in the universe which we can go through and return to our homes. You can secure your families against the Masters, protect them, stay with them if you wish. Then you can return here, if you wish, and help in the destruction of the Masters."

He watched them, feeling his skin bronze, wondering how many understood him, how many would join him.

"I hate the Masters as much or more than any of you, and I still wish to be with my family again. I want to know they are safe. Then I can begin my mission to destroy the Masters. When I am finished, this planet may no longer exist! I pledge it!"

Several creatures gave something like cheers, myriad noises emanating from all kinds of throats.

Toog glanced down at Bar'Gafu, wondering if the little brown thing could actually lead him home.

"Will try," said the Heis-Tegagan in response.

Toog looked up at the assembled creatures.

"Any of you who feel as I do, who wish to do as I do, I welcome. Follow me through the Masters' cube to your own worlds, to your homes. I know the way, and I will lead you there. Decide now if you wish to return to your homes, or else use the remainder of your life pursuing the Masters to their destruction. Those who would follow me home, step forward now!"

The brisk afternoon wind tugged at the wide sleeves of the garment Toog was given. He straightened the sleeves, cut down for his size, crossed his arms over his bent legs and lowered his blue head.

He gazed at the camp from a jumble of rocks which

bordered the plateau. Xmburrhaltin sentries walked their path around the camp. Other beings went about their tasks as Toog contemplated the morning's decision.

He wished Grauun would have chosen to join him. That would have helped turn the others. The Xmburrhaltins had stuck by their leader, as Toog knew they would. At least he was accompanied by Bar'Gafu, Arkor, the two Dikondran lizards, the Hu-man, and the green female, Basha. A few creatures seemed unable to decide, perhaps not understanding. He had not cared who went with him—except Bar'Gafu, who knew the Process—but it would have given him a sense of being right. He meant what he stated: he would return to destroy the Masters but only after he had secured his family. Most of the creatures chose to stay and fight, to sacrifice themselves to save their families and their homes from the Masters.

"Two choices," Bar'Gafu had spoken to him afterward. "Like two nose vents. In and out, the same."

Toog had talked with Grauun the previous night, telling his adventures. He told about his return to the cave through the deep snow and the return of Djuttu. He described the rescue of Bar'Gafu and Zem'Gafu, and of Djuttu's death, and Bar'Gafu's embracing-of-negative-energy, and his decision to go home with Bar'Gafu's help. He described the Masters' raid on the cave and the chase through the canyons, over the mountains, and their escape to Grauun's camp. The Masters would never come this high, he and Grauun agreed.

In turn, Grauun told Toog of their raids on the Masters' work camps, fighting the Masters wherever they could. Bar'Gafu's rescue had been made easier because most of the Masters in the prison were away fighting Grauun's army. They had talked late into the night.

Sitting on the rocks, Toog realized he was quite tired. His

blue skin had faded in places to a dull gray. He ran his hands over his rough skin, no longer the smooth silvery surface he had during his life on Sebbol. He was ugly now. He leaned back on the rocks and his hands, pressed against the rocks, gradually turned the same brownish color. His feet also took on the color of the rocks they touched. It was a strange trick First Goddess played on him, making him look like a rock.

After talking with Grauun he had gone to the tent they had given him, making a detour to the latrine. He found Bar'Gafu there, the only creature he had met that allowed him to talk about his family or his life before the Masters captured him. That talk lasted even later into the night, as they returned to the tent and continued inside, dismissing the odor that always trailed the Heis-Tegagan.

Drawings of his family appeared on the walls of Toog's mind-cave as he closed his eyes, settling against the rocks. Pulling his weapon close to his side, he allowed himself to slip into sleep.

A noise made his finger wedge against the trigger of the pulse-gun. His eyes spiraled open, remembering where he was. What had been the clinking of the bolt in his dream had only been the sound of pebbles knocked from rock to rock as the female from Ababeraz approached him.

Toog strained as he sat up, his blue back stiff from lying on the rocks, common whenever an Aull was too long out of the *skarg*. He put the weapon aside.

"They held worry in the hands of the camp," explained Basha at seeing Toog's distress: his eyes glowing pink, nose flaps quivering, blue skin paling. "Now so you make a calm."

Toog shifted his position on the rocks as she lowered her body beside him, a giantess towering over him. He could be a midling, he measured, easily fitting into her arms while taking sustenance at the valves of the mounds on her chest.

"ˢN'f," spoke Toog in casual Sebbou. Seeing she did not seem to understand, he spoke using Ra'aa'al's method, directly mind to mind: "I have no harm." After a moment, Basha dipped her head to indicate her understanding.

"Hard fabric coverings hide not the burning blood nor torn flesh," spoke the Ababerazan female, as Toog's inner Ru wrote the words in Sebbou on the wall of his mind-cave.

"*Aed*," Toog responded, agreeing. You can't hide your hatred and pain even inside a tent.

He gazed across the plateau, thinking how it resembled the high plateau of Ila in his dream. The sky was darkening, the sun setting. A small orange ball, appearing so different from the large bronze star of Sebbol which they called Uf. This weak sun floated on the cold horizon, spraying red and purple light across the distant mountain peaks. He wondered how such a terrible place could have this moment of beauty.

"Come where from you?" Basha asked in a breathy voice.

"From Sebbol," he replied, rearranging her words into passable Sebbou. The wind picked up, tossing his sleeves about his arms. He pointed to the sky. "It would be over there." He waited for her to decipher his words. "If the clouds did not block our view. I very much wish to return there, to be with my family again."

"Lonely you can be," she spoke slowly, thinking of the words.

Toog's skin settled back to blue as he relaxed. "It has been many years that I have been here on the Masters' world. It is difficult to see my family on the walls of my mind-cave now."

He looked out over the plateau again as though he

expected to see them coming toward him: his grown daughter M'ah helping her aged mother, L'ra. His heart tripped.

"Tell me about your world," said Toog, turning his focus to the Ababerazan female, tilting his head up to see her green face with its long nose and large dark eyes, thick lips and yellow teeth.

"Nothing there is telling." Her eyes flashed dark red and let go sorrow-rain which she wiped away with her hand.

"Nothing? That is difficult to believe. We all have stories locked inside. In all the time I have been here, only one creature has been willing to listen to me, and I appreciated the patience. I wish to give the opportunity to you. It is our stories which keep us alive. The urge to continue the story pushes us on."

She ran her pointed tongue back and forth over her lips as she pushed a finger into one nostril, then the other, and shook off onto the rocks what her finger collected.

Seeing her hesitation, Toog thought telling her story might require too much conversion. So he reached up, stretching his blue arm—longer than seemed possible— and pressed his hand against her forehead.

"I was in the forest," she spoke aloud in her language, but also heard by his inner Ru, "away from my home, fleeing my village, and the spouse who would kill my babe and me. The babe was made by another—a warrior, not the home male. It is common for us. So I hid myself in brush to push out the babe and in that moment I saw the Masters. Suddenly they were there—as though they stepped through a doorway. They saw me and grabbed me, before my babe was completely out of my belly. They threw me down on top of my babe. I thought my babe had no chance to live after that. The Masters put a spell over me and brought me here. Then you, Toog, and Grauun, rescued me from them. I thank you for that, though I remain in danger being on this world."

Toog lowered his hand from her forehead as she wiped more liquid from her nostrils. The connection had already been made.

"I am warrior, so I fight." She made a spear-throwing motion. "I have killed twelve Masters. I will kill more."

"You will not return to your home?" asked Toog, continuing in the manner Ra'aa'al had taught him.

Basha's face turned dark. "It is better to stay and fight them."

Toog flashed bronze. "And when you return home, what will you do? Return to your spouse?"

Her lips tightened and her hand went to her chest, pulling the edge of her soiled green gown aside, as though checking that her chest mounds were still there, each the size of Toog's head.

"If I return I will kill him for the trouble he caused. Most males of our kind are small...like you. We keep them like pets and they do simple work. The females are the strong ones, protecting our villages while carrying babes. But my spouse was a coward. Never would fight—we have many enemies. Away to the House of Scrolls each night! He lived in dreams. So I chose a warrior from my phalanx and bent him over a stone and rode him like a *sorrio!*"

Toog's blue skin brightened, his nose flaps relaxing.

"Warriors should be with warriors," Basha continued. "It is the saying of the High One, the Mistress with no Master. If we can fight we should take the field, she tells us. If we fight we will make strong babes. It is necessary, because many nations rise against us. We fight all of them, win against all. The war against a'Hlanfr lasted seventy-seven years but we won. We captured many male breedstock—"

"You are a fighter," Toog spoke, a hot sizzle running through his body as his skin mottled gray and blue. "But not your mate."

Basha grinned, let her long tongue wipe her lips. "Maybe he was taken by the Masters, too, or killed by them. None have seen him among the captured here. The same fate probably fell upon my lover, too. He would not stand guard for me during the birthing. Males can be so slim and soft, like *aloum*!"

The gray overcast parted, the sun below the horizon now, and a few of the brighter stars blinked above as Toog gazed up at them. Where was Uf?

"May I see your hand," asked Basha.

"Why?" he questioned, regarding her.

"I wish to know what you saved me from."

Toog extended his hand toward her as he turned his head away. She took his blue hand in her green hands and caressed it, as though trying to brush away any lingering pain, staying away from the gap between the second and third bones.

Basha approached the hole tenderly. Healed completely, a callused lip remained around the hole. Her fingers probed the hole and Toog turned his face to her, watching her touch him, feeling her gentleness. His belly began to lighten, glowing pink.

"I want this mark," Basha spoke suddenly.

He pulled his hand away. "Why?"

"It is the symbol of hatred for the Masters, of our contempt for their species. I want this mark in my hand to show that I, too, am pledged to their destruction. I want to feel the pain you have felt. I want to know how cruel the Masters are. They killed my babe."

Toog's eyes pinked. "I do not understand this desire you have."

"One reason. I want to know your pain, to be as you are."

His pink eyes bulged. "How am I?"

Basha drew her fingers down over her cheeks. "I find you strong yet gentle, fierce yet compassionate, determined yet just. You are as I wish a spouse of mine to be." Her mouth up-turned. "Except you are small and...so blue. Like a *hap grol*...which we hunt for food. People in my village would caw at me!"

Toog's skin turned darker, his eyes no longer bulging. "I have a full-mate, which is a serious life-long relationship. It comes with permission to create orbs in the *skarg*. And we did."

Basha burst into high-pitched chortles. "Toog, you are lonely. I am lonely. All creatures need comfort. If you were dumb I would care for you as my pet. Yet you are intelligent. Grauun says you are a cunning thing." She looked him over. "I do not know how your kind does the joining. My kind push together like raging *fex*, locked in battle until we have no more strength. If I rode you like a *sorrio* you might be crushed. We can comfort each other somehow. There must be a way. How can beings of different species help each other? What does your kind do?"

Toog was already turning pink as his belly vent quivered.

"There is a thing we touch in a certain way," he spoke. "Yet it is comforting only in a certain season. That season is not now."

He watched her staring at him, her eyes focused on his lap.

"You do not have...*lath*?" She spoke in a soft voice, as though it was a secret. She pointed to the smooth area

230

between his upper legs. Only the line marking his closed vent showed—though it had thickened. "In our older warriors their *lath* sits heavy there. They show it to females who pass them. Some old warriors can barely walk, it is so big. Yet they are best for making the babes."

Toog lowered his hand over his lap, worried his pinkening belly would give away his interest. "Inside. It comes out when the season is right. This world does not have that season."

"A shame of crying," said Basha. "Even without babe-making we can touch, like two sticks that make fire."

Toog flashed bronze, faded to blue. "Now is not a good time for any fire. There is much to do before we can go home."

She breathed hard, nodded, let her torn gown slip down her chest. "Like you, I have lost my mate, and my babe. I need to rage—or my *skulin varra* will not be in balance. If I am to fight I must stay strong. I must rage for a time. It is our way."

Toog pushed her curious fingers away from his pinkening belly as the green mounds on her chest, free of the ripped gown, heaved before his blue face. He did not know if she pushed them out to him or he had leaned toward them. White fluid leaked from the valves.

"I cannot comfort you, Basha. Not only am I too small to endure your rage, but I am also promised to my family. No thoughts can block my vow to return to them."

She sucked in air, expelled a long howl that shook the stars.

Toog worried that she might become violent and attack him, so he sprang up, grabbing the weapon beside him.

She also jumped to her feet, howled again. Clouds were shoved together overhead. The rocks shook under her feet.

She waved her arms like she was throwing stones. She wiped the fluid dripping from her chest mounds all over her body.

"Toog of Sebbol!" she cried out. "First to escape!"

He took a cautious step back, holding the pulse-gun ready. As she calmed and turned to him, her face glowed, her mouth up-turned.

"Maybe someday each of us will find another to bond with," she spoke in a raspy, strained voice. "For now, will you accept me as comrade?"

Toog shaded blue, lowering the gun. "I can do that."

She thrust her hand to the sky. "Then I shall have your mark!"

Toog gazed up into her wild eyes.

"Bolt me!" she shouted.

He pointed off to the camp. "Arkor carries his bolt with him at all times, always to remind him of his hatred. I used mine to cut through the door of my cell. I left it in the neck of a guard. Are you sure you want this?"

She clapped her hands. "Yes! Yes!" then added the Sebbou word "*Aed! Aed!*"—scraped from his mind-cave wall.

"Then we shall do this symbol-making tomorrow morning. Others may decide like you. We will count them."

Toog waved toward the camp, a few fires glowing in the twilight.

"It is late, and tomorrow will be a long day."

Basha grabbed him, lifted him into her arms like a child, pushed out her pointed tongue and licked down the side of his blue face. Pressing her nose against his nose, she exhaled into his vents and he had no choice but to breath in—then out into her nostrils.

"I hope soon...or some day," spoke Basha, holding him

up, "you will not be afraid to rage with your kind or another kind—and, yes, that day will come, my little blue friend."

the balance

▲ ▶ ▲ ▶   10

The morning came early to the camp, with the sun blazing bright in the sky, the cold wind falling silent. With the sunrise came the procession: Toog and Grauun in the lead, followed by Arkor then Bar'Gafu. Others followed in a loose formation, all marching to the pile of rocks at the edge of the plateau where Toog had gone to brood the previous day

Toog had discussed the idea with Grauun during dinner the previous night. Most of the leaders were in agreement, feeling the symbol was important for those who had not spent time in the prison or at a work camp. Having decided on the ceremony, they started early so the rising sun might serve as a witness to their vows. Grauun explained the meaning of a rising sun to vow making. Vows made in darkness can be forgotten.

They halted before two large boulders standing beside a pile of smaller rocks, both worn by the wind and rain and snow. Grauun selected two large stones. Each creature's hand would be placed over the space to allow the bolt to go into the gap between the stones.

"Creatures from across the universe," Grauun spoke loudly in his growling voice. "This we do so we never forget our hatred of the Masters. Let those who have been saved from the Masters' cruelty be marked with the Masters' mark, that they pledge their lives to the destruction of the Masters!"

"So be it," Toog seconded.

The Ababerazan female, Basha, stepped forward first from the ranks and climbed the rock pile to where Grauun waited. She knelt before him as Arkor pulled the bolt from his belt, presented it to Toog. Basha extended her muscular arm, her hand placed over the gap, palm up. Grauun took Arkor's bolt from Toog.

"This we do against the Masters!" Grauun roared, making a huge fist. "To the balance!" He slammed his fist down upon the bolt, driving it through Basha's hand.

She screamed, but only once. "Destroy the Masters!"

"Destroy the Masters!" the others responded, shouting angrily.

Basha stood and faced the crowd below, displaying her hand, the bolt still impaled and blood trickling down her arm.

Grauun took her hand and pulled the bolt loose.

She smiled as she climbed down from the rocks.

Several Xmburrhaltins rushed forward, arguing about the order in which they went to be marked. Finally, deciding the order, they marched up to the stones, one after another, each to pledge their lives to the destruction of the Masters, eager to be marked with the Masters' mark. Soon all had marched up to Grauun and were marked.

Only two of the uprights were not marked. Bar'Gafu, whose twig hands were too small to endure the bolt, was excused. And the Hu-man from Earth, the Timothy

Cromwell being, refused, claiming the injury would impair his ability to fight. No-one was forced to be marked, yet a few who had decided against it the previous night had decided for it when caught up in the fury of the ceremony.

The five-legged Piilactrian trotted nervously below the rocks, whickering. *Pain-pain-pain. Must go home.*

Bar'Gafu pointed a tiny hand down at it. "Heard those have a gland somewhere that the Masters think is cure for disease."

Toog nodded, feeling sad for the five-legged beast.

"Same for the Cetrean," said Bar'Gafu. "The bile is rich."

"What would they use our bodies for?"

Toog lingered by the blood-stained rocks after everyone had returned to the camp. He breathed the crisp air and watched the day pass, feeling the winter season ending. He thought of home as the others prepared for the raid on another Masters village. The planning had been underway before Toog arrived so he chose not to go this time, getting much criticism from Grauun.

"Next time," Toog assured the Xmburrhaltin.

Instead, Toog lounged upon the rocky ridge surrounding the plateau, healing himself from his escape through the mountains. His body ached, his legs were sore, his fingers numb.

Toward midday, he was visited by Bar'Gafu, who brought him a lunch of dried meat strips and plump berries.

"Are you limping?" Toog watched the little brown pod ascend the hillside.

"Not meant to walk long paths."

Bar'Gafu sat beside Toog, regarded the rocks before him.

"These rocks will be red forever."

"And green, blue, white."

Toog nodded, began to eat the lunch.

"Time," Bar'Gafu spoke after a long pause, "is becoming short for me. Already existed for three-hundred-twenty of my world's years before captured, brought here. Must teach you the Process before unable."

"Yes, Bar'Gafu," Toog replied, "we will talk of this soon."

"Not understand. Will not be here soon!" Bar'Gafu shook a clump of slime from a hand. "Am dying. Dying! Yes! Was limping. Leg has no feeling, will not move as should. Soon will be like Zem'Gafu: completely paralyzed, unable to stand. Am not embracing negative energy. Am bowing to truth!"

Toog regarded Bar'Gafu, realizing his seriousness.

"Will be able to walk another five days, then will be twenty days more until death. No amount of nourishment will help."

Toog spoke quietly: "How complex is the Process?"

The brown body wrinkled, eye rising on its stem. "Depend on mental power. If as strong as Ra'aa'al, no difficulty to succeed."

"Ra'aa'al taught me how to speak to other creatures by using my mind, not my mouth. He taught me how to strengthen my mind. Is that enough?"

"Perhaps. Let us determine."

"What do you mean, perhaps? You keep building my hopes high then pulling away the foundation level."

"Need to measure your mental capacity. Only then can know if can work the Process."

"I can do it, Bar'Gafu. I must do it."

"Then will try to teach you the Process. If fail, not to blame. Will be dead."

Bar'Gafu found a stick and drew in the dirt atop the flat stone in front of them. He made two circles side by side that met at one point on their arcs. He sat back, admiring his work.

"Universe has two sides," the Heis-Tegagan started. "You and I, and each of our worlds, are located in this side where stand now." He drew an X in the left circle. "This is the positive side of the universe. Other is the negative side. Must embrace negative energy sometimes. The two sides are similar in form but are different from each other in their arrangement. Meaning your world, Sebbol, is not in the same place on both sides, yet parts of the planet are on both sides."

Toog looked intently at the drawing. "How can it be true?"

"Have known creatures that travel from planet to planet in large machinery, swimming through the ether ocean. But this is always done with these planets located in the same side of the universe."

"In machines?" Toog asked, astonished. "How?"

"The machines duplicate within their boundaries the same environment as their home planet. Travelers live in machines as travel from planet to planet. But these machines do not fly fast enough, so takes great amount of time to traverse ether ocean. And the creatures can grow old if the planets are not close. But need not discuss machines, because there is better way: the Process. Need no machines for the Process. Yes, the Masters use machines, their magic cube, but that is because their minds are not sufficiently strong for the Process. But you and I need no machine."

"How can it work?" Toog leaned down, studying the circles.

"Before explaining the Process, look at these circles drawn. See where they touch? At just this one point? They touch at one point and only one point. This single point is called a tangent—*heis* in my language. The Masters built their machine on top of a tangent they discovered. Marks one particular tangent on this world. Are many tangents on each world. Millions of tangents. Some may be found. The Masters have seven cubes. A powerful mind, however, can force a tangent to appear almost anywhere. The cubes seem only tangents discovered—in our region—all naturally formed."

"Let us use one of the cubes then."

"Occasionally the cloth of space tears in a certain location, forming a natural tangent. In other places, can tear the cloth for ourselves, when and where wish to—"

"I talked with the Ababerazan. She told me when the Masters came to her world, they appeared to step through a doorway in the air."

"Yes, the cube they have is like a doorway. Rather, opens the doorway. Portal. Passage. On one side is their world. Can step through to other world—your world, my world, and do terrible things there. Yet powerful mind can tear the cloth of space anywhere. Can go from *heis*-Tegag to *heis*-Sebbol. No machine. What am trying to teach you. The Masters are weak, thus require a machine to tear the cloth for them."

"You said you knew how to operate the cube. Why not teach me how to operate the cube?"

"Told you will teach you the Process. The Process does not require the cube."

"But is the cube easier?"

"Only first step. Let you go to next world, whichever may be, but may not be your home. Will need to *make* tangents yourself—or be able to identify natural tangents in next world to find tangent to your world. Remember Grauun's map? Many worlds there. Using the Process can go from one planet to next planet—to your planet."

"So I must walk across many worlds to reach my home?"

"Each tangent is a bridge from one world to another world. But each tangent connects to only one other world. May need to travel great distance to find tangent which will connect to next world. Tangents are difficult to find. In ancient era Tegagans would trip over them, so many around, find ourselves in other worlds and confused how to return. Then learned how to find, how to return. Studied how to use. Then happened to open wrong tangent and found the Masters coming to save us. Thought they were our saviors, each of them ready to exit, but they were not. Apologize for letting the Masters off their world, for not stopping them. Look at us. How could we stop them?"

Toog bronzed. "How can I find a single tiny point on an entire world?"

"Not one tangent, but many—many. Every point on a planet is a tangent to another planet, or to other point on same planet. Any tangent will do to start a journey. After, your mind must guide."

"But that could take years! I don't have much time."

"*Time?* Are burning time right now, Toog. If stay here, have no time at all. Better to die by trying than just to die? That is what you said before."

"I did say." He rubbed a furrow into his blue face, nose flaps quivering. Suddenly he stood. "This is impossible!"

"Have not changed," said Bar'Gafu, brown slime oozing out of both ends. "You have. Am using the view used to seeing so can understand. Perhaps, now near death, find less easy to accept. More than three-hundred years have existed, always being of service. Was teacher, then Heis'aq'i priest, on my world before the Masters came. By helping you, my life will have one final purpose. Serve you because the Masters could not find use for my kind."

Toog sighed, kicking dirt over Bar'Gafu's drawing.

"Why angry?" Bar'Gafu asked. "Can learn the Process."

Toog's face bronzed, returned to blue. "Then continue."

"Understand shape of universe now?"

Toog nodded, sitting again on the rocks beside Bar'Gafu.

"Understand form of tangents?"

"Yes." Toog sighed impatiently.

"Then can teach you the Process—as taught by three parents nearly...how long is? Three-hundred years, when only a crumb of waste. Was taught the Process as soon as could make stench. Was long ago, but sure can teach you. Are your mental powers as strong as you say? As strong as Ra'aa'al?"

"Nearly so." Toog smiled, nodding.

"The Process is what you do with your mind to tear space apart and project body through tangent opening. Do with power of mind, which can be greatest force in the universe. Bio-chemical, electro-chemical energies created in the brain of an advanced creature, applied to engineering problems, can move mountains—sometimes planets. Or, as you say on your world, to 'raise the stars'."

Toog's face flashed bronze. "$^sT'_n\ Ra'_q$."

"You remember expression from childhood? Took from your mind, from memories of childhood training, so can understand. Is true. This power, when focused on right spot and increased to right magnitude can rip curtain between two sides of universe. At such a moment, while rending this curtain, step through to other world."

"Like so many magical beings suddenly appearing and then disappearing in our ancient tales—"

"Rules to follow which will assist in working the Process.

Will teach. The remainder—mental energy—will have to build. First rule will help find first tangent. Forget the Master's cube. Now close eyes, Toog, and think of a place— a place you have seen directly. Easier that way. Form picture in mind. Do not allow that Ru shadow to draw for you. Make own picture, with much, much detail. Concentrate. Conjure scene from memory. Bring into focus. See every detail."

"I can only think of home," Toog revealed as squeaks.

"See picture?"

"Not clearly, not accurately. It has been too long. I cannot recall it clearly. Only feelings—moods—ideas."

"Try, Toog, try. Feeling is brush on canvas. Draw now. Must picture something. A dwelling, your dwelling. Your chamber in that dwelling. Your sleep-mat in your chamber. Think!"

Clouds swirled within Toog's mind, flowing through seven colors, billowing and darkening, forming edges, hardening into substance, the colors becoming real.

"I have something. It is my repose place."

"Good. See it clearly?"

As he watched, the scene firmed, became fixed, images crystalizing, forming hard edges—as though he could reach out and touch it and it would be solid.

"Wait...yes." He sucked in air. "Yes, I can."

"Are details clear?"

"Becoming...." Toog pressed his hands to his face. His inner Ru was scribbling as fast as it could on his mind-cave's walls.

"How does it look? Describe."

"It is very dark. There is a patch of light that keeps fading in and out. That is the look-vent. I am on the repose-mat, next to my full-mate, L'ra. It is double-warm. I am covered in skin-rain. I have thirst. I cannot repose." He squealed. "Oh! I remember: the night they came for me."

A long steam hissed over the rocks.

"Return," Bar'Gafu whispered. "Not ready."

Toog's eyes spiraled open, blinked away eye-rain, breathing deeply as though he had run a long distance. "Not ready?"

The Heis-Tegagan's eye flexed on its stem. "Allowed your Ru buddy to draw. Must do yourself. Send away the magical imp."

"I tried, but my inner Ru insisted on drawing."

"Must shut away the Ru. Not helpful. A support being, yes, understand. Yet not helpful in working the Process."

"I will send it away." Toog frowned. "My inner Ru is angry, but will agree to take a nap."

Bar'Gafu's eye gave a nod. "Must keep emotion away from the Process. Otherwise, will deceive. Such deception can lead on wrong path, a path that can end in death. Must be sure of correct path."

Toog sucked in air. "I can do it, Bar'Gafu."

"Try again." Bar'Gafu waved a tiny hand. "This attempt, will try something closer. Need to see a place in magnificent detail, as though actually there. Then, while in focus, tighten mind's electro-chemical energy to a point directly before you—as if wishing to send beam of energy straight to that point—yes, as if want to destroy. Then increase magnitude of that energy. Focus power into a tighter beam. Understand?"

He nodded, eyes closed, blue face bronzing.

"That rock over there." Bar'Gafu raised a twig arm, directing Toog's gaze to a gray outcrop a short distance away. "The one that rises above the others. Saw it before closed eyes? Try to see as something other than what really is. Concentrate on the new image. Think of its shape, its size, its texture. Detail, Toog, think in detail. Have it?"

Toog's mind reformed the image, conjuring a shape, molding it into other shapes, squeezing the mass, making new structure, adding strength, making it real.

"Yes," he replied, eyes tightly closed.

"Continue to concentrate on it. Keep locked in center of your mind—and no inner Ru! Center it until your mind grows numb or until becomes whatever object you think it is. The object you want it to be. Concentrate. Maintain the rock or whatever it has become in your mind, then push everything else away. When what is left is real, slowly open eyes, but do not let your concentration wane. Must be able to do this with eyes open—so don't trip over small stones as traveling."

Toog's face was placid, bronze, his concentration tight.

"It does look real, Bar'Gafu. It does."

Bar'Gafu's bottom opening sputtered. "Must be able to see in mind and see with eyes same moment."

"I am ready." Toog's face had returned to blue.

Bar'Gafu let out steam from the lower vent. "Open eyes."

Toog loosened the seal of his eyes, made them spiral open. He glimpsed a red *drouk* standing behind a white fence with green hills behind, lines of *lathu* dividing the fields. Then the *drouk* disappeared almost as soon as he saw it. He stared at the rock outcrop which he thought was the *drouk*'s head. So close. He recognized the green hills as the rocky slope of the plateau's ridges.

"Have succeeded," said Bar'Gafu. "For one moment."

Toog continued to stare at the rock outcrop. "I saw the rock over there as the head of a *drouk*. A red *drouk*—symbol of good fortune. Behind the beast, the rocks turned to grassy hills. There was a white fence...."

Bar'Gafu scoffed. "Symbol of your doubts."

"Is this the Process?"

Bar'Gafu's eye nodded. "Part."

"But it seems so easy now." He let out a string of squeaks. "I just think of home and I am suddenly there."

"Not so simple." Bar'Gafu grimaced, gas spilling out of both top and bottom openings. "Do not take lightly. Even what just did will cause great fatigue, particularly since beginner."

Toog stretched his arms, shook his hands. He tensed his back, relaxed. "I feel fine."

"Will catch you. Believe what say."

Toog pondered the rock again. "My concentration broke. That is why it faded just as I opened my eyes."

Bar'Gafu's eye blinked. "Correct."

"How do the Masters do this, then?"

"In their cube. Controls which operate machines assist them in focusing energy to split the curtain. Their tangent is natural, so always open. What did now was create own tangent. The Masters' cube opens and holds open the curtain for them to pass through—because their minds are not strong enough to do."

"Then my comrades will have to use the cube."

"Likely difficult, considering the Masters control it."

"How can our comrades ever operate the cube machine? So many different beings. How can they operate the controls? Can we ever manipulate the machine and make it work for us?"

"Yes. Very simple. Most difficult part of using cube is getting the Masters to let use it. After Masters enter, they stand within the cube, one at a time, pressing controls in the following order: the red button, then the green, then blue, then white, then the same red button again. Next press the keys that correspond to the numbers assigned to the being using the cube, and keys for identification. Select destination same way. Then pull down, towards you, the big lever to the right of the control panel, then press the large black square on the left side of the panel, then push down the smaller lever in the middle. That begins the process for them. Feel surge of energy flow through the cube, generated by the machine. Fills room and increases—bodies shake, energy rattles—until wall in front appears thin and can see through it, then disappears and see other world. Step forward and be there."

Toog's face furrowed. "How do you know this, Bar'Gafu?"

"Read minds of the Masters. Forget how long here. Can learn much in such period of time."

Toog stood, stretching his blue arms skyward. He noticed the webbing between his fingers had shrunk to nothing. A bad sign.

"One more question, Bar'Gafu: What *is* the next world, the first one on the other side of the cube's doorway?"

"Depend which cube use." The eye rose on its stem. "The cube we arrived in is called...let me think.... Yes, think we have creature from there. What was that species? The Timothy Cromwell being. That one. So alike the Masters. Yet its world is called E-ar-th'. Need to consult Grauun's map to be certain. The Masters drew a map to find way around the negative side of the universe."

"So the Masters cross this world called E-ar-th' on their way to our worlds?"

"Correct."

Toog rubbed his blue cheek, nose flaps quivering. "And when we are there, then what happens? Each of them will wish to go a separate way after stepping on that E-ar-th' world. Do I have to show each of them the way to go on to find their own tangent?"

Bar'Gafu sighed, standing, wobbling on stick legs, one bent.

"Would seem. Told you would take a long time."

"Yes, I know." Toog bowed his blue head. "Thank you. Will we have another lesson tomorrow?"

"There are many lessons yet," said Bar'Gafu, body squirming.

As the Heis-Tegagan expelled an awful black fluid from both upper and lower openings, Toog gazed at the horizon across the plateau, beyond the camp, saw purple clouds framing the orange globe of the sun as it sank into evening.

"It is late," Toog said, stretching. "Day is short, night long. We should return to the camp. The raiding party has returned by now. Time for dinner."

Bar'Gafu nodded. "Much to exit."

Toog turned, smiled dryly, closing his nose flaps against the fresh odor.

"I simply concentrate on a place I know," he squeaked, "focus my mental energy on a point in front of me until I split the cloth of the universe, then step through to the other side. Is that it?"

"Yes, have order of operations correct. Now must come much practice."

Toog stood stock still, head tilted back slightly, eyes closed. He recalled the tent they had given him, the mat on the ground, and he counted the threads, the tear in the corner, the lump of dirt beneath where his hip rested, the way the battery lamp shone from its place hanging on the center post, the swaying shadows that crept across the ground inside the tent—and he stepped forward. His blue foot felt a hot sizzle. He looked down and could not see his toes. Alarmed, he drew his foot back and saw his toes again.

"Will see again at camp," Bar'Gafu hissed. "Old way, step by step go." The Heis-Tegagan gazed up at Toog, its eye stem fully extended. "Almost did."

"I saw the inside of my tent." Toog closed his eyes again.

"Try again," said Bar'Gafu. "Not so far."

Toog swam sideways, caught in a rip-current, yellow water-vines tangled around his sleek silver body; then he was tripping over his blue feet and tumbling to the ground, his shoulder bumping the pole in the center of the tent, knocking it askew. It drew the ceiling of the tent down. He righted himself and got up on his leg joints, gazing about the abode they had assigned to him and Bar'Gafu.

"Toog!" Arkor called immediately as Toog stepped from the tent, the resized greatcoat dragging behind. "We have a surprise for you—something we got on the way back from Batagai."

"What is it?" Toog asked, confused at how he had arrived in his tent. He stretched his blue arms straight up over his head, feeling the haze-fatigue of tangent-tearing. *It worked.*

"Come with me," Arkor replied, nodding his big head.

They moved between tents as the thrill of a successful raid was evident throughout the camp, monsters happy and boastful. Passing through the camp, Toog caught a glimpse of the green Ababerazan female rolling around in a tent with a Xmburrhaltin. Basha appeared pleased with her partner.

To the center of the camp went Toog and Arkor, following the screams of captives. Three of the Masters had been stripped of their uniforms and laid out on iron rods, the arms and legs already separated from their bodies by the team of Mogadans preparing them for grilling.

They arrived at Grauun's tent and Arkor held open the flaps for Toog to enter.

Toog's eyes bulged. There before him was Grauun and two Xmburrhaltins holding up the legless torso of a Master by its shoulders. It seemed still alive, eyes white with fear, red blood dripping from its lower end. They had tried to seal the wound with fire but were not completely successful. Its arms were tied behind its body.

Grauun turned at Toog's arrival. The Xmburrhaltins set the Master on the ground, leaning against a supply box.

"We are sorry we could not bring you a whole one. We had to burn off this one's legs to keep it from running away."

"Why did you bring it here?" Toog eyes pinked, regarding the scene. His inner Ru crawled out of a dark passage, weeping and kicking the wall of his mind-cave.

"You give questions, it gives answers." Grauun laughed. "They always ask us questions. Let them answer our questions now. Do that hand-to-head thing you do."

Toog bent back his arms, let the coat slip off, returned his arms forward, as he regarded the wounded Master. Arkor grabbed the coat off the ground. It always felt better to be without the heavy garment, ready to swim the *skarg*—

"But can it speak?" asked Toog. "It appears lost in fear."

"Who wouldn't be afraid after what we did at Batagai?"

"What did you do?" Toog asked, cautiously.

"We stormed the place, took them completely by surprise. We killed probably fifty of them, burned them with our pulse-guns, tortured a few of them that we missed the first time. We told them who we were, who was doing this to them. Then we chased after a few trying to flee. We shot the legs right out from under this one. I believe a couple of them escaped, but it's a long way to another village."

"Extra difficult with no legs," the Xmburrhaltin called Nogum laughed.

"This one appeared to be in charge," Arkor added. "It shouted commands to the others."

"It killed one of our gang. The Vuuth," said Grauun. "And wounded two of ours, one Xmburrhaltin and the Drell. The Piilactrian, although probably intelligent, was useless. Just kept watch."

Toog regarded the half-Master: a legless body with head.

Despite his hatred of them, Toog could feel pity for this creature who was losing red fluid from its body. He saw in the Master's eyes the same fear, pain, and agony he had felt many times since his arrival on their world. He was surprised to pity this creature.

"Ask your questions," Grauun growled.

Toog drove away feelings of compassion and regarded the Masters as Grauun did: a vile enemy that lay helpless now in their camp. The end of the stream, the depths awaiting. It could smell the marsh behind the mountains.

Toog's face flashed bronze. "I want to talk with it alone."

"Why?" Grauun exclaimed. "What could it say that would hurt me? What might it say that could benefit you but not me?"

"It is not either choice," Toog lied. "I want to torture it myself for a while. I never had the opportunity to torture a Master. I owe this ambassador of theirs a lot of anguish."

Grauun howled, joined by his Xmburrhaltin comrades.

"Ah! Yes, Toog!" Grauun growled, his toothy grin frightening the captive. "You sound more like me every day.

Now if you could grow fur." He turned to his hairy comrades. "Come. We will return shortly."

Grauun motioned the others out of the tent. Nogum was the last to exit, pausing to lean down and growl at the captive.

The Master was at the edge of desperation, Toog saw. To be captured by monsters! To be cut in half and clearly on the path to death! What a state to be in! And now this little blue freak coming to stare at him!

Toog glared at the Master, its half-body wriggling on stumps where its legs had been. Toog had never seen one of them so close, so baldly set before him, without needing to fight hard for his life. This Master had a plain face, dull pink but more red on its cheeks, small dark eyes above a large nose, curved lines of hair above its eyes, flat forehead above. Its wide mouth twisted through the waves of pain, teeth gnashing, and the front of its jaw seeming to point accusingly at him. Only once did their eyes meet—and Toog felt a stab of agony and fear cut deep into him, as though he saw his own reflection in the Master's eyes.

"You have pain," Toog spoke in Sebbou, expecting that the Master's mind-cave would echo the meaning of his words. "And agony. I see that. You know I can see that. Because you know I have felt it, too. I have experienced this pain that you now feel."

The Master seemed not to understand, remained too agitated to communicate.

Toog stood before the Master, blue head even with the top of the Master's head, its half-body on the ground. Its face showed teeth, tightly clenched, eyes red with hate.

"*Ty u nikh glavny?*" the Master barked out, putting on a brave face. It twisted its haggard lips, clearly trying to communicate in its terror. Failing, it expelled some fluid from its mouth which fell upon Toog's bare foot. "*Kakaya malenkaya urodlivaya marionetka! Detskaya igrushka.*"

Instantly Toog's blue arm shot out, stretching a little beyond its limit, the heel of his hand smacking the Master's forehead. His hand stayed there as his fingers stretched up and over and around its hairless head, fingertips flattening into suction disks, pressing. The Master became alarmed but was powerless to resist.

Toog's eyes bulged as he leaned forward, nose flaps waving as he took in air. His face bronzed.

His inner Ru had written words on the walls of his mind-cave. Toog read them with displeasure: 'You are their leader? What a small ugly puppet. A child's pet,' the Master had spoken.

The Master showed alarm, hearing its own words spoken back to it, realizing the little blue monster understood its insult.

Why do you do this? Toog asked, the echo whirling around his mind-cave. *Why do you hunt other species? Why do you need slaves? Do you not have enough of your own kind for work? I cannot understand. Tell me.*

The half-Master tightened its face, a spasm of pain overtaking its attention. "*Khuy tebe!*" It screwed its face into a mask of hate. "*Ya skoro umru. M'nene nuzho otvechat.*"

The little blue being understood, hand against the Master's forehead, seeing the words of Sebbou written on the walls of his mind-cave. The suggestion that he go and mate with himself made no sense. The acceptance of impending death did. His inner Ru waved its hands furiously in warning. Yet, instead of displaying anger and hate, Toog gazed into the red eyes of the Master until its resolve softened.

Please tell me the reasons, Toog communicated.

As if overcome by a magic potion, the Master sank against the box, its body limp, eyes rolling up, vile breath fluttering out of its mouth. It tried to speak but had no more will, ready to die.

Speak freely, Toog invited. *I want to understand.*

A series of deep breaths, face showing anguish. "Our species, as you say, is superior to all others, so it's our purpose to subdue and conquer them. That's what we are taught from day one."

Toog's inner Ru reached down, grabbed some stones from the dirty floor of his mind-cave, banged them together, starting up a rhythm that shook him.

Do you feel superior now? Toog pressed his hand harder against the Master's forehead.

The Master shrieked—

Arkor rushed into the tent. Toog was torturing the half-Master to good effect, the toothy creature recognized, incisors clacking. The blue being had a hand on the Master's forehead, obviously sending streams of fire through its mind. Arkor stood in awe.

The half-Master was shaking as its body was shutting down. "As a wounded thing, no, I'm not superior now. But as a species, we are supreme. It's our destiny to make other species work for us, to be our slaves, and die for us. Including all the little blue monsters. Like you."

Toog kept the pressure of his hand on the Master's forehead, fingers pressing in from the sides. *Is it your mission to tear us from our families? Is it your purpose to lock us away in prison cells and use us whenever you choose? Is it your right to destroy us when we have done no harm to you?*

His inner Ru was shouting, scraping fingernails raw against the stone.

How can you believe it is your purpose to take me from my full-mate and springling? Have you no code of right and wrong?

The Master glared at Toog. The death-clench overtook its body, rattling its throat. It spilled red fluid out its mouth and its heart and lungs collapsed, releasing a final breath.

"No," was the last word spoken—scooped out of the air by his inner Ru's crinkly talons. The word was thrown to the floor of his mind-cave and heavy stones were set on it.

The Master was doomed when Toog first saw it. He did not kill it. Yet he felt his blue body turning bronze, muscles sizzling with cold fire. His eyes bulged until they hurt. Now it was done. It was good to recall how hate felt. Life had been too easy the past few days and his hatred had slackened, but it was back now in full fury.

He stormed from the tent, found Grauun approaching.

"Are you finished, Toog?"

"I will not be finished until I see my family again." He rushed to his tent, full of hate yet unable to let it go, unable to calm himself so he could rest.

Arkor followed, parting the tent flap cautiously.

"Are you ill?" asked the tooth-faced comrade.

"No, just hate-filled," Toog replied, blue head in blue hands, eyes returned to normal. "It burns."

"What did the Master say to you?" asked Arkor.

"Not much information." Toog did not look at Arkor. "He told his beliefs. What the Masters believe. We know that already."

"Yes, I've heard their speech before," Arkor replied, shifting on his flat feet, flopping his half-tail. "It's a religion for them."

"I cannot understand their idea." Toog's nose vents fluttered. He rubbed a vertical furrow in his face. "How can any creature believe it has the right to rule over any other kind? How can it be possible?"

Arkor squatted on his big haunches. "Listen to a tale from my youth. As hForro-Nu of Vbam near the Mkel-Po, a great verse writer, tells: On my world long ago there were two tribes. They were different. One had short tails and long ears, ate plants and hopped, while the other had long tails and short ears, ate meat and ran. There were only two sources of food for the second tribe: the long-eared creatures or their fellow meat-eaters. So the meat-eaters captured and bred the long-eared creatures for food, even though the long-eared creatures had never harmed them."

"You are one of the meat-eating creatures." Toog looked up suddenly. "I see you eating the meat of the Masters that have been captured and killed."

"Yes, but we must survive. You have eaten the flesh of these beings that once captured us."

"My teeth have grown sharp. My belly churns with poison."

"You have the ability to adapt to your environment," said Arkor. "Your gods must like you."

"First Goddess watches over me." Toog regarded Arkor. "I must return home and make a praise-gift for the temple."

"You have temples!" Arkor let his teeth chatter. "Our kind is like the Masters, the dominant species on our world, yet they conquered us. Now the long-eared, hopping kind thrives on my world. They have no enemy now."

"But you had to conquer them for food."

"To enslave is to enslave, whatever the reason, no matter how straight the reason might be. It is the same."

"You had to eat to live. Not all reasons stand tall."

"Maybe we could have learned to eat plants. There is always another way. We just have to look for it."

"Now you sound like Bar'Gafu." Toog's face bronzed. "Where is Bar'Gafu?" He stared at the Heis-Tegagan's dirty sleeping spot.

Arkor clacked his teeth. "Didn't he take lunch to you?"

"Yes, he did. I was at the bolt ceremony place," Toog replied, his blue hand rising to the top of his round head. "We discussed the trip home. How to—"

"But he has not returned."

"Not returned?" Toog's flashed bronze, standing. "I left him some time ago, on the side of the plateau. I left without him."

Arkor frowned. "He was ailing when he left camp. Perhaps we should look for him."

"I will return to the edge of the plateau. I should not have left him. He said his legs were becoming too stiff to walk."

"I will go with you, Toog."

Outside the tent, they saw Nogum dragging the corpse of the half-Master toward the center of the camp, where the Mogadans were grilling.

"I will not eat that one," said Toog.

As they were about to exit the camp, the Hu-man from Earth appeared, acting wary, clothing wet from body fluids.

"Ah! M'lord Toog!" cried the Timothy Cromwell. "Out for a stroll, I see. Indeed, a good time to stretch my legs." He glanced back toward the center of the camp, then lowered his voice: "I never like getting in the way when they prepare those fellows for dinner. I dare say, I'm very much like them. I wouldn't wish those Mogadans to mistake me for one of the Masters. When they started passing around the eyeballs, I simply had to leave."

"Then come with us," said Toog.

The rocks were difficult to see in the growing darkness. Clouds subdued the fading amber sun, but the trio eventually got to the place where Toog had spent the day with Bar'Gafu. The large gray moon of the Masters' world lazed above them.

The trio carefully crept up the rocky slope, part of the rim that encircled the plateau, past the ceremonial boulders where members of their gang had been marked. They got to the flat stone where Bar'Gafu had drawn the two adjoining circles.

Toog stretched out his head, turning in every direction. A brown pod among the brown rocks would not be easy to see.

"Bar'Gafu!" he called.

They paused to listen for a hiss of gas, wriggled their noses for a whiff of odor. The breeze seemed clear.

"I do not see the little thing," said Arkor, glancing around.

"I catch a vile scent," the Hu-man offered. "Over there."

Toog climbed onto the next higher rock in the pile, stopped.

"Look!" he erupted, pointing down between the rocks.

Arkor hefted himself onto the higher rock and glanced where Toog pointed.

There was a gap between the rocks, enough that someone could stand there as though riding in a machine-wagon.

"Is it?" asked Arkor.

"Bar'Gafu...," Toog squeaked.

Between the drifting clouds, the pale moon showed the space where the remains of Bar'Gafu oozed in its own puddle. A lone eye on a short stem, a few tufts of wiry hair, and cartilage lay in the dark pool.

Toog turned away quickly, fighting the up-spew.

"What an awful stench!" cried Timothy Cromwell, putting his hand to his nose, standing below them.

"Bar'Gafu had perhaps twenty days left," said Toog. "That is what he told me. A life of three-hundred sun-cycles, the last of them in a prison cell."

"But you freed the thing," said Arkor, "so it died free."

They stared at the mess.

"This was not just him getting old," Toog muttered.

"I saw one of these Heis-Tegagans before," Arkor said. "At an execution. It looked just like this...after being shot by one of the Master's weapons. The pulse-gun heats them, makes them burst like a seed pod."

"Are you saying that Bar'Gafu was shot by the Masters?"

Arkor's incisors gleamed in the moonlight. "Yes."

They ducked down among the rocks.

"Of course!" Toog regarded Arkor. "The captured Masters, the ones that escaped. Maybe they followed you to the camp."

"They've likely been watching us," said Timothy Cromwell. "They don't wish to miss us again. Good on them."

"I will alert the camp," said Arkor, getting up.

"Be quiet," said Toog. "We do not want them to know that we know they are close. Keep the camp quiet. I will return soon. I want to look around more. Any sign the Masters were here."

"I shall go, as well," said Timothy Cromwell. "Probably I can run faster than our large beaver friend."

Arkor stumbled down the hillside and started waddling as quickly as he could across the plain. Timothy Cromwell was already in full sprint and quickly left Arkor behind.

Toog began to climb up the hillside, grabbing onto the rocks to keep his balance. He glanced at the long horizon at the edge of the plateau. He thought he saw movement, but he could not be sure. He continued to navigate the boulder-strewn slope until he could peer over the ridge into the adjoining valley.

Laying with his belly to the dirt and head raised just enough to allow his eyes to see over the top, Toog spotted the formation of machine-wagons below. He counted the Masters: perhaps a hundred. A bunch congregated around a large weapon he had never seen before. It resembled their pulse-guns but was much larger. Its main cylinder narrowed to a point at the firing end but had a round bubble shape at the opposite end. Mounted on a cart, its length was more than a Xmburrhaltin's height.

Toog wanted to get a better look. He crept across the rocks on his fingers and toes like a *lurg*. As he lifted his head again, he came face to face with a young Master, head wrapped in a tight brown covering with some kind of optics device hanging in front of its eyes. It seemed to be watching the camp from the opposite side of the rocky ridge.

The optics was suddenly filled with Toog's blue face.

Only a brief moment their eyes meet—long enough for Toog to realize he forgot to bring a weapon.

Immediately, the young Master, surprised to find a bug-eyed blue face staring at him from such close distance, flipped up the optics device for a better look. In the same instant, Toog's blue arms shot out, one grasping the Master's throat, clenching it between his long fingers and knocking the optics device away. His other hand clasped the pulse-gun hanging from the Master's shoulder by a canvas strap and tried pulling it free as the Master frantically gripped the barrel.

The Master lurched forward to desperately claim the weapon as Toog pulled it away, falling backward off the rock. The hand battle tilted them further and they tumbled down over the rocks with the Master on its back reaching up, Toog on top reaching down.

As he squeezed the Master's throat with one hand, Toog felt a burning sensation in his hand sweep over the Master's throat, causing the young Master to writhe in pain and cry out. It tried to jerk away, letting go its tight grip on the weapon. When the Master's hand went to his throat, checking for injury, the two fighters spilled further down, landing hard on the lower rocks.

In the struggle, the Master's finger, stuck in the trigger guard, ripped the trigger backward. An orange blast shot past Toog's shoulder. The light streaked up above the plateau.

Crashing down the embankment, the entangled wrestlers hit boulders and scraped against patches of gravel and sharp slivers of stone.

Toog heard the Masters below shouting, remarking on the shot that was fired, giving away their position.

He released his hand from the Master's throat, saw it reach for the knife on its belt. With no time to block an attack, Toog's hand stiffened, his longer second finger's joints locked, claw at the tip sharp. Despite shaking with some kind of electric burst, the Master guessed this monster was going to grab the knife and so it rolled onto its side, pinning the knife against the ground.

Toog released his other hand from the pulse-gun to push the Master away. Seizing the opportunity, the Master raised the gun and struck Toog hard across the back of his neck with the gun's support frame. The angle was not the best so the blow did not strike fully, but Toog felt the support frame break against his neck, newly firmed as though he wore scales.

The young Master wrenched itself away, struggled to its feet to continue striking Toog with the gun's broken arm support, in doing so pulling him up, leaving him hanging from the Master's arm.

The Master swung the gun down against Toog's body, raining blow after blow—until Toog plunged his stiffened hand, clawed second finger leading the attack, deep into the Master's belly. He shoved his hand straight through until the claw forced its way out the Master's back.

The Master let out a wrath-call of the universe as it dropped the weapon and collapsed, releasing Toog.

Several Masters were scrambling up the slope, mounting its crest and starting down Toog's side. One slipped into the gaps between the rocks and screamed. Others slowed to help their comrade.

Toog pulled his arm from the Master's body. His arm dripped with blood. Pieces of shredded organs were caught on the three spines that rose on the back of Toog's hand as he withdrew it. He grabbed the pulse-gun that had fallen on the rocks at his feet, held it up.

The Masters bounded over the uneven rocks.

Juggling the pulse-gun, Toog pulled the limp Master's body to its feet as best he could and let it fall downward over the rocks onto the ascending Masters.

Toog followed that diversion with several blasts from the pulse-gun before he sprang down his side of the slope like an *api*, landing flat-footed on the soft plain. He ran on his rubbery blue legs. He tripped over stones and slipped on loose gravel, but caught his balance without falling, and soon reached the camp.

"We must leave immediately!" Toog shouted, entering the camp, but saw they had already been warned. Everyone was packing to leave or else busy preparing to defend the camp. The Xmburrhaltins had positioned six rail-guns aimed at the distant ridge, two barrels of bolts between the stations.

"The creatures that are going with you, they have already left," Grauun shouted through the bustle. "They go to the east ridge—should be there soon. Arkor is still here."

They heard a sharp grunt.

"Toog, you must lie down," Arkor insisted, coming to them.

Toog checked himself. "I cannot. There is no time."

"But your neck and shoulders are dark, and you are covered in blood, like you were beaten! What happened after I left?"

"I had a fight with one of the Masters. Watching us from the ridge. They are camped on the other side, a hundred of them. And they have some kind of large weapon. I think they plan to use it on this camp."

"What weapon?" Arkor asked, directing traffic.

"It is like a giant pulse-gun," Toog responded.

"Time is short!" Grauun growled.

"Yes!" Arkor roared, rushing away.

"Grauun." Toog turned to him. "This is it: we part again."

"Yes," Grauun grumbled, and took a heavy step toward Toog, paused, then embraced him with his big furry arms. "I will miss you. You have been a good comrade to me—like a brother. A little blue brother."

"Grauun, you helped me survive," Toog cried, parting from him. "You have given me hope, and...and I can never forget that."

"I will continue to destroy Masters. If there are any left

when you return, I will let you kill them."

"It will be a long journey," Toog spoke. "It will be many years before we see each other again, if indeed we do."

"Watch the *kjo* on your tail," Grauun growled. "The pesky beasts are always hungry."

"And you, too!" Toog found eye-rain running down his face. His eyes felt hot. "When I return—and I will return, Grauun—you and I will go Master-hunting. I promise!"

Grauun raised his furry hand in salute. Toog waved goodbye and turned to go gather his few possessions.

In his tent, Toog threw basic survival items into a knapsack. He gathered his pulse-gun, an extra battery pack, and a knife, and left the tent.

Passing among the tents, Toog glanced off to the ridge where he had fought the Master. A group of them were there now, not hiding at all. They had managed to mount the ridge with their long, pointed weapon, struggling to keep it steady on the uneven ground. Showing unusual patience, the Masters aligned the big weapon on the camp, lowering the tapered front end, as though focusing it directly on Toog.

"Arkor, where are you?" he cried out, searching the camp.

"I saw him last in Grauun's tent," Timothy Cromwell spoke up from the frantic crowd.

Toog turned to Grauun's tent.

"M'lord," the Hu-man called, running after him. "I've changed my mind. I want to go with you!"

"Then join me," Toog responded in a rush, looking around.

"I couldn't tell him." He pointed to Grauun's tent. "But I can tell you: I don't think he shall survive. I've a bad feeling and I don't wish to perish with him. Surely, you must understand."

"We have no time to talk. If you are joining me, hurry away now. Go to the east ridge—where the others went."

"Thank you, Toog. Thank you."

Toog watched the Hu-man run away.

At Grauun's tent, he tore open the tent flap.

"Are you leaving yet?" Toog demanded.

"I'm gathering the maps. We need them," Arkor explained.

"Be sure you take the one showing the tangents. It is the most important one."

Arkor finished stuffing the rolled maps into a pack.

"Ready!"

They hurried out of the tent, running through the camp, shouting farewells.

They ran across the plain toward the east ridge. Glances to the south showed them the Masters preparing their weapon. The long tapered cylinder was glowing red.

Toog and Arkor scurried up the rock-strewn slope—

An ear-splitting hiss erupted from the weapon followed by a mighty roar which deafened the entire plateau. A blast of red light had shot down from the ridge and engulfed the camp like a cloud. A great explosion following the blast.

Toog and Arkor were thrown against the ground and held there until the air pressure dissipated.

Toog struggled to sit up, a dull ache across his shoulders and a sharp pain in his neck. He gazed across the plateau where the camp was in his memory and saw only a gaping crater.

Arkor moaned, weakly brushing fallen rubble off himself. His front teeth had been broken by the blast and falling debris. One eye tried to look at the twisting red cloud rising up from the plateau. His other eye was smashed.

"Toog...," he called.

Rolling onto his sore leg joints, Toog crawled to Arkor, seeing his wounds. "I am here."

"Toog," he moaned, then could not speak. *Tell my kin I tried to clear the stream. Tell them to keep the dam secure and that I...I will meet them...downstream....*

Toog watched Arkor expire—a long, gurgling breath— then stared at the wide crater that used to be the camp, feeling heat from the rising cloud burning his skin. He knew that Grauun and the other Xmburrhaltins, Basha, the Dikondrans, Mogadans, and others there had been turned into vapor.

His inner Ru collapsed on the floor of his mind-cave, wailing.

The black coffee was hot in the camo mug, held in gloved hands, about to be lifted and sipped—as the commander's deep voice crackled through the control room's wall speaker, startling the staff: *"Yest' problema v trudovom lagere nomer tri Verkhoyansk."*

The man in the khaki uniform with the short beard, graying at the corners, sipped the hot coffee anyway. Sitting at the desk below the speaker, he glanced up as though he was surprised to hear any sounds come from it. Taking another sip, he sat down the mug and spun around in his chair, instructed his staff of four to run through the standard protocol to check that all their instruments were in proper working order and presenting data.

More trouble at Verkhoyansk work camp number three, muttered Master-Sergeant Andrei Ilych Yakovlev, People's Army of the Soviet Federation of Eurasia, Seventh Division, Second Security Brigade. He reached for and spoke into the communication device on the desk, responding to Senior-Lieutenant Lozhkin's alarmed report.

Yes, there was a disturbance at the work camp, Lozhkin

confirmed. Some prisoners had fought with guards, a few tried to escape. In the end, all were caught or killed. Such incidents, although regrettable, did happen from time to time, making necessary a review of the protocols. Again.

Behind Yakovlev, his staff tried to repress their groans.

This time one prisoner was returned to the prison rather than to the work camp or executed outright. That went against protocol as stated in Rules Manual ver. 5, sec. 7.2c. The prison commander was called to Headquarters for questioning. During that absence, the prisoner that had led the rebellion at the work camp managed to escape. Somehow. Again, protocols were not followed.

It was not a random occurrence. The prisoner helped others escape. The exact number was not yet known. There was an embarrassing number of them these days. It was becoming dangerous outside the prison and other facilities in the region, requiring the assignment of another security brigade.

It would not be so if I were in charge there, Yakovlev thought, listening to the report.

The escaping prisoners would have been rounded up like cattle. Sensors on the ground and in the sky, drones sent aloft to scan the region, were able to track their movements. By the time sensors pin-pointed their location, they had gathered many of the other escaped prisoners and formed a militia.

Then, while the 3rd Laser Battery went to intercept the band of escapees, a vital facility of the Army was attacked.

Yes, they should have put Yakovlev in charge when he was first assigned to this arctic *oblast*. He sat back, picking up the coffee mug, half amused by the mistakes of his superiors and half concerned he would have to clean up after them again. And get no recognition.

All because of the mysterious facility they were there to guard. *Razdatochnayah Korobka*. The transfer box—that was how they referred to it. Or, simply, the *korobka*. A huge concrete block 12 meters high, 12 meters a side. The gray cube encased the highly sensitive machine—but he was not allowed to know more about it. He was just a soldier, a guard, doing his duty protecting the machine. It required constant maximum security, his team was told. What the scientists and government officials might do inside it was none of their concern. He had been to it only once: when he first arrived and was given the tour of their areas of control.

"Inside are many experiments," his supervisor that day had said, "all to assist our great nation in its future expansion."

Expansion seemed to be the key word. Yakovlev remembered it, thought of it for weeks as he settled into his duties. Expand to what? Where? What more is there?

The *korobka* was guarded with the highest security. Besides the physical barriers erected around it, the compound was patrolled by dogs and armed guards. At first. Eventually the lack of any serious incidents precipitated the gradual reduction of the patrols until nearly all manned security was withdrawn. Enhanced sensors were then implemented along with a system of automated weaponry around the perimeter. The occasional wolf or marmot was shot to pieces. He laughed at those reports, glad he did not have to stand guard in sub-zero temperatures outside the facility watching for intruders.

"Pan-American terrorists could be sneaky," the old colonel had reminded him before being transferred back to Novosibirsk and a warm office in the protected Zhukovka complex.

Yakovlev envied him, wondering how long the world

had been growing cold. First they had said the world was growing warmer and everyone would die. Scientists predicted constant deadly storms. Yet only snow came, piled up, the cold settling in. He had read the science papers his son had shown him—before Dmitri Andreivich was taken away, arrested for protesting government plans to build nuclear power plants in the arctic region, far enough away from population centers yet vital to maintaining a failing economy.

No time for nostalgia, Yakovlev told himself, recalling the last view of his son as they led him out of the courtroom. Then five years of prison time and somehow he died from a virus the day before he was supposed to be released. Many died of common diseases in those days. Like his wife, Lena Pavlovna, who passed in a Voronezh hospital during the third pandemic, while he was on duty in Donetsk, trying to keep the peace as wave after wave of refugees fleeing the wars in the West were processed for relocation in the Caucasus.

They ran out of medicine and more died from diseases as well as starvation. That was when he was ordered to reduce the number of mouths to feed by killing those who were too far gone, many of them children and the elderly. Many children were orphans whose parents had recently died. He could not clear out the camps like that. He protested.

"There is no room in this country for a soft heart," his menacing supervisor had warned him, drawing a long knife from a scabbard on his belt and holding it to the nearest child's throat. "You and me, or this sickly waif. What is your choice?"

The child died quickly and Yakovlev was on the next train east, papers in his pocket assigning him to arctic duty and a demotion in rank.

He earned his rank back within a year and ran the command post like a highly productive factory, doing everything by the book, following protocol, and never had a problem. As long as he did not ask questions about what they were all doing so high in the arctic, only a few kilometers from the frozen sea. He was a guard. He did not need to know what he was guarding.

So I will wait another year and apply for transfer, Yakovlev mused, boots up on the corner of his desk in the command center, perhaps someplace nice and not so cold, like Crimea.

Except that there was a breach of protocol.

"My boots will get dirty today," he muttered, dropping them to the floor with a loud thump. He tossed down the last of the coffee. At least he would be taking his annual leave soon, a week down in Yakutsk, small consolation for the harsh duty.

"Check that location, secure it, report back," Lozhkin ordered. "You know what to do."

A reactionary force was often called out to check on the outer facilities, often for nothing more than a stray animal brushing against a wire fence and tripping the alarm. They were far from any town and there were no indigenous people this far north in this arctic wasteland.

"It seems now is good time for some fresh air," he announced to the awkward grins of the staff in the command center.

Yakovlev called in his squad leaders, gave them the mission. A little more than their usual training exercise, he cautioned. The two younger sergeants grumbled about another chase of the gooses that always fly away. These two were straight off the front lines in Mongolia, he knew, so he gave them some slack. They did not know how lucky they were to be snatched from endless war with China up to the arctic frontier.

"We do what we are ordered to do," Yakovlev growled.

He didn't like going out into the arctic cold any more than the younger men did. There would be punishment if he did not go. Yet what could be worse than a day trek across this frozen landscape? What worse assignment was there in all of Eurasia? He could think of a few: Mongolia, fighting Chinese forces, or the German front, facing the Pan-American armies. From all sides, it seemed, they were being threatened, even as the planet was growing colder and vegetation, therefore food, was withering. Now the wars were about food and the land to grow it.

Sergeant Malkin, who Yakovlev thought would make a good leader someday, unlike the others, asked about their protective garb. Of course the usual cold weather uniforms would be worn. The thin mesh fabric was imbedded with a lining which shielded them from the cold. Battery packs could power the network of heating coils that ran through the uniform, further warming the soldiers. A loose over-garment would shield them from wind. And radiation.

If they had to get close to the Korobka they would need to don the heavy, specially lined robes that blocked the waves of radiation the device spun off and wear the breathing masks and goggles. A lot of hassle.

"I don't think we will be so close," Yakovlev replied. "Better we travel light. Field uniforms only. Battle helmets, too. And bring the laser cannon. We can get in some training, save us a trip out next week."

He wanted to be back to the base before dark, when the temperatures dropped dangerously low. Standard arctic field uniforms, fine for a short excursion during daytime, would not protect them under those harsher conditions.

"It'll be a short patrol," he muttered. "We'll return soon."

A few minutes to collect equipment and the three squads were ready to deploy. First by trucks, as far as the road went, then on foot.

At the pass between the ridges dividing the Tokuma area from the Tomtor region, Yakovlev split the three patrols. First squad stayed with him while Second squad went south, circling around the ridge. Third squad set up a defensive position at the pass, ready to rush in as reserve fighters or block the escape of any of the enemy active in this region.

They knew what they were facing. Number three work camp was notorious for the cruelty shown to prisoners from far away lands. From beyond the gap—through the *Razriv*. Creatures big and small, roughly mammalian and reptilian, and others that could not easily be classified. Studies were done on these odd beings. If the creatures could serve as manual labor, they had a purpose. Others might yield some possible new medicine from their fluids or cells. The scientists stayed busy.

Once in a while a creature would decide to rebel and often call others into rebellion. That happened at the #3 Verkhoyansk work camp and several creatures had been killed.

Now Yakovlev's team was called to engage the ragtag army of escapees and kill them. There was no plan to capture and return them to work. Clearly some of them were intelligent enough to understand their destiny and not want to follow that path—

Yakovlev nodded, suddenly aware of his drifting thoughts. He took a deep breath, held tight to his laser rifle as they marched along the rocky trail through barren snow-streaked hills. No trees or bushes gave any indication of life on this world. Only the snow, ice, and bare rock. No creature could live out here unprotected for more than a few hours.

The platoon came to a bridge over an ice-covered stream and crossed quickly, all twenty of them and their gear. The last three soldiers handled the laser cannon, a relic of the final days of the European War. The threat of nuclear annihilation had brought the truce. It had lasted for fifteen years—so far. But the laser artillery—two men carrying the long weapon, one carrying its tripod—gave a small squad an amazing amount of firepower.

When they arrived at the designated coordinates, marked by a fist-sized drone in the sky, Yakovlev climbed the slope and using his digital optics saw the camp below. It looked like a well-ordered battalion of Soviet troops. Of course, the creatures had stolen the tents and other equipment they used to survive in this arctic environment.

First squad moved up to the top of the snowy ridge beside Yakovlev and set up the laser cannon.

Yakovlev lay against the frozen slope, the optics panel flipped down from his helmet showing him the layout of the camp in detail. Heat signatures ran the gamut for these creatures. He marked traffic patterns by indentions in the snow. He marked the occupation of tents by heat signatures. From the data, Yakovlev chose the tent most likely to be their headquarters. The optics panel zoomed in on that tent and, switching to audio enhancement, he could gather sounds from the tent but did not understand the strange languages. How did these creatures communicate with each other?

In a few minutes it would not matter.

"Ready, Master-Sergeant," a crewman spoke.

"When you have a lock on the heat signatures on target number one, you may fire," he responded. "Start with level five."

"Five?"

"Yes, five. No reason to be kind to these monsters."

"Level five it is."

"Evaporate them in one blast and let us go home."

Scanning the distant, opposite ridge through his optics panel, Yakovlev detected movement. Zooming in, he spied two hairy creatures almost staring back at him, though they could not have actually seen him with their eyes from that distance. These furry apes were common, useful in the work camps. Really should get them, too.

Yakovlev grunted. So they would miss those with the laser. They would catch them later.

"Fire."

A low hum rose behind Yakovlev, then a whirring that hurt his ears and finally the loud spurt of energy.

The valley below was lit up with a red beam from the laser cannon that caused the target to burst into a great ball of flame, producing a tremendous roar that shook the entire valley. The targeted tent exploded and the frozen ground under it erupted through the campsite like tentacles, cracking the earth, throwing everything into the air.

Yakovlev buried his face in the snow, not expecting the extra loud boom. Must have ignited something hidden inside the tent, something that was itself explosive. When he looked down at the camp, nothing remained but a smoldering pit of debris. Around the periphery he could see dismembered bodies that had fallen back to the ground—wearing Army uniforms.

Was this a set-up? Using captured soldiers and a fake camp?

Yakovlev kept his composure. With a nod, he glanced back at the laser crew. "Well done."

"Thank you, Master-Sergeant."

"Pack it away and prepare to go down for clean up."

The squad members did as he ordered.

"There were two creatures on the far ridge," said Yakovlev to the squad leader. "The apes. We need to go after them."

He selected four squad members and started down the slope with the soldiers hurrying to keep up with him.

The winding path cut through the shoulder-high snowdrifts and had become dusted with more snow during the night. Their boots made tentative impressions, as they marched in loose formation, weapons ready. Bands of monsters were known to ambush patrols, a reason none of the soldiers wished to go on patrol. Some soldiers had been forced to retrieve whatever parts remained of comrades after such attacks. Body parts strewn about, some chewed on.

Where are those days of global warming? Yakovlev pondered as he brought up the rear of the patrol. If only he could return to his family *dacha*, put his feet in the stream and throw a fishing line into the water, napping until he felt a tug.

They had marched a kilometer before Private Andropov, on point, halted and the others paused behind him, scanning the snowy hills for an ambush. Yakovlev stepped cautiously forward to tap the private's shoulder.

"What do you see?" asked Yakovlev quietly.

"I don't see," said Andropov, "just smell. Smoke, like a fire for cooking."

They both took sniffs of the frigid air. Yakovlev nodded.

He turned and gave hand signals to the patrol. He

directed Krushenko to mount the crest of the hill and have a look.

As Krushenko reached the crest he dropped low, crawling on his belly until he was able to gaze over the top of the hill and see what lay beyond.

Suddenly a loud snap echoed against the ice and snow.

Yakovlev stared up the slope at his corporal, saw the body laying there. Something fell from the sky, hitting a patch of ice and rolling between Yakovlev's feet: Krushenko's severed head, face smashed in by whatever had struck him and sent his head airborne.

Before Yakovlev could give a command, the hill was overrun by monsters. A dozen beings of different species rushed down the snow bank, half running, half sliding, weapons firing at his patrol. He looked up, half a heartbeat only, then ducked down, knees to the snow—

A big, hairy ape-thing held a rail-gun, the heavy weapon usually mounted on a vehicle. Others used pulse-guns, stolen from convoys. Before Yakovlev could assess and act, it was finished, his patrol dead. Except him. Andropov had fallen on top of him. The pulse-gun had sent a beam into his chest and it burned through almost to Yakovlev under him. He could feel the heat touch his parka, melting the plasticine fabric, producing a bitter odor.

But he lay still and silent as the monsters checked the bloody results of their ambush. From under Andropov's body, Yakovlev watched the monsters kick each of his men, turn them over, add another blast to one of them as they worked up the line toward him. He wished he could start digging a tunnel straight down into the snow and escape but that was not possible.

The ape-thing with horns stopped at Andropov's body. Using the business end of the rail-gun, the ape-thing poked at then flipped over Andropov's body, exposing the second body.

Flat on his back, Yakovlev raised his hands in surrender.

The ape-thing growled in its gruff language. With the rail-gun trained on him, two more humanoid-type beings grabbed his arms and pulled him to his feet. They examined the blast mark. The front of his jacket was singed but he was unharmed.

His escorts jostled him along the snowy path, quicker than he was willing or able to go. The ape-thing growled angrily behind him. Then, when he seemed to be dragging again, Yakovlev felt a punch to the back of his head and the world spun around him.

⬤

Yakovlev awoke. With his eyes closed he worried he was blind. He heard the shuffling noises of a camp, creatures coming and going. Stung by the sour odor of rotten meat, he assumed they had made a meal of his comrades. He shuddered at the thought, which caught the attention of his guards. One came over to him and jostled him. He grunted and they seemed amused. He shook where he sat, dropped down on a hard surface, his ankles tied together, his hands tied behind his back. A heavy stone rested in his lap, pinning him down. He had let go his urine as he sat there and it had frozen in his clothing.

He heard something speaking intelligently, though it was not a language he could understand. Apparently at the command of this speaker, his guards removed the cloth wrapped around his head which had covered his eyes and nose. He dared open his eyes, only slits at first, testing his sight.

What he saw around him were cave walls, frost painting them, ice in the cracks, snow and ice beneath him. He had been sat down near the entrance so the whiteness of the exterior was blinding if he turned that way. The opposite direction, back into the cave, was dark yet lit by lamps at intervals. Monsters of different sizes and shapes moved past him, entering and exiting. A few beasts slowed to regard him, a curiosity.

The ape-things were there: big, brutish creatures twice his height and three times his strength. But also there were beings of various species, some wrapped in uniforms taken from soldiers on earlier patrols. Why had they let him live? If only he could understand what they were saying. He could not imagine how such different creatures could communicate, or how they would not fight among themselves like his people had done down through the centuries. Instead, they had come together for a common purpose: to attack his men.

A pair of ape-men stood in front of him, gazing down at him. To Yakovlev, they seemed like bullies in his gymnasium days, always harassing the weaker pupils. He had never been a victim but he understood the situation now. Another ape-man joined them. Then another. Four stood in front of him as he shivered from the cold and shook in fear. He did not believe his body could feed these four big creatures adequately.

The beasts growled among themselves, glancing down at him as they argued. Their talk got louder. One pointed a giant furry hand at him, accusingly. A yellow claw grazed his cheek, but his frozen flesh barely bled.

Just as Yakovlev was about to faint, expecting the ape-men to pull him apart for their dinner, the four beasts were parted by a small silvery hand. As the gap grew wider, the owner of that hand slipped through and stood before him with the wall of ape-men remaining behind the little creature.

The silvery hands faded into blue up its arms. Its entire body was blue and shiny. On spindly legs—like its spindly arms and rubber-mallet hands—it squatted to have a look at him—rather like a frog about to leap. Although its head was blue, several strands sprouted there and hung down like hair but thicker, almost like fingers. More of the blue strands grew out and covered its shoulders and torso. The tips of the strands, especially those on its head, were silver.

Hearing the click of a rail-gun ready to fire, Yakovlev looked up, fearing the sight of a weapon trained on him by one of the ape-men would be the last thing he would ever see. A fitting end. How many of their comrades had he and his men killed?

Instead, it was the calm face of the blue creature regarding him that stunned him. The strange being shifted from a bluish-silver to a silvery-blue as it studied him. Must be one of the dumber creatures, thought Yakovlev, likely just a pet of these ape-men. This blue being looked like one of those typical aliens everyone was afraid of decades ago when talk of flying saucers and UFOs were of interest to the public—then dismissed as mental illness. A large, round head, hardly any neck, a rounded torso with a slight pot-belly, thin legs and large, flat feet. Big, perfectly round eyes but no lashes or brow ridge. No prominent nose although there were two holes where a nose should be with flaps that closed and opened. And a tiny mouth hole which also moved as it breathed, thin lips that seemed to have a hard edge on them, maybe used to grasp its food, he decided. Could be intelligent—or just curious like a lost puppy.

I am Toog.

The message clicked inside Yakovlev's head, even as he saw the little mouth of the creature move and his ears heard some kind of sing-songy sound. He didn't know how to respond. Should he speak his reply? Or merely think the words?

You are one of the Masters.

Yakovlev hesitated, worried about the kind of response he would get, then nodded.

His mind had automatically translated 'Masters' for 'Razdatochnayah Korobka komanda bezopasnosti' as he heard the words spoken in his mind rather than his ears. But his mind also heard the Russian words like an echo, as though each ear piece of a set of headphones gave different audio. The effect was confusing. He rethought the words.

"I'm Master-Sergeant Andrei Ilych Yakovlev," he spoke out, weary voice trying to enunciate his Russian words, "of the Army of the Soviet Federation of Eurasia, Seventh Division, Second Security..." and he fell silent.

The silvery being with blue strands sprouting from its head and naked body stared at him a moment before standing fully. The creature could not have been but a meter and a half tall. Something like a small pet, thought Yakovlev, or like a character from one of those French animations. Its blue eyes turned pink around the perfectly round orbs.

It raised one hand—two pairs of blue fingers—and the ape-men backed off.

Yakovlev was surprised. How could this little *boy* command those ape-things?

The hand the blue being held up showed the prominent hole in the palm. The cute mouth was not smiling.

You did this to me, came a voice in his head, thin and light.

"I didn't," snarled Yakovlev defiantly in Russian. "I was out here, manning the station. But I get your meaning. One of us did it. But not me."

The creature stared at him, wide eyes expressionless, its skin fading back and forth between blue and silver.

"Sorry," Yakovlev muttered after a moment.

A long string of words quickly followed, not angry in tone but still agitated, sounding in his ears as beeps and buzzes and in his mind as poorly formed Russian, like a child would have learned in primary grade one, but he got the meaning.

"I agree," said Yakovlev when the stream of words ended. He cleared his throat. "We are wrong to do that, to do everything. But I'm small person in this big plan. I only guard the station. Before you all escaped, there was no threat to the station." He shook his head. "Believe me, I don't want to be here any more than you do."

The Xmburrhaltins grumbled, shuffled behind the blue boy.

You have family? asked the blue creature, fading to silver.

"I had. Long ago."

Family died? asked the silver one, squatting again.

"Yes, dead now."

I have family, said the little one. *I want to return to them.*

Yakovlev nodded sadly. "I understand."

Other creatures had gathered around the silver/blue one, towering over him. The gang of monsters appeared formidable, staring down at him: just one human, bound, helpless. Not such a 'master' now, eh? He wondered why they called him and his kind the Masters. He took it to refer to his military rank but now he was not certain.

The silver one, slowly turning blue, as if hearing his

private thoughts pointed a long silvery finger at him and spoke aloud:

"On my world, called Sebbol, it is legend that the Masters will come and carry away the offspring who act badly." His blue eyes narrowed. "It is not only legend but truth. The riddle is why you come to my world. To each of our worlds." He waved his hole-hand at those gathered around him. "And why you choose us. Why me? Why them? What is the purpose?"

Yakovlev heard the translation clearly in his head, getting the ideas by some kind of telepathic means of communication—until the grumbling crowd became too loud for him to hear the voice in his head. The silver one, phasing to blue, waved them to silence.

"I really don't know." Yakovlev grunted resignation. "I wish I knew what they're doing there, in that Korobka. Nothing but a bunch of scientists operating a complex machine. I just guard the damn thing. Others have a plan, maybe, but I don't know what it is. I don't know why you were taken from your world—"

How do we return? came the demand from this blue thing.

Yakovlev could only shake his head.

"Let's kill this one," said one of the hairy ape-things. "It smells delicious. And my belly is empty."

Yakovlev heard the gravelly words in his head, using an odd accent of Russian. So many creatures speaking so many different languages, each instantly translated in his head, producing a cacophony of words that quickly overwhelmed his mind.

Other creatures added comments to the conversation and they spilled into Yakovlev's head like a river whose dam had broken. He tensed, expecting to be hauled up and dismembered at any moment. He could not look up at their faces, especially the big ape-men monsters—

We are called Xmburrhaltin, came the words shoving into his head. *We are not monsters.*

Their fangs were dripping in anticipation of the meal.

How do we return? asked the blue boy, waving the crowd to silence again.

Yakovlev tried to calm his wildly beating heart. "I guess you go back through the way you came here."

We do not know the way, said the blue boy, silver patches appearing on its arms.

"Right. Probably you were unconscious when they brought you here." He took a deep breath, the icy air burning his lungs. "There is a door. A doorway—more like a tunnel but shorter. I've never seen them bring creatures through it, but I've seen the schematics, and the diagram on the monitor screens—so I can watch for any problems. I know the basic layout."

The blue one waved him to silence, turned back to the big ape-creature. "Bring Cromwell."

Yakovlev watched the ape-creature push the errand off on a lesser monster. He didn't know what was going to happen next but it seemed whatever might happen would be delayed a few minutes.

Yakovlev looked up as a new being arrived and the Xmburrhaltins made a space. The little blue being stepped aside as a tall insect-like thing resembling a mantis ushered a human to him.

A real human, clothed in a ripped, dirty costume of an older era, was roughly pushed up to Yakovlev. The man was unlike any of the creatures he had seen in the ice cave: fully human, although his manner of dress was odd and the man's hair was long, disheveled, dried blood on one side of his head and down one arm. Where did they capture this person?

Speak to this Master, said the little blue being both in audible words full of squeaks and chirps and the pure ideation flashing in his mind like a light switch flicking on.

I must simply be in a horrible dream, thought Yakovlev, hearing the command.

"What shall I say?" the man spoke in English. He stared down at Yakovlev, eyes wide, surprised to be presented to someone so much like himself. "Who might this gentleman be?"

The blue one's small round mouth moved, yet Yakovlev heard no words in his ears or in his mind. The newly arrived man turned to him, offered a slight grin, dismissive of his task.

"Do you speak English?" asked the man. "My name is Timothy Cromwell. Pleased to meet you. I dare say!"

Nothing came into Yakovlev's mind, only in his ears. He gave a shrug, awkward with his wrists tied behind his back, leaning against the ice, the heavy stone on his lap.

Yakovlev had spoken to the blue one using his native language, Russian, and the creature seemed to understand. It was some kind of mental telepathy, he guessed. They had experimented with the technique in the Moscow Academy. Many of the monsters around him seemed to have gained the ability. He focused his mind, spoke the Russian words only in his mind.

Speak to this one, the blue being instructed him, meaning to this man named Cromwell, obviously understanding his words clearly.

Yakovlev spoke to the human in Russian.

The human jumped back. "Ah! Yes, well, this man seems to be speaking Russian. I don't understand Russian, but I recognize it. I did a bit of travel over to that eastern province before the war, and.... Umm, yes, well, er...." He straightened himself, smoothed his ruffled clothes. "Good afternoon, sir. Umm, *Dobra dyen*—I think that's it. I learned a few words while visiting Saint Petersburg."

He stopped suddenly, squinting at Yakovlev.

"This man is Russian?" He was asking the blue one. "Is he one of us? Like me?"

No, this is a Master. Or a creature used for guarding the facility. It is a Hu-man like you.

Cromwell heard the communication in his mind while hearing the strange beep and churl language spoken by the blue one.

"Yes, well, all right then." He put his hand to his chin, thinking a moment. "He is Russian. Yet he isn't one of us. Not like me, a human. Yes, he is like me: a human. Yet there are many kinds of humans, certainly. Who are we really?"

The man glared down at Yakovlev.

"What do you call this place?" he asked the Russian. "*Chto eto za mesto?* I think that's right. I asked what he calls this place."

Yakovlev, puzzled, replied that they call this place Ust-Yansky, in the Sakha region of Siberia, part of the Soviet Federation of Eurasia.

Cromwell listened patiently and asked for repetition twice.

"He says that—"

"*Eto Respublika Sakha, Ust-Yanskiy okrug.*"

"Yes, this is the Sakha Republic, the Okrug of Ust-Yansky. I'm not certain where that might be, however. But the rest of...what is it? the Soviet Federation? of Eurasia? I'm not at all aware what that is. I know Eurasia, of course. A vast landmass which spans most of the planet. Which must therefore mean that...."

The man grew faint, caught himself. Two Xmburrhaltins held him up by his arms.

"It must mean that...I do not find myself on an alien world, after all, but rather on...on my own world. We call it Earth. I told you, M'lord, that I come from a planet named Earth. Now this man.... He says this planet is Earth. I cannot understand."

Yakovlev spoke again, pointing his chin at the human. He seemed to be indicating the man's clothing. "*Odezhda starogo obraztsa,*" he said with a disapproving sneer.

"It is not! Quite the contrary. Yes, 'twas expensive—when first I purchased it. I dare say!" Cromwell's face reddened. "This garment is quite common in my city, for a gentleman of my class. I have worn this since the day I was captured. Captured...by you!"

He held up his hand, showing the hole in his palm, the mark of war he'd accepted after his companions were killed through months of fighting. He threw himself at Yakovlev, but the other creatures held him back as he cursed the captive.

"You're Russian." Cromwell shook his head. "This is Russia, part of it, such as it is. Siberia, I dare say! And yet...here I am, not only a traveler of space but also of time." He glared at Yakovlev. "Tell me, sir, what is the year now?" He repeated the words he knew: "*Kakoy god?*"

Yakovlev grinned like he had been caught in a lie. "*Eto dve tysyachi pyat'desyat pyatoye.*"

"Oh dear! He says it's...." Cromwell felt weak, put his arms out to catch himself against the icy wall above the seated Yakovlev. His ill stomach erupted, sending its watery contents down upon the Russian.

What has made you ill? asked the blue one.

"Shock. I-I have a rather weak constitution." Cromwell shook his head, dropping to a knee. "Apologies for my unseemly display. The shock overcame me."

What is the shock? asked the blue one.

"The year. Too advanced. It is far into the future from my own time." Cromwell regarded Toog. "I was born in the year seventeen-forty-two. More than...than three-hundred years ago." He grabbed his chest. "How can I be in this year? 'Tis the devil's work."

The blue one, flickering into silver on his shoulders and hands, pointed his hole-hand at Yakovlev.

Here is your devil. One of many. Forced you into the future.

The little blue being stepped away from Yakovlev and he feared what would happen next. It seemed clear this blue entity, though looking so innocent and weak, was somehow their leader. Its arms turned from blue to silver as they crossed over his small, smooth, blue torso, free of nipples and navel.

All family you knew are now dead, the blue being addressed Cromwell, with Yakovlev able to hear also but unable to understand the English, *though you remain on your own world. Perhaps it was mistake for you. For us, we were brought here for purposes we know not. And we cannot escape. We cannot travel away from this world.*

Yakovlev cleared his throat and spoke in Russian: "You want to go home? Go back through the tunnel."

How? asked Toog in Yakovlev's mind. *To each of our worlds? Which direction are they? How many steps to arrive?*

Yakovlev addressed Cromwell in Russian. When he saw the man did not understand, he repeated his message in simpler words.

"He says if we let him go free, he will help us go home," Cromwell reported. "He knows the machine's location, and can show us how to enter it."

Yakovlev spoke again.

"He says he wants us to go home, too. He recognizes we do not belong here. Except for me, perhaps, but I do not belong in this time period, either. I know nothing of the machinery used here."

Yakovlev continued speaking and the blue one waved him to silence after a moment, then directed the Xmburrhaltins to pick him up. The stone was removed from his lap. Two ape-men carried him by his arms and shoulders well above the cave floor, and they all went deeper into the cave. He saw that a storm was blowing hard outside, the entrance to the cave a curtain of flurries.

Down the slippery path they went, winding among stalagmites and ducking stalactites as the ice gave way to rock. They came to an open area where creatures huddled together, eating—waiting to go home. He saw what they dined on: some were arms or legs or ribs of what looked like humans. The tattered uniforms told him they once were members of his brigade. One creature that was hunched over dared look up at him, flashing rows of teeth in its flat face. Another took a step toward him but halted at the growl of his escort.

The blue one led them into a smaller enclave and Yakovlev was sat down on a short stalagmite. His wrists were untied, his arms swung around in front of him and tied again. At least it was more comfortable, thought Yakovlev. He did not have much confidence in how long the blue one would delay his inevitable transformation into the monsters' dinner. Out on this forsaken wintry landscape there was little else to eat.

The blue one spoke again, his mouth producing the same beeps and chirps as before but accompanied by ideas bursting into clarity inside Yakovlev's mind. They were pictures. He saw himself inside a cave in his mind. He was writing on a rock wall, drawing pictures of a figure acting on his behalf. He was not sure whether he was doing the drawing, making art on the wall, or the blue boy was projecting this cinema to him so he might understand. He let it go on and they came to the end of the wall. The drawing stopped and the figure that was supposed to be him, complete with uniform and a crudely animated face and hands, stood back to admire the new drawings.

Yakovlev stared at the blue boy. *Your name is Toog, correct?* He merely thought the words this time.

Yes, I am Toog. The blue being responded mentally.

You are leader here? Yakovlev asked within his mind, mouthing the words, still standing in that cave beside the drawings.

Toog raised a silvery hand, waved two of his fingers.

I am their leader.

Yakovlev nodded. Inside his mind-cave, a short silver being appeared, resembling the real blue being that stood before him in the real cave. This figure was half the size of the figure of himself in this mind-cave. The silver being indicated the first drawing on the wall, the farthest one on the left, and the cave-Yakovlev stepped up to it.

The silvery being in Yakovlev's mind-cave pointed to the first drawing.

Explain, came the instruction in Russian, a ghostly echo from the mouth of that blue mind-cave figure.

h o s t a g e

 **12**

As Yakovlev found pieces of words from the tiny piles of word-dust in his mind-cave, he managed to place them into a proper arrangement on the floor. The silver being occupying his mind-cave adjusted its slender arm and hand to point to different drawings, sometimes stretching out its arm like a rubber strand: the longer it stretched, the thinner it became. The drawings represented the prison, the station he guarded, the cave where they were, and the machine which possessed the means of passage. At the end of the passage drawing was a depiction of the planet Sebbol. Behind the blue and gray sphere were other planets. He counted twelve of them, different colors and sizes, each a home to those beings around him in the real cave.

Here is what I know, Yakovlev's mind-cave figure spoke to mind-cave Toog. *About fifty years ago, people discovered some holes in Siberia—this land here. Investigation resulted in study of magnetic fields in those holes.*

Outside his mind-cave, the menagerie of creatures waited as Yakovlev communicated to Toog and Toog then communicated everything to Cromwell and other members gathered there.

He continued: After twenty years, scientists determined that the magnetic fields in the holes could be harnessed for energy. Attempting to construct a power plant which could use the magnetic field to drive turbines caused 'a rip in the fabric of the universe'. That was how it was described. Workers were sucked through the opening and lost. An opening to another world lay before them. Further exploration led to the realization that the rip could allow access to other worlds.

A brigade was formed with the intention of transferring to other worlds. Brigade members wore protective suits that shielded themselves from radiation. Over tight-fitting suits they garbed themselves in metallic-embedded robes which further protected them. They wore goggles to protect their eyes from the bright illumination that occurred when the opening seethed with energy. They were armed with pulse-guns and rail-guns, as well as traditional ballistic weapons, though on some worlds gunpowder did not work. From each world they took some of the indigenous life forms. Eventually, a dozen different worlds were accessed and beings were brought back.

At the same time, a facility was constructed around the rip in the 'curtain of the universe'—*Razryv vo vselennoy*, or just Razriv, they called it: the 'gap in the universe'. To common eyes, it appeared as though the sky itself had been torn, and through the gap, another world could be seen— just like looking through a window. Two other places were found on the opposite side of the planet, in northern Canada. So a race was on to explore and exploit the new frontier before the Pan-American Union could lay claim to the resources of alien worlds.

Rather than allow the phenomena to be exposed to the harsh arctic elements and possibly disappear as randomly as it had appeared or worsen its unpredictable effects, they decided to contain it. They constructed a housing unit around it. The labor force needed was readily available among the beings obtained from the worlds the brigade had accessed. Additional magnetic fields were found and exploited. They were determined to draw energy from them. Instead, the brigade gathered even more beings from worlds they could access. There was no particular criteria for selection: proximity, unique appearance, demonstration of intelligence, suitability for manual labor. Or perhaps some scientific use. Medical uses.

The magnetic fields seemed to expand even as they tried to contain them, and with expansion, the arctic wasteland became unstable. This frozen landscape soon became a desert of noxious gases. At first scientists believed the gases would destroy life only within the infected areas. Then they came to understand that as the infected areas spread, they would gradually encompass towns and large tracts of land, productive land, forcing evacuations.

The problem could spread around the Earth, scientists knew, so the magnetic fields in the high arctic became possible escape routes. The brigade's mission changed from exploration and exploitation to search for and preparation of a suitable world for Humanity—beings like the Masters, people of the Soviet Federation of Eurasia. A new home. For our survival. Selecting a world, exterminating its residents. Terraforming as needed.

And the captured beings from a dozen different worlds? They could be used as labor for as long as they were useable. Get weak, leave them in a ditch. Get injured, same. Starve, they can eat the ones who died and were dropped into ditches. None of them were worth any consideration; they were animals, beasts, a weird collection of creatures from a dozen different worlds—and not all were human or even humanoid or were able to adapt to the frozen tundra of the Ust-Yansky Okrug.

Then there was a rebellion at one work camp, and a breakout at the prison. Some prisoners escaped—

Miniature Toog, standing in the mind-cave of Yakovlev, stopped. He lowered his pointing hand, turned blue, eyes pinched together like a stubborn child.

"Like I said before, I'm sorry," said Yakovlev through the mouth of his mind-cave self and his real mouth speaking Russian. "I'm sorry for all of that. I didn't know everything that was happening here."

You knew how to operate the laser cannon, the blue one communicated.

"Yes—as is my job specs. Based on our training that you are the enemy. Now I know. You just want to go home."

We have families, said the real Toog, though the mind-cave Toog mouthed the same words. *We want to go home. Show us how to go home.*

Yakovlev bowed his head, the mind-cave suddenly blinking into darkness. He lifted his tied hands up to his face and wiped his eyes.

"I do believe he is completely honest with us," Cromwell spoke. "His task was only to guard the station, as he stated. He was not privy to the scientific information, nor had he any part in making those policies of exploration. Nor did he know the adverse effects the phenomena might have."

Did you go through the tunnel? asked Toog in Yakovlev's mind.

The Russian shook his head, then looked up. His face was pale. He dared not lie.

"I went one time." He glanced from Toog to Cromwell to the Xmburrhaltins, back to Toog. "It was accident. I was guarding the machine and they were demonstrating how it worked for some administrators. It worked, yes. They were sucked through. Me, as well. I hung on, only a few steps into it, then I clawed my way back to this world."

His spoken Russian seemed to have registered in the minds of Toog and his lieutenants.

"What did you see?" asked Cromwell before Toog could send the message mentally to him.

"It was a storm of swirling winds, blue and white. I could not see the land itself, nor any beings. I'm not sure whether that was the next world or the effects of the transference."

We must examine this machine, said Toog to everyone there without uttering an audible word.

◆☙

"My good fellow," spoke Cromwell, keeping his voice low to avoid anyone noticing he was addressing the prisoner, "I have questions which, among all who are here, only you might be able to answer. Mmm.... *Ponimayu*? Understand?"

"*Vy ponimayete*," Yakovlev corrected, with a slight grin. He looked down at his feet. "Know only small *Angliski*."

"Ah! So you've been holding back your talents."

Cromwell glanced each direction. Creatures from several worlds were engaged in their tasks. A Xmburrhaltin stood guard a few steps away.

"I don't blame you. These fellows can be quite prone to violence and, mmm, always hungry. The lassies, too. You might have noticed the females with their great breasts covered in fur. One took me in her big arms and treated me as though I might be her baby, forced her teat into my mouth. It was not a pleasant experience, I dare say! Indeed, food is the most critical aspect here, yet they have often captured supplies from convoys, and I have managed to endure from those meager rations. The others—aye, they dine on flesh, on your comrades. And their own, too, if desperate. It is a hard thing to witness. One must keep an eye open while sleeping. However, good fortune has been with me ever since they ambushed the caravan taking us to the prison, thus saving me from a gruesome fate. The blue one likes me."

He held up his hand, took a moment to admire the hole in it.

"See this? You can't be one of the leaders unless you have suffered this torture. I was never in the prison, or a work camp, not like most of them, so I avoided it initially. They offered the mark to me. I accepted rather than be seen as not one of them, you understand. They applied an iron staff to make this crude hole. Call it an initiation. I needed to fit in."

Yakovlev grunted. "Me, don't make—do it—hand—"

"Do not tax yourself, sir. I cannot make much sense of your mumbling. 'Twould be better if we could communicate as Toog does. We are poor humans. Without such advanced abilities. The mind connection trick. It's witchcraft. Only a few can do it. Yet we dare claim superiority over these various space oddities. We are so high and mighty! If only God Himself could see this dire truth! Aye—God Himself! He made us in such variety, and He knows our flaws. And these others? The Lord does have a bold humor. Now tell me about the world between your time and mine."

Yakovlev gave him a strange look, not understanding.

Cromwell was about to speak again when a shadow reached both men. They saw the ugly creature with a lumpy red face and stubby black horns protruding from its cheeks and across its forehead. Black veins appeared just beneath its red skin. The devilish being hovered behind them, long fangs hanging from its hideous mouth, saliva dripping in hope of a bite or two.

"That is a Vuuth," said Cromwell, thumbing at the ugly creature. "Not my favorite among the cast here."

The creature spoke its gravelly language, unintelligible to them, and shifted its squat form back and forth on thick legs, a stubby tail waving behind its red body.

"Some—bad animal—here," said Yakovlev.

"Animals?" Cromwell dared laugh. "Each of them was chosen for their unique features, I suppose, chief of which being intelligence. The ability to understand and you're your commands. The apex predator of each world. I think this fine fellow behind us would definitely be a predator. The one they call their leader seems harmless enough. The little blue man."

Yakovlev had lost him again.

The shadow disappeared, replaced by a short presence.

Let me help you, Toog communicated in both their mind-caves. He raised his rubbery blue arms and placed one hand on Cromwell's forehead, the other to Yakovlev's forehead.

Instantly, the Russian soldier was thrown hard into a cave in his mind, yellow stone walls covered with the same drawings as before. A miniature twin crawled into the cave, as if rolling out of bed half-awake. The mind-cave Yakovlev stood wearily and stared at the wall drawings, reading them. He expected a small Toog to enter and guide him. Instead, a miniature Cromwell appeared, sprouting up from the cave floor like a stalagmite then stepping free. Little Cromwell stepped toward the small Yakovlev and they shook hands.

"Tell me the history between your time and mine," asked little Cromwell in perfect Russian.

"It is so long," replied mind-cave Yakovlev in English. "There would be so much to tell and we do not have much time. We might be dinner at any moment."

"Time is always available here. Some of us have been here for a decade or longer, from the very first mission. I was one of the fortunate ones."

The mind-cave Yakovlev nodded, a motion that became a head bow, then a full drop into a respectful prostration.

"I am sorry for what you have suffered—all of you, the whole group of creatures from the other worlds. I never understood your suffering. I had no knowledge of plans to capture such creatures—lifeforms—from other worlds. I do not know the reason, but it is the curiosity of scientists, I suppose. Yet I'm not a scientist. I'm a soldier too long on the front line. And this—this strange manner of communication is a...a miracle."

Rising, Yakovlev drew on the wall as he spoke, more of an artist than he thought he could be. His hand worked feverishly, creating maps and scenes and characters that acted like the animations he had seen in his youth. He explained the major events of his life and how they matched events in the world. He had never been a serious student, did not know all the history, he had to admit, but he explained how the old Soviet Republic gained a tyrant as the new Tsar, how the world turned warmer, permafrost melting, and how the methane frozen in the surface layers released into the atmosphere, caused much illness, and how the plan to find a new home developed. The world turned colder, the skies overcast, sunlight blocked. Before the old Soviet Republic was a time of great suffering—the result of wars with the Pan-American Union. With Europe divided between them. And to the south was the vast Chinese Empire. It seemed the world had been cut up between the three entities, with Africa the battleground. Before that time there was an older nation which collapsed into chaos. Before that older nation was an empire ruled by a family that lasted three-hundred years. Before that time was a world of poverty and war—

"Three-hundred years?" little Cromwell quizzed, poking a finger at the drawings on the wall. "I detect a theme: poverty and war."

Then the man from ancient Earth told of his life in the Colonies on the American continent, what he understood would eventually become the heart of the Pan-American Union, with its capital city named for a victorious field marshal who became its first king.

"I was a locksmith by trade," Cromwell continued as his smaller self drew on the walls of their shared mind-cave. "Yet I dabbled in science. In fact, sir, I had great interest in the topic of electromagnetism. I thought some device might be engineered which could be applied to the public good. My brother was a merchant seaman, had a company in England. I lent a hand in trading and thus never plied my locksmith craft. I went on trade sojourns with him. One journey was to Copenhagen and on to Saint Petersburg, where I stayed for a year. I picked up some of the language. I attended many theater productions. A fascinating place!"

Sorrow swept over his face and he had to pause.

Yakovlev didn't know what to think, so he waited patiently, taking the pause to glance around the cave at the many creatures who might kill and eat him.

"And one day," Cromwell continued, his voice strained, "after I'd returned to Boston, I went down the wrong alley and was accosted by two fellows in long brown hooded robes. By their appearance, I thought they must be from a monastic order. Or else the government, affecting disguise. I insisted I wasn't a member of any seditious gentlemen's club, but they took me away nevertheless—through a doorway in the air, and here I am. So far from home."

A miniature figure of Toog entered their shared mind-cave and held a small globe aloft.

"This is Sebbol," spoke mind-cave Toog, letting the blue-gray globe spin in the air just above his open palm. "My home. I have a full-mate there. I have a springling there. I did no wrong. I obeyed the laws of my community. Now it is many sun-cycles between there/then and here/now. What has become of them? Have they grown old waiting for me? Do they search for me in their mind-caves? Have they gone to the dream land forever? What shall I do?"

Toog released his touch upon both men's foreheads and the mind-cave dimmed, then closed, leaving both humans fatigued and faint where they sat.

"We must go home," said Toog with both his mouth and his mind.

Yakovlev gave a nod, communicating: *I will help any way I can. I want to go home, too, but mine is more difficult, I fear, than yours. I will be stopped, possibly arrested.*

And I, Cromwell responded telepathically. *How do I get home? I am a traveler of both time and space. My home still exists yet it is far away across the ocean, and back across the stream of time. I am quite out of place there. And out of place here, certainly.*

You are welcome in my home, said Yakovlev, clapping a hand on Cromwell's shoulder. *If I can find it, many days' travel from here. In Ukraine.*

They heard the words echo in both languages, barely able to understand each other. Yet they no longer needed to speak. Yakovlev, surprised by the strange effect, regarded Toog.

Now you are able to communicate with each other, said the blue being. *We are all one family.*

"I wonder," Yakovlev sent the idea as a communication stream to Cromwell, "how he is able to be the leader. So small and only one claw on one finger of each hand as weapons. And is he...naked? He.... I take him to be male yet I'm not sure."

"Oh, he is the leader, all right," the American colonist replied. "They all respect him, the first to escape. Thus, he is thought to be the toughest of them. And I hadn't considered whether he is male or female. Does it matter?"

"Does he have a plan?"

"A plan to escape, perhaps. We all wish to return to our homes and families."

"Look at the hair he grows all over his head and body. I think they would be called hair, but they are much thicker. Almost could be tentacles."

"Yes, his kind seems to have developed from an amphibious species. One time I saw him take one of the strands in his hand and squeeze it. It popped like a vessel full of liquid. What fell to the ground burned the rock, made it break apart. Like an acid."

"Amazing," Yakovlev responded. "So many strange creatures. Many strange weapons. I am afraid and curious at once. For a being from outer space like blue boy, maybe it is a condition for the cold climate."

"Yes, that may be," Cromwell communicated, lowering his mind-cave voice as though he'd forgotten that no one could hear. "I'm no scientist but it would make sense. If he came from a tropical world, his body may provide its own adaptation. His feet have thickened, like they grow the soles of boots, even as the hair grows over his head and body to keep him warm."

"They look like tentacles without suction cups."

"When he was in the tent they laid flat against his skin, but when he goes out in the cold, they expand, become thicker."

Toog heard their voices wafting through the cave, distinct from the others, and he focused on them: the captured Master and his friend from ancient times who looked like one of the Masters but was not. They examined him, remarking on his body, on the changes to it he never expected.

Yes, he suffered in the cold, even hiding in the cave. He feared death. Eventually a node appeared on his body, and another and another, growing into long strings which pressed against his blue skin. The blue appeared to help protect his delicate skin from the weak sunshine that cut through the clouds once in a while. It darkened to help him blend with the landscape. Its properties held in warmth, kept out cold. And his feet, wearing no covering like the Masters wore, had grown a hard underside that could fight against rocks and other rough surfaces and help him grip slick surfaces. His toes had grown longer by a knuckle to better grip slippery rocks when he climbed.

A light flicked on behind his eyes and he turned inward to greet his inner Ru, coming into his mind-cave as though arriving at the end of a long journey, setting down a heavy bag.

Fear not, said his inner Ru, for you are special among the Aull of Sebbol. You have hardships others do not, so you have been granted special protection to accomplish your task. You must complete it or Sebbol will not survive.

●
 ▾

Toog stepped between two tall stalagmites and slipped down into a hidden crevasse which opened a little to provide space to extend his arms. He knelt on one bent leg, his foot spreading to grasp the soil. His eyes spiraled closed. He opened his nose flaps, breathed the acrid cave air.

What is happening to me? he called to his inner Ru.

Dark clouds swirled around his mind, a storm pulsing and crackling. Flashes of bronze light struck him as he fell into his mind-cave. The walls were blank yet a stick of chalk rolled on the floor. He reached for it, and tumbled into the cave like a loose pebble.

He had always been silver from head to toe, although he knew he might shift toward blue when he was stressed. He had seen that on this world. Yet there was a lot more happening to him now which he neither expected nor understood. He called again to his inner Ru. His skin had been as smooth as water yet now it had a viscous texture. He had no coverage over his body as many animals did, yet now the strands had sprouted from his head and body, growing long, curling tight against his skin. And they turned blue!

Was he dying? Or was it the effect of being on this world for so long? And his appendages were changing, becoming less rigid and more flexible. He could reach for something now and, if his fingertips did not quite touch it, his arm would stretch further to enable him to grasp what he desired, then snap back to its usual length. And his feet had flattened, becoming wider, suction pads on the bottom, as though he needed them to traverse slick ice. It seemed as though his body was changing to fit this cold environment.

Even his circuitry was altered. He could feel the nerves of those around him if he attempted to communicate. He could sense the way the signals went around the other creatures' bodies and, if he wished it, he could shut off the stream and the creature would not be able to think or feel or continue to live—if he pressed hard enough in his mind.

His inner Ru held up a hand to the mind-cave wall, and with a flick of fingers the wall broke open. His inner Ru slid its hand into the space. *If you wish to cause pain, press here in the mind-cave of the other being.*

He also knew the silver tips of the many strands growing out of his skin could fill with electric power, and when their silvery tips were touched by another creature they could shock and kill. He had never known he had such abilities to kill before. If he had, he would take himself away from his family to protect them from an accident. Yet this world demanded he prepare himself to survive, to fight back. His inner Ru explained everything yet he insisted he did not want to kill—

You have killed in their manner whenever your army has taken the advantage in the field, did you not?

Toog lowered his head, found his neck stretching thin as his head dropped and his eyes assumed the level of his leg-joints—which were no longer joints which only bent one way but rubbery appendages which could fold in any direction. He wanted to wince at the awkward pose, yet his mouth would not turn that way. He knew his inner Ru was correct.

Transformation is not unnatural. It is not wrong. It is not something you should fear. His inner Ru formed a bent-mouth opening, tongue out and pulsing pink. *From the most distant time Great Goddess Aull has put inside you, into every Aull, these defensive means. When you need them they will appear.*

Toog straightened up, took his stance to its maximum, tried to make himself rigid—like the night long ago when the Masters came for him. Ready to fight. Even with new weaponry, would he ever be able to return to his home before he died?

Everything we know spins on the rear-horn of a hungry gulk, his inner Ru imparted.

From the top of the ridge the Korobka did not look like much: a massive cube sitting in snowdrifts, itself white with a hint of gray at the entrance where it was tinted by shadow. Outside it were four guards with weapons. Two of them lazed with their backs against the front wall. Two others stood, sharing a vapor tube and blowing smoke that curled slowly into the gray sky. They passed the time joking about their harsh circumstances. Stuck in this frozen wasteland just to guard a big box! Not even knowing what was inside, just a bunch of machinery. Yakovlev had seen it before. Like him, these fellows were likely the lowest of the cadre, sent to this arctic post as punishment.

Extending behind the cube was a line of black rock faces, forming the other line of the Y-shaped ridge. That section of cliffs was hung with myriad frozen streams. From their view, it seemed a tight fit for such a special device, wedged into the entrance of a gorge. The only reason to put the cube in that awkward space was that there must be a magnetic field present. On the sides facing them, however, the ground was flat and covered with withered grass and lichen, and patches of snow. That flat area extended away from the cube for several kilometers, across the tundra, up to the next snowy ridge. Between the cube and the ridge ran a muddy road, up to the cube, then continuing on and turning into the gorge.

Yakovlev pointed out the arrangement, suggested from a soldier's perspective how to attack it. He had no doubt the guards would start shooting at the first sight of monsters.

We are not monsters, Toog communicated.

Yes, but they call you that. Yakovlev grimaced, looked away.

Regardless how close they could get, say, the end of this ridge, Yakovlev explained, the distance was too great for an all out charge. They could not get to the guards before the guards could react and shoot them. Many would be killed, Yakovlev noted. And these big Xmburrhaltins were not fast.

"What is the plan?" asked Cromwell, breaking the mood.

Yakovlev shrugged, laying against the snow.

Toog studied the cube, his eyes spiraled open fully and bulging, wondering what amazing things were inside. The passage home perhaps. He seemed focused on the third or fourth step, not the first or second: eliminating the guards, then entering the Korobka.

"I go...to there...talk," spoke Yakovlev in his poor English, laying on his belly against the snowy slope with his eyes just peeking over the top. He spoke to Cromwell, also on his belly, and focused within. *Let me go down there and talk with them.* He glanced at Toog, laying on the opposite side of Cromwell. *I will distract them, then you attack. Please do not kill them. They are simple guards, not these so-called Masters you hate.* He added a pleading smile.

Before they left the ice cave, Toog had consulted the map drawn on the wall of his mind-cave by the visiting mind-cave Russian, who stepped fully formed out of solid stone and began to work the stick of white chalk on the beige wall, showing the route to the nearest Korobka—the interdimensional portal. They made a plan which featured Xmburrhaltins bearing rail-guns. As they hiked three days over the frigid landscape they lost two of their band, unable to endure the frozen landscape.

When they had halted in a protected gulch the first night, Toog pulled loose a blue strand growing from his blue head and took the tip of it in his hand. The tip glowed silver; it did not project any light but displayed a more intense silver than usual. He lifted the tip of the strand and pushed it against the back of Yakovlev's head.

The strength of the sting almost caused Yakovlev to tear away. It reminded him what he imagined a scorpion's sting to feel like, yet it filled his head and ran hard down his spine, a burning sensation, then faded to dull numbness at the site of its attachment: the rear quarter of his head, behind his ear. At that point, Toog pinched off the end of the strand, leaving a fingertip's glob of silver rubbery substance stuck to Yakovlev's head.

I connect to you, you connect to me. Mind-cave Toog waved his blue hand at the mind-cave Yakovlev, standing dumbfounded and covered in chalk dust before the map on the wall.

Yakovlev had grimaced but understood, nodded.

Toog moved off, checking with others in their band. Only a few came on this mission. Having no idea how well guarded the Korobka might be they were not preparing to attack it. First, Toog only wanted to have a look. For their reconnaissance they took only ten creatures, half of them Xmburrhaltins.

I lead you to here because I wish you go home, spoke

Yakovlev through the pinched-off strand's mind-link with Toog. It hurt a little each time he had a thought but he quickly got used to the effect: the first syllable produced a small burn, what followed burned less. If he spoke more there was no painful sensation.

If you lead us into a trap, you will painfully die, Toog's mind-cave voice echoed back to Yakovlev as they lay on the snowy slope gazing down at the Korobka. One of the Xmburrhaltins picked up the communication and grunted at the Russian soldier.

I will talk with them, Yakovlev spoke, nervousness in his voice, *and distract them, and you come out and capture them. Leave them alive, I request, and I will act as though you have forced me to show you the Korobka.* He nodded at Toog. *Watch for my signal.*

What you say will be our plan, Toog responded.

"How about me?" asked Cromwell, catching the mind-talk.

"Soldier see you. Look different," Yakovlev replied in English, his voice low. "Maybe shoot you."

Cromwell nodded. "Indeed." He watched as Toog and Yakovlev retreated down the slope, then spoke after them: "I shall await your call, sir." Tightening his jaw, he turned to the dirty Xmburrhaltin beside him. "Ah! What a fate! To fight and die in Siberia! Three-hundred years in the future. Next to a damn abominable snowman."

The Xmburrhaltin grumbled, showed his rows of teeth. The Vuuth laughed.

They made their way down to the end of the ridge, out to the dirt road. On their side of the cube the flat ground gave them no cover. The side where the guards congregated had to be the entrance, yet for Toog, who had investigated the

Korobka on that northern beach with Grauun, there again seemed to be no door. Only a spread of gravel as a driveway gave any clue.

The guards would see them approach from the end of the ridge if they happened to look in that direction.

Toog measured a span of sixteen Xmburrhaltins laying end to end from his team to the guards in front of the cube—

I count fifty meters, Yakovlev communicated.

Only the four-legged members of the team were fast enough to cover that distance before being shot, Toog responded.

You wait behind the end of this ridge, where the road turns, Yakovlev advised. He would go out and gain their confidence, make them unaware of the monsters about to attack. The long-necked Froju would keep watch, the Xmburrhaltins standing ready behind her spiny rump.

With a mind-tap from Toog, Yakovlev stepped out boldly as the others remained hidden behind the end of the ridge.

Yakovlev walked with determination, hunched in his parka, hood up, as though he was hurrying to get out of the wind yet not willing to break into a run. The thought flickered through his head that he *could* run—run fast and escape the menagerie of creatures that would kill and eat him. A sudden spark burned at the back of his head and he knew his mind-cave link was always open, his scheming thoughts and innocent ponderings no longer private.

So be it. He was honest in wanting them all to go home. Leave this Earth. He wouldn't wish to share it with them. In that way he was on their side. He also could feel for them, knowing the suffering of creatures forced into this wintry world, unsuited for the climate, and for those who'd been abused in the prison or the work camps.

"*Ey!*" Yakovlev called out as he got closer, raising a hand.

The four guards saw him, two of them raising their weapons. The two sitting scrambled up. One grabbed a communication device from his belt.

"*Privet tovarishchi!*" he shouted, a friendly greeting meant to disarm them. He also out-ranked them. One guard seemed to recognize him, waved.

The guards lowered their weapons, the other putting down the communication device, hooking it on his belt.

Without slowing, Yakovlev turned off the muddy road, frozen and uneven, and onto the short gravel driveway leading up to the cube. He waved his hand again and when he stood before them shook hands with the ranking guard.

"Thank goodness I found you," said Yakovlev in Russian, rubbing his hands together against the cold.

They milled about, talking, shivering.

"What're you doing out here in the middle of nowhere?"

"Oh, my truck broke down," said Yakovlev. "I've been walking for many kilometers!"

"You see any monsters out there?"

Yakovlev grimaced. "No, none."

"They haven't used this machine in months."

"The monsters are in the next district, thankfully."

"Still hate being here. Much too cold. And no vodka until Saturday."

"What's the status of this one? In operation?" asked Yakovlev.

"Oh, they fiddle around with it sometimes. I think they might be gearing up for another trip. Who knows?"

"The Ministry is kinda down on exploration these days. Too much bad propaganda, you know."

"Yeah, now people know about the monsters they bring back. Big uproar, as you can imagine."

"Well, some of them are dangerous."

As they chatted, Yakovlev moved casually to his right, one step at a time so the guards turned with him to remain face to face. Soon their backs were toward the creatures hiding behind the bend of the road.

"You hear about Third Laser Battery? Attacked by monsters!"

"Yes, terrible."

"Then the response team got attacked, too."

"Is that so?" Yakovlev responded. "Perhaps they were not so prepared."

"All lost, they said."

Yakovlev kept a straight face, wishing the news didn't include him. One guard eyed him like he was recognized. Of course, his uniform's name tag gave him away. It was half-ripped off already so he finished it, stuffed the cloth strip in a side pocket.

"I had to take this parka from my dead comrade, sorry to say. Killed in the crash. Mine was ruined—mud and engine oil."

"Crash?"

"You said it broke down."

"Yes, the truck. Went off the road, into a ditch. Monsters set a trap on the bridge."

The guards seemed sympathetic. They also had their backs to the squad of monsters.

"Any chance of catching a ride back to headquarters? I need to file a report as soon as possible."

"Not for three more days. You'll have to stay with us in the compound 'til then."

"What compound?" asked Yakovlev.

"Over there, around those rocks, back in the gorge."

"A poor lodging. But it's out of this horrible arctic wind."

"Night duty is terrible! I'd give my first-born son to get out of night duty."

"We stay there, one week's duty, then return to town."

"The scientist quarters are nice, though."

"Who is your commander?" asked Yakovlev.

"Old Lieutenant Gorky, about fifty years old."

"Hah! Yes, that old fart keeps getting demoted."

"I must endure by-the-book Lieutenant Lozhkin over at Security Brigade HQ, which is worse."

"Can't be bad as Gorky, a real bastard. Like today, he denied us lunch just because we were too slow getting ready for duty this morning. I mean, it was friggin' minus-forty at dawn!"

Tall shadows fell over them. Yakovlev spun on his heel, but the Xmburrhaltin was upon him, swatting him down to the snow with a backhand slap. The beast reached for the nearest guard, tore his head off in one grab-and-twist, and began drinking the fountaining blood. Two shots fired from the next guard's weapon, the rail-gun bolts striking the huge beast in the ribs yet not stopping the attack. The Xmburrhaltin hit by bolts grabbed the guard, raised him up then brought him down hard against the ground, breaking his neck, fracturing his skull.

Other Xmburrhaltins, who had come sliding down the snowy slope directly at the cube rather than running up the road from the end of the ridge, swung their big arms around the other guards. Cromwell and two other upright creatures, the four-armed Fruth and the stocky, nearly transparent Gurrul, tied the guards' hands, removed their weapons and communication devices, threw the guards down on the frozen ground as Toog arrived.

The Russian got to his feet, brushed the snow from his parka.

"I asked you not kill," Yakovlev demanded, his Russian heard as Xmburra in their mind-caves.

I was hungry, the Xmburrhaltin responded mentally, licking its red lips. *You never was hungry?*

Yakovlev reddened with anger—

How to enter? came Toog's voice in Yakovlev's mind.

Yakovlev pointed to the bend in the road, leading back into the gorge. *There is a compound with soldiers*, he communicated. *Maybe they will come. Maybe the guard called them.*

Toog's mind-voice became more agitated. *We must hurry. How does it open? How do we go home?*

"I don't know," Yakovlev spoke, glancing at Cromwell. "Make him understand. Other guards will come."

"M'Lord, he says...." Cromwell stopped, seeing Toog's intense stare fixed on the Korobka.

The creatures stood before the huge structure, gazing up at its height, equal to three Xmburrhaltins standing atop each other. On the front of the cube appeared a very tall door which likely would roll up. Like the cube on that northern beach, there seemed to be no way to get inside, no clear door that could be opened. No handles or levers, no buttons to push. Liwo, the gazelle-like Binko from Molk, sprinting around the cube, reported with her four horns glowing that all sides appeared the same: flat gray surfaces, smooth as ice.

It must be magnetic. Yakovlev's eyes narrowed. *This is not the korobka I visited before, but they must be similar.* He studied the front of the cube but kept glancing to his left, expecting soldiers from the compound to come rushing at them. *They will come soon.*

The guards tied up on the ground cursed him.

"Shut up!" he barked in Russian. "I'm fixing mistake."

Yes, righting a wrong, Toog repeated.

Klarr, the Di'h from Jmarh'h, clawed forward, raised one of its three primary barbs and an electric pulse shot out like lightning, striking the front of the cube but to no effect.

When I visited korobka before, communicated Yakovlev, *one scientist held up a device which must have produced a code which opened the door.* He continued examining the front wall's perfectly smooth surface, seeing no controls to open it.

"Anyone in need of a good locksmith?" Cromwell dared chortle—and felt a punch to the gut which bent him over. "Apologies."

Code, Toog's mind-cave voice communicated. *Numbers. Measurements. Equations. They will match, break the code.*

Yakovlev wasn't sure what Toog meant, but he stepped aside as the blue being moved to the front of the cube.

Toog selected one blue strand from among all that hung from his head, held it before his eyes, then let it drop back to the others and chose a different strand. Its tip glowed silver, pulsing wildly as he pushed it forward. The tip turned bronze as it came within a hand's width of the cube's surface. The wall began to vibrate.

"Whatever this magic is, all the devices have gone mad," cried Cromwell, holding up the guard's comm device to Yakovlev. The gauges were spinning erratically.

"Stand away," said Yakovlev.

They all heard his message telepathically and moved.

Toog stood before the front wall, holding the bronze tip of the strand close, almost touching the surface. The wall vibrated, became a fierce shaking that felt like an earthquake under their feet. The wall rattled, upper corners moving, bending inward as it dimpled. The lower corners wrinkled. Cracks spread to the center and in one *swoosh* the front wall caved in, bending at the corners, breaking apart at the center, the metal tearing open, leaving jagged edges. At the same instant, Toog's small body was blown backwards—into the furry chest of a Xmburrhaltin, who caught the blue one and set him down gently.

"*Yebena mat'!*" Yakovlev's mouth gaped in shock.

Yakovlev thought Toog would faint from all of the energy expended to break open the door of the Korobka. But the blue one stood straight again like nothing had happened.

A piercing alarm sounded within the structure. Yakovlev glanced back toward the entrance to the gorge where the compound was that housed the other soldiers.

"Now they know for sure," he grumbled in Russian, wishing he had a weapon of his own. Again the guards tied up on the ground cursed him. He glared at them. "If you want to live, you'll stay quiet."

The entrance created was open just enough for the smaller creatures to enter, like the Hu-mans and Toog, but not the Xmburrhaltins and the four-footers. They would need to wait outside. Yakovlev warned them about soldiers coming from the compound. If they did attack, they would need to fight while Toog was inside.

Let me clear the way, spoke Yakovlev through his mind-cave figure. *There may be scientists inside and they will be frightened how the door opened in this manner.*

Go, Toog responded.

Yakovlev pushed the metal flaps down with his gloved hands and heavy boots, then bent low and stepped gingerly through the jagged gap. What appeared to be metal had left sharp edges he was careful to avoid, lifting his knee as he climbed over the lower edge of the portion still fixed to the cube's wall. He caught his lower trouser leg on a sharp edge and ripped it open before extricating himself, tripping into the cube's interior.

Cromwell got in positon to go next but Toog raised a blue hand to the Hu-man's shoulder, directing him away.

"But I assumed...."

Wait.

"When you solve the riddle, sir, I shall be here, prepared for my return home."

Toog followed Yakovlev's movements, folding down upon newly bent knees, his rubbery legs forming a joint in one leg and a similar joint at a higher point on the other leg to accommodate the necessary angle. Toog passed easily through the gap, unfolded himself into an upright stance once he was on the other side. He stood tall—as much as an Aull from Sebbol could, up to Yakovlev's chest.

The soldier stared straight ahead at a long passage, longer than it should have been. Toog saw how it appeared to extend much farther than the cube's outer dimensions would indicate. It seemed to go on forever: a white four-walled corridor without any doors, control boxes, signs, or other beings occupying it.

Yakovlev was astonished. *This is different from the korobka I visited. There were control panels about here on the walls.* He pointed, then had to hold a hand to his ear against the alarm's screeching. *One of the administrators showed me the buttons to push to deactivate the alarm.*

Toog held up his blue hand, four fingers curled together, making a fist, and with a blink of his eyes the alarm ceased.

That is a good trick, Yakovlev intoned. *We must keep you around for just that.*

Now go, Toog communicated, his hand pointing ahead.

Down the corridor?

Yakovlev saw that the passageway angled downward as

it went deeper, apparently descending into the ground. It could lead to an underground facility, he thought. Yet the cube was not large enough for it. Was anyone down there?

Someone down there knows we broke in. Maybe they will call soldiers.

I am not afraid, Toog communicated. *Are you?*

Now I am.

Yakovlev started off, stepping lightly but with a steady pace.

Toog could not match the soldier's speed. He tried to stiffen his legs, to make them move faster, yet they would not hold their configuration. His body felt watery, as though he needed to concentrate to maintain his form. It almost felt as though he was pushing himself through the *skarg*, the strong liquid pressure against his body.

Yakovlev paused, waiting for him.

Toog's blue body was darkening in places, turning purple. A few strands on his head curled upward as though detecting something. The silvery tips blinked with curiosity.

Do you feel it? Yakovlev communicated. *Magnetic pulse, I think. Subconscious vibration. The machinery is in operation.* He saw how his companion vibrated, twin images flickering like some kind of animation film.

It will shake me apart, came Toog's response. *My fluids will boil. My body will burst.*

Should we go on? asked Yakovlev.

We should. There is no turning back. Toog pressed on. *My inner Ru will guide me.*

Yakovlev again wanted to ask him about this 'inner Ru' the blue one kept mentioning, but he needed to stay alert. More guards could come at any moment. The strange vibration he felt, although annoying, wasn't much different than being close to some of the experimental laboratories in his youth. Machinery. Nothing to fear.

But something is on, operating.

He turned to see Toog's body in flux. His blue torso shook like it was locked in a centrifuge. Toog's face was distorted, eyes and nose and mouth switching positions, strands swirling about his head. Yet he continued to step forward, determined.

We must go back, Yakovlev communicated.

Can not go back, the blue one responded.

Another step.

Another—

Two guards appeared, seemingly straight out from a hidden side panel that opened and closed, indicating there really was more space underground than might be suspected at first. They wore white coveralls that displayed on the front the red circle and blue triangle logo of the Academy of Interdimensional Exploration. Private security team, thought Yakovlev. So the cube had additional areas below ground. That explained a lot. He tried to remember the schematics he had been shown; the great machinery that ran the cube was located under it. He recalled the diagram showing four long tubes like jet engines, turned upright, driving the mechanism that could tear open the universe.

The private guards held up their stubby pulse-guns like trained soldiers as they jogged casually up the corridor's slope to intercept them.

"Sorry," Yakovlev spoke in Russian, grinning at the guards. "I guess I'm lost."

They didn't seem to appreciate his situation. He actually was lost—lost in so many ways.

"I'm hostage," he cried out to ease their suspicions.

No, they didn't care if he was lost nor that he was any

kind of hostage. The Korobka had been breached. There was no hiding the damaged entrance behind him. Who else could have done that? Only the blue being standing beside the soldier.

By habit, Yakovlev reached for the sidearm which was no longer in his holster. *I need a weapon*, he cried out in his mind-cave.

Stand behind me, Toog responded.

The vibration diminished and he regained solidarity, standing firm on his spindly legs, blue hands weaponless.

What? How can...?

Yakovlev, not believing he was safe, nevertheless had seen quite enough since he was captured by the monsters. He dashed behind the little blue being, then wondered whether he should crouch down.

Before he could decide, a cloud of blue mist filled the air in front of them, hovering, then expanding to fill the corridor from side to side and top to bottom, like a curtain hung between them and the guards. It was something like the spray of squid ink, thought Yakovlev. It had to have come from the blue one, blown out from his tiny mouth.

Yakovlev could see through the blue mist. The guards gasped, dropped to the floor with thuds, grabbing their throats. He rushed forward to take their weapons, coughing and choking in the blue haze.

Move out of the cloud, came the instruction.

"*Da, da!*" He dropped to his knees, coughing out the blue mist, one hand over his mouth and nose. *I know it is bad for my lungs,* he communicated, *like for those two. We are the same species. Are they dead?*

The blue mist coalesced after a moment into granules that were swept to the edges as fine powder by the airflow in the corridor. The vibrations ceased, as though someone had turned off the machinery beneath them.

They will sleep for a short-cycle, Toog communicated.

Yakovlev stood, regained his balance. *You have many talents.*

My inner Ru guides me. The blue one seemed to grin, his facial features returning to their proper positions.

"*Da*," said Yakovlev. "I get it now."

On they went, down the gentle slope of the corridor, what must have been thirty meters. They had to be below the surface by now, thought Yakovlev. The earlier vibration lessened as they went on, the air warmer in the corridor.

Yakovlev slung one of the pulse-guns gathered from the guards over his shoulder by its strap and held the other gun, ready to fire. He kept glancing back toward the entrance. How soon until they come? More soldiers, coming to deal with the breach of their precious Korobka. Yet could he shoot one of his own men, his military brethren? Whose side was he on? He felt some admiration for the creatures brought here against their will, and how they fought to return to their homes. That was noble. Yet he couldn't promote them against his own kind.

A man's scream made Yakovlev turn. Up the corridor at the broken entrance, through the gap of jagged bent metal he saw one of the tied-up guards standing, blood fountaining from an armless shoulder. Giant pincers of the mantis-thing that had first tried to force open the cube's door reached out again to snip off the man's head. The screams ceased—but the thunder of rail-guns filled the space, loudly pounding against the cube's walls, then—

A great metallic noise suddenly erupted at the entrance, the pressure wave flattening them against the wall. The floor shook. The walls took on the intense vibration. Down the corridor was darkness, as though the power source had gone out, lights no longer illuminating the corridor. The noise covered any cries from outside the cube. Yakovlev shoved a finger into his ear to shake out the numbness.

Toog slipped off the wall, his blue flashing bronze and back to blue as he focused on the entrance. The anguished cries of different creatures cut through the numbness of the explosion.

"See? There!" shouted the guard who had been tied up, now joining the response team as they climbed through the broken metal. "I knew he was full of shit! Said his truck had engine trouble, then said he was in a crash."

The response team stood with weapons poised as they regarded the two unauthorized figures. More boot-thumps came from below, from the dark end of the corridor ahead of them.

The Masters come, Toog's mind-cave voice spoke calmly.

I'm sorry, Yakovlev responded.

The team of soldiers rushed at them from the entrance, called to duty when sensors detected the break-in. Took them long enough to mobilize, Yakovlev noted sternly.

He glanced at Toog. The blue one must be realizing his comrades outside are probably already killed.

A squad of four guards approached slowly, emerging from the darkness of the lower end of the corridor in white uniforms, weapons held ready. One knelt to check the fallen comrades, still unconscious but alive.

The team of eight from the entrance halted several paces from their out-of-place comrade in uniform and the little blue being with the odd kind of hair, hands and feet. The soldiers did not seem surprised, used to seeing creatures from other worlds. They kept their weapons set to fire.

The leader of the entrance team asked Yakovlev if he was injured. Yakovlev hesitated, couldn't answer, shook his head. The team's sergeant held up a radiometer, checking the levels, gave a nod, waved two of his team forward. The sergeant asked again.

Here was his chance! Yakovlev held a pulse-gun in his hands, had another hanging over his shoulder. He could spin around and lay a blast into the blue being and finally be free. But he would painfully die, he recalled. Maybe. The silver glob behind his ear itched, warmed as if getting ready to explode.

Grinning awkwardly, Yakovlev lowered his gun, pulled off the one on his shoulder, set them both down on the floor. He raised his hands: at first to surrender then to simply shrug.

I don't know, he communicated, then realized they could not hear him.

The squad coming out of the darkness down the corridor also paused, weapons poised. What is this situation? The two groups of soldiers must have wondered why this Master-Sergeant was there with this little blue monster. But the entrance had been torn open—how? And why? What were they doing here in the Korobka?

Smelling the hot scent of a pulse-gun ready to fire, Yakovlev rushed at Toog, pushing him hard against the wall with a fierce grunt.

"Now I've got you, you little blue bug!" he cried out in Russian, holding his forearm across Toog's throat and his other hand at his belly, catching a couple blue strands between his fingers.

The soldiers relaxed; he was one of them.

"This is their leader," said Yakovlev, fighting hard to ignore the burning sensation from the silver nodule stuck to the rear of his head. "They captured me, so I had to play along, be nice boy for them. Ha-ha! But be careful, this one is electric."

The soldiers from both groups closed in, formed a semi-circle around the pair.

Why do you betray me? came the message from Toog's mind-cave figure to the miniature Yakovlev standing in his own mind-cave.

Both the real Yakovlev and the mind-cave figure scoffed.

"Can you believe they just want to go home?" Yakovlev laughed, speaking Russian to his comrades. "They captured me, made me bring them here so they could escape, but I had no idea they could break in. Special powers. But I don't know anything about this Korobka thing, how it works, how to get inside, or the dangers."

"You did the right thing," said the sergeant leading the entrance team, Lensky by his name tag. He glanced back, checking the entrance as though expecting reinforcements.

"Let's bring this blue one outside," said Lensky. "We have a special container for this kind." He grinned at Yakovlev. "You will get medals for this, I'm certain."

"I'm glad you came," Yakovlev cried out happily. "I need to get back to headquarters and file a report."

"I knew something was odd about you," grunted the outside guard who had been saved.

"It's a dangerous world," Yakovlev growled back at the guard. "You have to be clever."

The soldiers took over from Yakovlev as he picked up the pulse-guns off the floor. Two soldiers held Toog by his spindly blue arms with gloved hands. Two others kept their weapons—a pulse-gun and a rail-gun—fixed on Toog. A nylon rope noose was slipped over his round blue head, settling on his slumping shoulders, then hitched snug.

Not too tight, spoke mind-cave Yakovlev, then realized only Toog could hear him.

As they led the blue being up the corridor, the chest-aimed rail-gun moved around to cover from the rear.

Yakovlev held back, scratching the silver glob stuck behind his ear, waiting for pain.

"Let me check our comrades down the corridor," he spoke, with a wave to Lensky. "They are only knocked out, not dead."

"We'll send a medic once we are out of here with this monster," said Lensky.

The guards snickered at their captive.

"Like a walkin' talkin' cartoon character," one of them remarked in Russian, but it was converted to Sebbou in Toog's mind-cave. All their Russian words were converted by his inner Ru so Toog knew what they were saying. The soldier chuckled but was shut up by Lensky.

"I've seen this kind before. At the work camps. They never live long here," one soldier explained. "Start out silver, then turn blue. That means they're going to die soon."

"Tropical species don't last long."

"He's like a little blue frog trying to walk upright," said another.

"Keep alert," commanded Lensky. He took his comm device in his hand, spoke into it: "We have secured the monster, a blue frog type. Bringing out now. Have the container ready. No idea how it broke into the Korobka. Major damage. Other monsters have been terminated. Send medic. We have casualties."

Within Toog's mind-cave, his inner Ru was shedding streams of sorrow-rain, had dropped the chalk on the floor and crashed to its knees.

The group moved in tight formation up the corridor toward the torn-open front wall, step by slow step, making sure they maintained control over the monster.

Yakovlev trailed deliberately.

I am a safe distance now, he communicated.

Understood, Toog responded.

His dull blue skin began to glow, like a luminous sea creature, causing the closest soldiers to take a step back. They had handled alien creatures before. This one had some tricks but it was so small and comical looking that they had no concerns. A few strands growing from his head curled up like snakes, their silver tips shining.

"Look at him," one soldier laughed. "He's frightened."

"Some of them put on an act to scare us," a comrade added.

"He won't bite you, at least. Not with that tiny mouth."

"Be serious," Lensky ordered. "Stay sharp."

As the group came to the front wall where the torn jagged metal edges stood out, the glowing of the blue being's skin intensified. One soldier noted it, another laughed.

"He knows where he's going!"

The glow seemed to lift off Toog, like a thin layer of clothing hovering just above the skin all around him.

Two soldiers stood back, staring.

"We'll have none of that blue magic from you," sneered the corporal and slammed the butt of his rail-gun against the head of the little blue being.

Lensky cursed at the corporal. "No killing, you idiot. These odd ones are bound for the laboratory."

Instead of falling unconscious, Toog's round head had bent inward like the chrome bumper of a truck, then slowly sprang out again, perfectly repaired.

"Hey! How about that?" cried the corporal. "Just like my little sister's plastic dolls."

"I'm calling the lab," said Lensky, reaching for the comm device on his belt, "tell them to expect another blue frog within the hour. They said before that they need to dissect them while they are fresh."

As the corporal stood in amazement, chuckling, the glowing blue cloud around Toog's body intensified—then exploded!

The blue shock wave threw everyone away from him, some of the soldiers blasted against the jagged edges of the torn-open door, the sharp metal impaling them or slicing clean through their bodies. The soldiers behind him were knocked back so hard they hit their heads on the floor and lay too dazed to rise.

Toog no longer glowed. Standing free, he lifted off the noose from around his neck, dropped it on the floor, and turned to locate Yakovlev far down the corridor, away from the energy pulse. Raising his hand, Toog's fingers extended and formed what resembled a two-prong antenna. A silvery current crackled between the prongs.

Yakovlev guessed what was about to happen.

The energy stream shot out, touching him right in the center of his chest, even that far down the corridor, and he crashed to his knees, held stiffly in the electric field. When Toog released him, he fell forward, his face hitting the floor.

Yakovlev rolled onto his back, spasms shaking his body. When the spasms stopped, he lay still, breathing hard.

I need you to help me, came the message. *Therefore I chose not to kill you now.*

I understand, replied Yakovlev weakly. *Thanks.*

With the blue lightning crackling down the corridor, panels popped open along the white walls down the corridor. Behind each panel they saw rows of buttons, small screens, switches and levers to operate. Toog stepped toward Yakovlev.

Why have them along this long corridor? Why do they appear identical? They had the same thoughts at the same time, as their miniature figures met in their shared mind-cave.

"There are five Korobka I know of," said Yakovlev weakly in Russian, converted to Sebbou in Toog's mind-cave. He slowly got to his feet. "The one I visited was the most westward of them. We are now in the most eastward one. It has a different design. Likely it was built last, so what they learned from the others they changed for this one. New and improved."

How does it operate? How do I go home?

Yakovlev rubbed his head. "There will be more coming."

Then we must hurry.

"Maybe there is no time." Yakovlev glanced up the corridor at the jagged broken entrance, the mangled bodies. "We broke into their precious Korobka. People will come. With big weapons for us!"

My comrades are gone, Toog communicated. His inner Ru sat on the floor of his mind-cave, covered in sorrow-rain.

In a way they have gone home, Yakovlev responded, raising his arm and holding out his hand, ready to clap the blue one's shoulder like a comrade. But he hesitated, withdrew his arm.

Toog's blue skin flashed bronze twice, returning to blue each time. Unconcerned, he stepped up to the next panel that had popped open. The door slid apart, half to each side, revealing a small data input system featuring a biometric scanning pad. The keypad and other controls seemed to allow for adjustment of the device, perhaps to select the destination. He raised his hand, webby fingers spread, silver fingertips widening and flattening into suction pads.

Yakovlev held up his hand. *What will happen?*

Toog's hand hovered over the biometric scanner. Perhaps it was a way of unlocking something: the person would be identified through biometric scan and something would become operational. Or it was a device which would identify what kind of creature touched it.

Yakovlev was afraid of that. "Maybe if they read you, they have safety protocols which might be dangerous. The corridor could be flooded with poison gas to kill every living thing in it. Something like that."

Toog paused, silver sparks flickering within his blue hand as his inner Ru translated.

How would they know an Aull from Sebbol is visiting?

"Because they have a record of every creature they've taken, and every world they've visited," Yakovlev replied. "It's in the computer record of this place."

How to access the information?

"If you know Russian, then you c—"

Toog grabbed Yakovlev's hand, pulled it to the panel on the wall. Yakovlev resisted.

"It's not that simple. I don't know the pass codes or which files to look in. And they have my record, too, most likely."

I only need someone to input Russian code.

Toog grasped Yakovlev's hand, pressed it to the biometric scanner. Instructions in Russian flashed by on the left as the screen blinked green. Yellow circles appeared, showing where to place fingertips. The circles pulsed as data streamed down the left side of the screen. His smug face appeared in one record as well as details of his service. The red X indicated he'd been terminated from those positions. Finally the data flow stopped and the circles faded away.

Yakovlev lifted his shaking hand from the scanner, held it there a moment as if assessing the experience.

"Now they know I'm here. I'm likely finished. Promotion is kiss goodbye."

They both looked around, up and down the corridor. Nothing had happened. No new soldiers came running at them. No secret doors opened. No poisonous gas was released. No robot killers unleashed. The guards knocked unconscious remained dazed up the corridor, one rolling over and moaning in pain, holding his head, the others presumed dead. The pair below them in the corridor still asleep, one snoring.

"I must be too ordinary to unlock anything," Yakovlev spoke to himself. His handprint didn't achieve anything.

Yet they had not pulled down the red lever on the side of the panel. Toog pointed to it. His inner Ru stood tall and proudly recited Bar'Gafu's instructions: 'Press controls in the following order: the red button, then the green, then blue, then white, then the same red button again. Next press the keys that correspond to the numbers assigned to the being using the cube, and keys for identification. Select destination same way. Then pull down towards you the big lever to right of control panel, then press large black square on left side of panel, then push down small lever in middle. That begins the process for them. Feel surge of energy flow through the cube. Bodies shake, energy rattles until wall appears thin, see through it, then disappears and see other world. Step forward and be there.'

Yet this was a new kind of Korobka, Yakovlev had said, and there were not any of the buttons Bar'Gafu had noted. The Heis-Tegagan never mentioned a biometric scanner, either. There was no big lever to the right or a big black button in the middle, but there was a small lever on the left with a red handle. It must be important; it was red.

Toog reached for the small red lever and pulled it down before Yakovlev could stop him.

"Wait!" exclaimed the Russian.

The screen lit up, showing rows of sixteen small squares of different color patterns. There was plenty of space remaining for more of the square images. A total of forty squares would fit on the screen, Toog calculated. So twenty-four more worlds could be added—

"*Vybrat' tsel'*" spoke a feminine robotic voice. The words were also displayed on the screen. 'Select target.'

Yakovlev translated for him in his mind-cave.

I want to go home, Toog communicated. *To Sebbol.*

The voice did not respond. Toog spoke his home's name in squeaks and chirps but still no response from the machine.

Yakovlev reached around Toog, pointed to the blue-green-gray square half-way down the left side. "This icon."

Already they were feeling the Korobka's vibrations rolling up and down the corridor. Yakovlev had a bad feeling. The engines were churning below them, building up power. He didn't know what was going to happen.

"Are you going to push it?" Yakovlev held his breath.

Toog raised his blue hand then paused to gaze at the soldier.

I can go home now? A vague smile appeared on his face.

"I don't know how it works." Yakovlev expelled a loud sigh. "But this icon is for the world you want. If you push it maybe you get data about your world. Or maybe you—"

Toog extended his longer finger.

"Wait," snapped Yakovlev, holding up his hands. "If you push wrong buttons or set wrong destination then the portal might open in reverse, suck the other world into this very corridor. Then the power in this unit could start chain-reaction, maybe cause explosion. Could cause systematic repercussions across Eurasia—the huge network of underground tubes across Siberia all filled with methane—and maybe blow up entire planet. If one tube ignites, then all tubes ignite and kaboom! Goodbye Earth."

Toog's eyes bulged, his mouth round. *Your kind did not consider that possibility when it was built?*

"Uh...*nyet.*" Yakovlev took a breath. *They did not think ahead.*

Toog's face flashed bronze. *If I input wrong codes this machine will explode?* His skin started glowing blue. A silver spot formed on his head.

It is possible. Yakovlev grimaced, actually afraid.

Toog's blue hand hovered over the scanner pad. *And then come explosions across this planet?*

Yakovlev was shaking his head. *Again, possible.* He put his hands on his hips. *But I don't advise.*

Then the passage to my world, and all worlds, will be closed.

The little blue being from planet Sebbol dropped his hand down upon the scanner.

"Stop!" Yakovlev exclaimed, but it was too late.

Yakovlev grabbed Toog's wrist, tried to wrench his hand off the scanner but felt a sharp pain at the back of his head. A second burst of pain made him fall back, tumbling to his knees. One hand reached back for the rubbery glob behind his ear, scratching at it, trying to get it off, but it wouldn't budge.

Beneath them the machinery surged, roaring around them. The screen glowed green once more, with circles appearing. But only enough circles lit the screen for the four fingers Toog had. He moved his fingertips over them.

As data flickered down the side of the screen, the lighting in the corridor dimmed. The dark end of the corridor lightened, however. A blue-green-gray haze filled the square as the walls, floor, and ceiling became a frame around the scene: a place of lush flora, murky water, boiling sky, bronze clouds over brown mountains, creatures in the air and on the land and in the water seeming so real.

Toog's eyes widened, bulging out of his blue head. He swept the strands out of his face, and stared at the scene before him, formed in the square of the corridor.

"Sss ^{ss}$_{ss}$ ee^{ee}_{bb} $bb$$_{oo}$ o o $_l$$_l^{l}l$........ ... ."

A high-pitched squeal like nothing Yakovlev had ever heard before. He stepped aside, surveying the screen and the flickering data streams over Toog's shoulder.

We call it Tau Kita 6...what you call Sebbol.

Toog lifted his hand off the screen and the image started to fade, first into reds and golds, then into darkness. He quickly slapped his hand back on the screen, pushed his fingertips into the circles, and the scene returned with the corridor shaking.

How? cried Toog's mind-cave miniature.

His inner Ru appeared, looking flustered, as though it had run through a rainstorm, bronze water running down its robe, reflecting Toog's mood. Now you understand the desire trick, how you can possess one thing yet not possess one thing. Yet you must do both things at once. His inner Ru held up both hands, palms open, and shrugged.

Toog stared hard at the biometric screen, then glanced down the corridor at the blue-green world of his home swirling there.

Is it real? Can I go there? called Toog.

Yakovlev grunted, not believing. "I was told on my first

visit that when the settings are correct, they just walk into the other world. Like tunnel. Never believed it could be possible, but I'm a soldier, not a scientist."

I am a gardener on my world, Toog responded.

He stared at the biometric screen again, took several strands in his other hand, selected one at a time, pushing their tips down to the circles on the screen. As he released each fingertip, he stuck a rubbery strand tip there. When his hand was completely free of the screen, he reached out and pinched off the tips so they were no longer attached to the strands. He turned again to see the scene in the corridor.

The image remained!

Now run, he communicated, and hurried on his blue legs as best he could until he expected to crash into an invisible wall ahead but, instead, fell and fell and fell....

A comm device crackled up the corridor, hooked to the lower half of Sergeant Lensky, divided at the waist by the jagged metal.

"*Vzvod chetyre, otvechay*," an agitated voice cried out, asking for the team to check in. Despite the noise of the Korobka's machinery, Yakovlev got the rest of the message: Team 4 didn't check in, so Team 5 is coming. There was no one to answer. A final command followed: 'And take Master-Sergeant Yakovlev into custody.'

He took only a heartbeat to consider his options.

Popping open a small door on the side of the panel, as he had seen them do at the demonstration he had witnessed previously, he slipped the remote control wand into the side pocket of his trousers.

He glanced at the pulse-gun dropped on the floor up the corridor, his throat tightening. Too far to go and grab it.

Dismissing it, he charged at the blue-green scene swirling in the square frame of the corridor, leaping only at the last instant, just as the blue one had done, and falling farther than he thought he should be falling based on the scene he glimpsed before he leaped.

▲ ▶ ▲ ▲   13

He might have hit his head, maybe breathed the wrong gas, ate some bad food, or perhaps he had traversed an interdimensional doorway from one reality to the next. Anything was possible.

When Toog opened his eyes, he saw the amber sky above, clear and unblemished by gray overcast. Words stuck in his head, words he had vouchsafed while on that horrid world. He expected to find *skarg* at his feet and *oum* in the air. Instead the air was parched, the land barren. He wondered if he had pushed the wrong buttons and gone to the wrong world. The scene in the corridor had appeared to be his world. Or it was only a trick of the Masters.

What he found was his blue body slumped against red dirt with red mountains in the distance, and a dark red sun, larger than he remembered, blazing fiercely down upon him. He tried to rise, but his legs were too weak, as though he had swum a full sun-cycle through all the *skarg*s of Sebbol. His head wavered, like it was full of *lool*.

A red *duidir* crawled over his foot. He moved to flick it off, hesitated. Reaching for the insect, he pinched it gently between his fingertips and, because his fingertips had developed special abilities in his former environment, he could detect the genetic code of this tiny life form. It was a creature of Sebbol.

So I am truly returned to Sebbol....

The bug went still between his fingers. Toog set it down on the dirt and it fell over, remained still. Yet he had not crushed it or in any way harmed it. Perhaps residual energy still pulsed in his fingertips. He rolled onto his belly to examine the thing. Six legs and a long body, no wings, four antennae, stinger in place.

Toog noticed his blue strands had shortened, not hanging in his face as he lay there. Their silvery tips had closed off and were blue like the strands. Perhaps it was happening because he was back on his world. He no longer needed the protections Great Goddess Aull had designed for him. Now returned, he could live the simple life he had lived before. He could work in the garden, gather food, sell it in the market, and enjoy his family. He thought of his full-mate L'ra and the springling they made, and he thought long before he could recall her name: M'ah. But time had turned and they must be gone, and their kin gone, too. His eyes leaked sorrow-rain, which made the dirt wet.

In the moisture came forth at first one then more of the stringy *ylla*. He watched the little white worms wriggle forth from the soil, poking out and sniffing around for their mother. They stretched tall toward the sun-light. Yes, the land looked very dry, a desert. He guessed he must be far from his village. The little worms were awakened by his tears wetting the soil. And just then his mood shifted and his tears ceased. No more moisture fell and the little worms retreated into the soil, gone.

He noticed his blue feet showed some silver on their

soles and toes. His fingers also had a bit of silver, as well. His head hurt and he put his hand there only to discover that most of his strands had receded into his head, leaving only nubs. He never knew he could evolve such features. Now he could not believe he was returning to his previous form. A good sign he was home.

And yet what home? How far to his village? And who might be there to greet him? It had to have been years since he was taken away. Would anyone remember him? Would they doubt him when he declared he was Toog? Would any of his family remain to welcome him? Or would it be exactly as the Heis-Tegagan predicted?

He stood, stretched, discovered his arms would not extend beyond their normal length as they had on that other world. They were stiff now, no longer rubbery and malleable. The same with his legs. He rubbed his hand over his smooth head—the nubs had receded. He regarded his silvery palms and his mouth up-turned.

Scanning each direction, he could not get a bearing. He could not decide which way to go. Nothing looked familiar. The mountains in the distance could be the mountains near his village, except for one small gap that he could see which the mountains near his village did not have. If he could go there and climb to the top—they were not so high, he decided—then he might be able to see better and choose a path home.

And then, just as Toog shook himself from the weariness that had engulfed him since his arrival, he heard a loud thump and turned to see another creature fallen out of the air, landing hard on the red dirt, and rolling to a stop almost at his feet.

Yakovlev lay flat on his back. The hot sun bore down on his face and one hand went to his chest as if checking for injury.

Toog gazed down at the soldier, noticed how the strands had grown out of the creature's lower face, strands which were very thin and had no silver tips, that had not been so long when they first met in the ice cave.

The soldier opened his eyes, blinking, and brought a hand up to shield his face from the bright sun-light.

"*Gde ya?*" asked Yakovlev. Where am I?

Toog extended his arm. Usually—what had been usual on that other world—his arm would stretch all the way down to the Hu-man's head, his arm becoming thinner as it got longer, but that was no longer possible. So he crouched until his silvery hand could touch the head of the alien creature.

This is Sebbol, Toog communicated.

Yakovlev seemed to get the message in his head.

"*Ya boyalsya etogo,*" he groaned. I was afraid of that.

Toog remembered that day as he climbed up the dry mountain slope, his smooth skin quickly scratched and bruised, his head and face turning from silver to bronze— and the big creature behind him struggling to keep up, straining to breathe the air of this world.

He remembered how the shaman told him that P'ua was not suitable for him. They had been granted permission to practice the mating ritual yet no orb appeared. The shaman declared P'ua flawed and set her aside for another: his full-mate L'ra. He and L'ra quickly made an orb. *I only want a life where I can make orbs with my full-mate*, he recalled wishing. P'ua could not be his full-mate, or anyone's, so she was sent to the shadows, only a partial-mate for anyone who needed to prepare for the mating ritual or who snuck through the *skarg* for a brief *booz*—just to keep their *org* loose and shiny. Others shunned her until one day she left—walking out of the village one morning and never returning. Most expected she would be eaten by a *gortor*, as she often liked to lounge by the *abo*, or be carried away as dinner by a pack of *druka*. That was a common fate for an Aull who wandered away from the village alone. They had been warned.

Yet Toog knew it was her by the band of metal, a gift he made for her, fixed around the arm bone that protruded from the red dirt in a wide depression which no longer held water, a *skarg* dried into desert in the years Toog had been away. Just under the red-crumb surface he found head bones, cracked, half of them missing. Possibly a hungry *duur* had scooped out her skull, made it hollow like a drinking cup, and let the *ul* slide wet down its throat before scampering off. He gazed down at the remnants of his former life, someone he used to know, realizing he was too late.

He still wanted to climb the mountain to get a look at his world, all red and brown and gold like the *thax* the shaman had told them about when they were young. When Aull acted badly they would find themselves in *thax*, where they would dry into husks and blow away as dust.

"So there is life on this planet, after all," mugged the other gruffly in its native language, seeing the bones.

Toog did not reply but stepped away, continuing the journey home. It could not be far.

"It looks like Mars—like pictures of Mars I've seen," spoke the other.

Toog wished he could shut off his inner Ru, to stop the translating. But there was the possibility the other might speak something important.

"All red desert," the other intoned, gazing around. "But it's warm here, not cold. Too warm, too dry. Can't breath it easily."

More complaints. Always complaints.

"I think the gravity is too much here," the other complained. "I can't walk easily nor breath this thick air."

Toog tried to ignore the verbal noise.

"How long is day here? I'm tired already. When does it get dark? I want to sleep."

Toog stopped, waited for the other to catch up.

A long-cycle is thirty short-cycles, Toog communicated.

"Thirty? You mean thirty hours?" asked the other, breaking into a chuckle. "Too long. How long is a short-cycle?"

A short-cycle is nine-hundred-ninety-nine beats of an Aull's heart.

"But my heart beats...what, about sixty or seventy a minute, I guess," said the other. He counted out a minute. "So what is that then?"

The heart of an Aull beats ninety for one of your minutes.

"So...ninety beats times sixty minutes...is...hmm...." He rubbed his head. "Wait, what? So that's like two hours.... So your short-cycle is two hours, not one!"

Correct. Thirty short-cycles makes a long-cycle.

"And around around we go," said the other, waving his hand in circles. He tried to laugh but broke into a wheezing fit. When he recovered: "So it's how many days in year here?"

Sebbol goes around Uf in six-hundred-sixty-eight long-cycles.

"Too long! It's crazy! No, I sure wouldn't want to live here. When does this summer season end?"

Toog closed his tiny mouth. Red sand was blowing, brown dust boiling into clouds, drifting away. The red sun blazed down.

Sebbol used to be wet and full of colorful flora, with many collections of water, a place of fertility, a home.

"If you say it's so...."

The mountains seemed lower, washed away by the blinding winds every ninety sun-cycles, according to the shaman. That was their fate. Yet Sebbol was a tropical paradise, lush with flora and soaked with moisture—except when the sun turned angry and crystals fell and the land scorched, which was about every third generation.

Or when the Masters came.

The soldier laughed at a private joke, then turned to Toog. He spoke in his language but the words were written in Sebbou on his mind-cave wall by a tired inner Ru: "You know what would be funny? If they stepped onto different world, one that had advanced civilization. You know, where the natives were far more advanced than us. And they got bigger guns, too. And bad attitude. That would've ended the exploration business quick."

He glanced at his silver host, apparently ignoring him.

"Yeah, instead of a desert planet like this, suppose they went to other world and found big city with many tall buildings, and flying cars. Cannot conquer that. Then what would they do? You ever wonder that? Then I wouldn't be here."

Toog glared back at the other, never a friend, no longer needing its help. Though it did not hammer the bolt through his hand, it was the same kind and might someday be the one to hammer the bolt through other creatures' hands. The only thing holding back his electricity was the fact the other did aid him in escaping. Yet the rest of his gang remained there, captured or killed. Maybe a few got away and survived in the frozen wilderness. He could not help them from here.

If they had come with him in the Korobka, they would all be here on Sebbol now, most of them suffering, Toog realized.

"Wait, wait," called the other desperately.

Toog halted. He gazed up the slope, measuring how much farther it was to the top.

You should have eaten more worms when you had the chance, Toog communicated, referring to when he dug in the ground and pulled up a nest of *ylla* after drops of his *smaul* had drawn them to the surface, then crunched several of them in his mouth before offering a handful.

Then the soldier had insisted on eliminating the fluid in its body and took its *org* out of the cloth, pointed the thing at the ground just as Toog cried out in his squeaky voice not to do it. The golden liquid poured out, gathered on the red dirt, made a puddle—

The ground shook and the soldier toppled over, wetting its cloth, as the puddle disappeared into a crevasse that expanded until a *kuur* rose up like a quick-sprouting tree and bent down with seven fangs showing, forked tongue flickering, and deep purple eyes glowing. Toog raised a spear of energy and sent it at the *kuur*, which deterred it enough for the soldier to scramble away. They got up and ran, the soldier faster than the Aull, yet they escaped.

I won't waste energy cursing you, communicated Toog after they were safely away.

From the top of the red mountain, Toog surveyed his world in each direction. He could not see any village, the blazing light of the angry sun making long-vision difficult. He feared his skin would dry out, his eyes burst, his bones all that remained to mark his passage. He slunk into the shade of an outcrop and thought of the days he had hidden in a cave, shivering from the cold, and his body responded by growing strands to cover him and turning his skin from silver to blue. Already he was re-adapting to this new environment by turning bronze. The flaps of his throat vents had grown longer to better protect against errant sand and dirt. He had grown thin flaps which stretched over his eyes. Yet he did not want to have to adapt to a new world; he wanted to return to the old world of moisture and vegetation he had known.

They found an old road cut over the ground and followed it, never encountering any other travelers. He did not recall the road, had never been this far from the village, but if the Masters came this way then he would, too. They came in the night, probably to hide their approach, so they must have been able to navigate their way in the darkness. The first sign was sound, then beams of light. Those curious enough to venture out of their abodes were captured, taken away, never to be seen again.

Unless they escaped. But who would remember him? Who would tell the tale of his departure, perhaps to be a warning to others? And now that he was returned? What work would he be able to do to be accepted again in the village? His full-mate would likely be given another partner. So he would be nothing. Perhaps someone would mark a scroll for him and set it into a lock-box for all time.

Instead, a tall stone monument rose in the center of the village. Toog saw it before entering the village, from outside the low wall that encircled the place. The abodes within were left empty and silent. He recognized the configuration and it was true. This abode and that one, each in their proper places. The shaman's abode. The marketplace. The garden plots, dry yet still measured in squares of duty. He was home. However, he was too late. None remained. He hurried from abode to abode, checking for any living resident, yet found none. Each abode seemed quickly abandoned, possessions left behind, as if the residents expected to return soon like an ordinary day.

The monument beckoned. A figure standing atop the block had a resemblance to him—to Toog, a gardener who vanished one night, never to be seen again. On one side of the block a plaque had been placed. He could not remember the script of his childhood yet his inner Ru appeared, hesitant and weeping, to tell him its meaning:

Toog went with the Masters as personal sacrifice, willingly to teach them harmony among all beings, as determined by the High Shaman of First Goddess, and only when the Masters had learned harmony would Toog return, and all will have a great feast on that day.

He dropped to the red dirt, legs bent, arms crossing his body, silver head bowed, and his eye-rain ran thick into the ground yet no *kuur* rose to dine there.

Toog never taught harmony to the Masters. The High Shaman was wrong. Perhaps that was the reason his village died. First Goddess was displeased and struck down everyone. If only he had been able to teach the Masters about harmony. He never had a chance to do that; he would have tried, he knew, if given the opportunity. And if he had known that was his purpose in traversing the interdimensional portal. He would have happily taught them everything he knew about gardening, how to prepare the seedlings, tending the growth, the harvesting, even about the best recipes for food dishes he could create. And they would share with him, too, all they knew about...

What did the Masters know about?

He looked over at the soldier, slumped on the ground, all covered in red dirt, wheezing, appearing half-dead.

The Masters knew how to kill, how to torture, how to abuse, how to make devices which allowed them to travel to other worlds and capture other beings, how to conduct tests on the creatures they captured. Surely there was more they could do, more they could share, but to what end? He wanted to return there at that moment. He wanted to return and take the great weapon that had destroyed Grauun's camp and laugh at them, then push the button and watch the world explode. He would go with them. He had nothing left to live for—

"Is this it?" the soldier called to him, voice weak. "Is here your home? Seems dead zone now. All gone."

Toog would not expend the energy necessary to respond.

"Long walking for nothing...."

Yakovlev sat on the red dirt, his sweaty back resting against the abode opposite the one where Toog had resided many sun-cycles in the past. In those days, Toog would never have thought there could be a poor example of a Master lazing like a *frou* in the middle of the village. He complained about the air: too thin and dry to breathe, yet Toog remembered how thick and moist the air used to be, so thick you could see it drifting by. Now the soldier had stripped off his upper cloth and cut short his lower cloth in response to the heat. When complaints of hunger came, Toog reminded him it was easy to open his exit vent and release fluids which would draw the *ylla* up for him to dine on. He finally tried the local delicacy, then lay ill for days.

Usually they would cook the *ylla* and eat it with a good portion of *spix* to ensure the *ylla* did not bite back during digestion.

And the long-cycles turned in this way.

Yakovlev sat outside the abode, back against its curved wall. He stared up at the night sky, an ocean thick with stars and no city lights to interfere with counting them. But he soon grew bored with counting.

"Hey, silver surfer!" he called out, raising his arm, pointing, first finger extended, "I see six moons up there. Why you have six? We only have one. It's not fair."

There was no use in ignoring the other. It would continue to ask questions through the night. So Toog responded from the doorway of his abode: *We have six moons because we have six goddesses, and they need places to live.*

"You have six goddesses?" He scoffed. "That's too bad! Any gods? There must be at least one god to keep them happy."

Perhaps, Toog communicated, *but life comes from goddesses, say the tablets.* He directed the other's gaze to the large gray-green moon hanging over the distant mountains. *First Goddess lives there.* He pointed to the pink moon. *Second Goddess lives there.*

"They all live alone? How sad for them."

Toog indicated the dull red moon and the purple moon. *Third Goddess lives there and Fourth Goddess lives there. Fifth and Sixth Goddess live on the two gray-white moons over there. We seldom hear from them.* He let out a sigh, wishing they would speak up more, give advice which First and Second Goddess had never considered.

"Perhaps you call them goddesses." He tried to chuckle.

"But it's only pretending." The other slid down the wall and dropped flat on his back on the red dirt. "You want to believe they are goddesses, but they are only pretty rocks in the sky. Magic powers, you think, but it's only fancy play of light and shadow, eh?"

No, they live there. They have a temple on each moon.

"Okay, temples I can believe. But no people there, ha!"

They live alone...watching over us...helping us.

"But they need a man sometimes, don't they? Some hero fresh from battle, yeah? A mortal soul to corrupt."

Toog chirped, then gave a whistle that Yakovlev said sounded like a cardinal's song, but Toog didn't know what a cardinal was.

Our goddesses are Aull, not Hu.

"Hu? Hu-what?" Yakovlev growled, rolled over. He breathed hard. "You mean human? Like me?" He coughed, spit out dust. "I bet they would like me, your goddesses. You think? I wonder if we can go there, up to those moons, through the Korobka. Any place is better than here. What am I going to do here? Wait to die? Not even anything to get drunk on here."

Toog stood over Yakovlev one morning, gazing down upon the ill creature. With a squat to bring himself closer, he reached out and placed his silvery hand upon the sun-burnt forehead of the poor example of a Master.

Their shared mind-cave opened and in marched the miniature Toog. Crumpled on the floor, covered in yellow dust, was a tiny Yakovlev, small puffs of breath popping into the cave. There was writing on the wall of the mind-cave, little Toog saw. The words he did not recognize but the image beside them was clearly a rough attempt at depicting the machine which had sent them to Sebbol, the Korobka. Perhaps the words were instructions, steps to follow to use the Korobka.

"Awake?" asked mind-cave Toog of mind-cave Yakovlev.

The little being stirred, shook off the yellow dust that had gathered, twisted its head to address Toog: "Better to not be awake here."

"What do these words mean?" asked Toog, pointing.

The other stared at the wall. "I don't know. Maybe a story about wishing to go home."

Mind-cave Toog pouted. "I have that story in me, too."

"Yes, common story: the little silvery being from planet Sebbol who wants to go home from land of torture. It's like legend. You made it home, little fellow. Congratulations."

Toog held back sorrow-rain. Truth hurt. "How about you?"

"Me? I'm dead already."

"Why did you follow me?"

The other tried to sit up, fell into a coughing fit.

"Did you think you would find your home here?" asked Toog.

"I didn't know what I would find," mind-cave Yakovlev finally responded. "But sure I'm first to visit other world for so long, yeah? Likely I will get big medal for this feat. No, my friend, I thought the others like me came this way— though they wore protective masks and shielding robes— so I wanted to do it." He coughed, found blood in his hand. "Besides, after you left they were calling for me to be arrested. Yeah, for helping you. So I had no place to go."

"Your own kind would capture you? And hurt you?"

"Yes, we do that. It is our special trait."

"Then I am glad to be Aull." Toog studied the weak

Yakovlev. "But you cannot be Aull. You must be what you call Hu-man. First Goddess made us all the way we are, and none can change."

"First Goddess, hmm? Is there another goddess I might speak to about this problem?" The mind-cave Yakovlev tried laughing, which brought another coughing fit.

"I suffer, too, in this new world. If you had come to the world I knew, you would find much moisture, many waters, a vast coverage of vegetation, and many fruits to eat."

"A swamp, eh?" Yakovlev rose to one knee, trying to catch his breath. "I'd go for that about now. A good swim would be nice."

Mind-cave Toog smiled. "We are born in the waters and swim free until our parents lift us out of the waters." His belly changed from silver to bronze as the memory of lifting their female orb from the *skarg* with his full-mate's hands interlocked with his warmed through him and faded.

Yakovlev finally stood tall though unsteady.

"I need a good drink, too. A bottle of vodka would be nice."

Toog pointed again at the writing on the wall. "What does this mean?"

Yakovlev squinted at the wall. "I think it says how to go back. Strange things come in dreams. Like little blue men. I must've been wondering how to go back. Crazy thing this cave."

Toog frowned, his nose flaps quivering. "You can go back. That is your home, not here. I must stay here, even though it is now a dead place. I will await death here. Like Bar'Gafu said. There are no others here so I will die alone as a dried husk."

"Then you might as well return with me."

"To a life of torture?"

"Yes, that's not a good thing." He scratched his beard. "Nor is staying in the cold wilderness with a band of other creatures. You have no options, my friend."

Mind-cave Toog brushed eye-rain aside, closed his nose flaps, turned away. He stepped toward the exit, a dark tunnel leading out of the mind-cave. A shadow colored the far wall, enough to make him pause, but when he looked closer, it had disappeared. The weak, unsteady figure of little Yakovlev remained, leaning against a wall for balance. Then Toog stepped out.

He fell back on the dirt, exhausted by the ordeal. Yakovlev was the same: he had sat up, put his back against the abode, that crazed expression scrawled upon his burnt face, like he couldn't believe he was actually on another planet dying slowly. If the poor air didn't strangle him, radiation was slowly burning him from the inside.

You must go back, Toog communicated through his squeaks and chirps that Yakovlev heard in his mind-cave as Russian.

"I think so, too," the soldier replied.

Toog stood, regarded the other, remembering all that he had endured as a captive of the Masters.

I want to hurt you, because your group hurt me. But I am not like you, and I do not want to be like you. So I will control my inner Ru.

"I didn't hurt you, little man," Yakovlev spoke in Russian, his voice slurred. "I didn't even know what they were doing to all of you, not for a while since I was there. When I did learn the truth, I did nothing. I did nothing because you were just creatures from other planets. Not like us, so didn't count. Beasts of the field, farm labor animals, lab experiments, and so on."

Now you know we have intelligence, no matter how our

body form is.

"I know that now. So do—" His voice cracked, his throat too dry. "So do they now. I'm sorry. I apologize for the way they treated you. I will tell them not to do it again. I'm sure they will listen to me." A painful chuckle emanated from his gullet.

You will die soon if you stay here, Toog communicated. *I will help you. I will go back, too. I must make everything right. First Goddess gave me a task. I must complete it.*

"What task?" Yakovlev gagged when he tried to speak more, then: "I mean, what can a little silver toad do?"

Toog took a step back. *I must destroy the Masters.*

Double-warm was the dark interval and air the thickness of *skarg* sludged over the village, strings of *oum* creeping here and there among the abodes set in rows between the food-gardens and the merchant-stands. The tall stone monument had cracked. In Toog's dream the second-summer *chakari* squeaked low over the short-cycle, then rose to such a gravelly din that he could no longer hear them. Not until their noise ceased.

He awoke on a dirty repose mat in his abode, the ancient swing-basket swaying overhead, making squeaky noise as hot breeze blew in. Another squeak of a different tune tickled his ear. He got up and searched for its source. In the broken rubble he found another swing-basket whose frame had fallen over yet still allowed the swing-basket to move. He touched the basket, gazing around the abode, realizing his full-mate L'ra had a second orb. Then he recalled the dream, when the one named N'oh visited him.

Many generations have come and gone, Toog discussed

with his inner Ru. With each life, memories were made, and a pinch of them left for the others in the form of stories, and objects collected which point to stories.

Their body forms were also left, his inner Ru reminded. The body breaks down into dust eventually and only stories remain. Each small mote mixes with grains of dirt and sand, becoming one with the planet, with the universe once more. *Out of the swamp we came, and to the swamp we must return*, his inner Ru said. Someday the sun will die, too, and long after that moment a new sun will blink to brightness. Then every stray piece of Aull embedded in the soil of Sebbol will blossom into existence once more.

He was the last of his kind, the final Aull, Toog told his inner Ru. Who would know his story? Who would find his bones? Would they wonder who he was? Would they build a monument to him? He had not served them well.

It is not for them to decide if you served them well, said his inner Ru. *It is only for you to solve the riddle of the Masters. That is the task First Goddess has given to you.*

The Masters' Riddle? he asked his inner Ru.

Yes, and until you solve that riddle, I begin to die. And if I should die before you find the answer, then you shall die, too.

Rise now, Toog communicated with the prone Yakovlev, fading away short-cycle by short-cycle. The soldier stirred.

Yakovlev cursed in a rough voice, coughed and spat, watched a thirsty worm rise from the soil seeking moisture. He cursed at the worm and slammed his fist against the dirt.

"What do you want?" he growled in Russian. "Just let me sleep until I'm dead." He was breathing hard.

I will take you back to your world, Toog communicated, *before you die and leave your dust here.*

"Dust!" He cursed more, hearing the word in his mind-cave. He pushed himself up to a knee, his hand rubbing his forehead then his back. He stretched himself up and stood on both legs, swaying a moment before settling into balance. "Damn, my head hurts."

The air is not right for you, Toog communicated. *It does not have enough of the particles you need. I understand why the Masters wore special breathing devices when they came. And wore the special robes with magnetic layers to protect them from the radiation.*

"Yeah, it's true, who would ever want to live on this red piece of rock," Yakovlev cursed, looking around him, seeing the red-brown landscape everywhere. He glared at Toog: the silvery being stood to only half Yakovlev's height, looking like a chrome car bumper. "I guess your skin reflects the sunshine. Is that it?"

There are many mysteries among the choices Great Goddess Aull has made, Toog communicated, starting off.

"Now what's that supposed to mean?" Yakovlev called out, then grumbled as he took long steps to catch up to the little silver being.

They skipped the detour to the top of the mountain to survey the landscape, but the trek still took a long time. Toog pressed on with his spindly legs, joints hardening and aching. The sun blazed down upon him, turning his silver to bronze. His nose flaps stayed open as his wind tubes sucked in the hot, dry air. His throat vents burned.

Always trailing behind was the dying soldier, stumbling and falling, getting up and trying to take several steps before losing his balance again. Many times he would stay on the ground after a fall, resting and breathing hard. His face was red. The portions of his arms and legs not covered by cloth were also red, his skin forming boils in places and flaking off in other places. He often cried out in pain or desperation or both.

Toog patiently waited while he caught a rest, then led him onward, returning along the same path to the point where they had arrived.

"But how you know the way?" his frantic companion called. "The dust has blown over our footprints."

My feet recognize their steps, Toog communicated.

It might be true, thought Yakovlev, staring at Toog's bronze feet, once silver, previously blue—and never covered by shoes. Maybe his feet had some kind of tactile memory.

"But how will we open the portal again?" Yakovlev moaned.

It will open for us when we arrive.

"Ho! You think so? But how you know so much science? It's advanced technology. I don't even know it."

The reverse is understood if the forward is known.

"Now you're talking in riddles!"

Toog halted, let the Hu-man close the gap between them. Toog spun around. *You say there is a riddle?*

"Huh? What?" Yakovlev had to catch his breath, bent over with his hands on his knees, sucking air. "Riddle? What riddle?"

You said there is a riddle. What is it?

More hard breathing, raspy noise that hurt Toog's ears.

"I don't—don't know any—riddle." He fell back on his bottom and collapsed flat on the dirt, arms and legs spread out.

Toog went to him, squatted and pressed a hand to Yakovlev's chest. The muscle inside pulsed irregularly, had a whir to it, like a machine out of alignment, the spinning gradually wearing down the cylinder. It would stop soon, he calculated.

We must return to your world, Toog communicated. *Or you will die here. This world is not meant to hold your dust.*

He focused on his mind-cave and his inner Ru peeked out of the shadowy passage as if being interrupted from dinner. Help me keep this one alive, he asked his inner Ru.

With a weary shake of his head, his inner Ru pointed over to the drawing already on the wall, a detailed diagram of the Hu-man's inner structure. Press here, tap there, push upward here, said his inner Ru. If he does not reset, push hard here then again here. And here. Monitor the movement of fluids through the gap here and here.

Toog thanked his inner Ru and followed the instructions.

"What was that?" Yakovlev gasped, sitting right up and putting a hand to his chest.

You can go longer now, Toog communicated. *I reset the muscle in your chest. It was not getting enough air. Now you can get more air and the muscle will pulse more efficiently.* He stared at the soldier. *Now we continue.*

Yakovlev sprang up like he was on his own world, the gravity about the same. He shook off the dust from himself and took several deep breaths.

"Yeah, that's better," he exclaimed in Russian.

Toog was already several steps away. Yakovlev jogged to catch up to him, pleasantly surprised he could without losing his breath. They kept up the pace and traversed the passage across the plain, pausing to bow before the bones of P'ua.

Soon they reached the place where they had first arrived on Sebbol. Yakovlev was not certain and gazed in every direction. He tried to measure their position against the angle of the sun but did not become more convinced.

Then he saw it: the cube floating in the air about head-high. Just a solid black cube smaller than his fist—almost translucent when seen from the wrong angle. Hovering in the air—no, fixed there, as though nailed to a wall that could not be seen.

Yakovlev was puzzled. "What is that? What do we do with it?"

Toog stood under it; he fit in that space. He looked up at the underside of the cube, but it appeared the same on every side.

Here is the place where we arrived, Toog communicated. *I do not know what the small cube is.*

Yakovlev put his hands on his hips, studied the cube.

It had to have something to do with the portal, of course. When the Masters passed through the foreshortened corridor inside the Korobka and arrived at another world, Toog thought, they must hold the doorway open for them to return. That was the purpose of this cube sitting in the middle of the air, he realized.

He wanted to touch it but his hand could not reach it without the stretching he was able to do before. He raised up on his feet. If he did touch it, would it do something? Open a door into the corridor? Or perhaps him touching it would close the passage forever as a security precaution?

"Ah!" said Yakovlev suddenly. He pulled at his leg covering, put his hand into a hidden space in the cloth, and retrieved a small rectangular device the length of his hand and thickness of his finger. "This," he said, holding it up. "The controls."

Toog stared at the device Yakovlev held up and aimed at the cube as though the device was a weapon. He put his face against the device, looked along its edge as he pushed first one button then another.

In an instant, one side of the black cube opened, folding up. Another side folded down. Other sides folded open, left and right. Each open panel further unfolded, making the cube grow and grow until the entire thing became a flat panel the height and width of the corridor in the Korobka.

Looking into the darkness of the final opening, they could see nothing. There was no corridor. No swirling scene of the inside of the Korobka.

It is the way, Toog communicated, yet he hesitated.

"You sure?" The soldier shifted his boots in the dirt. "It might be a dead end. Or we go to another world."

You must go so you will live, Toog communicated. *I should stay here. It is my world. I am meant to stay here. I will soon join the dust of my world*—

"Stop your woe talk!" Yakovlev regarded his little escort. He gave a sigh. "Yeah, I understand. You have no choice. Die here or come with me back to the world where you were prisoner or slave. Maybe they will execute you for escaping and the army you put together to attack us—attack them."

Or I should return to find my comrades and help them return to their homes, Toog responded. *Those who remain will want to go home. That has not changed.*

Yakovlev stepped forward, reaching his hands up to grasp the edges of the corridor's opening, like climbing into the back of a truck.

"Either come with me, like you say to complete your mission," Yakovlev said with a wry grin, "or you come to enjoy the fine arctic weather we have."

Into the darkness he leaped, his hands grasping the side walls the last to disappear.

Toog stared into the dark square and took a slow half-step forward, hit by a sudden blast of humid air.

Crumpled on the floor, but without the blast-furnace heat and acrid air of the previous world, Yakovlev rose to a knee, putting a hand to his forehead.

He recalled reading the first news about the holes. A special environment zone. Natural phenomena which excited scientists. A hole of unknown origin, perfectly round, bottomless. Another hole was discovered in another arctic region. Neither sinkholes nor natural caves, explorers were initially overcome by fumes seeping from the holes. Methane. A colorless gas that filled the air for miles around, making it difficult to breathe. And it blew east—around the world. His head churned with the information, like a bad school lesson returning to torment him.

If it works in reverse, the other world coming through to our world, then you get a Tunguska blast, the voice of his teacher echoed in his head.

Yakovlev didn't care what they found, only that the ancient permafrost was melting and releasing previously frozen pockets of methane. The gas was rising into the atmosphere, joining other gases. Investigation of its sources led to the discovery of the first interdimensional doorway. The folding of space-time, they called it, around magnetic vortices made it possible to cross to other worlds. With a greater understanding of the process, scientists created the device which stabilized and directed the energy, making it possible to walk from one world to the next—or any world that could be connected through manipulation of a particular space-time vortex, essentially a very short worm-hole, sometimes called an interdimensional tangent or doorway or portal.

"*Vot on! Vernulsya iz svoikh priklyucheniy!*" someone cried out just as Yakovlev opened his eyes and focused on movement up the corridor. 'There he is! Returned from his adventure!'

Ahead of him were soldiers in white uniforms, weapons held ready. One soldier had a rail-gun trained on him.

"*Ne strelyay, Ya nevinoven,*" Yakovlev cried out, but he found his voice weak. 'Don't shoot, I'm innocent.'

He pulled himself to his feet, standing tall, his hands held up. Turning slightly to check the corridor behind him, he saw that the darkness hid what might be there. But an instant later he saw faint motion, waves in the air, and out of the dark end of the corridor came a little silver being that was his alibi. He pointed back at Toog.

"There's the dangerous being! Tried to escape," Yakovlev called out in Russian. "I stopped it."

Toog moved innocently forward, his silvery skin starting to mottle blue. Hardly a dangerous creature, anyone could see.

"Thanks to God for being able to return home. I've been stuck on that damn desert planet for nine days," Yakovlev explained, raising his voice to his comrades. "And each day is sixty hours long. It was terrible. I almost died there. I had to eat worms to survive."

He glanced at Toog, at his armed comrades, at Toog.

"But I caught him. Finally!"

Yakovlev rushed back and grabbed Toog, shoved him against the wall, raising him off his feet and putting a hand tightly around his throat. The creature continued to turn blue—a response to the different environment of the Korobka and the cold outside it. He looked better in blue, anyway, more playful, like a child's doll.

But as Yakovlev grasped Toog's throat—explaining to

the soldiers what had happened, convincing them he'd done nothing wrong and was actually helping—a set of spiny barbs sprang out from each side of the blue being's neck, catching Yakovlev's hand and piercing it with seven of the eight spines.

Yakovlev howled in pain and tried to wrench his hand free, but he could only extricate his hand from five of the spines. Using his other hand he pried his hand from the remaining spines but lost bits of flesh as he did. He cried out for them to shoot the dangerous little monster—but he stood too close.

The soldiers raised their weapons as Toog slid down the wall, feet planted on the floor.

"No, don't shoot!" ordered the squad leader. "Not in here. It could damage the facility." He waved two soldiers forward. "Bring them both to the front."

Yakovlev went peacefully, holding his torn, bleeding hand.

Toog, feet on the floor again, was jabbed by the barrel of one soldier's pulse-gun. As the soldier motioned him away from the wall, Toog stepped over to Yakovlev, who was moaning in pain. Toog clasped Yakovlev's wounded hand, clenched into a fist, thumb inside. Toog's blue fingers stretched around the hand and squeezed until the fist fused into one knobby appendage.

The pain ceased and Yakovlev gazed at his blue tormentor, then at his fist, now a blunt, clubbed end to his arm. He shrieked in horror.

Another barrel pressed hard to Toog's body.

"March!" the squad leader commanded.

As they approached the front of the Korobka, Yakovlev noticed the entrance had been repaired. He wondered how long he had been away. A repair like that had to have taken a while, yet they seemed to know him, maybe were waiting for him, knowing where he had gone. The data system knew he was there, his hand on the control pad, his biometric signature recorded. Then he was gone.

"It's good to be back," Yakovlev said with a grunt, fighting the pain as he held his fused fist. He still needed these soldiers to go easy on him. "How long was I away? It must be a new record."

The squad leader glared at him with hard eyes, as though waiting for Yakovlev to return had been a chore.

Yakovlev anticipated another reduction in rank—which probably didn't matter given his damaged hand. His shooting hand. Unable to perform his duties, he would be kicked out. Retired or worse. Then what could he do?

"Three months," came the answer finally.

The squad leader paused at a control panel along the wall near the entrance and punched in a code, put his hand on the biometric pad. When he hit another button the front wall began to slide up into the ceiling and the frigid world of an arctic winter blew inside.

The men put up their hoods, fixed their collars, slipped on their gloves, taking turns guarding the two prisoners.

Yakovlev kept begging them to release him. He did nothing wrong. Couldn't they see how this little blue demon attacked him? That should prove he wasn't helping the monster escape. No, he was bringing the monster back to be imprisoned. He was a hero!

Once outside, shivering in his cut-off pants and sleeveless shirt from the desert clime, Yakovlev saw the mound of burnt *something*. At the edge of the black mass he detected body parts. Different creatures killed, their bodies burnt. Had to be dozens of them, the mound as high as his head. He noticed Toog's lingering gaze at the mound.

They were the blue one's army. The ones that accompanied him to find the Korobka, and possibly others who came later looking for him and were put down. Nearby sat a battle drone, no longer armed, its four rotor-wings motionless. The ground was littered with rail-gun bolts, and spotted with pulse-gun blasts turning creatures into various colors of stains. They must have returned, searching for their leader, thought Yakovlev, and gotten into a battle with his men—these *Masters*. It didn't have to be that way, he thought. Just let them all go home.

Putting Toog at the front of the mound, like he was posing for a photograph, it was clear the soldiers intended to execute him right there rather than return him to the prison or send him to a laboratory.

"Wait," said Yakovlev, but unable to put strength behind his voice.

Gray snow was falling over them as Toog completed his blue transformation. Nothing yet sprouted from his head or body that looked like tentacles. Nothing electric, Yakovlev guessed. That would take more time.

The soldiers formed a semi-circle, two rail-guns and four pulse-guns trained on the blue one.

Yakovlev took quick breaths, deciding what to do. The little blue being saved him when he was dying on Sebbol. And brought him home. Yet hurt him permanently here. But he had acted badly, he knew. Just saving his own skin. Even so, he couldn't just let them shoot the little blue being for...for being an alien, only that and nothing more. The creature only wanted to go home. Like we all do. Like he had, thanks to the blue boy. He wanted to shout for them to stop, to let Toog go free. But where would such a creature go if he were free? There was five-hundred kilometers of frozen wilderness in every direction.

Unfettered as he stood before them, Toog's blue body gained a tinge of bronze on his front side, skin firming against attack. He raised a blue hand as if surrendering, fingers spread apart, as his little blue mouth formed an O with pink lips. He blew out a nearly transparent substance as an expanding bubble that then flattened before him, making a kind of shield.

"Fire!" the squad leader commanded.

The soldiers shot their weapons—but the rail-gun bolts hit the flat bubble and bounced off. The pulse-gun beams splattered across the bubble-shield, turning it orange.

"Fire again!" shouted the squad leader.

Again they could not penetrate the shield.

"It's some kind of force field," a soldier explained.

One soldier went to pull down the shield, grabbing it with his gloved hands, but fell dead with a bright spark.

"You and you," ordered the squad leader, "tear down that wall!"

The two soldiers hesitated, earning a curse from the squad leader. He marched up to Toog, keeping a space between them, and lifted his service pistol over the top of the shield. With the barrel pointed down at the little blue creature's head, a red dot settling between its glowing silver eyes and above quivering nose flaps, the squad leader pulled the trigger.

The bullet hovered in the air, stopped like it was caught between magnetic fields. Then, as the squad leader watched in dismay, the bullet turned slowly and launched itself straight through the shield into the squad leader's chest. He dropped to his knees and fell over in the gray snow.

The soldiers rushed to their leader as Toog stepped away, the bubble-shield dissolving into the air. He moved around the mound of burnt bodies and turned down the snow-dusted road, wearing nothing against the cold but his sleek blue skin. Knobs formed on his head, on his shoulders, the start of the strands which would cover him and keep him warm as he searched for his lost comrades and helped them return home.

From the side of the road, Yakovlev watched in both horror and amazement as Toog departed, the snowfall growing thicker, until he could no longer see the little blue being.

s a c r i f i c e

14

Years later, having searched the district for his comrades, visiting every campsite and cave and finding mere scraps of abandoned or destroyed supplies but not a singed hair or burnt bone of those fellow creatures once captured by the Masters, Toog made his home in a narrow cave near a different Korobka, further north, in sight of the frothy sea, a place of perpetual winter.

He adapted to the clime, his glorious silver turning a royal blue, and his blue turning steel gray, then into a dull white, and gradually a white that was nearly translucent—especially when he might lay upon the ground at the top of a snowy ridge to spy on the comings and goings of the Masters around the Korobka. By then, he could achieve such a faint appearance that he might even stand close to them and never be noticed. The strands growing from his head and from his body were just as transparent and kept him warm enough. They also shielded him from detection by devices which might pick up the pulse of his heart or the flow of air from his vents. His feet had thickened, his toes more splayed, his claws sharper to grasp the icy paths. His hands had stretched to add an extra knuckle to each finger and he had a stiffer palm pad which he could use as an extra finger.

Yet they knew he was there, watching them. Sometimes one of them would turn and scan the landscape as if looking for him, then stop, eyes directed to where he hid. One in particular, who always wore a red hood, seemed to be able to see him through whatever haze settled over the land. That one would raise a hand as though signaling to him. He dared not respond. If he got up to flee, his translucent form would be noticed.

"Do not be afraid," that one communicated in a strange accented Sebbou, "for we do not capture others now."

Toog had almost replied that time.

"All the beings held here have since gone home," that one communicated, standing in front of the Korobka, looking in his direction. Perhaps it was a trick to capture him.

And as the cycles passed, Toog saw the changes unfold. The Masters' robes became close-fitting suits, dark blue with white markings, red patches on the arms. They wore round globes over their heads, clear in the front, though they still put glass disks in front of each eye inside the globe helmet. The weapons they carried remained the same. Sometimes, they had a laser-cannon, once in a long while something more ambitious, as though they had a large contingent of creatures to destroy. Yet he never saw more beings from other worlds in his travels around the district. He watched the Korobka yet never saw the Masters bring back any new creatures. Even his old prison looked abandoned.

Perhaps they had changed, thought Toog, as he sat deep within his cave, poking at his inner Ru who lay in tattered rags on the floor of his dusty mind-cave, another dark nothingness without food in his belly. Perhaps they no longer took beings from other worlds and brought them here for experiments and slave labor in work camps. Perhaps they could see the true forms of those creatures' mind-caves, spoken with their inner Ru, and found the right passage through the dark nothingness to the light of Great Goddess Aull's silver torch. Perhaps she would welcome them to her paradise. He was not certain he would like to share such a paradise with the Masters, just as he had once shared the desert of his dying world with that soldier— whom he helped twice and still the soldier betrayed him.

Was that enough? Were they in balance now? Which way did the universe lean? Would the *skarg* and the *oum* and the *chakari* ever exist again in his life? What count remained of his life?

His inner Ru did not respond but lay retching on the floor of his mind-cave.

Have you nothing to say? Toog insisted.

You have chosen, came the reply in a raspy voice.

There was no choice. There was only one way. What will Great Goddess Aull think of me?

To speak honestly, it is likely that Great Goddess Aull would not wish to be bothered with your special situation. Maybe not even First Goddess would want to hear your cry. His inner Ru rose up on an elbow, feeble hand pointing at him. *When you could have saved Aull from destruction you turned back and embraced your enemy.*

I did not. I was saving myself. Toog shivered, wrapped his arms around his folded legs. It was only one choice.

Yes, exactly. His inner Ru sat up, acting as though the aches were too strong, making a painful face. *And this is all you have achieved. Killing your inner Ru.*

You are not dying. You are merely hungry.

The hunger is not for food but for satisfaction. With a grunt of anger, his inner Ru pushed itself up and stood tall yet wavered, putting a hand out to the wall for support. *I stand for you, yet you must do the walking. You must take the journey back, and in that trek you will learn the answer.*

The answer to what? Toog sat up, hands clasped.

To the Masters' riddle! And his inner Ru pointed over to the dark passage as if indicating where he should go.

Toog shivered, felt pale blue. I remember you telling me I must solve a riddle, but I have no answer. I have not heard this riddle.

It is not a riddle to hear, but a riddle to solve, and his inner Ru stepped to the dark passage and disappeared.

Toog sat for a short-cycle then grasped the box he'd stolen from one of the Masters' vehicles, looking again inside it but not finding any more crumbs to consume. Each of them had a box and a bottle. Being nearly translucent, he could sneak up to the machine-wagon, usually at night, and snatch a few boxes and bottles. He often heard them call him the 'night thief'. Soon he noticed a box and a bottle would be deliberately placed on the ground before the wagon rolled away. Yet it was not enough to fill his belly more than twice.

That was the problem. Not enough nourishment to regain his color—much less the strength to fight his way through the Korobka. If that was the journey he was meant to take, then he would do it. But first he needed to eat. There were no tiny *ylla* or huge *groll* here, only ice and rock. In the sun-break cycle he would venture forth and seek ample sustenance from the closest source he could find: a good fleshy strip of a Master, no matter the horrid taste.

The dark nothingness held no sound for Toog but a steady hum of calmly settling snow outside the cave's tiny entrance. He rose and felt his way to the entrance, his fingers sensing a message. Dropping to his leg joints and extending his pale arm outside, he found a small box there, the same as what the Masters carried with them: a long-cycle's ration. He took it within and quickly consumed the food inside the box: dried meat slices, some kind of plant material, cooked grain, and a container of milk turned sour. Only as he slowed to savor the final bits did he ponder who had brought the box to him. That some Master had found his hideaway and delivered just what he needed seemed an odd possibility.

Are you satisfied now? came a light voice that might have been a whistle on the wind.

Toog sat back, touched his belly, expanded for the first time in several long-cycles. A bubble of gas also expanded in his belly but he vented and felt no discomfort. He was glad he found food without needing to attack a Master and strip flesh from the creature just to survive.

Are you satisfied? asked the voice. *Are you ready for your journey?*

Toog expelled frustration. *My journey?* He called his inner Ru to question the proposition but his inner Ru remained silent.

Worry not, said the voice weaving through his head like the winding passages of his mind-cave, somehow finding the way to the wall of knowledge and instruction.

You are not my inner Ru, Toog communicated. His tired body stiffened as if preparing to fight. *Where is my inner Ru?*

A figure in a long robe entered his mind-cave, held up a hand to signal calm, waved the other hand at the wall of knowledge and instruction. The figure proceeded to draw a detailed map on the wall, clearly marking the Korobka closest to his cave.

This is your journey, the figure in the long robe stated. The figure reached up and lowered the hood, revealing the mild silvery face of an Aull, a beautiful female of Sebbol. *Do you understand? Do you see the way? I will guide you.*

Toog tried to stand, bumped his head on the low ceiling. *My inner Ru! Where is it? What have you done with my inner Ru?*

The female figure turned to face him fully, opening her long dark robe to reveal a silvery body with a transparent belly, the organs gurgling inside. It was a show of submission, of honesty, of trust—to expose your vulnerable parts.

I am your outer Ru, she communicated.

No—you are not. You are in my mind-cave!

No, Toog. The female pointed to the dark passage beside the wall of knowledge and instruction. *I am outside your cave.*

Toog bumped his head again as he jostled himself upright.

Come out, Toog. The figure in his mind-cave disappeared into the dark passage. *Let us begin the journey home.*

The thread was delicate yet because it connected her to him, she was careful holding it, giving it slack when needed, keeping it taut when necessary. The dream land was a special place, and she must obey its rules, no matter how much she wished to hurry and wind in the thread to bring herself closer to him, eager to see him, to slide her hands down his back.

I am N'oh, your second daughter, who you never met except in the dream land, she told him. *I am real but not a physical being.*

Toog opened his eyes, let them bulge to better see the image before him. She was Aull, a close imitation of L'ra, his full-mate, in her silvery youth. He darkened toward blue as he stood up outside the low cave entrance.

In the dream land I met you once before, communicated Toog to the glowing image posed in the snow, flurries drifting about her dark face and shoulders. Her robe of energy waved in the wind.

I was given a task, N'oh communicated. *To find you and guide you home. You must return home or Aull will fail forever.*

"It cannot be true," spoke Toog. "I was there. I went there. I returned home and nothing existed. Only red desert. No Aull remained alive."

That place must have been far into the future. She turned to go. *You went too far, Great Father, a thousand sun-cycles into the future. I will guide you to the correct plane.*

"I long for the *skarg* and the *oum* and the balance," spoke Toog.

Come then.

As she moved down the slope, maneuvering among the rocks and patches of ice, her glowing body faded to a darker image, yet Toog could see her in the night and follow her down to the valley floor where the gravel road ran between the Korobka and the prison complex. They turned east and continued.

A dark moon rose behind gray clouds as they traversed

the road, winding through snowy hills and rocky ridges, down icy slopes and up the other sides, step by step, as the cold wind blew. It had to be a dream land trek, Toog was certain.

When they approached the Korobka, Toog saw lights around the white cube, illuminating the whole area. Two machine-wagons were parked in front of it. Several of the Masters milled about. Some of them wore military uniforms, but others wore scientist uniforms. A few of them were unloading large boxes, setting them by the entrance, which was closed.

You know this machine, don't you? asked his outer Ru, the dream land spirit of his long-lost daughter N'oh.

Not the same one I used before, he responded.

This is the correct one for returning to our present Sebbol, N'oh explained. *Yet sixty-two sun-cycles have still passed.*

Toog stared down the road at the Korobka, huge gray cube as the others were. He wondered if it operated the same way. On the walls inside were panels which opened and he tried to select the best settings. He failed before, not knowing how to set the controls. He did not wish to return to the red desert world.

We need you now, Great Father.

Toog stared at the cube. *I am one being. What can I do?*

You carry the treasure of Great Goddess Aull, she replied, *yet you never have known it. It resides in each of us but few Aull ever find it and even fewer can use it.*

Toog grimaced at the thought, skin glowing silver, returning to pale blue. The snowfall had ceased.

"Hey there, little fellow," called the one who had seen him before—even when he had been almost translucent.

She turned on the light inside her globe helmet, revealing herself: short yellow hair around a pale face, eyes blue like his skin used to be, a long nose without flaps, a wide mouth with borders that up-turned at the sight of him standing in the snow.

"I've missed you," she spoke in the language of Yakovlev. "I'm Anastasia Grominskaya. I'm a scientist. I operate this machine."

Toog must have seemed ignorant to her, standing like a child a short distance away, dark nothingness at his back. She spoke slowly and carefully pronounced each syllable. In his mind-cave, his inner Ru was asleep down a dark passage. Behind him his outer Ru stood with a faint silver glow that only he could see.

"Do not be afraid, little one. We only want to send you home," spoke this Master. Tapping the side of her helmet, she seemed to indicate her head, or mind-cave, as though signaling him to tune in to his. She continued silently but inside his mind-cave came a full voice: "You are the famous blue being I've heard so much about. You are hard to find. Called a dangerous criminal. That is what I've been told. Yet you appear harmless. You're rather cute. Did you know?"

A soft joy-noise filled his mind-cave, causing a pleasant echo, and Toog relaxed. This one was different than the others.

"You may not remember," she spoke, "but you were ordered killed for your part in the rebellion at that work camp. Fourteen years ago."

He remembered that day. A little gray being like him leading a fight against the Masters! It was nothing but a dream land drawing now.

"I called just in time to save you. I wanted the chance to study you, your species." More pleasing noise. "But they lost you in the prison and I could not study you."

Toog recalled. Then he escaped. And others escaped.

They formed an army and fought the Masters.

"Now the Ministry of Special Projects has finally decided to end this program. Too expensive, especially given the other, more crucial needs we have now. No more venturing to other worlds through this machine, and others like this. No more capturing creatures. We are shutting the program down. And closing all of these machines. I studied you the best I could—yet always from afar. I could pick up some of your thoughts and some of your language. You are a very interesting species. The result, anyway, is the end of this program—because of you, little friend."

She showed her up-turned mouth again. The vibrations were steady, even. She believed what she communicated.

"The Ministry set up a perimeter around your habitat zone, forbade anyone from entering. We have been able to study you better. Did you notice? Your existence convinced us, the scientists and politicians, of the wrongness of our actions. Someone heard about you, your story, and made a comic book of your adventures. The little blue being from another world! It was quite popular with children. They made fluffy blue dolls of you. My son has one, though he's hugged it to rags by now."

Toog held his head up straight yet his eye-rain leaked out, twin streaks of fluid running in lines down his face.

"However, before we close down this interdimensional portal," Grominskaya spoke, "perhaps you would like to return home."

He took a hesitant step forward, his front illuminated by work lamps at the front of the cube.

Yes, Toog communicated.

Grominskaya clapped her hands. "Excellent!" She turned to another Master wearing the protective uniform with the globe helmet. Gazing at Toog once more, she spoke: "Do you know what to do? Or shall we assist you in the protocol?"

I went to the wrong world, Toog communicated. *I used a different machine.* He thought for a moment. *Master-sergeant Yakovlev, one of your kind, helped me.*

"You entered before?" asked Grominskaya.

Yes, we did.

"This Yakovlev...? He was a scientist?"

No, a soldier. His group attacked my group. We captured him and he helped us. But he was not one to trust.

Grominskaya spoke with her comrade, then turned to Toog: "Yes, we have a record of the incident." Her assistant handed her a tablet. "It says he retired from army service due to injury. Oh! In fact, he was the one who told us about you. He told about your adventures together. It was on all the official mindcasts, which got him a contract with a publisher. No wonder! Yet he died not long ago, age forty-three. Too much radiation damage, I suppose. You need not concern yourself with him." She handed the tablet back.

Toog was not sure what to think. Yakovlev had helped him go to his world, but he had helped the dying soldier back to his home—and became trapped here for that act—

"Nooooo!" shrieked Grominskaya.

A sharp pain entered Toog's body as he realized someone stood behind him, holding a long metal pole.

"The only way to kill this kind!" growled the soldier wielding the metal pole. The jagged broken end made a spearpoint. "It killed my brother!"

The metal rod had been thrust down into his body, scraping just inside the skin on the back of his head then through his shoulder into his chest, breaking two ribs as it passed into his belly. The sharp end protruded to the side of his genital flap. The force of the thrust dropped him to his leg joints on the icy ground. He could not move, skewered on the spear.

I am sorry, but I cannot help you, communicated his outer Ru, her raised hand too slow to block the stabbing. She only managed to get her hand stabbed through also, like they did in the prison when Toog first arrived. Her hand was attached to him now by the spear.

Grominskaya cursed the soldier, rushing to Toog with sorrow-rain spotting the front of her globe helmet. Her gloved hands went to his shoulders, her eyes searching for how to save him. Again she shouted at the soldier behind Toog, and he removed the metal pole cleanly in one swift pull.

The pole was stained with a dark green fluid thick with bits of solids. The out-sliding pole had brought the substance up the length of metal—as his outer Ru's hand got free. When the dark green fluid reached the soldier's hands, it burned his skin. He immediately threw down the metal pole. When it hit the ice on the ground and bounced, one end then the other end, the dark green substance was flung off the pole, splattering the soldier's face. Not wearing the protective uniform like the scientists, he cried out. His hands went to his face. But his hands were touched by the dark green fluid, and bringing them to his face only worsened the horrible effect: the fluid, acting like acid, burned through flesh and melted eyes, then dissolved the bone of his skull as he shrieked his wrath-call of the universe.

＊

The shock of the attack still shaking her, Grominskaya warned the others to let the fauna be. They all saw for themselves what could happen if they dared strike an innocent-looking creature. Three soldiers were tasked with bagging the body.

Grominskaya and a medical person she called Belochkin laid Toog flat on the ground. Belochkin examined the wound. It was a clean entrance, a single cut straight down through his body with a small exit. They rolled Toog on his side and the doctor held an electronic device over the entrance wound. A faint hum rose and fell as he moved the device along Toog's side. Nods and frowns. They rolled him onto his back again and checked the exit wound with the device. The humming stopped. The doctor shook his head inside his globe helmet.

"You must save him," Grominskaya pleaded. "If not for this one, they would never have thought the program a failure. He must live and return to his home—her home. I'm not sure."

Toog noticed eye-rain slipping down the scientist's face. She twisted the helmet around and lifted it off her shoulders. She swept her blonde hair back with her hand, blinking. Her red mouth formed an awkward up-turn—a decidedly artificial display meant to encourage him. She put fingers to her eyes, wiped one then the other.

"Nothing I can do," said Belochkin, putting the medical device away in his bag. "We don't know how to treat this kind. That was the reason for our experiments—"

"Shhh!" she blurted.

Toog studied this female Master and her shaman, decided they were not true Masters. They could only be imitations. Yet the one that had injured him, stabbing him from behind like a criminal, had gotten his reward. Death with pain.

"Look," said Grominskaya, pointing at the small exit wound. "His blood is white. Like milk. It runs from the wound to the snow." She met his eyes, bulging orbs that could not hide his fear, or his cold thoughts of death. "Please, Yuri, we must do something. Stop the leaking of his blood, at least."

Belochkin took a thick medical stylus from his bag, set it over the wound, pushed a button on the stylus and an orange streak of light projected from the end of it. He directed the light over the blue flesh of Toog's lower belly. The skin mended. Yet Toog's face tensed, his blue belly turning purple, his eyes darkening. When the orange light from the stylus ceased, his color returned to blue.

Toog's outer Ru stood away from him, across the road from where he was attacked, holding up her arm and gazing at the hole in her hand. She could see the sky through the gap. She could see all the stars above, twinkling so coldly between gray clouds that touched and parted, touched and parted. Lowering her hand she saw the Masters kneeling on the ground beside Toog. He did not look well. She moved toward him, drifting over the patches of ice and frozen gravel of the road, a bit above the ground, outlined in a steel gray that pulsed slowly but did not glow.

"Help me get him into the Korobka, out of the wind and cold," said Grominskaya.

She and the doctor, and a pair of soldiers coming at her call, each took a limb as another soldier set down his weapon and took a square plastic panel from the rear of one machine-wagon and set it on the ground beside the little blue being. With a count, they raised Toog and the panel was slid under him. Then all of them lifted him on the panel and carried him inside the entrance of the Korobka.

"Close the door," she instructed.

One of them punched a red button on a panel on the side wall that began the process of lowering the high door.

Toog's outer Ru could not hurry, could not catch up in time. The door dropped faster as it fell and slammed shut as she got to it, just in time to touch the door's surface, feel the cold metal of it and fall back a step, surrounded by soldiers standing guard.

Inside, Grominskaya replaced her helmet, locked it around her neck as she gazed down upon the little blue being, her eyes wide with wonder. She knelt beside him.

"Fascinating...." She reached for an instrument in her pocket, something meant to pinch, and put it carefully to the flap in his lower belly. Using the instrument, she grasped the flap, lifted it. The flap stiffened as she pulled it away from where it seated against his belly. "So fascinating...." She looked up at Belochkin. "Give me a probe."

He handed her the medical tool and she held it like a knife to poke at the little bit of flesh hiding inside the cavity normally blocked by the flap.

"Fascinating," she kept muttering.

As she poked the bit of flesh, it firmed and rose up—outward, if Toog had been upright. The flesh widened into a flange, its outer edges wet with a clear substance that made the flesh glisten.

"I'll bet this could be developed into industrial glue. What do you think, Yuri?"

The doctor shook his head, folded his arms over his chest.

As Grominskaya continued to poke, the fleshy digit brightened from blue to pink and suddenly spurted a cloud of pink globules as small as grains of sand, all suspended in a viscous gray liquid. The substance hovered in the air a moment, then collapsed, splattering over his belly, some of the substance getting on the front of Grominskaya's white coverall.

Yet in the mating ritual, safe in the *skarg*, the globules would wait for his mate's belly vent to open, then hope that one of the globules would be sucked into the opening of the long, unfolding tube she would present and be drawn up to the base of the tube where it would initiate conception. Their merged materials would grow until the orb was large enough to transmigrate out through her thinning belly wall into the *skarg*. Then, when the orb had grown further, it would be retrieved from the *skarg* and placed in a swing-basket in their abode and grow to be a springling, then a midling—a walking child.

"Fascinating," she intoned, listening in on his thoughts. She gave him a nod. "Thank you for that explanation."

Using the examination tool in her hands, she urged the fleshy digit to recede, then gently lowered the flap over it, all the while mumbling her wish to have gone into Alien Anatomy while in university rather than Interdimensional Exploration. But her die had been cast and she had gotten her position far away in the arctic wasteland. At least she had been able to visit six worlds.

"This!" she exclaimed. "This is why I went to school! To study creatures like this, Yuri. And to find viable uses for whatever features they possess that we can use."

"Yeah, yeah, for the Motherland," Belochkin grumbled. He stood up behind her. "What do we do with this one? It's nearly dead."

"No, look!" She pointed at his belly—above the flap.

In the bright lights of the chamber in the Korobka, Toog's belly appeared nearly transparent. They could see his organs—three lungs and a heart with three chambers, a stomach with three compartments, and three other organs they could not quite identify. Fluids in three colors flowed through a network of tubes. And the bone structure appeared flexible, malleable, the ribs sporting phalanges which shifted like fingers, tightening or loosening as needed. They could see the dark green line of the wound, too, as straight as the metal pole. At the lower end, where it had exited, the wound had been sealed by the doctor. Gradually the wound was healing up the line, turning dark blue like a beaker filling up.

"He is not dead," explained Grominskaya. "No, he is healing himself. If only we were able to do that, Yuri. Think of how the battlefield would change."

"We cannot keep him here to study," said Belochkin. "It is the standing order to return all aliens to their home worlds."

"Yes, I know, but...if only...." Grominskaya stood, gazing affectionately down at Toog. "This one.... I've monitored him for quite some time. I feel like...like he's a pet, really. My pet."

Toog's eyes had closed but opened again as she rose from tending to him. His eye-rain started again and his face pinked in pain. He called for his outer Ru, the squeaky sounds from his tiny mouth barely making a language.

"I know it hurts, dear one," said Grominskaya.

"How do you do that?" asked Belochkin, arms uncrossing over his chest. "Talk to alien creatures?"

"It's lexical telemetrics," she replied like a professor. "Some can learn the technique. We communicate a set of linguistic values, like with mathematics, which can be translated into any language. Like X equals 'pain'. Language is only a system of signs and symbols, and sounds, after all. Once you learn a system it's easy to convert one set of patterns to another. Of course we lose all nuance like idiomatic meanings, but basic communication, for example 'stand up and speak', transfers well enough."

She glanced at Belochkin, then back down at Toog.

"We speak Russian but this one hears his own language, what he calls Sebbou. The same with French." She smiled down at Toog, knelt and put her hand on his forehead. "*Nous vous enverrons chez vous*. Or English: *We will send you home*." She returned to Russian: "And he hears my idea in the language system he knows. Don't you, little friend?"

As she lifted her hand from his head, her fingers tickled him, drawing a thin coating from his skin, something viscous yet clear. She raised her fingers to her nose, sniffed.

"Sweat?" asked the doctor as she stood up beside him.

"I think it's a mating scent." She wriggled her nose. "Very strong, wouldn't you say?" She held out her fingers for him to sniff. "Strong enough to be detected through water."

The doctor regarded the little being, less transparent and more blue. "Or in a murky swamp."

"Yes.... This substance, whatever it is, could have industrial uses. The viscosity level is amazing. If only we could breed them, Yuri. If we had a female...."

"And we have pledged to send them home," Belochkin reminded her.

"Yes, Yuri." She pondered the thought, face tense, then clapped her hands to get the attention of her assistants. "Let's make ready the passage. We have a guest we must return home."

Immediately, the staff began their work, each standing at a wall panel making calculations. The cube hummed around them. The hiss of pistons moving machine parts beneath the floor, the glowing of electronic signals. A low droning filled the Korobka, shaking the floor as Grominskaya and Belochkin, along with two assistants, lifted the plastic panel and carried Toog down the corridor's slight slope into the darkness of the far end. Lights blinked on as they went and blinked off as they passed.

Finally they set him down and Grominskaya knelt there.

"Look how he heals. Almost complete. His body repairs itself. A wound as fatal as that...yet after an hour, nearly healed. Only the entry wound remains."

She saw the flap of skin on the back of his head, peeled away as the pointed end of the metal pole caught it. She asked for the stylus the doctor had used to seal the exit wound and applied it to the entry wound. Within Toog's body, the dark green line of the wound had mended and faded into medium blue which matched the rest of his body.

"Are you ready to walk?" She chuckled to herself. "Or do you hop? Or leap? Or swim?"

She got up, stepped over to check the status of the operation on a nearby wall panel, opening its door and deciphering the data feed. With the push of a few buttons and the tweak of a dial, she nodded, satisfied.

"Twelve minutes, little fellow." She grinned at him, but his blue face showed no pleasure. "Don't be afraid. You will soon be home again. Promise." She wiped her eyes. "And we are so...so very sorry for all you have endured. Goodbye. I wish you well, my friend."

She alerted everyone to check their uniforms, to prepare for the operation. The radiation burst was harmful if they were not protected. When each of them had given confirmation, she hit the big switch on her wall panel and a scene opened at the dark end of the corridor: a hazy, humid brown swamp. As they watched, long strings of cloudy material floated by.

Toog raised his head, saw the *skarg* and the *oum*.

They picked him up and stepped through and set him down again, retrieving the plastic panel and leaving him on the mushy, pungent soil. His mouth up-turned and he out-breathed a long joy-noise.

As the team turned to go, Toog uttered a small squeak, raising his hand, half blue and half silver. Only Grominskaya paused to regard him. His long fingers curled in the air, drawing her to him.

"Wait," she called to her team as she knelt beside him on the wet soil, curiosity in her eyes.

Suddenly, he grabbed her forearm, pulled her hand down to his head. Before she could snatch back her hand, a great flood of data burst through her, burning up her arm to her shoulder and into her brain, an explosion of words there. A whole library of information, she realized. She saw a miniature version of herself standing there as tablets sloughed off the yellow walls of Toog's mind-cave: the complete story of his life on her world and on his world, the long account of the Aull of Sebbol.

She fell backwards on the ground, her bottom pressed into the moist dirt.

Toog let go a mild chirp.

She gazed upon his silvery face and knew the proper reply in Sebbou. She tried to chirp back to him. Close: *I'm almost ready to sleep*, she actually communicated, but Toog could guess what she had meant. Yes, she would tell his story to everyone, make them understand his kind are not children's pets or circus tricks, lab experiments, or slave labor, but separate and unique beings who live perfect lives on their own world and never imagined needing to solve any riddle.

▲ ▶ ▲ ▶ ▲ ▶   15

On the soggy black soil lay Toog in repose.

In repose lay Toog for many short-cycles, absorbing moisture from the *skarg* and watching *oum* of many shapes and sizes float by. Soon he slipped into the murky yellow-green waters of the *abo* and swam with ease—until he narrowly avoided a bite by a startled *frou* and crept back onto the *saak* bordering the *abo*.

"Are you ready?" spoke his outer Ru in perfect Sebbou.

Toog startled at the voice, sat up.

N'oh stood tall, her long robe waving in the humid soup. She glowed like First Goddess when paying a visit to the Aull, an outline of bright gray sparkling energy around a darker gray figure without definition or detail.

Toog up-lifted his arm, open-hand fluttering like a *mez* in the *op* of a dry *abo*, what they called a *dour*. It was too soon. His strength returned after several short-cycles of dark nothingness and a long-swallow of *faef* from the *abo*.

"The journey is not yet finished," she spoke, raising a long straight staff she held in the hand which had gotten the hole forced through it. "A walking of many short-cycles awaits. And the sights will alarm you. This *abo* is your last gentleness."

Toog pulled himself up, shook off the *lool* from his skin.

N'oh led the way, her feet bending blades of *tull* as she went, a slight waft from her movement, from her long robe of pure energy.

Toog stepped awkwardly over the soft soil, sliding through the muddy tracks, and splashing in the occasional *lool* wherever it formed. A higher, firm road ran alongside their path but he enjoyed stepping into a *weeth* at every opportunity, just to steal more moisture. In his body, although healed, the dark green bile that filled his wound had hardened, causing his movements to be stiff, throwing off his balance.

As they traversed the reach, short-cycles passing like *oum*, and the land became drier. Even so, Toog squealed joy-noise when he recognized the *rabs* and *lools* of his district. Ahead were the abodes of his village, gray domes forming a pattern which pleased First Goddess. His eyes spiraled open wider and bulged to see details but the view was obscured in humid haze. Breeze brought clouds of *saak* and *wa* before him, but it was not yet *yu'u*, the season of falling crystals.

His outer Ru remained silent as she halted at the entrance, at a gap in the low wall that encircled the village. The abodes were overgrown with creeping *zum*. Looking in each direction, the gritty noise of *saak* scratching over the domes' surfaces was all he heard. She waved him on through, followed him as he went directly to the center of the village, to the market where the tall statue with his likeness stood.

Blowing *saak* had marred the face of stone Toog but he could read the plaque. It was the same as on his previous trip. He felt alarm. Was this the right time and place? When he had discovered the monument with Yakovlev in tow, it seemed a cruel joke—*sF'z* in Sebbou. How they mocked him! No, he was captured and taken away and forced into slave labor. He was not a hero, not their savior. He was not taken to be a shaman and teach them harmony. How could they get such a strange idea?

Shall I tell you? his outer Ru communicated.

Toog turned to her: the gray shape roughly appearing as Aull, a glowing outline which illuminated the village as the short-cycle faded. On the horizon, far beyond the village, he saw the old sun falling behind distant ridges, the dark nothingness soon over-washing them. Now he had no fear of the Masters ever returning. Yet where were all the villagers? Would none come out to welcome him home?

They cannot welcome you, Great Father.

She watched him go to the nearest abode and peek in the open doorway, seeing nothing in the interior darkness. He went to the next abode, and the next one, and the next. He paused and back-turned to regard his outer Ru.

"This is no better than my previous visit," he spoke.

She lifted her gray hand, a spasm of energy burning bright for an instant. Her hand directed his vision to the abode he had just peered into. A silvery light flowed from her fingers into the abode and Toog gazed within.

He stepped inside and saw what remained of the villagers. On the mat lay two forms, bodies straight as if in repose, and the light shining from his outer Ru's hand allowed him to see how their skin was brown and shriveled like an old *purnak*. Heads lay sunken like old *mando*, as brown as *trez*, eyes closed and flat, nose flaps wrinkled shut, mouth holes shrunk to slits. The bodies appeared hard and stiff—like the *snorvix* the next village always sold in the season of falling crystals after herding them, slaughtering them, and drying the flesh.

"Are they dead?" asked Toog.

Come with me, his outer Ru called.

She led him to another abode, gestured for him to enter. The same sight: a pair of leathery bodies stretched in repose, too dry to be alive. Toog in-breathed death.

"It is *thax*," he spoke solemnly. "Nothing worse for an Aull than being slowly boiled alive." His orbs fluttered. "Or becoming too dry."

Now I will tell you everything, Toog.

His outer Ru took him to the abode which once was his. He had feared to look upon it and so had gone to the others first. But N'oh forced him to follow. When he stood over the body there, flat on the mat, like a worn branch of *frex* that had off-broken and floated in the *lool* for many sun-cycles, his outer Ru spoke.

This is K'au, of your counting line, four lives from you.

"What happened to them?" asked Toog.

His outer Ru flickered with energy, the light which outlined her form glowing intensely.

We need you to produce eye-rain. Much eye-rain. It is the only way. So I will tell you a story....

The sun-cycles turned and the families of Laat, Maak, and Buun grew and grew, gaining more springlings. And the village grew like fresh planted *sporra* and the sons of Laat and the daughters of Buun led the community. On the same counting line, the children of Maak prepared the village for the next arrival of the Masters.

And Toog, you were honored in the village council by the high shaman. A figure was crafted which stood twice the height of you, arms spread wide, face up-gazing at First Goddess. The figure sparked fire in the hearts of those who up-gazed on it. Bellies became hard, like the stones of Guul'va, and arms and legs tied together double-strong. Tools were made for fighting and food gathered from the gardens for the siege everyone expected.

The community built stone mountains around the village and topped the peaks with flying barb-sticks. Meanwhile, the gardens dried and plants withered. Midlings ran naked and cloth went unmended. The community practiced its defensive formations every long-cycle, pair-practiced attack motions each short-cycle. The Masters would arrive soon, everyone knew.

Yet they did not come. Everyone knew you had subdued them, taught harmony to them, and made them weep.

And the springling of Toog, and those Aull from the village who had long-past must have disappeared to teach the Masters about harmony, and left many pictures on the walls of every mind-cave. And this springling down-sat among the *fluu* as everyone gathered around her, this one named N'oh, and they listened to her words, describing the pictures everyone knew from the many tellings.

You tell it true, my inner Ru reminded me.

Silence, you old *wuk*! I will tell it in my own way, the way my mother told me, the truth of my great father Toog.

Then it shall be a lie.

Better a lie than a telling of cutting words and aching bellies.

I cannot allow you to tell it that way.

Then you can go to your hiding place. Or start a journey into the dream land.

You do not respect me.

Now I hear some wisdom from you!

I am leaving now.

Great Mother F'ae up-lifted her arms and up-turned her face to the sky. The sun-light bathed her old bronze face in golden-green. Those gathered around her chanted the invocation to summon the goddesses.

And I told the tale...

How you led the alien cohort against the Masters, holding a square marker in your hand, set on a square machine pad with numbers running quick, and the Masters pleaded with you to keep your hand away from the marker, and they begged you to grant them mercy, offering sincere apologies for their harsh treatment of you and your cohort, insisting they were only seeking habitable places to migrate for their own survival, yet you were not impressed.

I told them this:

Again Toog raised the device, holding it at the level of his eyes so he could keep the Masters' platoon in sight and still see the lights on the device.

It was already switched on, generating ignition energy. He knew the sequence but only the orange light blinked.

Again the Masters pleaded with him.

Then Toog saw the orange light hold steady, changing to red. The time for action had come. The red light blinked.

No, Master-Sergeant Yakovlev cried out. *Don't do it!*

The red light flashed, then held steady.

With a shallow inhale, Toog pressed his long second finger to the square marker and at once let go all his fear, all his sorrow, all his regrets, merging them into a hammer that struck down upon that sliver of plastic that covered the complex electronic synapses beneath. He felt a sting of lightning shoot up his arm.

Yakovlev and the others cringed.

Nothing happened.

The wind blew against them with more insistence. They stared at each other across the frozen, rock-strewn plain.

Then everything happened.

Toog's orbs closed tight. *I did not do that.*

His outer Ru laid a heavy hand on his shoulder. *I know.*

Then why did you tell it?

Toog's outer Ru could not face him, her face nothing more than a gray slate within a shapeless form, eyes mere vortices of energy drawn from the power of the universe.

"The villagers needed a story to give them hope," she spoke. "Everyone knew you went away to teach the Masters harmony. Yet some of our community did not believe the Masters could be taught harmony, so I told a story of strength—how you fought against the Masters and in the end destroyed their world."

"And they believed the story?"

His outer Ru rose a bit, her hand glowing like a lamp over the market, illuminating the space.

"Yes," she spoke and a long out-breath followed. "Because they were dying. Only a story of hope would comfort them. Yet they died anyway."

She lowered her gray hand and clasped her hands together. The silver glow extinguished as dark nothingness over-fell the village, only a red line of fire leaking on the horizon.

"Plague came upon us. None knew its origin though we suspected it came from the Masters. In shaman tablets were no stories and no cures. The high shaman advised us about an ancient potion and we made it, drank it. For some of the community, new flesh grew inside the belly—grew until it could not be contained and burst, tearing them open. These we had to burn and the ashes we did not drink but let fly on the wind."

"But the wind would carry it to other villages...."

"Yes, and they suffered the plague like us."

"I should have been here...."

"For others, the extra flesh did not grow within their bellies. The 'wasting caul' we named it. They could not eat food. They could not work or play, could only fall into repose. And their bodies wilted like *fuut* in the dry season. And the dry season pulled them, and water left their bodies, their bodies shrank—as you saw in the abodes—until they were as you see them now."

Toog up-stood from the dirt, out-extending his spindly arms as if he were pressing the edges of the universe apart.

"We need you to bring us your sorrow-rain," spoke his outer Ru. "I told the story to bring sorrow-rain from you."

"Sorrow-rain?" asked Toog, lowering his arms to his sides.

His outer Ru waved a hand at the abode before them.

"There is need for sorrow-rain. Your sorrow-rain."

She stared at him, seeing puzzlement in his face.

"On the shaman tablets are descriptions of the universe. The dots and lines we cannot see are magic behind us. In one recipe the pattern is found in sorrow-rain. And more."

She held out her hand, took his face in her shapeless fingers.

"Can you recall how, long past on that world, you went into a hidden pool within a hidden cavern not far from a prison where you were hidden away? How you swam in that pool not knowing what it was or what might be in it? The strange liquid of a foreign world? How you emerged from the pool with illness, your silver turning blue, with the inner fire to fight the Masters?"

Toog did not need to think for long. Years before. His

inner Ru knew everything about him, so it did not seem strange that his outer Ru also knew his history.

"Yes, I recall."

"There conjured in you the potion described in the shaman tablets. A fire which does not have flame. A burning which does not consume. A toxin for them, a healing potion for us. A waste collection pool from the Masters' machine. Leaking into the depths of their world. And you were not harmed."

Toog's orbs expanded in wonder, glowing blue in the dark.

"You have the cure within you, Great Father."

His head stretched to each side in disbelief. His orbs felt moist, the start of sorrow-rain.

"Come," spoke his outer Ru.

Into the abode they went and Toog leaned over the face of the wilted body there. He thought of the stories, remembered his adventures. How he struggled. How he hated. How his full-mate L'ra never again felt his touch or saw his silvery face. And his daughter M'ah never knew him, nor her own springlings, nor their springlings. Or his neighbors—all believing he did something wonderful and saved them from the Masters! And his comrades in the snow and ice of that wasteland—lost!

His orbs filled with sorrow-rain, and drop by drop spilled down upon the leathery face, wrinkled like *tof*. And after many drips the brown fingers of the figure twitched. The orbs wiggled. Foul air out-breathed from the nose vent as the flaps out-folded. The tiny mouth spread apart as fingers flexed.

"It is truth!" cried his outer Ru.

Startled at her cry, Toog shifted beside the repose mat and sorrow-rain hit the ground. A sprig of golden *suppo* emerged, curling in each direction, seeking moisture, hungry for the healing potion.

"As your sorrow-rain wets the soil, life springs forth!"

Toog's mouth up-turned as he stood beside the repose mat. Below him the figure was becoming flexible, softening, filling with life and moving about on the mat. He stepped to the other side and applied the same measure of sorrow-rain to the next body, and the result was the same.

He moved to another abode, repeated the same sorrow-rain treatment. N'oh continued telling him stories to keep the sorrow-rain spilling. Some neighbors were too far decomposed, they had believed, yet drops of Toog's sorrow-rain brought the piles of brown dust back into form, a body and a head, restoring fullness and silvery sheen to them. Then life!

As he finished wetting the bodies in each abode, his outer Ru escorting him around the village, she spoke in his mind-cave:

I have gone long from this place. Great Goddess Aull has granted me this pause to find you and bring you here to save our kin.

Her gray form wavered as Toog continued to shed sorrow-rain over each of the dead.

I grow weak now, yet we have brought the cure home. There is a text on the shaman tablet. It is a riddle. A prophecy. It is a story about the one who disappears among the stars yet returns with the touch of the goddesses. It must be you, Great Father.

Toog stopped, regarded her. "You said there is a riddle?"

The gray form darkened, its edges becoming diffused.

"Can you tell me?" He got up off his leg joints, staring at the gray form. "Do not go away. Do not leave me."

I cannot hold together much longer. Yet there is much to

do. Go to each village and remember the stories I have told you. Make sorrow-rain and let it return each Aull to life.

"I will," spoke Toog. "But what is the riddle of the Masters?"

You know it, Great Father.

The gray form withered, folding into a box, then a line which stretched tall before bending sideways, folding into itself, shrinking to a spot in the night air before blinking out.

"N'oh!" he squealed.

The sound echoed in the dark nothingness and he felt alone. Not even the rising of villagers from their abodes brought him comfort. A few of them waved a hand at him. Others showed their up-turned mouths. Some attempted to out-step from their abodes, stiffly but with improving flexibility. Toog blinked at them. A whole village returning to life. He stood tall, up-stretched, wide-looking in each direction for his outer Ru, yet he saw nothing.

Have you learned the riddle of the Masters? a voice asked.

He stopped—and in that moment believed he was on the Masters' world again, hiding deep in a cave, his silver body freezing before he had turned blue and grown the strands that warmed him and gave him powers he never asked for, never knew he had, and that this visit from N'oh was only a dream.

Or he was already in the dream land himself—forever.

You take in the poison, the voice goaded him.

His inner Ru had awakened, crawling into his mind-cave.

Then you make the potion that cures your kin.

Toog pinched his blue lips, felt the moisture covering his body thicken. He knew the answer. And in that realization, everything he had experienced came together, colluding in his mind-cave to form a new tablet that sloughed off the wall. The mind-cave Toog caught the tablet, held it in his silver hands. He could read it, could gaze upon the marks and know everything.

His inner Ru feigned impatience. *Do you know the answer?*

Toog read from the tablet in his hands. *Yes.*

As Toog went from village to village, bringing each dried husk of Aull back to life, the seasonal rains came. Through many long-cycles, the land returned to life. Trees grew leaves, flowers sprouted from the ground. Gardens filled with food. Depressions collected *lool*. The cold gray sky of that other world was gone and the amber sun-light of Sebbol was bright and warm. Springlings squiggled through the *skarg* and leaped along the *saak* of the *abo* while older females picked berries, dug roots and males herded beasts.

And in one village Toog found an extra-mate named G'oi, who was abandoned when the Masters came and took her full-mate, never to be seen again. She escorted Toog through his tasks. So he eventually requested the shaman make her his full-mate. And G'oi agreed, so the shaman granted the bonding.

"All goddesses grant me the power to command you and you to seek the *skarg* as one," said the shaman, with a large crowd of villagers gathered, "and enjoy the warmth of each other there."

A cheer went up: "To the *skarg*!"

Knowing the future, Toog advised villagers to prepare. Many channels and reservoirs were built to maintain the flow of *lool* to and from the *skarg* and the *abo*. Plans to harness the passing *oum* were made. When the dry seasons extended to fill the sun-cycles, they would survive.

And as the sun-cycles turned, the valley crackling into a writhing kaleidoscope of floral colors, the second-summer *chakari* squeaking, Toog and G'oi rubbed together in the *skarg*. Although too long-lived to make a springling, they took comfort with each other, remembering what First Goddess had written on the wall of the mind-cave they shared: *Fill your throats with joy-noise and be like fruit-trees, blossoming in season, and always welcome what is sweet.*

APPENDICES

For more information about Siberian sink holes and the problem of melting permafrost releasing methane into the atmosphere, see the following sources:

http://unfccc.int/ghg_data/items/3825.php

http://www.realclimate.org/index.php/archives/2014/08/how-much-methane-came-out-of-that-hole-in-siberia/

http://www.huffingtonpost.com/james-grundvig/methane-blowholes-the-nex_b_5688019.html

CAST LIST

Toog's Family:

Toog = *L'ra*

M'ah = (Naar) Keet   &   N'oh = (Guur) —

Toog'la/Raam = *K'ae*

Gaag = *H'ou*

Laat, Maak, Kiid, Buun

Other major players in order of appearance:

Ra'aa'al – an exo-body being from Ra'a'am'mas'sandiit
Trexon – a furry ape-being from Xmburrhaltis
Grauun – a furry ape-being from Xmburrhaltis
Djuttu – a Wexa, a fox-like being from Yvo
Bar'Gafu – a pod-being from Heis-Tegag, mate of
    Zem'Gafu and Tan'Gafu
Arkor – a Bex from Becha in the Buz-Lop system
Timothy Cromwell – a Hu-man being of Earth
Basha – an Ababerazan from Ababeraz
Andrei Illych Yakovlev – master-sergeant in People's
    Army of the Soviet Federation of Eurasia
Anastasia Grominskaya – scientist with Ministry of
    Special Operations
Yuri Belochkin – physician with Dr. Grominskaya

On the Mating Practice of the Aull of Sebbol

(Courtesy of Dr. Anastasia Grominskaya)

The species of intelligent being known as Aull, indigenous to the planet Sebbol located in the Tau Kita system, is a dioecious creature: i.e., fauna having two sexes, male and female, differentiating only late in the birth process. Evolving from an amphibious proto-being, reproduction continues to occur within a watery environment where one sex gives a portion of its genetic material to the other sex and their genetic materials merge into a single entity, typically allowing the fertilized substance to grow within the body of one of them.

In the case of Aull, the male possesses a small tube (a nominal penis) which projects from the body, by way of a vent in the lower abdominal area, upon tactile stimulation within seasonal parameters. By contrast, the female Aull possesses a much longer tube (an extending vagina) which unfolds from a similar abdominal vent, opening upon tactile stimulation, but only during the mating season.

To initiate mating, the male will release from his penis a cloud of pink viscous fluid containing dozens of gray granules (synonymous with sperm; in appearance more congruent with ova). As mating usually occurs in the watery environment of a marsh or similar pool (*skarg* or *abo*), the male's "semen" remains intact and does not dissipate, waiting for the female to collect it. Normally the pair of mating Aull are in close proximity; however, on occasion the male may depart, leaving his pink fluid buoyed in the water and viable for up to three days before breaking up and dissolving.

The female's role begins when she unfolds her longer tube ("vagina"), often three or four sections of this tube bent within her abdominal cavity. This extended vagina begins a process whereby the granules in the pink fluid are sucked into her tube, drawing as many as she can upward to the base of the vaginal tube. Some are lost or damaged during this process so only a few arrive to meet the spherical orb already in place there with its many sticky fingers ("egg"), embedded in the lining of this womb area.

A strong granule will present itself to the egg, pulsing to achieve some momentum and often bumping other granules away. The egg will reach out to grab a granule while still attached to the wall of the womb, catching it with a poke of its dozens of fingers. Once stuck to the end of a finger, the egg will pull in the finger and completely envelope the granule, drawing it gradually into its innermost area. All fingers fold inward from the egg's surface when signaling fertilization. The fertilized zygote will then develop by dividing and doubling itself until it achieves significant dimensions.

During this pregnancy period the female Aull will generally leave the comfort of the marsh or other watery mating venue and go about her usual activities. Once the egg has grown to a certain size so as to distend the female's belly, the outer skin and musculature will progressively thin to only a membrane's thickness, allowing the spherical fetus ("orb") to pass through her abdominal wall into the watery environment to which she must return. Moisture is key in preventing damage to the female's body. The fetus will push out of her abdomen as a sealed orb which is allowed to grow further in the watery environment.

At a critical juncture in the process, the parents gather their orb from the marsh and place it within an artificial environment, typically a basket within their abode. The orb continues to expand until the offspring's limbs poke through the sphere's membrane. Once the "springling" has breached the membrane, the membrane is removed and the parents enjoy the continued growth of their offspring.

Soon the offspring can swim, later crawl, and even later stand and walk on firm ground as a "midling".

On the Inner Ru

(Courtesy of Dr. Anastasia Grominskaya)

In the language of the Aull of Sebbol, Ru means 'guide'; the understanding is that of a spiritual guide, one who leads through knowledge, the powers of suggestion, or in the case of the Aull by drawn images. The inner Ru is meant to convey a spiritual entity which resides within the Aull and is not a physical being separate from the body of the adult Aull. The form taken in society is that of a miniature Aull who resides in the mind: indeed, a physical part of the surface yet able to move independently within that space.

The inner Ru possesses the features and functions of what human philosophers have called a *homunculus* (literally "little person" in Latin). The homunculus is a representation of a small human made popular in 16th-century alchemy and 19th-century fiction, historically referring to a miniature, fully formed human.

In the Aull, this partner actually exists within the brain in the same area where the pineal gland resides in the human brain. The inner Ru is physically born along with the Aull, much like an *in utero* twin that is reabsorbed into the head of the surviving twin, and exists throughout the life of the Aull.

The entity is sparked into consciousness in an Aull's youth, summoned through ritual by the local shaman. This entity has access to the elements of the universe, incorporating all the sciences and expressing itself chiefly through imagery.

The inner Ru may become injured by deliberate mental

disconnection with the host Aull or when the body of the host Aull becomes injured. Working together becomes difficult and the inner Ru may hide or become contrary. The Ru may be willful in certain situations yet it can never destroy its host.

A Sebbou Glossary

(Courtesy of Dr. Anastasia Grominskaya)

abo — a marshy lake; a body of water (generic)

aed — "yes"

ag — nose (the short, flaccid snout of the Aull, having two flaps for closing against water or bad air)

Aull — the name of the race of beings on Sebbol

boog — a large bat; commonly affected by excessive heat, wild and erratic behavior

booz — a playful mating

borrox — a kind of three-horned antelope

clee — a long whistling cry common to Aull babies

chakari — a cricket-like insect

chii — a marsh plant with large seed pods often used as food or ridden by young Aull

chool — a flowering thistle

choot — the daytime

chun — a footed snake-like creature with a flexible hood around its face

doong — an insect (generic term)

dour — a dried up swamp; in the process of drying up

drao — a mush of decaying berries that drop to the ground

drii — a round free-flowing bush; tumbleweed

drix — a swarm of red bees

drouk — a horse-like creature

druka — a wolf-like animal

duidir — an ant-like being with a long body

duup — a thick fern forest

duur — a large hippopotamus-like predator

em — blood

emno — paint made from lizard blood

erol — marsh

eruth — a popping exhalation

enu — species ("race"); kind, type, category

faef — a cloud of algae-like water flora that drifts in the air

faen — a kind of pink crystal

fiz — an insult; a cruel joke

flaam — a blue bamboo-like plant

flao — a large ground-blossoming plant

fleal — tall ferns growing as a forest

fluu — a short, stout volcanic exit

forai — a high-pitched chant uttered by Aull when excited

frex — a swamp tree usually with many roots

frou — a giant swamp slug

futar — a colorful songbird

fuug — a small footed snake-like creature

fuut — a plant with white petals

gaum — a tar substance used to light fires

gop — sin; forbidden; against Aull custom

gortor — a large crocodile-like creature

goud — a rhinoceros-like creature

groll — a large grazing beast

groof — small round insect often grilled and eaten

grurt — a playful curse, an insulting joke

grut — a collection of fertilizer made from animal waste

grum — a giant land crab

gurg — a large worm-like creature

gulk — a giant toad

guum — a water-horse

gumu — the clitoris

haal — a long exhale producing a whistling noise; audible
  sign of surrender

hafo — a long-winged bat

hareh — a dust whirlwind

hox — boiling pools of water and mud

hux — a predatory beaver

im — heart (internal organ)

THE MASTERS' RIDDLE

im-tha — heart-fire; "love"

ivi — fate, destiny

jaax — a vicious fox-like creature

jo — area filled with high stalks of grass

jumi — confidence

jurt — a tall, thick, tough-wood tree with few branches or leaves

kalar — a large horned beast with big hooves

ka'loul — sweat; perspiration

kark — a silver gemstone

kuur — a giant sand snake

lalo — meadow, grassy area amidst a forest

lath — a bush (generic term)

lathu — bushes (generic term)

lool — a body of liquid infused with crystal particles; "water"

lu — genitalia of Aull (generic term)

lurg — a large cockroach

luts — a flying snake-like animal

luur — lake kelp, having long strands

mando — an oblong pink melon with large black seeds

maot — a large river fish with spines

meax — a long-legged flightless predatory bird

mez — an eel-like aquatic animal, known for calling its prey by waving its tail

nur — a long-necked tiger-like beast

nuum — mud pit

o — a bowl

op — the underneath area, of a pond or a cave

org — the male sex organ, projecting from an abdominal opening with flaps

ouk — gummy vomit balls expelled from certain animals

oul — harmony; balance

oum — a warm particulate that forms moisture pods

ourk — an elephant-like reptile

paaz — a stink-turtle

palati — knowledge; lessons

parg — perspiration from skin

per — mountain; Mount+(name)

pook — milk vents (nipples)

purnak — a small red fruit usually dried before eating to make toxins inert

puut — a long red melon grown high on the puut'va tree

puut'va — a tall woody tree with large red melon-like fruit.

rab — hill, especially a solitary hill on a plain

rai — sun, star

rai-wud — year ("sun-cycle")

reez — sticky fecal paste

re-kon — a bird of prey

reng — dry scrubland

Ru — guide

ruu — a ribbon of light; rainbow

saak — coarse sand, grit

Sebbol — a warm, lush planet in the Aull'va system

Sebbou — the language spoken on planet Sebbol (a.k.a. "Sebbolian")

Sebbox — the collective name of the lifeforms of Sebbol (people, fauna, flora)

shaar — a long-necked antelope

skarg — a particularly murky swamp

smaul — exhalation that includes mucus

snorvix — a long-legged pig-like beast usually domesticated

som — day ("long-cycle"); there are 668 long-cycles per one sun-cycle on Sebbol

spix — a leafy vegetable which is hot to the tongue; eaten with ylla to assure ylla does not bite back

suuk — a small 6-legged reptile

suul — a long-tailed bat

suupo — a mossy plant

suur — a large alligator-like reptile

tali — female chest tubes (breasts), not projecting from

chest of Aull

tem — hour ("short-cycle"); there are 30 short-cycles per one long-cycle on Sebbol

thu'th — a thump sound

tha — fire, flame, a burning sensation

thax — a place of heat and fear ('nothing worse for an Aull than being slowly boiled alive'); Hell in Aull culture

tin — raise, lift, make higher

Tin rai q — "raise the stars"

tof — a long purple vegetable dried in sunshine, ground into powder

tull — marsh grass

tii — a gnat

toom — a mammoth with straight tusks and horns

trez — decayed plants; "compost"

tuuk — a spherical thistle which floats in the air

u — (name)+language (suffix)

ua — the tongue

udu — a giant hairy monkey; ape

Uf — Aull name for the sun around which the planet Sebbol orbits

ul — brain matter

uma — the night

uv — the eye

vash — a geyser

va — a tree (generic term)

vau — trees, woods, grove

veedo — a unicorn antelope

vol — sulphur gas

wa — dirt (natural and unfiltered)

wal — soil (filtered, used for gardens)

weera — a biting gnat

weeth — a marshy place where animals often gather

wud — cycle

xasto — floor

yb — a large bag for holding liquid

ybou — a large blue plantain

ylla — a tapeworm

yu'u — a quartz-like crystal that is completely transparent

zab — "no"

zour — urine

zub — a large-winged soaring bird of prey having a red
beak and red tail feathers

zum — a vine

About the Author

Stephen Swartz grew up in Kansas City and dreamed of traveling the world. His writing usually features exotic locations, foreign characters, and smatterings of other languages besides English—strangers in strange lands. However, Swartz chose to study music first, including composing a symphony, and planned to be a music teacher before turning to fiction writing.

The Masters' Riddle began as an idea in his youth, then matured as a project for the National Novel Writing Month competition in 2014. In order to win, a writer must write at least 50,000 words. However, the story was not finished at that point. Working on other projects while teaching at a university in Oklahoma did not hasten its completion. The prolonged solitude of the 2020 pandemic and stay-at-home mandate which allowed the time necessary for the completion this epic tale.

Acknowledgements

Much thanks to my friend and grad school colleague Liliya Bormotova, for checking the Russian phrases in the manuscript.

The author is grateful for notes on Sebbol and the Aull left by Dr. Anastasia Grominskaya in a time capsule which may have been inadvertently placed too near an interdimensional tangent, apparently slipping backwards to the early 21st century as well as across the continents.

The author found appropriate sound support for the writing and revision of the novel by electronic duo Carbon Based Lifeforms (albums: *Twentythree*, *The Path*, *Derelicts*). The song "Frog" from the album *Interloper* was influential in fixing the protagonist's appearance. Additional aural support was found on a YouTube channel called Sovietwave Mix, especially *What Could've Been...*, *Retrosounds*, and *Mother Russia*.

STEPHEN SWARTZ

Also by Stephen Swartz

Contemporary Literary Fiction

After Ilium

Aiko

A Beautiful Chill

A Girl Called Wolf

Exchange

Year of the Tiger

Fantasy & Science Fiction

The Stefan Székely Vampire Trilogy

I. A Dry Patch of Skin

II. Sunrise

III. Sunset

*Epic Fantasy *With Dragons*

The Dream Land Trilogy

I. Long Distance Voyager

II. Dreams of Future's Past

III. Diaspora

STEPHEN SWARTZ